RYNN'S WORLD

WHEN THE ORK hordes of the warlord Snagrod, Arch Arsonist of Charadon, lay waste to the planet of Badlanding and devastate the Crimson Fist forces sent to stop them, Chapter Master Kantor is forced into a desperate defence of the Fists' home planet, Rynn's World. Tragedy strikes. An errant missile destroys the Space Marines' fortress-monastery, killing most of their number outright. With a handful of battered survivors in tow, Kantor must cross a continent and reunite with his Second Company if he is to have any hope of defeating Snagrod's orks and preventing his Chapter's total annihilation.

RYNN'S WORLD

STEVE PARKER

To Nick Kyme, for all the fire support!

A Black Library Publication

First published in Great Britain in 2010 by
BL Publishing,
Games Workshop Ltd.,
Willow Road,
Nottingham, NG7 2WS, UK.

10 9 8 7 6 5 4 3 2 1

Cover illustration by Jon Sullivan.

Maps by Adrian Wood & Rosie Edwards, based on originals by Steve Parker.

A CIP record for this book is available from the British Library.

UK ISBN 13: 978 1 84416 802 6
US ISBN 13: 978 1 84416 803 3

See the Black Library on the Internet at
www.blacklibrary.com

Find out more about Games Workshop
and the world of Warhammer 40,000 at
www.games-workshop.com

Printed and bound in the UK.

IT IS THE 41st millennium. For more than a hundred centuries the Emperor has sat immobile on the Golden Throne of Earth. He is the master of mankind by the will of the gods, and master of a million worlds by the might of his inexhaustible armies. He is a rotting carcass writhing invisibly with power from the Dark Age of Technology. He is the Carrion Lord of the Imperium for whom a thousand souls are sacrificed every day, so that he may never truly die.

YET EVEN IN his deathless state, the Emperor continues his eternal vigilance. Mighty battlefleets cross the daemon-infested miasma of the warp, the only route between distant stars, their way lit by the Astronomican, the psychic manifestation of the Emperor's will. Vast armies give battle in his name on uncounted worlds. Greatest amongst His soldiers are the Adeptus Astartes, the Space Marines, bio-engineered super-warriors. Their comrades in arms are legion: the Imperial Guard and countless planetary defence forces, the ever-vigilant Inquisition and the tech-priests of the Adeptus Mechanicus to name only a few. But for all their multitudes, they are barely enough to hold off the ever-present threat from aliens, heretics, mutants – and worse.

TO BE A man in such times is to be one amongst untold billions. It is to live in the cruellest and most bloody regime imaginable. These are the tales of those times. Forget the power of technology and science, for so much has been forgotten, never to be re-learned. Forget the promise of progress and understanding, for in the grim dark future there is only war. There is no peace amongst the stars, only an eternity of carnage and slaughter, and the laughter of thirsting gods.

PROLOGUE
Transmission

There won't be time to broadcast again, so this is it. We've held out for as long as we can, but they'll breach within the hour, and this array, the only real hope we had, will be lost to us. There isn't time to scuttle it properly. Sergeant Praetes wants us to leave immediately. The greenskin artillery barrage is creeping closer by the second. They've already obliterated the government buildings and the collegium, and neither of those is far from here. But I have to try, just one last message before we pull out for good. If we're lucky, the orks will reduce this facility to rubble behind us, not recognising its value.

I've already started moving the last of the Lammasian squads out of the north gate. I'll retreat with the rearguard as soon as this is sent. The final party of civilians and wounded troopers left yesterday with an escort of able-bodied men from the 18th Mordian. There aren't many left. That goes for civilians and soldiers both. I'm down to a handful of combat platoons cobbled together from what's left of three shattered regiments.

It has fallen to me to lead them. Six days ago, I assumed overall command, and not by choice. The entire cadre of senior officers was wiped out in some kind of greenskin stealth attack. That might sound implausible given the nature of the foe, but on my honour, they were in and out like ghosts, leaving a room full of headless corpses behind them. I suppose they wanted more foul trophies, though Emperor knows, they should have enough of them by now.

My own head would be hanging from the belt of some greenskin savage right now were it not for my duties. I was executing a trio of faithless deserters at the time.

I see the Emperor's hand in that.

My own faith, the fuel by which I continue to fight, tells me that He must be watching over me. All things are part of His great plan. I will not allow myself to fall into a deadly despair. I know that Rynn's World is not far from here, barely two weeks' travel as the warp flows. If the Emperor wills it, the Crimson Fists may have received word of our plight already. Lord of Mankind, grant that they are en route even as I speak.

It is not an unreasonable supposition. We have been transmitting steadily, every hour, on the hour, since the first of the greenskin assault ships cut across the sky. Surely someone has heard our call.

(Sound of muffled artillery fire and explosive impacts.)

Damn the filthy xenos! Their shells are definitely getting closer. It won't be long now. I... I can still barely comprehend the numbers we face. The orbital defence grid was overstretched from the start. The sky went dark with their ships. I should have executed someone for that; according to records, the missile and plasma defence batteries hadn't been inspected by a tech-priest in over three hundred years!

At the very least, there should have been some kind of warning. Why was there no word from the relay station on Dagoth? I can only imagine that the orks struck there first, and with such speed that there was no time to alert the rest of the sector. Now Badlanding pays the price.

If anyone receives this – it doesn't matter who you are – you must send word to the Crimson Fists. Do not try to aid us alone. Only the Adeptus Astartes can help us now. This is no fight for a lesser force. An ork incursion of this magnitude… it has to be a Waaagh! And, if it isn't checked here, it will grow. By Throne, will it grow.

Lord of Mankind, don't let it be too late.

To the Space Marines of the Crimson Fists, I say this: if you receive this message in time to offer us any hope of rescue, know that we have abandoned Krugerport for the cave networks beneath the Scratch Mountains just north of the city. We'll dig in there for as long as we can. There is no other refuge left to us.

Our supplies are expected to last another week, perhaps two if we–

(Sound of distant stubber-fire answered immediately by the closer, louder crack of las-weapons. Urgent shouting from multiple individuals at once.)

The artillery has ceased. They're making an infantry push!

We're pulling out. I'm sending this without encryption.

In the name of the Immortal Saviour, I pray that some-one hears it.

Hurry! Get this message to Rynn's World! If we are to die here so that others might be warned, then so be it. But let our deaths not be in vain.

This is Commissar Alhaus Baldur signing off.

Munitorum Identicode (verified): CM41656-18F
Timestamp (IST): 17:44:01 3015989.M41

ONE

'When a man dies before his time, how much is truly lost?

More than just a life, certainly. A branch withers and bears no more fruit. Futures are erased. Paths close that can never be re-opened. Would his offspring have been saints? Killers? Both?

When a man dies before his time, the answers go with him.

This begs the question: should not all men be saved?'

Extract: *Diary of a Survivor*
Viscount Nilo Vanader Isopho
(936.M41-991.M41)

ONE

Arx Tyrannus, Hellblade Mountains

'UPHEAVAL,' SAID RUTHIO Terraro, staring down at the cards he had pulled from the deck. They lay in the pattern known as *The Burning Star*, a dark omen in itself. He did not remember touching a single one, nor had he consciously chosen their arrangement, but the absence of those memories did not surprise him. The deep trance was always the same. So was the awakening. Like a vivid dream of falling to one's death, it always ended with a shout and a shudder and a gasping for breath.

That he still emerged from the trance this way angered Terraro, for it was the mark of a Librarian yet to fully master his gifts, and the other Codiciers had already moved beyond it. But if it bothered the giant figure on Terraro's right, there was no indication.

'Upheaval,' echoed the giant. 'Go on, my brother.'

'A struggle against great odds,' Terraro continued, turning from the cards. 'Oceans of blood. Storm clouds, dark and heavy with impending violence. Below them, a fork in the road, signifying choice. Two paths, one leading to day, the other to night. So it has been the last four times, honoured brother, and with only the most minor variations. Do you wish me to try again?'

The giant, Eustace Mendoza, Master of the Librarius, moved to the Codicier's shoulder and stood over him, glaring down with dark, hooded eyes at the ancient cards. Their stylised images seemed to move, to dance in the glow from the golden candelabras, while the rest of the chamber remained thick with shadow.

'No, Ruthio,' he said, his voice a deep baritone. 'That will not be necessary. Your interpretation corroborates Brother Deguerro's visions. The currents of time and the immaterium will reveal nothing more to us tonight. The Epistolaries and I will discuss the matter at the next council. For now, you must return to your quarters and have the Chosen attend you. Full plate and arms, do you understand? We must look our finest. First light will break in four hours, and the Day of Foundation shall be upon us. There is a great deal of ceremony to observe.'

With a nod, Terraro gathered up his cards, pushed his chair back from the broad oak desk, and rose to his feet. Standing two metres tall, he was still a head shorter than the Master of the Librarius, but equally broad across the shoulders. On one of those shoulders, his master now placed a big calloused hand and, together, they walked from the room.

'Until the coming day is over,' Eustace Mendoza told Terraro as they passed into the echoing, lamplit corridor beyond, 'the future will have to wait.'

ALESSIO CORTEZ, WHO by his own confession lacked the slightest interest in the musical arts, found himself deeply moved by the hymn that now echoed from the Reclusiam's dark stone walls. It was as mournful as it was ancient, its every beautiful note a heart-rending lament to the battle-brothers the Chapter had lost, not just in the last hundred years, but in all the long millennia since its glorious inception.

Cortez had heard the hymn just three times in his life, for it was only sung on the Day of Foundation, but his perfect recall of those previous times did nothing to dull its effect now. All those deaths, all the one-sided farewells, they came back to him, just as they were meant to. This was the time to mourn properly. This was the time to remember the sacrifice his noble brothers had made, and his heart was heavy with the sorrow of it. More importantly, it was also filled with pride.

There was no guilt to dampen that feeling. He had survived three and a half centuries of war, and he was long past survivor's guilt. An Astartes lived or died by his skills and attributes, his teamwork, his unending dedication to perfecting the art of war and to the oaths of honourable service he had made. Death was inevitable, even for a Space Marine. It was just a matter of time. Immortality was the province of the Emperor alone, regardless of what anyone else said.

He looked across the Reclusiam to the opposite arm of the transept, studying the servitor-choir from which the hymn continued to pour forth. What pitiful creatures they were! Their skinny, limbless bodies were fixed to short pillars of black marble which concealed the mechanical workings that kept them half-alive. Every eye-socket was bolted over with iron plate. From every mouth, a black vox-amp grille protruded, and from each pale, hairless head, ribbed cables extended, linking them together in perfect synchronicity, their rudimentary intellects united and focussed only on the song.

On the gallery to Cortez's right, high above the Reclusiam's entrance, yet another servitor sat, hardwired into a massive mechanical steam organ that boomed out dour musical accompaniment.

Wretches all, thought Cortez. But perhaps it is better they sing our sadness for us than that we try to sing it for ourselves.

He almost grinned, thinking that his own rough voice, if forced into song, would do no honour to the dead. In fact, it was more likely to cause insult.

This was not an original thought. He made the same joke to himself every century, and let it pass just as quickly. Matters which did not involve the killing of the Chapter's many foes seldom held Cortez's attention for more than a few seconds.

Pedro was always chastising him for that.

The hymn came to an end now, its final sorrowful note reverberating in the minds of the congregation for moments after the sound itself had ceased. Cortez let it go, feeling unburdened somehow, and turned his attention towards the apse, to an altar of gilt-edged black marble where High Chaplain Tomasi now stepped forwards and began reciting words of remembrance from the Book of Dorn.

He was an impressive figure, Marqol Tomasi. As High Chaplain, he needed to be, for he was often required to command the absolute attention of large congregations such as this. There was no room for self-doubt or diffidence in a man of his station. It was his duty, and the duty of his subordinate Chaplains, to safeguard the faith and obedience of every last battle-brother and serf in the service of the Chapter. When he spoke, others had to listen, had to believe in him and in the religious strictures he espoused.

Cortez respected Tomasi a great deal, perhaps even liked him a little. The High Chaplain was a ferocious close-quarters fighter with almost as many high-profile kills to his name as Cortez himself claimed. But, more than this, they shared a certain outlook on life, characterised by its elegant simplicity. The enemies of the Emperor must be sundered, and the honour of the Chapter maintained. With these two things taken care of, all else was moot. What more could there be? Why did Pedro concern himself with secondary and tertiary matters, like the annual petitioners, or planetary law reforms, or pan-sector trade relations? What did any of that matter to a Space Marine?

After a few minutes, Tomasi stopped reading aloud from the *Book of Dorn*, and stepped around to the front of the golden lectern on which it rested. His armour was utterly black, polished to such a sheen that it gleamed like a dark mirror in the light from the wall sconces and the thousands of votive candles on either side of the apse. His ceramite breastplate and pauldrons were adorned with the gleaming bones of fallen foes and with wax-and-parchment purity seals, each delineated with a blessing written in blood. His helmet, with its distinctive faceplate – an extremely detailed rendition of a skull cast in flawless, polished gold – was clipped to his belt, leaving his harsh, deeply-lined features in plain view. Even among the Crimson Fists, few dared to hold that fearsome gaze for long.

This was the part of the service where Tomasi called out to the Emperor and to the Primarch Rogal Dorn to look down on the congregation and bless them in all the bloody work ahead. He spoke of the Chapter's hated enemies and of the slaughter they sought to perpetrate, the rape of worlds, the subjugation or destruction of all mankind.

His words took their intended effect, gradually charging the air as if an electrical storm were building. Cortez felt something rise within him and knew it was hate, pure and powerful and always there, his constant companion, fuel for the fire that burned inside.

Every century, scores of Crimson Fists gave their lives in battle to protect the Imperium from the foul maladies that infected it. From the outside, stabbing inwards with inexplicable hatred and barbarity, myriad alien races sought to undo all that the Imperium had struggled for ten thousand years to build. From the inside, perhaps the most contemptible of all, came the unforgivable corruption and madness of the traitor, the mutant and the foul, ungrateful heretic.

Aye, damn them all, Cortez cursed, fists clenched at his side. There will be no mercy for them, no quarter given. Their blood will turn the very stars red.

Tomasi was a master at this. Once every century, with the whole Chapter gathered here at Arx Tyrannus, he turned their brotherly grief into something far more potent, far more valuable and deadly. Cortez knew this feeling better than most; he had lived with it longer, and had embraced it without reserve. On all too many occasions during a lifetime filled with violence and slaughter, he had lain broken and bleeding in a bunker or in the back of a Rhino transport, and had heard the Apothecaries mutter that he would not survive his injuries this time. Every single time, his body had fought through the most horrific damage to mock their pronouncements, found the strength somewhere to heal itself and rise again and carried him back to war to execute the Chapter's never-ending duties.

He knew exactly where that strength came from, and he hoped his 4th Company would learn to embrace their hatred as he had. Not just in word or deed, but deeper, in the core of their souls, where it would bring them through horrors they would otherwise not survive.

Thinking of the battle-brothers under his command caused him to avert his gaze from the altar. He looked out along the central section of the great nave. In all, exactly nine hundred and forty-four Space Marines stood there, every last one dressed in full battle-plate, each pauldron and vambrace polished to perfection for this most important of days. They looked glorious, assembled together in their perfect ordered rows, facing the altar with their eyes fixed on Tomasi as he lifted a beautifully crafted bolter over his head and gave thanks to the Emperor and to the forges of Mars for the Chapter's long-serving weapons of war.

Among all the blue-armoured forms, Cortez picked out his own company, easily identified by the deep green trim on their pauldrons.

Under his leadership, the name 4th Company had become synonymous with the kind of decisive, all-or-nothing gambits which Cortez had always favoured. So others thought them reckless and brash – what of it? The surfaces of their armour were acid-etched with more glories, decorated with more honours than any other company save the Crusade Company, the elite 1st Company of the Crimson Fists.

As a sergeant, Cortez had once been a part of that glorious elite. All company captains earned their command that way, proving themselves worthy through years of exacting service under the Chapter Master's immediate personal command. But it was among his beloved 4th Company that Cortez knew he belonged, commanding some of the finest battle-brothers with whom he had ever marched into battle. Iamad, Benedictus, Cabrero, old one-eyed Silesi, vicious, unrelenting Vesdar. They were all born killers.

His focus rested momentarily on each of them, and he allowed himself the smallest of nods. Fine discipline. He expected no less. Not one of them moved. Not one spoke. All were utterly fixated on the solemn ceremony as it came, now, to its close.

High Chaplain Tomasi finally lowered the venerable gold-chased bolter from above his head and boomed, 'For each drop of our blood that is spilled, may crimson floods spill forth from the wounds of our enemies. For each scratch on our sacred armour, may their flesh and bone be cleaved apart by our blades, pulverised and shattered by our fists. The Imperium will endure. This Chapter will endure. Each of you shall endure. This we pray in the name of the primarch who shaped us, and in the name of the Emperor who made us.'

'For Dorn and the Emperor,' the assembly intoned. 'For the glory and honour of the Crimson Fists.'

Cortez lent the full power of his voice to the response. Standing beside him in the western transept, the other members of the Chapter Council did likewise.

'So we pray,' added the High Chaplain, more subdued now. 'So shall it be.'

Tomasi turned and nodded to a towering figure standing in a shadowed alcove to his left, then retreated from the altar to the reliquary at the rear of the Reclusiam, there to return the magnificent relics he had used during the service to their rightful place.

The tall figure on the left emerged from the shadows now, striding forward on long legs to take centre stage in front of the altar. Revealed in all his splendour, he was a breathtaking sight to behold. Light glittered from his gem-encrusted breastplate and from the shimmering golden halo behind his head. Golden skulls and beautifully embossed eagles graced his gorget, knee-plates and greaves. From his armoured waist, a tabard of red silk hung, proudly displaying the Chapter icon, a clenched red fist on a circular field of black. The ancient purity seals that hung from his pauldrons fluttered as he came to a stop.

Immediately, with the exception of the members of the Chapter Council, the congregation dropped to one knee.

Cortez and his council brothers simply bowed their heads, a privilege of their rank, and waited for the figure to speak. The voice, when it came, was strong and deep, warm like the currents of the South Adacean, a great bass rumble that was impossible to ignore.

'Stand, brothers. Please.'

Cortez had spent most of his life listening to that voice, doing as it commanded and, on no small number of occasions, debating fiercely with it. It was the voice of his closest friend, but also of his lord and leader. It belonged to Pedro Kantor, twenty-ninth Chapter Master of the Crimson Fists, and, barring perhaps the eight mighty Dreadnoughts who stood with their engines idling at the back of the nave, by far the most impressive figure in the Reclusiam that day.

'We have observed remembrance,' said the Chapter Master, 'for all those honoured brothers lost to us in the last hundred years. Their names have been inscribed on the walls of Monument Hall, and the records of their deeds have been committed to the *Book of Honour*. Any of you wishing to pay personal tribute after today may approach one of the Chaplains at a suitable time and request the proper prayers and offerings. This I strongly encourage you to do, as is our tradition, as is our obligation.' His eyes scanned the rows of silent Space Marines. 'We are the Crimson Fists,' he told them. 'We do not forgive, and we do not forget. The dead live on in our memories and through the progenoid, and our deeds must always – *always* – serve to honour them.'

In salute to the fallen, the Chapter Master balled his right gauntlet into a fist and clashed it three times against the sculpted left pectoral of his exquisitely crafted cuirass.

He watched the assembled warriors mirror him. 'We salute the fallen,' they intoned as one. 'We honour the dead.'

The Chapter Master waited for the echo to finish ricocheting from the shadowed rafters high above, then said, 'In a moment your captains will lead you out. We shall assemble on the Protheo Bastion, there to witness the Miracle of the Blood and receive the first of the day's battle-blessings. There will be no repast this day. The Day of Foundation requires us to fast, and you will all hold to that. After receiving our blessings on the Protheo Bastion, we shall return here for the initiations and the Steeping.'

Was it Cortez's imagination? For a split second, he was sure the Chapter Master had flicked a discreet glance in his direction before he continued, saying, 'We shall be joined today by members of the Upper Rynnhouse, who are travelling from New Rynn City to pay their respects to our Chapter and its traditions, and to celebrate the anniversary of our Founding with us. Some of you have made your objections known regarding this, and to these I say this; do not underestimate the importance of our relationship with the Rynnite nobility. In accepting the great responsibility of this star system's political governance, they have lifted from our shoulders all those burdens which do not befit men of war.'

He paused briefly before adding, 'See the value in that, as I do. They shall be landing at Tarvo Peak shortly and are here by my invitation. In all likelihood, you will not need to speak to them, but, if you do, you will show tolerance and courtesy. Remember, in a galaxy such as this, they are but children, and we are their protectors.'

Cortez frowned, certain, now, that much of this was directed his way. He and Kantor had locked horns over permitting the spoiled, self-indulgent aristocrats inside the sacred walls of the fortress-monastery, but the Chapter Master's word was law. With little choice, Cortez had ultimately backed down, stalking off to vent his frustrations on a combat drone in the training pits.

Cortez believed it was far better to be feared than loved. He knew Tomasi would have agreed. Better to maintain as much distance as possible from the weakling masses. The shameless way they threw themselves into utter dependence on those stronger than themselves sickened him. And what did inbred, soft-bellied socialites know of the meaning of sacrifice? What did the Imperium mean to them, save the security, comfort and personal profit it brought? Even those rare nobles who opted to spend a few years in the Rynnsguard only did so for the right to wear a dress uniform on festival days. Their terms of so-called active service were famously short and without incident.

The Chapter Master resumed speaking, abruptly cutting across Cortez's train of thought.

'My brother Astartes,' he said. 'This service is ended. Go with honour, with courage and with the Emperor's blessing, remembering always your sacred duty.'

'By your command,' replied the ranks.

The incense-thick air of the Reclusiam soon shook with the sound of armoured boots on stone as each of the captains led their companies through the sanctum's vast bronze doors. Cortez's turn came, and he moved out of the transept and down the central aisle, leaving only Captains Ashor Drakken and Drigo Alvez to follow.

Cortez threw the servitor choir a last brief, disdainful look as he left, noting that they had already been powered down. In their stationary silence, they now seemed little more than a row of hideous alabaster busts.

At a nod, 4th Company fell in behind him.

As he marched them under the great arched portal and out into the wide, snow-carpeted courtyard beyond, Cortez looked to the sky. Two hours ago, when the service had started, it had been a starless, midnight black. Since then, morning had broken over the Hellblade Mountains, bringing snowfall and a crisp, icy air that refreshed him, purging the unpleasantly rich incense from his nostrils.

As he marched, he wondered if, by the next Day of Foundation, his own name would be etched on the walls of Monument Hall. He had never feared death, always throwing himself headlong into even the most hopeless of battles with far more thought for the objective than for his own survival. Perhaps, coupled with his bottomless reserve of hatred for the enemy, that was exactly *why* he always survived. To fight without fear of death was liberating. Not that he was foolish enough to believe the myths that had sprung up around him, of course – myths in which the men of his company, marching in unison behind him, seemed to take a great and obvious delight.

Cortez the Immortal, they called him out of earshot.

He was certainly *not* immortal, despite popular speculation. One day, he knew, he would meet his match, and the preposterous rumours would be proven false. A part of him almost looked forward to that. If nothing else, it would be a most memorable fight.

When that day finally arrived, he wanted only two things from it.

The first was to die well, to sell his life dear with power fist smashing through armour and bone, pistol barking in his hand and a bloodcurdling battle cry on his lips.

The second was that the brothers who received organs cultured from his progenoid glands would honour him with their deeds, one day becoming heroes of the Chapter themselves.

It pleased Alessio Cortez to imagine such things.

Neither hope seemed particularly unreasonable.

When he and his men were halfway across the courtyard, his attention was suddenly diverted. A small, robed figure burst from a stone archway to the right, stumbled, and fell face-down in the snow. He got up immediately, ignoring the clods of white that now caked him, and continued his run in the direction of the Reclusiam's main entrance. The cog symbol on his left breast identified him as a serf belonging to Javier Adon's Technicarum. The runes underneath it showed that he served in the tower known as the Communicatus.

'You there!' Cortez barked. 'Halt!'

The man's legs froze before his mind even had time to process the words, such was the razor-sharp edge of authority in Cortez's voice.

'Are you so eager to die, Chosen?' asked Cortez, glaring over at him. 'You must know what will happen if you step beyond those doors.'

The men of 4th Company came to a smart halt behind their captain. They, too, stood facing the lone figure.

If the little man set one foot within the sanctum's walls, he was as good as dead. The strictures prohibited it. With the exception of the rare individuals who served the Sacratium, and servitors, only a full-blooded Astartes could enter the Reclusiam and live.

The man bowed low to Cortez, then once again to the battle-brothers behind him, and said, 'Honoured lord, I am imprinted with a message for the Chapter Master. Its urgency was deeply impressed upon me by the Monitor. I… I am ordered to deliver it no matter the consequences to my person.' He indicated the Reclusiam's wide entrance. 'I thought perhaps to catch Lord Kantor as he leaves.'

'He will not come out that way,' said Cortez, punctuating the remark with a small thrust of his chin in the direction of the great bronze portal. 'And Durlan Cholo knows better than to bother our lord on the Chapter's Day of Foundation. What kind of message warrants such urgency, I wonder?'

The serf fixed his gaze on the ground at Cortez's feet and replied, 'I was placed in trance for the imprinting, lord, so the content is unknown to me. I know only what the Monitor told me. He was most insistent that Master Kantor hear it at once.'

Cortez moved closer, his armoured boots crunching virgin snow, until he stood looking down on the little man from only a few metres away. 'Relay the message to me,' he said. 'I will go back inside immediately and pass it to His Lordship on your behalf.'

The serf weighed the offer for only a heartbeat. Any longer would have been a grave insult, for every living soul in Arx Tyrannus knew that Pedro Kantor loved and trusted Alessio Cortez above all others. To Cortez's knowledge, there were no secrets between the two of them.

His decision made, the serf smiled gratefully and dipped his head. 'The famous captain is both kind and wise. I shall sign the activation code to you now. Speak it back to me, lord, and I will automatically recount the message.'

Cortez nodded and watched closely as the serf's fingers fluttered, making a series of rapid symbols on the air.

'I have it,' said Cortez. '*Fifteen Theta Cerberus*.'

The serf's body immediately stiffened as if it had just received a massive electric shock. His head rolled to one side, his eyes glazed over, and he began speaking in a voice that bore no resemblance whatsoever to the one he had used only moments before.

'Emergency communication from Imperial commercial transport vessel *Videnhaus*. Omega-level encoding. Relay of deep space pulse-burst signal transmitted by Commissar Alhaus Baldur. Identicode verified. Message content follows...'

The voice changed again, dramatically.

Cortez felt a flood of mixed emotions wash over him as he listened to the little serf replay the words of the desperate Commissar Baldur, words that had been flung out into deep space weeks ago. The message had taken its time, but it had at last reached its destination. The odds that there were any defenders left alive on Badlanding were slim, to say the least. Then came mention of the ork Waaagh.

Cortez felt his pulse quicken. He heard blood rushing in his ears. Restless energy welled up inside him, charging his muscles, readying him for combat on the strength of the words alone.

A Waaagh!

Yes, this was something Pedro Kantor had to hear at once, regardless of ceremony, regardless of everything this day signified. The orks wouldn't wait. Ceremony and tradition meant nothing to them. There were few things in the galaxy more lethal and destructive than a full-scale Waaagh. Even now, the greenskins might be forcing their way further into the Loki Sector, smashing aside unprepared naval patrols and planetary defence forces. Badlanding would be an ideal beachhead.

The serf came to the end of his message and returned to full consciousness with a start. For a moment, Cortez thought the man would fall over in the snow and have some kind of seizure, but he steadied himself and looked up meekly. 'If my lord wishes me to repeat…'

Cortez shook his head. 'What is your name, Chosen?' he asked.

'Ha- Hammond, my lord,' said the man, clearly flattered to be asked. 'Hammond, if it please you.'

'Return to the Communicatus, Hammond,' said Cortez, 'and tell Cholo… tell the Monitor that Captain Cortez sends his gratitude. You have fulfilled your duty with distinction. On my honour, I go now to relay your words to the Chapter Master.'

Hammond's eyes started to glisten as the compliment registered. With some effort, he managed to hold back tears of joy and pride while still under Cortez's gaze. He bowed low once again, then made the sign of the aquila upon his chest and said, 'My lord's intervention has spared this unworthy life. He is as munificent as he is skilled in war. Truly, may the Emperor's glorious light ever shine upon him.'

Cortez silently prayed that his munificence and his skill in war were *not* equal. He would be dead many times over if they were.

He dismissed Hammond with a nod towards the stone archway through which the serf had come, then turned and walked back towards the Reclusiam's entrance. Over his shoulder, he called out, 'Sergeant Cabrero, lead the men to Protheo Bastion and wait for me there. I will join you momentarily.'

'At once, your munificence,' said Cabrero, almost managing to suppress a grin.

Cortez grinned back. His spirits, he realised, had been lifted by the very thought of going to war, and not just against any old opponent, but against the savage, filth-eating orks. Now *there* was an enemy who knew how to fight!

'You'll find out how munificent I am tomorrow on the training fields,' he told Cabrero.

The sergeant looked a lot less jovial at this prospect. He saluted stiffly, right fist to breastplate, and led 4th Company away as instructed.

Cortez walked back the way he had came, boots retracing the trail he and his men had just cut in the snow.

Ashor Drakken was emerging from the shadows of the Reclusiam's granite portico, leading his 3rd Company out into the wintry air. As Cortez marched in his direction, Drakken remarked dryly, 'Aren't you going the wrong way, brother?'

Cortez slowed only a little as he passed his fellow captain. 'This cannot wait, Ashor. Be ready to attend council. A session will surely be called.'

'Not today,' said Drakken, voice edged with arrogant certainty.

Cortez said no more. Grinning like a wolf, he turned, strode on and disappeared through the sanctum's doors.

TWO

Tarvo Peak, Hellblade Mountains

RAMIR SAVALES FORCED himself to straighten up. The mountain air held an icy chill this early in the morning, particularly now that Primagiddus, the Month of First Cold, was here, and he realised he had been hunching over to protect himself from its bite. That wouldn't do. One did not meet the planetary governor and the members of the Upper Rynnhouse standing stooped like an old man, whatever one's actual age.

Pulling a battered brass chronometer from his hip pocket, he checked the time. The shuttle still had a few more minutes to go before it could rightly be called late. He saw, too, that his fingers were reddish-pink, raw with the cold, and tried to rub some warmth into them.

Every year, the winter was getting marginally worse, or so it seemed to him. Life in the Hellblade

Mountains became that little bit harder, and the Month of First Warmth all the more welcome when it came. But he knew it wasn't the climate that was changing. Not really. It was his body, plain and simple. His best years were well behind him. Soon, he would have to approach the master about selecting an apprentice. Pride and simple stubbornness had delayed that particular conversation for far too long already.

He had been waiting for almost an hour now, standing on the periphery of the Tarvo Peak landing pad, just beyond the thick yellow line that marked the edge of the safety zone. The pad was a broad circle about a hundred metres across, projecting slightly outward from the gentle lower slope of the mountain like an oversized discus, supported from underneath by massive iron stanchions as thick as any of the limlat trees that grew in the far north. Tiny red lights winked in unison all along its circumference, and, painted in the very centre with its wings spread wide, was a massive white icon – a stylised eagle with two heads. He had supervised the repainting of it himself last summer. Its lines were still fine and sharp, though the day's snowfall was just starting to cover them.

Above the mountains, the clouds were the colour of wet slate. Bright, fat snowflakes spiralled down onto the shoulders of his all-weather greatcoat.

Underneath the coat, Savales wore a formal dress tunic, midnight-blue like the armour of his lords and decorated at the breast with the icon of the Chapter. It was a great honour to wear that icon, but the tunic wasn't doing much to keep him warm. Idly, he wondered how much more comfortable he might have been in the robes he usually wore about the fortress. His winter set, woven from thick *raumas* wool, were much more suitable for this weather. He donned the dress uniform only once or twice a year, and was thankful that most of those occasions fell within the spring and summer seasons.

A freezing gust of wind from the slope behind him cut through his coat and made him curse out loud. He turned to look over his shoulder, but neither the wind nor the curse seemed to bother the silent, stationary figures standing in a long double row behind him.

Servitors. Nothing bothered *them*. They patiently awaited his command, each pair holding a lacquered black palanquin between them.

Savales faced front again, muttering to himself.

Damn it, he swore, have I really become so fragile?

To think that he had once been an aspirant, had even passed the Trial of the Bloodied Hand. He might have been a battle-brother now, practically impervious to pain and discomfort, but the critical implant process had failed. Without the sacred implants, no matter how good a fighter he was, he was still just a man, and his destiny was to live and die as one, and to feel the cold in his aching old bones.

The seventeen sacred implants that would have made him a Crimson Fist…

He had been only fourteen summers old when the Chapter's Apothecaries had attempted the first procedure, and he would have given anything, anything at all, for it to have succeeded.

How cruel the fates had been!

How many nights since then had he dreamt of the life he might have led, sharing in the strength and glory of the armoured giants who had traversed the gulf between stars to find him and test him? How many nights had he awoken, cheeks damp with tears, weeping quietly into the dark silence of his room, lamenting all that might have been?

He had passed every test administered, mastered every task set. Death had done its best to stop him, and had taken all but one of his rivals, but it had not been able to reap the soul of Ramir Savales. He had survived, and he had earned his rightful place among the mighty while the other boys, all but Ulmar Teves, lay paralysed, drowning or bleeding to death in the stinking black marsh-waters of their home world.

The last test had been the hardest. The vicious sting of the bloated barb-dragon had almost pierced his skin. Just one microgram of its burning venom would have brought him unbearable agony, then madness, then finally death. Three times that lethal barb had almost pricked his wrists as he grappled with the noxious creature, but he had won out in the end. He had earned his place. No one, least of all Savales himself, had imagined that his own body, his own blasted flesh, would undo all his dreams.

With the cold momentarily forgotten, his face twisted at the thought. Fifty-seven years had passed, and he could still hear the words of the hard-eyed

Apothecary who had leaned over the table to which he had been strapped – words that had all but crushed his soul:

It is not to be, young one. Your body rebels. The implants will not take.

You are not destined to serve as we do.

You will never be Astartes.

It stung him even now, a wound that had never fully healed, though it had dulled significantly over the long years. Back then, he had wished for death to take him, to end the agony of his disappointment. It would have been the ultimate kindness. Instead of death, another kind of salvation presented itself, and it had come from an unexpected quarter. Pedro Kantor, Master of the Chapter, Lord Hellblade himself, had come to the teenage Savales in person as the boy sat weeping in the solitude of a dark stone cell deep below the surface of the Chapter's mountain home.

The master had spoken of the worth he saw in the broken-hearted youth, of potential that should not be wasted. So Savales was not to be an Astartes, the master had said. Regrettable, certainly, but perhaps the Emperor had another destiny laid out for him. The Chapter did not survive by the blood of its Space Marines alone. In his wisdom, Pedro Kantor had offered the failed neophyte another means by which to serve.

The young Savales had been apprenticed to the lord's aging major-domo, Argol Kondris, eventually replacing him when the older man passed away.

Ordinator of the House, the master's seneschal, highest ranking of all the Chosen – it was as grand a destiny as any mere mortal had the right to hope for, an honour beyond words. Savales had given thanks to the Emperor and His saints every single day since, just as he had prayed for the safety and long life of the one who had given him his glorious second chance, the very one who had charged him with greeting the Rynnite nobles out here on this bitter winter morning.

Yes, he thought, it is on the master's behalf that I stand here now. It is my duty, and that duty is a great blessing. So to hell with the blasted cold!

Mouthing Saint Serpico's *Ninth Litany of Resilience*, he lifted his eyes to the sky once more and tried to pierce the veils of falling snow for sign of an approaching craft.

Nothing.

His brow furrowed. He was about to check his chronometer again when he heard, ever so faintly, the distant, throaty hum of powerful turbine engines. The noise grew steadily louder and, seconds later, a black bulk resolved itself in the distance, just a shadow at first, but growing more solid, more detailed, as it closed the gap.

So it begins, thought Savales. At least they are on time.

Within minutes, the roar of the shuttle became deafening. As it swung in for its descent, vertical thrusters scorching the surface of the pad, its underside blotted out a good portion of the sky, and

Savales allowed himself a moment in which to be impressed. The Peregrine was a fine craft, almost thirty metres long, he judged, and perhaps fifteen in height, with a wingspan to match. Its prow was decorated with a gleaming eagle sculpted from solid gold. Unlike the icon painted on the landing pad, this one boasted only a single head. The craft's sleek gunmetal flanks bore the crests of the planetary government and each of the families that ruled the nine provinces, all beautifully rendered in gems and precious metals.

As the engines powered down, shifting from a rib-shaking roar to a gentle purr, Savales adjusted the lapels of his coat, smoothed his thinning grey hair, tugged his sleeves down, and stepped forward. He could feel welcome heat radiating from the massive turbines and willed his body to soak it in. Then, as he stood there in the shadow of the long, pointed prow, he heard a new sound – the whine of electric motors. The shuttle's belly eased open, forming a ramp down which two men marched in the bright, cream-coloured livery of the Rynnsguard. At the bottom of the ramp, each stepped aside, one to the left, the other to the right, and rested highly polished lasguns against their right shoulders. They did not make eye contact with him.

Savales felt a smile twitch the corners of his mouth. Overgrown pageboys, he thought with a private chuckle. They wouldn't last half a day back on Blackwater. The drechnidae would eat them alive, if the marsh-wallocs didn't get them first.

But that was unfair, and he felt a momentary stab of guilt. Lord Kantor had taught him better than that. The planetary defence forces *did* have a role to play. The nobles needed their bodyguards, and there were always some segments of the populace that needed to be kept in line, even here on Rynn's World, both of which were duties far beneath the notice of the legendary Adeptus Astartes.

More footsteps rang on the polished metal plates of the ramp now, and a pair of slender ankles appeared at the top, soon joined by more as the planetary governor and her entourage began descending towards Savales.

He took a deep breath, straightened his shoulders, and readied himself to greet the most powerful bureaucrats on the planet, hoping to Holy Terra that they wouldn't do anything stupid while they were here.

LADY MAIA CAGLIESTRA'S palanquin was well cushioned, but the ride was rough and the mountain road was often steep and uneven. Still, nothing could dampen her spirits on this most auspicious of days. She had waited all her life for this. To imagine that she would finally enter Arx Tyrannus. She almost felt like singing. Only decades of well-practiced restraint, of rigidly adhering to the rules of conduct her late mother had so sadistically impressed on her, kept her from externally expressing her joy. Ninety-seven years old – though anyone asked to guess would have wagered her a strikingly beautiful forty – yet she felt as giddy as a child on the morning of the Harvest End festival.

Even the icy air and the dark vista of the brooding black crags to either side of the road merely served to heighten the experience. These were the Hellblade Mountains, the domain of the legendary Crimson Fists.

He was here.

She had waited seven years just to see him again, and soon he would be before her, resplendent as always in his ceramite plate of blue and red and gold.

At a signal from the man who had introduced himself as Ordinator Savales, the hooded servitors carrying her conveyance came to a complete stop. The convoy had reached the end of the mountain road. Leaning out of her palanquin's left aperture, she saw that the column stood on the precipice of a yawning black chasm which separated them from their destination.

The Ordinator walked back to the side of the governor's carriage, and, bowing slightly, said to her, 'We've reached the main gates, ma'am. I thought you might like to watch the bridge extend.'

From the palanquin's shadowed interior, Maia smiled up at him and held out her hand. Her senior secretary, whom she affectionately called Little Mylos, was already hurrying forward from the rear of the column to attend to her, but he was too late. Savales gently helped her to her feet. As she grasped the seneschal's forearm for support, she remarked to herself on the ropey hardness of his muscles.

He must have been a fine specimen once, she thought. I wonder how old he is.

Once she was standing, Ordinator Savales gestured to his left, and Maia turned her eyes to follow. There before her, towering above the far lip of the chasm, were the great outer gates of the fortress-monastery Arx Tyrannus.

For a few seconds, Maia Cagliestra forgot to breathe.

'By the Golden Throne,' she gasped at last.

None of the pictographs in her extensive library could hope to do the sight justice. The gates were at least a hundred metres tall. As a child, so very long ago, she had read all about them. She knew that they had once comprised the prow armour of the legendary starship, *Rutilus Tyrannus*, the original spacefaring home of the Chapter in the long millennia before the Crimson Fists had been given domain over Rynn's World. Even today, the heritage of those gates was unmistakable. They still bore the vast shining aquila design that had decorated the front of the mighty craft.

The gates were set between two massive, square-cut towers that bristled with artillery and missile batteries, all pointed upwards at the dark grey sky, ready to fend off a threat that Maia couldn't imagine ever daring to approach. Even the foulest and most violent of the xenos races surely weren't foolish enough to attack a Space Marine home world.

Extending from either side of the towers were the fortress-monastery's gargantuan ramparts, thrusting up at sharp angles from the black rock, as

timeless and immovable as the mountains themselves, as if they, too, had been formed in some
distant, pre-historic age. The walls, like the gates,
had been built from the stuff of *Rutilus Tyrannus*,
and were studded all along their length with devastating long-range weaponry, much of which had no
doubt once graced the port and starboard batteries
of the ship.

How many enemy craft had those guns obliterated
in their battles between the stars, Maia wondered?

High on the slopes of nearby peaks, she saw other
structures, smaller but similarly fortified against
attack. The appearance of most of these gave little
clue as to their purpose, but one bore large arrays of
deep-space receivers and transmitters, and she recognised it from her books as the Communicatus. As she
looked, a bulky Thunderhawk gunship hove into
view just below the cloud line, arriving from the
north-west and slowing to land on the roof of a large
cylindrical building that jutted from a hazardous-
looking slope to the north.

She heard Savales say something – she didn't quite
catch it – and turned to look at him. He had one finger pressed to a small mechanical device that
encircled his left ear.

'I'm sorry, Ordinator,' she said. 'Were you talking to
me?'

Savales didn't answer immediately. Any words
would have been drowned out by the tremendous
metallic groan that now issued from the far side of
the chasm.

Maia turned and watched, her mouth slightly agape, as the gates of Arx Tyrannus creaked slowly open and, from a broad horizontal housing in the rock below them, a metal bridge extended.

It was almost four minutes before the noise finally stopped. When it did, the bridge was firmly locked into place, spanning the width of the chasm, and the gates were thrown as wide as they would go.

On the far side, Maia saw large humanoid figures marching out to meet them. Her heart leapt. Surely these were the first Crimson Fists she would lay eyes on today. As they moved out from the shadows of the gates she saw instead that they were hulking gun-servitors led by one of the Chapter's senior serfs. They took up positions on either side of the bridge, facing inward like statues lining a long hall. They did not look in the direction of the nobles.

Perhaps reading disappointment on Maia's face, Ordinator Savales said, 'It is a rare occasion that no Astartes mans the gates, but today is just such an occasion, my lady. On the Day of Foundation, every battle-brother who is able is required to attend the ceremonies.' He gestured to Maia's palanquin. 'Shall we proceed?'

Maia was still a little overwhelmed by the cold, dark grandeur of Arx Tyrannus and didn't trust herself to speak, but she nodded and accepted the Ordinator's help in returning to her seat, absently noting his quiet strength for the second time. Moments later, as the palanquins passed before the dull, expressionless eyes of the gun-servitors, Maia felt a chill that even her thick furs could do nothing to abate. This was most definitely not the warm welcome she had imagined. On either side of the bridge, the lobotomised living weapons tracked the palanquins as they passed. Their weapons were powered up. Maia could hear the hum of deadly, constrained energies. Her skin prickled and her breath became tight in her chest. No one had ever aimed a weapon at her before, at least not overtly. There had been a few failed assassination attempts over the years, but she had only learned of those after the fact.

Now, she forced her eyes forward, willing her heartbeat to slow back down.

It didn't return to its regular rhythm until she was beyond the gates.

THREE

Arx Tyrannus, Hellblade Mountains

FROM HIGH ATOP the black stone walls of the central keep, banners of blue, crimson and gold rippled and snapped in a cold wind, each beautifully decorated with the proud heraldry of the Chapter's ten companies and the iconography of a thousand glorious crusades.

On the spacious, snow-dusted grounds of the Protheo Bastion, a hundred metres below those banners, the Space Marines of the Crimson Fists stood in perfect formation, each armoured warrior a metre apart from the battle-brothers to either side, all arranged according to company, squad and seniority.

Trails of steamy breath and exhaust fumes rolled into the air from the vents in their helmets and backpacks. Their broad-barrelled boltguns were held rigidly in front of them, gripped in gauntleted hands, muzzles pointing skyward.

Behind the Space Marines stood over six thousand of the Chosen, all robed in blue to match the armour of their masters, all with hooded heads bowed.

No one, neither Space Marine nor serf, turned or gave even a flicker of notice as Ordinator Savales led Lady Maia and her party beneath the vast south-western archway and out onto the grounds.

From the line of nobles following in Savales's wake, there came a jumble of gasps and suitably hushed exclamations. Savales let the moment pass of its own accord and kept walking, anxious that his charges be seated out of the way as quickly as possible. To that end, he led them north along the base of the towering inner wall, thirty metres back from the closest row of Crimson Fists, guiding the nobles straight towards a small wooden terrace that had been constructed by the Chosen specifically for the purpose of their visit.

Despite the brisk pace he set at the front of the line, he suddenly found himself addressed by the governor. She had come up alongside him, matching his stride easily with her long slender legs. 'They're incredible, Ordinator,' she breathed, making no effort to disguise the depth of her awe. 'I mean, I've seen them before in the capital, but never like this. Never all together like this. I... I don't think I've ever felt the Emperor's presence as surely as I do right now.'

Savales glanced at her, intending to express his agreement in the briefest possible terms, but the words died on his lips the moment he saw that the governor was actually weeping. Tears were running in two glistening tracks down her soft, powdered cheeks.

He and the governor came from different worlds, both literally and figuratively speaking, but here, in her reaction to the great spectacle before her, was something he could truly identify with. The assembled Astartes were a sight to stir the heart of any Imperial loyalist.

He didn't slow his pace, but his voice was kind as he answered, 'No one has seen the Chapter together like this for a hundred years, ma'am. Not even I. It is indeed a magnificent sight, as you rightly say. My heart is gladdened that it affects you so.'

The governor smiled a little self-consciously at that, then quietly dropped back beside her secretary, who offered her a small square of silk with which to dab at her face.

If the nearest of the Space Marines had heard the exchange – and of course they had, for their powers of hearing went far beyond those of a normal man – they showed no sign of interest. Both they and the Chosen remained as still as marble sculptures, awaiting the arrival of the Chaplains and the members of the Chapter Council.

Savales and his wealthy charges soon reached a set of shallow wooden stairs that led up into the small terrace. The Ordinator stopped beside them and helped Lady Maia up the first few steps, more out of propriety than anything else. The lady clearly had no need of a man's steadying arm, but took it anyway, no doubt as a point of etiquette.

'Your party shall have an excellent view of the proceedings from here, ma'am,' said Savales to her back as she stepped through the doorway at the top.

And it will keep you all penned in very nicely, he thought to himself. No one must interfere with the procession.

Once the last of the entourage from the capital had climbed the stairs, Savales ascended them himself and found most of the nobles already seated in the well-cushioned ebonwood chairs that had been laid out for them. A handful of the Chapter's most junior serfs stood silently in the shadows at the back, awaiting any command Savales might deign to give. As he looked along the front row, Savales saw that the chair closest to Lady Maia remained curiously empty. Standing in front of it, looking slightly put out, was Viscount Isopho, Minister of Trade, senior representative for the Province of Dorado.

'I don't understand, Maia,' he said, absentmindedly addressing her as if no one else were within earshot. 'It is quite clearly my seat. Why in blazes–'

Lady Maia threw him the kind of smile that Savales judged she must have used countless times to get her own way. It was dazzling and absolutely filled with promise. 'My dear, gallant Nilo,' she said. 'Your close company is always a great blessing, as I've expressed before. But I *had* hoped Ordinator Savales might sit beside me today, unless you feel that you can explain the various elements of the procession better than he.'

The viscount, a slim, dapper, thickly-moustached man in his mid-fifties, threw Savales a brief, hard glance. He was obviously incensed that the governor wished him to defer to someone who was still, technically, a member of the peasant class, no matter what Savales's status within these hallowed walls might be. After a few seconds the viscount mustered a fairly convincing smile of his own, bowed to the lady, and said, 'As you wish, of course.' Then he turned towards Savales, walked down the row of seats towards him, and said, 'Might one of your people bring another chair, Ordinator?'

Secretary Mylos, who was seated at the near end of the front row, leapt to his feet. 'There's no need for that, sir,' he said. 'Please, take mine. I'll be quite content to sit with the other aides in the second row.'

Isopho muttered something vaguely appreciative to Mylos, and dropped himself into the seat, dropping his smile at the same time.

Savales noticed Lady Maia gesturing to him and, with some reluctance, for he had no wish to talk during the procession, took the proffered seat next to her. On his right sat Margravine Lyotsa of Macarro Province, a slightly plump woman who was beaming with enthusiasm for the whole affair. 'Do you think the Chapter Master might wave to us as he passes?' she asked Savales.

It was a preposterous question, and Savales fought to hold back a sharp retort. Did the woman think this some kind of carnival? Instead, he feigned an apologetic tone and answered, 'I shouldn't think so, my lady. In truth, the Day of Foundation is a time of great solemnity and reflection, not celebration. As I tried to impress on your honoured personage during the journey here, we who bask in the glory of the Crimson Fists this day must make ourselves all but invisible during their observances. To draw undue attention, to interfere in even the smallest of ways, so much as a well-meaning wave of your hand, for example, would be a very grave insult to the honour of our protectors. We must conduct ourselves just as if we were in the Great Basilica. One refrains from calling out to Archbishop Galenda during his famous sermons, does one not?'

The margravine looked horrified at the thought. 'By the Golden Throne,' she huffed, 'I would never… Your point is well taken, Ordinator. I shall be as invisible as my countenance allows.'

Savales wasn't sure what she meant, but it hardly mattered. He was pleased to see the expression on her round face settle into something more appropriate to the solemnity of the occasion. It was then that he felt the lightest touch of fingertips on the back of his left hand and turned to face Lady Maia again.

'How long will they stand immobile like this?' the governor asked him, looking out at the rigid Space Marines. 'Not one of them has so much as twitched a muscle since we arrived. If not for their breath on the air, I would swear those suits of armour were empty.'

As Savales listened to her, he eased the old brass chronometer from his pocket and stared at its face in confusion.

It must be broken, he thought. This cannot be correct.

But no, one hand was still ticking off the seconds as steadily as it had always done. The chronometer was an ancient piece, inherited from old Kondris, and it had not dropped a second in all the years Savales had owned it. What its elegant metal hands told him now was that something must be wrong. He watched more seconds tick off, filled with a mounting sense of unease.

The morning procession should have started by now. And Lord Kantor, as Ramir Savales knew better than anyone else, was never late.

THE GREAT DOMED and pillared hall of the Strategium was quiet, but it was far from empty. Only two of the heavy, square-cut onyx chairs arranged around the massive crystal table at its centre remained unoccupied.

Where the devil are they, thought Cortez? He had been the third member of the council to arrive, and now he was becoming restless.

He had passed Hammond's message to the Chapter Master in the nave of the Reclusiam, and had watched the words take effect. The Chapter Master had reacted exactly as Cortez had known he would: calm, controlled, only the slight narrowing of his eyes betraying a hint of anger that news of the attack on Badlanding should reach Arx Tyrannus now, on this of all days. Inconvenient, yes, but none who had faced the might of the greenskins before and survived would dare to take such news lightly. The message's significance could not be ignored. Like a thunderstorm gathering on the horizon, its charge building on the wind, it seemed the threat of a major war here in the Loki Sector was closer than it had been in over a millennium.

Orks!

Give or take a dozen light-years, Badlanding essentially lay on a straight line between the Rynnstar system and the domain of Charadon, a star cluster that was absolutely infested with the savage beasts. If the transmission from the struggling commissar was to be believed, and a Waaagh was indeed gaining momentum on the fringes of the sector, then the Crimson Fists were the only force within a year's warp travel that had a chance of reacting in time and with the appropriate level of force. Founding Day or not, action in the face of a major Waaagh could not be postponed.

So where in blazes are you, Pedro, thought Cortez?

He drummed his gauntleted fingers on the table, the sound cutting sharply across a tense silence. A few of the other council members glared over at him in irritation.

'What?' he said in a challenging tone, but he stopped drumming.

After another minute of silence, he said, 'If we have to wait much longer I think I'll chair the meeting myself.'

Raphael Acastus, Master of Siege, Captain of the 9th Company, snorted out a laugh. No one took the comment seriously. Cortez was famously impatient and rarely disinclined to express it. But Drigo Alvez, Master of the Shield, Captain of 2nd Company, saw a chance to knock Cortez down a peg. He met his gaze and said, 'Actually, Alessio, that duty would fall to me. Still, I commend your enthusiasm. If only you could channel it into sitting still...'

A few of the other captains raised half-smiles at this. Cortez grunted. He and Alvez had no great love of each other. The 2nd Company captain was as dour and over-starched a Space Marine as Cortez had ever met, unimaginative in the extreme, but it was these very qualities that apparently inspired the Chapter Master's confidence in him. Besides, Alvez was wrong. It was, in fact, Eustace Mendoza, Master of the Librarius, who would preside over the Strategium in the event of the Chapter Master's absence. And if Mendoza were absent, the duty would fall to High Chaplain Tomasi.

For a moment, Cortez considered pointing this out, but before he spoke, his eyes flicked towards the old Librarian, and he noticed that Mendoza was looking straight back at him. The Librarian held his gaze, giving a barely perceptible shake of his head.

In Cortez's mind, the powerful psyker placed three words.

Leave it, brother.

Cortez responded with a tiny shrug and resumed drumming his fingers on the tabletop, once again drawing the eyes of the others toward him.

Ishmael Icario, Master of Shadows, Captain of the 10th Company, laughed aloud. 'Alessio,' he said, 'of every battle-brother I have ever known, none are as restless as you. Chapter Master Traegus said it best, I think. *Only in the absolute stillness of the body and the complete silencing of the voice can we hear the truth of our inner thoughts, and so hearing, know ourselves that much the better.'*

Cortez threw Icario a dangerous look.

Algernon Traegus had been the controversial sixteenth Chapter Master of the Crimson Fists, a particular favourite of Icario's, judging by the frequency with which the Scout captain quoted the late Master's writings. Many of the older members of the Chapter were wary of Traegus's teachings. It was Traegus who had initiated the controversial breeding programmes – programmes by which the Chapter's failed aspirants, those who had survived the trials and had not been rendered sterile, were bred with women of suitable genetic stock in the hope of creating male offspring strong enough to swell the ranks of the Chapter one day as full Astartes.

Unfortunately, the results had been unpredictable and disappointing.

Upon his accession, the seventeenth Chapter Master, Klede Sargo, had immediately halted his predecessor's plan, and no Chapter Master had attempted to revive it since.

Responding to Icario, Cortez said, 'I can hear my inner voice fine, brother. It speaks with the volume of a thunderstorm, and right now, it tells me there are xenos to kill. The sooner we engage them, the better.'

'And so we shall,' answered a sonorous voice from the far side of the hall. The words echoed for a moment, bouncing back from the frescoed inner surface of the dome. The seated Astartes twisted and saw Pedro Kantor closing two massive ebonwood doors. They rose to their feet as the Chapter Master turned and descended the steps of the main aisle, walking between steeply tiered rows of white marble benches, down onto the Strategium floor. With a long, easy stride, as if his heavy power armour weighed little more than cloth, he crossed to the onyx throne at the head of the table and seated himself, gesturing for the others to do likewise. The chair beneath him detected his weight as he sat, and gear assemblies sunk into the floor groaned and rattled as they pulled him in towards the table's edge.

The Chapter Master rested his heavy vambraces on the gently glowing crystal surface, meshed his armoured fingers together and leaned forward. 'My apologies, brothers, for keeping you waiting these extra moments. I wished to talk to the Monitor directly, and to send word to Ordinator Savales that there would be a slight delay to the day's proceedings. You all know by now the reason this impromptu session has been called.'

Captain Acastus stared pointedly at the only onyx chair which remained empty. 'Shall the High Chaplain not be joining us, my lord? Should we not wait for him?'

Kantor angled his head towards Acastus, and said, 'The great majority of this day's responsibilities fall on Tomasi's shoulders, certainly far more than fall on mine. He cannot be distracted before the Miracle of the Blood. I will apprise him later of what is said here, but we will hear Brother Adon's report without him.'

Having said this, Kantor nodded to a member of the assembly who, on appearance alone, truly stood out among the rest. This was the Forgemaster, Javier

Adon, Master of the Technicarum, the Chapter's supreme Techmarine. His great affinity with the machine-spirits was all too evident in the clash of meat and metal that he had become. His armour bore the iconography of both the Chapter and the Adeptus Mechanicus, and the powerful servo-arms which sprouted from his back gave him something of the aspect of a mighty mechanical arachnid. When he spoke, the sound reverberated from a grille that masked the lower half of his face, and his words emerged in a rasping, grating mechanical buzz without tone or inflection.

'Assembled brothers,' he began. 'At 07:58hrs on this Day of Foundation, our near-space communications array received and decoded a pulse-burst signal with an Omega-level Imperial encryption key. The signal was broadcast repeatedly at fifteen-second intervals, originating from a commercial transport that slid from the warp two astronomical units outside the orbit of Phraecos.'

One of Adon's mechanical appendages swung up and over his right shoulder with a whirring sound. It slotted a thick, digit-mounted data plug into a socket set in the table's rim and pressed it home with an audible click. At once, the quartz tabletop began to glow brighter, to pulsate with light, and a ghostly hololithic view of the local star system manifested in the air above it.

The assembled Astartes raised their eyes.

'The transmitting vessel's identicode has been verified,' Adon continued. 'The ship is known as the

Videnhaus and is properly registered. There is no reason to doubt the veracity of her transmission, though the encryption was added later by the ship's captain. The original message, we now know, was transmitted raw from the planet Badlanding.'

'And the content of that transmission?' asked Ashor Drakken, Captain of 3rd Company, Master of the Line.

There was a short burst of static, and the voice of Commissar Alhaus Baldur filled the air. 'There won't be time to broadcast again,' said the voice, 'so this is it...'

Forgemaster Adon played the message in its entirety while the others listened with rapt attention. By the end of it, Cortez could barely sit still. Hearing it for the second time, he found his urge to ship out for Badlanding was even stronger. Battle beckoned him.

'That is all,' said Adon when the commissar's voice stopped. 'There is no more.'

'It is enough in any case,' said Cortez. He locked eyes with Kantor. 'Send my Fourth Company, lord. Badlanding will be purged of the greenskin taint. We will descend on them like holy fire.'

'Send the Seventh,' said Caldimus Ortiz, Master of the Gates, with equal passion. 'If not alone, then in support of Brother-Captain Cortez.'

Kantor unlocked his fingers and raised both hands into the air, calling for calm. The captains always vied with each other for the honour of deployment. He expected no less, but his decision would, as always, be based on tactical analysis. He did not play favourites, despite his friendship with Alessio Cortez.

'Forgemaster, show us Badlanding in relation to Rynn's World. And give me an estimate of travel time, both best and worst case scenarios.'

Javier Adon remained still, but above the table the ghostly view of the Rynnstar system zoomed out with dizzying speed to show the relative positions of both Rynnstar and Freiya, the K-type star around which Badlanding orbited. Figures began to scroll down past each of the tiny flickering points of light.

After a moment, the figures stopped scrolling, and Adon said, 'If the warp is calm, and the tides and eddies favour us, one of our cruisers could reach high orbit around the target planet in approximately three hundred and sixty-eight standard hours.'

'That's almost two weeks,' growled Cortez. 'The greenskins might have moved on by then. We should mobilise at once!'

'If the warp is turbulent,' Adon continued, 'and the tides are against us, the journey could take many times longer. A worst-case scenario is beyond my ability to accurately calculate with the information I currently have. Perhaps the Master of the Librarius would offer comment.'

Eustace Mendoza angled his head towards Pedro Kantor. 'Local warpflow appears relatively untroubled at this time. The Librarius has detected no significant disturbances that would present a problem to travel.'

As he watched and listened, Cortez had the feeling that Mendoza was preoccupied with something else, and it wasn't just the Day of Foundation. In the shadowed corridors of the fortress-monastery, it was cautiously whispered that some of the other Librarians had been reporting dark omens with increasing frequency. Was the master psyker holding something back?

An impressive figure seated on the Chapter Master's immediate right cleared his throat, drawing all eyes in his direction. His power armour was highly ornate, and his left pauldron, rather than bearing any form of company-centric iconography, was fashioned into a great silver eagle with two heads. This was Ceval Ranparre, Master of the Fleet, Hero of Hesperidon.

'Two weeks then,' he said. 'Trust me, Chapter Master, as you have always done. I can get a force to Badlanding in that time, ill tides or otherwise. If you will permit it, I shall send *The Crusader*. Of all our fleet, she is the most reliable when a swift warp transit is of the essence.'

Kantor accepted the suggestion with a nod. 'Then I shall focus my attention on who is to go.'

'The Fourth,' said Cortez again. 'There is no time to debate it, not if we are to make any kind of difference to Commissar Baldur and his remaining men.'

Drigo Alvez snorted derisively at this. Cortez knew as well as anyone that the Imperial forces on Badlanding were almost certainly dead to a man.

Kantor cast his eyes around the assembled leaders. He laid his palms flat on the table and pushed himself to his feet. With his weight no longer on the black throne, the servos jerked into action again and moved the chair out from under the table. Standing there like a vision of ancient glory, an echo of the primarch remembered from the time of the Great Crusade, the Chapter Master towered over the rest of the council.

'Let us be realistic, brothers. This will be no rescue mission. Those men are dead. Our priority at this point must be to gather intelligence on the threat of this alleged Waaagh. We have put down many significant ork incursions over the years, and the cost in Astartes lives has ever been great. If there is a way to rob this Waaagh of its momentum before it threatens the rest of the sector, I want it found and exploited.'

As one, the figures around the table rose to their feet and clashed their fists against their ceramite cuirasses. 'In the primarch's name,' they intoned.

Kantor nodded, then turned from the table and began striding back up the broad steps towards the Strategium's double doors. At the top, he stopped, looked back at the council members, and said, 'Ranparre, issue preparation orders to the crew of *The Crusader* as soon as the Miracle of the Blood is over. Forgemaster Adon, have the Techmarines ready weapons and equipment for a company-strength force.'

'Aye, my lord,' buzzed Adon.

Kantor paused with one hand on the heavy bronze ring of a door handle, and added, 'The procession will begin in fifteen minutes. The rites must be properly observed. Make sure you are all in place before it starts. As for my decision regarding which captain shall have the honour of this task, I will let you know after the Steeping.'

There was a groan of iron hinges, then the heavy wooden doors crashed shut behind the Chapter Master's back.

In the sunken circle of the Strategium floor, the council members saluted each other and disbanded, each captain hoping that the honour of battle in the Emperor's name would fall to him.

'The procession is starting,' said Savales, relief evident in his voice.

Twenty minutes earlier, a message from Lord Kantor had arrived. A short emergency session of the Chapter Council had been called. The Ordinator had been on edge ever since. What could be so grave as to interrupt this holiest of days? His knuckles had been white, fingers clenched tightly around his chronometer until, now, at last, he placed the old heirloom back in his pocket.

'It is starting, ma'am,' he said again.

Maia leaned forward in her chair and drew an excited, trembling breath.

A tall, dark figure appeared, striding through a twenty-metre archway to the far left of the bastion grounds. All the Chosen standing in line behind their Astartes masters immediately dropped to their knees.

Maia's heart leapt. It was him at last! She felt like she would burst at the sight of him. He was shining with an incredible light, resplendent in armour so polished that it was almost too glorious to behold.

She had waited a long time to lay eyes on Pedro Kantor again. It had been seven years since she had last spent thirty all-too-brief minutes in council with him at the capital. He had seen many battles since then, but, if his armour had been damaged in the fighting, it showed no sign of it now. The Chapter's artificers were unequalled in their skill.

He was every bit the vision of strength and honour she recalled.

As if reading her mind, Ordinator Savales whispered, 'He is an unforgettable sight, isn't he? And look, here comes High Chaplain Tomasi and the members of the Sacratium. Do you see the crystal sceptre?'

Maia nodded. She could hardly miss it, a mass of sculpted gold and las-cut crystal that surely weighed twice what she herself did. For all its weight, the terrifying figure of the High Chaplain carried it with deceptive ease.

The Miracle of the Blood.

Maia's father had spoken of it only once. It was, he had told her, a thing too great, too powerful and significant, to be shared through a medium as limited as language. He had died hoping she would see it for herself one day.

Now, watching High Chaplain Tomasi march gravely down the avenue between the Astartes ranks, a chill ran up Maia's spine. The Chaplain was the stuff of nightmares, a vision of death, and she forced her eyes to stay on the beautiful sceptre itself, rather than gaze into the black hollows of his skull-helm's eye sockets for any length of time. By contrast, the sceptre's head was like a shimmering golden sunburst.

Rays of metal surrounded a perfect sphere of trans-
parent crystal, and that sphere was half-filled with
what appeared to be dried blood.

As Tomasi took step after measured step, following
the Chapter Master's exact path, he swung the head of
the sceptre slowly from left to right above him.
Behind him came a score of other Chaplains, also
dressed in black armour, faces likewise encased in
leering ceramite skulls. Some of these were hooded,
the lipless lower jaws of their death-masks protruding
from deep shadow. Others were not. All carried items
of holy significance. For some, it was censers that
swung like pendulums, filling the air with strongly-
scented blue smoke. For others, it was ancient tomes,
the leather covers of which were embossed with the
Imperial aquila and the fist symbol of the Chapter.
Others carried ancient weapons, no doubt priceless
beyond measure and surely once belonging to heroes
long gone but not forgotten.

All chanted blessings as they moved, their voices
merging, blending in a low hypnotic hum.

'Watch the sceptre,' Savales told her.

Maia fixed her eyes on it, following it left and right,
left and right. Gradually, she realised that something
was happening. A change was taking place within the
crystal sphere at the top.

'The blood,' she breathed.

As the High Chaplain passed, still swinging the
head of the sceptre in time with his steps, the dried
blood visible within the sphere began to revert to
liquid.

Maia gasped, unsure of what her eyes were reporting, but Savales's hushed voice confirmed it.

'The crystal sphere holds the blood of Rogal Dorn himself,' he said. 'Imagine that, my lady. We are witnessing the blood of the primarch reverting to liquid form, ten thousand years after it was sealed inside! A true miracle! That blood was preserved by an Apothecary after the primarch was wounded in the defence of Holy Terra. To see it change before us now...'

Maia felt faint, dizzy. Though she looked young, she was not. She became afraid that her heart would betray her, that this was all simply too much. The blood of Rogal Dorn, son of the Emperor Himself... Her mind spun with the significance of it. She could offer the Ordinator no response.

The other nobles, too, were deeply affected by the change in the crystal sphere. They had heard Savales's whispered explanation, and they sat stunned. Some wept quietly, their faith in the Imperial Creed somehow finally vindicated by this one inexplicable event.

Maia heard Viscount Isopho, his voice low and reverent, ask, 'But what does it *mean*, Ordinator?'

Savales kept his unblinking eyes on the sceptre as he answered.

'It means that the primarch is still with us, viscount. He still watches over the Crimson Fists. Mankind is not alone, even now, even after ten thousand years of war and darkness and ceaseless slaughter. And if the primarch is with us, then the Emperor is, too.'

Maia felt the hairs rise on the back of her neck. She believed it, everything the Ordinator was saying. The

Miracle of the Blood was like nothing she had ever known. Archbishop Galendra constantly insisted that faith was its own reward. But here... here was proof!

She sat stunned, her body numb throughout the rest of the procession.

For three whole days after her return to the capital, she refused to see or speak to anyone, such was the effect of what she had seen. It had shaken her, shaken the way she viewed so many things. She felt lost at first, needing to understand her place in the Imperium under this new light. When she finally returned to her official duties, it was with a dedication and commitment that even her greatest detractors could not deny. Her faith blazed inside her. Others saw it in her eyes.

Maia Cagliestra did not know it then, of course, but she would need every last bit of that faith in the grim, blood-sodden days to come.

FOUR

Space, Badlanding

LARGE PICT-SCREENS DOMINATED the curving forward wall of the command bridge aboard *The Crusader*, auspex data pouring across them like torrents of glowing rain down a hundred black windowpanes. On the largest and most central of them, no data flowed at all. Instead, its pixels displayed the image of the ship's senior astropath, a pale, wizened man by the name of Cryxus Gloi. He looked to be well into his ninth decade of life when, in fact, he was a mere forty-four years old. The rigours of his calling had robbed him of much, including conventional sight. His eyes had atrophied during the soul-binding, when his mind had been reshaped by the Emperor until all that was left were two dark, hollow sockets, but their loss mattered little. Gloi had sight of another, far more potent kind.

Captain Ashor Drakken stood in full armour, staring at Gloi's face on the screen, fists clenched at his sides. The honour bestowed by Kantor on his former company must be repaid. Drakken could not allow the mission to fail. 'There must be a way,' he growled. 'Master Kantor must be apprised at once. If this moon can hide us from their scanner arrays, surely it can cover an astropathic transmission.'

Gloi's brow furrowed. 'Nothing, captain, can cover an astropathic transmission. The moment I attempt to send any kind of word out, every ork psyker on those ships will know exactly where we are, I promise you. If you wish me to manipulate the ether without alerting our foes, we must return to the far fringes of the system where we last exited the warp. From there, I might safely send word, but no nearer. It would invite a ship-to-ship conflict that you and I both know we would not survive.'

Gloi was no coward. He had served on *The Crusader* for over twenty years, performing his duties flawlessly under battle conditions, and had earned the right to speak plainly to whomever he served. Those without the witch-sight seldom understood much about the warp. The smart ones quickly learned to trust those who did.

'Very well, Gloi,' said Drakken. 'That is all for now.'

He dropped the pict-link and turned to his second in command, who stood patiently by his side.

'Comments, Leo?'

Sergeant Leoxus Werner looked thoughtful. He was not a man to make pronouncements lightly. Both his gauntlets were crimson, marking him as a veteran of the Chapter. He had been decorated numerous times in his century and a half of service, and rightly so. His face was a map of deep, angry scars, every last one a testament to victories bought with blood, to a life spent purging the galaxy of man-hating alien fiends. The greatest mark of honour Werner bore was not on his face. It was on his left pauldron. Rather than display the Chapter's standard iconography there, Werner wore the exquisitely cast skull sigil of the legendary Deathwatch, chamber militant of the Holy Inquisition's Ordo Xenos.

He had served that august body for seven years before returning to his Crimson Fist brothers, and even then, he could tell them nothing of his time away. He had been sworn to secrecy.

Drakken never asked about it. He knew that Werner would honour his oath of non-disclosure until the day he died. Integrity was the sergeant's byword.

'Sixteen ork battleships that we can see,' said Werner, meeting his captain's gaze, 'and that's just on this side of the planet. Five of those are equivalent in size to the Navy's Emperor-class ships, and each of those, knowing the greenskin propensity for arms over armour, almost certainly has the edge in firepower. I find myself in agreement with Cryxus Gloi, brother-captain. All we have in our favour is our speed and the fact that they haven't sniffed us out yet – two advantages I think we ought to hold on to. If we were to go straight for them, prow guns blazing...' He shook his head. 'A cudbear doesn't pick a fight with five swamp tigers unless he knows something they don't.'

Drakken accepted this with a nod, but countered, 'Still, we didn't come all the way out here to count ships and turn back. Alessio Cortez would have a bloody field day with that. The Chapter Master gave me full discretion on this one, and I intend to use it.'

'A ground operation, lord?'

Captain Drakken's narrow lips curved into a cold smile. 'Precisely,' he said. 'Three Thunderhawks go in on their blind side. We stay dark for as long as we can. Once we have our reconnaissance, we unleash hell on the beasts, do as much damage to them as we can and pull out before they can coordinate any kind of proper response.'

'Our targets?' asked the sergeant.

Drakken turned towards one of the three large work-pits sunk into the floor of the bridge and strode towards it. Werner followed. The pits were filled with a mix of servitors and human officers, all connected by cables and head-mounted apparatus to the banks of glowing consoles in front of them. In a station close to Drakken's feet, a scrawny tech-priest sat in the thick cotton robes of the Adeptus Mechanicus's *Divisio Linguistica*. His sallow features were lit by the flickering green screen over which hunched. A morass of thin metal tendrils trailed from his socket-pocked skull to the data transfer ports set into the sides of his console.

'Adept Orrimen,' boomed Drakken. 'Have those cogitator-banks finished the translation yet?'

The tech-priest spoke without turning or moving his jaw, his eerie voice emanating from speakers set into the sides of his head. 'The translation is coming through now, my lord,' he rasped. 'Do you wish me to relay it verbatim, or would you prefer a summary?'

'Just give me something we can use.'

'Summary, then,' said the tech-priest. 'The broadcast is a message spoken in a dialect of the orkish tongue known to be used among several of the largest clans in the Charadon Sector. Clans using this form of the language include those labelled under Ordo Xenos classification systems as Goths, Blood Axes, Deathskulls, Evil Suns and thirty-three lesser clans so far recorded. The speaker identifies itself as the warlord Urzog Mag Kull, a known lieutenant of Snagrod, the self-proclaimed Arch-Arsonist of Charadon. The message is intended for all ork parties currently active in the spinward sectors of the Segmentum Tempestus and the trailward sectors of the Ultima Segmentum. It instructs all ork ships in these sectors to rally under the banner of the Arch-Arsonist. It also declares that Snagrod's Waaagh has begun, that it cannot be stopped, and that it is the divine will of the ork gods, Gork and Mork.'

With that, Orrimen finished his report, but when the silence became drawn out, he added, 'Does the captain wish to query?'

Drakken didn't answer. He turned back to face Werner, gesturing with a raised eyebrow for the sergeant's comment. Werner looked darkly dismayed.

'Sounds like Commissar Baldur had it right. But how many other worlds have they taken in the time it took us to get here? How many other worlds might they be broadcasting from?'

'Not from this one for much longer,' said Drakken. 'That signal is being boosted by the ships, but it's definitely coming from Krugerport. We will cut it off at the source. I want their ground-based long-range communications knocked out for good. Get our brothers ready, Leo. We have our target. We deploy within the hour.'

Werner locked eyes with his captain and said, 'It's clear we'll be facing tall odds down there, lord. Losses are likely. If I may, I'd like to request the honour of leading the operation personally.'

Drakken frowned, keenly aware that Werner was attempting to protect him.

'No, Leo. I'll be leading this one myself. Master Kantor gave me this honour. He expects a detailed report on my return. I will see Krugerport for myself. Of course, if you can think of another way to hurt them, another worthy target…'

Werner thought in silence for a moment, then said, 'Badlanding is a practically a dead world. Most of the water there is lethally toxic, and orks need potable water just as much as the human settlers did. Krugerport has a single large purification facility.'

Drakken nodded. 'Just inside the curtain wall of the south-eastern precinct. Yes, I saw it on the maps.'

'I think it's fair to assume that the orks are stocking their ships from it in preparation for the next phase of their incursion. Hitting the comms array will help to delay the Waaagh, but, if we strike the purification plant, too, we can force them to supply their ships from elsewhere. That will delay them even further. It may even force them to split their forces.'

Drakken thought about it for only a moment. It made solid sense. 'Very well,' he said. 'Any delay we can create will give the Chapter Master more time to alert Segmentum Command. Congratulations, Leo. It looks like you will be commanding a detachment after all.'

FIVE

Krugerport, Badlanding

SERVICE IN THE 10th Company, the Chapter's Scout Company, was about proving oneself. It was about the mastery of war and of the body. As a Scout, one learned to employ his implanted organs, to trust them, to become one with them. One learned to perfect the art of the kill. Years of service would prove a Scout's readiness, and then the call would come. He would be ordered to return to Arx Tyrannus to attend the Steeping. It was an ancient rite dating back to the time when the primarch had walked among them. Dorn had once welcomed battle-brothers into his ranks by cutting his palm and sharing his blood directly with them. Now his blood was a holy relic, sharing only its presence. Time had wrought its changes on the Chapter's rites. Nowadays, a Scout being elevated to full battle-brother status would dip his left hand in the blood of a foe he had slain himself. The ritual had changed, but the meaning and significance of it had not. The fist literally became crimson. It was the final step in becoming a full battle-brother, the final step before being assigned to one of the other nine companies.

Unlike some, Scout-Sergeant Ezra Mishina was in no great rush to be elevated. His duties had often called for him to act as a sniper. Long days waiting for a perfect kill shot had taught him patience. His years as a sergeant, guiding younger and far less experienced men, had reinforced the lesson. The call for him to attend the Steeping would come when the time was right. For the moment, all he cared about was doing his best, doing his duty as he was supposed to. Right now, that meant serving as forward eyes and ears for Captain Drakken's 3rd Company.

Mishina had been specially selected by Captain Icario to accompany the 3rd on this mission to Badlanding, and, if he were being honest, there was nowhere else he would rather have been. This was where he belonged, in the thick black shadows of a hostile town, stalking alien sentries with his silenced bolt-rifle slung over his back, combat knife in hand, eyesight augmented by the sensitive optical lenses of his night-vision goggles. Already, he had silenced the grunting breaths of half a dozen filthy greenskin scum. His boots and fatigues were flecked with their blood.

Five hours ago, with the local star, Freiya, still bright in the afternoon sky, the 3rd Company's Thunderhawk gunships had landed in a deep wadi some thirty kilometres to the south-west. They had flown in low with the sun at their backs, using its blinding glare to mask the telltale glow of hot plasma from their thrusters.

Mishina and the three Scouts under his command had then pushed out towards the town, scouring the land for threats well ahead of the tactical squads that followed behind them.

They had reached the town's shell-pocked, fire-blackened curtain wall just as the sun slid below the horizon. Perfect timing. The orks here were complacent. It looked like they had slaughtered the Imperial Guard forces to a man. As far as they were concerned, the fighting was over for now. That was perfect, too. They had neither patched nor barricaded any of the gaping breaches that their artillery assaults had blasted in the high sandstone walls. Mishina and his Scouts waited for the very last of the twilight to bleed away, for night to cloak them in its veils. When it had, they slid into the town in silence, killing the orks they caught unawares by thrusting their long combat knives neatly between the third and fourth vertebrae as they had trained so relentlessly to do.

With their nerve bundles neatly severed, the orks went down quick and quiet, the trademark kill of a true Astartes Scout.

Mishina had taken many lives in this way. It was as instinctive a process to him now as breathing silently and moving from cover to cover, all of which he did without need for conscious thought. He was pleased with the performance of the other Scouts, too, though it was far too early to start handing out compliments. Captain Icario had assigned him some promising men. Two of them had only ever experienced the slaughter of a greenskin through the sensorium-link downloads available in the Chapter's Librarium, but they had bloodied themselves for real this night, and there was more killing to come.

Careful to make as little noise as possible, Mishina placed a booted foot on the edge of an old wooden crate and boosted himself up to the flat roof of an abandoned single-storey hab. From there, he surveyed the layout of the town. The planet's solitary moon, in the shadow of which *The Crusader* still held station undetected, had not risen yet, but the Scout-Sergeant's goggles showed him all he needed to see with the clarity of a dull, slightly muddy afternoon.

Aside from the town's curtain wall and a smattering of prominent two-storey structures, Krugerport was built low to the ground, the vast majority of its buildings topping out at about five or six metres in height. Most of the streets were narrow, giving the habs the aspect of short, blocky figures huddled close together against the wind-blown dust. It was an ugly place, and not just because so much of it had been blasted to rubble. There was little sign of artistry here. A kind of scrappy functionality ruled, as if everything had been put together as quickly as possible and maintained on the very edge of working condition. There were no parks or museums.

Mishina had seen towns like this before. They were hastily built to exploit local resources, and, when those resources were finally gone, when the mines or promethium fields ran dry and the wealth dried up with them, the population gradually died too, shrinking to nothing in a remarkably short space of time.

The walls all around him were plain sandstone. They might once have borne bright posters calling for faith in the Emperor and diligence in one's job, but now they were marked only by the telltale signs of heavy street-fighting, of las and plasma burns, and countless black holes cut by the impacts of so many solid metal rounds. From his new vantage point, Mishina spotted a number of small market squares and plazas where it looked like a few token statues had once stood. These were little more than rubble now. Most of them would probably have been carved in the image of the Emperor and His saints, but it was impossible to tell the standard of quality to which they had been finished. The orks had smashed all of them to rubble, not with the hate-fuelled malice of traitors and Chaos-tainted scum but, more likely, in a mindless expression of their raw love for destruction in all its forms.

They were simple beasts, the greenskins. In Mishina's eyes, there was little more to them than muscle and aggression, and that was just as well.

From his perch atop the modest hab, he contacted the other Scouts and queried their positions. As each reported in, Mishina found himself nodding. None had been spotted by the enemy. No one had given himself away. Each had positioned himself in the location to which Mishina had sent him, and had done so in good time.

So far, so good.

Mishina ordered them to hold position and await further orders.

To the north, almost eight kilometres away according to the laser rangefinder incorporated into his goggles, he saw the tall, rooftop-mounted, wrought-iron latticework that identified one particular building as the Krugerport communications bunker. Atop the latticework's eighty-metre height, he saw a cluster of dishes mounting powerful broadcasting antennae. Near the base of the pylon, the orks had decorated the iron girders with some kind of rusty metal sigil. Painted red, it was made of iron plates arranged in the rough likeness of a leering alien face.

Increasing magnification, Mishina noted the fortified rooftops surrounding the communications bunker. Their corners were piled high with sandbags, and they bristled with heavy weapons, many of which looked like Guard-issue lascannons and heavy bolters.

That's going to mean trouble if they get the drop on us, Mishina thought.

Hulking forms moved to and fro by the light of cooking fires. The orks had spitted meat over these. It hung roasting, licked by orange flames, and Mishina noted with revulsion and anger that some of those spits carried hunks of meat that bore the unmistakable silhouette of human limbs.

The smell corroborated his worst suspicions. The scent was close to that of roasted grox, but sharper in the nostrils. He had smelled it before, a funeral pyre stink.

Turning away from the sight, and zooming out to normal magnification again, he tracked right and found what he was looking for. To the east, nine-point-six kilometres away, he easily identified the water purification plant by its bulky rectangular profile and by the vast metal tanks that stood arrayed along its southern flank.

Mishina raised a gloved hand to the comms rig on his left ear, keyed the 3rd Company's command channel, and said, 'Brother-Captain, this is Shadow One.'

Drakken's gravelly voice answered, 'Go ahead, Shadow One.'

'Shadow Team in place, my lord. Visual perimeter established. We've marked a path for you. Clear to follow us in whenever you're ready.'

'Understood, Shadow One. Moving up now. Keep me apprised of movement.'

Drakken is solid, thought Mishina. His is a name with more than a few legends attached. He's not prone to careless mistakes, I know that much. But even so, I have the damnedest feeling, like a mental itch. There's something I don't like about this. Perhaps it just seems too easy.

Or perhaps it's something else.

TRYING TO MOVE silently in MkVII power armour, Drakken knew, was like trying to reload a bolter with just your teeth – damned near impossible and usually not worth the bother. Sooner or later, the orks would wake up to 3rd Company's presence here, and when they did, the real work, the righteous work he lived for, would begin proper.

He led his Astartes through the breach in the curtain wall that Mishina and his Scouts had marked out for them. Orks wouldn't see those marks. The Scouts left little splashes of a liquid that was only visible in infrared. The helmet visors of the Crimson Fists picked up those splashes as if they were blazing neon lights, and the Space Marines followed them into the town of Krugerport, knowing that the path they followed had been cleared for them.

Once Drakken and his men were beyond the outer walls, the captain opened a channel to Sergeant Werner, who was about twenty metres to the rear, preparing to lead his own group in through the breach. Drakken had assigned him command of three ten-man squads. 'This is where we part, Leo. Follow the Scouts' markings, and may the Emperor watch over you.'

'As he watches over you, my lord,' replied Werner, then he and his men split off from the main group, disappearing into the inky shadows of a narrow avenue to the right.

Drakken watched the last of Werner's Astartes disappear, then gave the signal to his own squads to move out in single file.

The streets of Krugerport were, in the main, too tight for heavy vehicles to negotiate. In some settlements, this would have been a strategy to prevent enemy armour making headway during an assault. In Krugerport, however, Drakken had the feeling it merely represented the human tendency to seek closeness with others when in hostile places. This planet was a merciless rock, its winds choking everything with corrosive dust, its chemical seas capable of eating the flesh from a man's bones in moments.

So why had men settled here at all? It was no great mystery. There were two things in Badlanding's favour. First, the atmosphere was breathable, which made it a relatively rare and valuable find among the millions of worlds man had discovered since the first days of his expansion into space. Despite the vast size of the Imperium, the ratio of naturally habitable worlds to non-habitable was far below one per cent. The second reason Badlanding had been colonised was just as simple: the Scratch Mountains, towards which Commissar Baldur had claimed he would lead his survivors, were rich in seams of adamantium and proteocite, the latter a compound used in the production of rare ceramite, the material from which much of the Astartes battle-plate was made.

Thinking of the Scratch Mountains made Drakken scowl. He had brought eighty-three Space Marines with him on this operation, not to mention numerous serfs, pilots, technicians, communications specialists and the like, all of which were absolutely essential to the smooth operation of the Crimson Fists' fleet. Of the eighty-four Astartes, he personally led a detachment of thirty, Werner led another thirty. Four Crimson Fists from 10th Company were acting as advance scouts. Eight more battle-brothers had been assigned landing-zone patrol duties on the perimeter of the broad wadi in which the Thunderhawks rested well out of sight, and another ten had been sent in an arcing path well out from the town, skimming over the dust dunes in Land Speeders, racing to the last known location of the Imperial Guard forces.

What that latter force had already reported made for grim news. The cave complex to which Baldur had retreated was now nothing but a mass grave. Desiccated corpses, most with their heads taken for trophies, lay in heaps at the back of the tunnels. There were a number of ork dead, too, but not enough by half. It was clear that Baldur and the remnants of his forces had been backed into a corner and slaughtered to a man. They had been completely overwhelmed. How the orks must have revelled in all that killing!

Only the fact that he wore his helmet stopped Drakken from spitting on the ground in disgust. He hated the greenskins with a lethal passion. Throughout much of his life as a battle-brother, he had fought to purge Imperial outposts and trade routes of their savage kind, but year after year they would come back, making fresh incursions from frontier worlds on the periphery of the Loki Sector. It seemed an endless task. No matter how many one killed, no real headway was ever truly made. Success was measured in distance, in how far the alien hordes were kept from civilised space.

In two millennia, Rynn's World itself had known the footsteps of aliens only once, and not at all since the Crimson Fists had taken up residence there. In the subsequent years, a number of potentially devastating Waaaghs had been averted, defused by surgical strikes which had been masterfully conceived by Pedro Kantor. Drakken had earned great honours for his part in these, but the real glory belonged to the Chapter Master.

No wonder they call him the second coming of Pollux, Drakken thought as he scanned the shadows up ahead for traces of ork.

He had a deep and abiding respect for Kantor, though the bond of brotherhood was more tenuous between them than it was between the Chapter Master and Alessio Cortez. This wasn't something that bothered Drakken much. Friendship meant little to him, certainly far less than good solid leadership, as it should to any Astartes worth his salt.

He had no strong love of Cortez, that was for sure. The man was arrogant, opinionated, noisy and boorish, and his status as some kind of invincible hero of the Chapter consistently got under Drakken's skin.

It is the Blackwater thing, he thought to himself as he moved out from the corner of a sandstone hab and signalled his men to follow. The way they all stick–

Scout-Sergeant Mishina's voice cut him off mid-thought.

'Brother-captain,' said the Scout over the link. 'This is Shadow One. I have movement at the objective.'

Drakken's hand went up immediately, motioning for his men to move back into cover. 'Details, Mishina.'

'A convoy of ork light armour, brother-captain. It's moving along the main road towards the communications tower. The lead machines have already pulled up in the plaza out in front.'

'Numbers?'

Mishina went quiet for a few seconds, then replied, 'At least thirty vehicles that I can see, and dust clouds from more at the rear. If they wake up to our presence prematurely, my lord, we're going to have trouble. A lot of it.'

SERGEANT WERNER AND his party moved east at the base of the curtain wall, following the infrared splashes left by Scouts Vermian and Rogar, both of whom had been tasked with reconnoitring the route from the wall breach to the water purification plant.

So far, not a single bolt had been fired.

On a surgical strike like this, thought Werner, the longer it stays that way, the better.

He had to admire his 10th Company kinsmen. Every few blocks, with his visor's night-vision mode turning inky night into murky day, he would spot the crumpled bodies of ork sentries hidden in burned out doorways or stuffed between bullet-riddled barrels and crates.

In the shadows, nothing beat the quiet goodnight of a knife in the neck.

The Scouts were good. If they kept this up, Werner and his squads would get all the way to the purification plant without any of the alien filth raising the alarm. Once there, of course, any pretence at stealth would have to be abandoned. Things would become more overt. The melta charges would see to that. Once they were detonated, the whole damned planet would know that the Crimson Fists had come calling to dispense death and destruction in the Emperor's name. Werner expected a fierce firefight on the way out. The streets would fill up quickly with the bestial scum. But, once the Fists were beyond the wall again, it would be a simple matter of calling in the Thunderhawks for pickup and holding a defensive perimeter until they arrived.

Whatever happened after that was for pilots, gunners and Navigators to worry about. Werner didn't concern himself with things he couldn't influence. It wasn't his way.

He heard Drakken hailing him on the comm-link.

'Leo, respond.'

'Here, my lord. Go ahead.'

'Status?'

'About one kilometre out from our objective now. Scouts moving into sniping positions. Ork presence minimal so far, but I don't think it'll stay that way for long.'

'You're not wrong,' said Drakken. 'The comms tower is crawling with greenskin filth. I'm afraid we have to alter the plan as a result.'

Werner called his men to an immediate halt, and they went into overwatch, their bolter muzzles swinging up and around to cover every street corner, door and alleyway.

'I'm listening, brother-captain,' said Werner.

'We've got ork light armour that just came in from the north. I've checked with Sergeant Solari. He is adamant that his speeders weren't spotted and neither were any of his men. They're back aboard their

Thunderhawk now, waiting to offer us close support should we need it. Listen closely, Leo, I know we discussed a simultaneous strike, but our best hope of knocking out that communications tower now depends on you drawing some of the defenders away. I need your team to strike first, and to make as much damned noise as you can.'

Inwardly, Werner cursed. The captain's logic was sound, of course, the reasoning faultless, but it meant dropping his men right in the heat of things. Ork light armour might look like worthless junk, but it could move fast, and, when they functioned properly, the greenskins' heavy weapons packed as hard a punch as anything in the Imperial arsenal. The narrow streets would protect his men for the most part, but they would have to cross several wide roads on their way back to the rendezvous point. That meant a dash over open ground, probably under intense fire.

It couldn't be helped. Orders from a brother-captain might just as well be orders from the Emperor Himself. They were to be obeyed no matter what. Werner was a Space Marine; he would walk straight into certain death if his superiors ordered it. How he died didn't bother him at all. It was how he lived that counted. 'Leave it to us, my lord,' he said. 'I'll light the facility up so bright the damned orks will think the sun's come up early.'

'Good. Make it happen, Leo,' said Drakken. 'I want to know the minute you're in position. Command, out.'

Werner waved his Astartes on, and, with righteous murder on their minds, they closed in on their target.

MISHINA WAS ABOUT as close as he wanted to get. There was little more he could do for Captain Drakken's party now, save cover them with sniper fire and keep them apprised of enemy movements. There was no more quiet clearance work to be done. That phase of the operation was over. After muttering a short prayer of gratitude to his deadly blade, he sheathed it for what he supposed would be the last time tonight. It had claimed the lives of sixteen of the oversized alien abominations.

Not a bad tally for a night's work, he told himself.

He wondered how many xenos his sniper rifle would claim once the shooting started. More than sixteen, he hoped.

The other Scout assigned to provide forward eyes and sniper cover for Drakken's team was a fairly fresh initiate by the name of Janus Kennon.

Brother Kennon was young, and Mishina had expressed concerns to Captain Icario that the inexperienced Scout needed more training before a critical deployment like this. But Kennon's innate skills had apparently marked him out for great things. In over a hundred years, no other initiate had come close to matching his scores on the practice range, even in thick simulated fog. Kennon's accuracy and targeting abilities bordered on the preternatural, and Mishina got the impression that Captain Icario saw a potential protégé in the young Space Marine.

Kennon was currently crouching on the corner of a dust-covered rooftop about eight hundred metres to the north-west of Mishina's current spot, covering the ork defensive post on top of the comms tower from a western flanking position.

At least, that was where Mishina had told Kennon to go. Had it been anyone else, Mishina would have assumed his orders were being followed to the letter, but not so with Kennon. The boy was far too sure of himself. The captain's praise had gone to his head.

Mishina couldn't help himself. For a brief moment, he turned his goggles north-west and increased magnification.

He soon detected Kennon's heat signature… exactly where it was supposed to be.

Mishina felt the briefest flash of shame for doubting a fellow Crimson Fist.

Jealous, Ezra, he asked himself? Jealous of the boy's talent? You've no reason to doubt him. He went through the same psycho-indoctrination programmes you did. Trust in Captain Icario's choice.

These thoughts had barely filtered through to the front of Mishina's mind when Kennon's voice addressed him over the comm-link.

'Shadow Four to Shadow One. Can you hear me, sergeant?'

'I hear you, brother,' said Mishina. 'Speak.'

'Sergeant, I'm not sure whether you can see this or not, but a monster of an ork just dismounted from some kind of truck in the middle of the plaza. He's climbing a stair on the west side of the building. It must be the greenskin leader. The beast is as broad as Brother Ulis!'

Mishina doubted that. Ulis was a Dreadnought, one of the Chapter's revered Old Ones, and about four metres across from shoulder to shoulder. The largest ork Mishina had ever seen in person had been almost three metres across. It had taken a direct hit from a Predator tank to slay that bastard.

Mishina squinted up ahead, but, from this angle, he couldn't see the creature Kennon was talking about. He was about to move to a neighbouring rooftop for a better angle when Kennon reported, 'He's going up to the rooftop of the bunker. I have his ugly face right in the centre of my crosshairs, sergeant. Requesting immediate permission to take the shot.'

'Request denied, brother,' said Mishina. 'Hold position while I–'

'I can take him out, sergeant,' Kennon insisted. 'He must be the leader. One kill-shot could put their entire force in disarray. Again, I strongly request permission to fire.'

Mishina's words were as hard as bolts themselves. 'You will *not* take the shot until Captain Drakken gives the order. Is that understood?'

Kennon was silent.

'I said is that understood, brother?'

Reluctantly, not bothering to mask the contempt and disappointment in his voice, the young Scout replied that it was. Mishina immediately contacted Captain Drakken and said, 'Shadow Four reports that he has what he believes to be the ork leader in his crosshairs, captain. He is requesting permission to take the shot.'

Drakken barely needed time to think about it.

'Negative, Shadow One. Authorisation denied. Sergeant Werner and his squads are preparing to assault the water purification facility as we speak. I want those orks drawn off before we strike the comms bunker. Is that absolutely clear?'

It was. If Brother Kennon took the shot – hit or miss – the orks at the comms bunker would deploy all their light armour against the most local, most immediate threat.

Mishina could understand Kennon's eagerness well enough. It was a shot he would like to take himself, a single squeeze of the trigger, one muffled cough from his weapon's muzzle that would garner the kind of glory and honour few brothers in 10th Company would ever have a chance to claim. To think that a single shot might defuse, or at the very least, greatly delay a potential Waaagh…

Not just a triumph for Kennon, thought Mishina, but something the entire company could be proud of. There would be decorations for everyone deployed here.

At the very back of his mind, a tiny voice said: *Results come first. Let Kennon take the shot.*

Mishina had heard that dangerous voice before. He expected to hear it again many times throughout his life. He responded to it now as he always did. He crushed it to nothing, just as he had been trained, just as his mind had been rigorously conditioned to do. He drowned it out with a silent litany of obligation.

Think of the Chapter, he told himself. Think of the primarch, of the Emperor and Terra.

None of these were best served by indulging one's sense of personal pride. A true Astartes was better than that.

There was a sudden brief transmission on the comm-link's mission channel. 'Sergeant Werner's force is about to light up Objective Two,' Drakken barked. 'Brace yourselves!'

A sudden clap of thunder shook the rooftop under Mishina's feet, and a great flash of white light, supernova bright, lit the whole town from the direction of the south-eastern precinct. It was followed by three more in rapid succession, each shaking the entire town like the footfalls of a mighty Titan.

Mishina screwed his eyes shut and turned his head away from the direction of the blasts, anxious not to be temporarily blinded by the glare. Sergeant Werner's party had launched their attack on the water purification plant in spectacular style. Stealth protocols were no longer in effect.

When the sound of the melta explosions had dropped to a ringing in his ears, Mishina opened his eyes. From the buildings all around the comms bunker, a great cacophony of orkish grunts and roars could be heard, merging together with the revving of powerful, fume-spewing engines.

The sound of distant gunfire echoed from between the streets and alleys around the water purification plant. Mishina's supremely honed ears recognised the distinctive bark of bolters being fired from about ten kilometres away. There was an awful lot of fire being traded. He muttered a prayer to the Emperor for the safety of Sergeant Werner and his men. From the plaza in front of the comms bunker, the first of the ork bikes and buggies began to move off in the general direction of the gunfight, their engines growling and sputtering like mad animals.

That's it, you brainless muck-eaters, thought Mishina. Keep moving. Go and see what it's all about.

It was happening exactly as Captain Drakken had anticipated, and, for the first time since the ork vehicles had shown up, Mishina started to feel truly confident that everything would go according to plan.

That was when he heard Kennon on the comm-link again.

'The warlord is moving, sergeant. I can't wait any longer. I'm taking the shot!'

Mishina almost forgot himself. Scouts were habitually quiet individuals. Shouting tended to give one's position away. Even so, he almost yelled over the comm-link, 'Hold your damned fire! That's a direct order. If you take that shot, upstart, I'll see you flayed alive, by Throne! Do I make myself cl–'

There was a brief burst of blue-green light from the direction of the comms bunker. Mishina felt his primary heart skip a beat. He knew instinctively what the flash meant. Kennon had taken the shot anyway. His magnified vision confirmed it when Kennon fired a second time, then a third. All of Kennon's rounds had been right on target, but they had detonated with brief, bright, harmless flashes on some kind of invisible energy shield.

Zooming in further, Mishina could see the shield-generating apparatus strapped to the monster's back. No sniper was going to fell that beast. Kennon had just given himself away for nothing.

The ork boss spun in Kennon's direction, took a great lungful of air, and bellowed out a battle cry that seemed to vibrate the foundations of the entire town.

Absently, Mishina registered that Kennon hadn't been exaggerating greatly about the creature's size. It was a formidable looking thing, the great bulk of its blocky apparatus only adding to the effect.

A half-second after this thought ran through his mind, bright light stabbed into Mishina's eyes. The orks on the roof had turned searchlights out into the night, and the Scout-Sergeant's night vision goggles hadn't been able to adjust to the sudden brightness quickly enough. Mishina threw a hand up over his face. Stubber and heavy weapons fire begin spitting out in all directions. Countless alien throats began calling out threats and challenges in what passed for their rough alien tongue.

Any chance of splitting up the greenskin force at the comms tower was now lost.

'Shadow One to Captain Drakken,' said Mishina urgently.

'Don't bother, sergeant,' snapped Captain Drakken on the other end of the link. The ink-dark streets where the ork searchlights couldn't penetrate now began to strobe with muzzle flashes as the battle-brothers of 3rd Company moved up, claiming the first of their kills early in the exchange. 'If we live through this,' continued a furious Drakken, 'you can explain to the Chapter Council what in damnation just happened.'

Mishina loosed a bitter curse and promised he would see Kennon strung up for this. Then he knocked his bolt-rifle's safety off, checked that there was a live round in the chamber, and scanned the streets below his position, sector by sector, eyes alert for anything that threatened to flank Drakken's men as they stormed towards their objective.

Gunfire from both sides rang out for hours on end. The dry, dust-caked streets of Krugerport soon ran red.

'ASTARTES, FALL BACK!' bellowed Drakken.

He wasn't sure they could hear him, wasn't sure the micro-vox circuitry in his gorget was sending them his voice. His helmet had been struck by some kind of greenskin plasma round that burned right through, crisping the flesh of his left cheek.

His visor had gone dead. He'd had to strip the ruined helm from his head in a hurry, enemy rounds rattling like hail on his armour while he was temporarily blinded. Now, with ork stubber-fire blazing all around him, shells ripping onto the hab walls on either side of the street, he had to shout his orders.

The enemy kept coming, spilling from everywhere, no matter how much fire he and his Fists spat back at them. They had felled scores, perhaps hundreds, of the slab-muscled aliens already, but the charges continued. They trampled their dead into the blood-soaked dirt without the slightest reverence. A foul odour came with them, an odour Drakken knew well, stale sweat and fungal stink, worse than rotting garbage.

Drawing a bead on the largest, darkest-skinned ork he could see, Drakken pulled the trigger of his bolt-pistol. Nothing. Without pause for thought, he switched magazines, his armoured hands moving in a well-practiced blur. He took aim once more. The beast had covered ten more metres, lumbering forward on legs as thick as a man's torso. He fired, and a bolt thundered into the centre of the creature's sloping forehead.

It kept running. Orks didn't go down easily. A second later the exploding bolt blew out the creature's brain, and its heavy, headless corpse hammered against the dusty street spouting thick red blood.

Drakken took a second to look down the avenue behind him and saw that his orders had gotten through. His squads were making a staggered retreat in the direction of the breach through which they'd come. Sergeant Werner's group would rendezvous with them there. Whoever reached the gap in the wall first was to hold it and wait for the others.

Across the street, in the shadow of another hab, Drakken saw one of his Astartes, Brother Cero, laying down cover with a heavy bolter. The massive weapon chugged and chattered, throwing its lethal rounds out in great scything arcs, cutting the front ranks of the charging orks to ragged red pieces. The death toll was so great it caused the ork charge to momentarily falter, as those immediately behind the fallen tried to turn and force their way to cover.

Drakken took this brief lull to race over the open street and slide into cover beside Cero.

'Can the others hear me over the link?' he yelled in Cero's ear.

The rattle of the heavy bolter should have drowned him out completely, but the Lyman's ear implant could filter out and separate even the slightest of noises. Cero heard his captain, and replied without turning from his targets, 'They can hear you, lord. Sergeant Werner has just sent word that his party has secured the breach. They are holding it, but their Scouts report xenos moving in from all sides.'

'Then we have to move now. Why haven't you fallen back as I ordered?'

'Someone has to cover your own retreat, lord.'

'You can't move as fast as I can,' said Drakken. 'I want you to make for the corner hab to the south. Go now. I will follow once you've established a firing position. Move!'

Cero loosed a last brief burst of fire, then dashed out from the shadow of the hab and ran towards the end of the street where his brothers were engaging enemy forces from the east. As he ran, Drakken leaned out from the bullet-chewed edge of the sandstone wall, and began picking off the closest greenskins, his every shot taking one down, if not killing it outright.

Cero's legs pumped hard, but the great weight of the heavy bolter and its back-mounted ammunition slowed him significantly. He didn't see the vast silhouetted form loom up on the roof to his right. The first he knew of his attacker was when the bright beam of its lascannon – a weapon pilfered from the fallen Imperial Guard forces – sliced through both of his knees, cutting bone, flesh and ceramite armour with ease.

Cero tumbled to the surface of the street, roaring in agony, his cropped legs gushing hot blood.

Drakken turned and saw his battle-brother scrambling in the dirt, trying to recover his weapon despite the pain, desperate to return fire on the beast that had maimed him.

The beast in question had disappeared already. It was nowhere in sight. The orks to the north had witnessed the Space Marine go down. They surged forward, driven into a frenzy by the sight of their enemy's fresh blood and the sounds of his agony.

'Get some suppressing fire over here,' Drakken demanded over the link.

Had he been able to hear the voices of his fellow Astartes, he would have realised they were already being heavily suppressed themselves. The orks swarmed through the streets, their vehicles careening down the broader thoroughfares, pintle-mounted weapons spewing lead in all directions.

Drakken picked off three more of the closest threats. Ammunition was running out. He ripped a fragmentation grenade from his belt, priming it in the same movement, and hurled it at the enemy. Then he ran from cover, straight towards Cero where he lay in the middle of the street.

Behind him, there was a sharp boom, and a chorus of alien howls.

He slid to a halt at Cero's side.

'Leave the weapon, brother. Grab my arm. Quickly!'

'Run, my lord,' said Cero. 'I can still cover your escape.'

From a dark alley to the left, a massive green brute surged out with twin cleavers raised for a killing stroke. Drakken saw it too late. He didn't have time to swing his weapon around. The ork opened its razor-toothed maw and screamed its war cry as it made range.

Suddenly, its head snapped backwards, a neat hole punched in its right temple. It fell to its knees. A moment later, its head burst in a shower of red gore and chips of bone.

Drakken looked up, automatically triangulating the shot, and saw Sergeant Mishina on the corner of a rooftop nearby, the butt of his sniper rifle pressed tight to his shoulder.

'We must move, my lord,' Mishina shouted down. He fired four rounds up the street, striking targets with phenomenal precision. Four brass casings landed at his feet. Four orks dropped, their meaty carcasses tripping those closest behind them.

'Leave the weapon,' Drakken barked at Cero.

Cero released his heavy bolter and detached the ammo feed while Drakken uncoupled his bulky backpack.

'Hold on,' said Drakken, gripping Cero's wrist, 'I will drag–'

A blaze of white light cut straight through his words.

Pain erupted out of nowhere, a fire consuming his every nerve. He would have screamed, but his lungs were empty and wouldn't refill. Distantly, he heard Cero roaring in protest, his shouts accompanied by the sounds of gunfire.

Why was it all so faint, so far away?

His pain fled so quickly and completely that it was as if he had only dreamed it. Now it was replaced by a sensation of falling. He knew he had struck the ground when the sensation stopped, but felt no impact.

His inner voice spoke to him one last time, quieter than he had ever known it.

'So this is death,' it said. 'It is warmer than I expected.'

Scout-Sergeant Mishina turned just an instant too late to open fire on the captain's killer. He wouldn't have been able to save Ashor Drakken anyway. He only caught the briefest glimpse of the ork as it charged off down another street, looking for its next prey, but it was enough to recognise it.

Urzog Mag-Kull. The hulking warlord on which Kennon had opened fire, precipitating this whole damned mess.

Mishina's rounds would have bounced off the monster's force-field just as Kennon's had done. He would have fired on it anyway, given half the chance.

Brother Cero was still alive down there, his lower legs shorn off at the knee, unable to escape without aid. He cradled the armoured body of his dead captain in his left arm. In his right hand, he gripped the captain's boltpistol.

Mishina could hear him repeating one word – *No!* – over and over again, desperately denying the captain's death, or perhaps what he perceived as his role in it.

The orks were closing in unopposed now, less than two hundred metres away from Cero, slowed only by the fact that many shoved and wrestled among themselves to get to the front where all the killing was to be done.

'This is Shadow One!' yelled Mishina over the mission channel. 'Captain Drakken is down! I say again, Captain Drakken is down!'

He chambered another round and dropped to a crouch, determined to hold this position where he could at least try to protect Cero and hold the orks back from defiling what was left of the captain's body.

Sergeant Werner responded, fighting to keep his voice level, not wanting to believe what he had just heard. But he had to believe it. The brothers of the Crimson Fists were not prone to lie.

'Your position, Shadow One?'

Mishina spoke as he resumed firing. There were so many targets in range now that it was impossible to miss.

'Two kilometres north-east of you,' he answered. 'Hurry! I can't hold them off alone.'

From the corner of his eye, he saw movement to the west. He felt the hab beneath his feet shuddering, saw a great cloud of dust kicked up by the passage of heavy vehicles. They were travelling straight towards the breach, straight towards the rest of the Astartes force.

By the saints, cursed Mishina.

To Werner, he said, 'Forget about us, sergeant. I've just spotted a large armour column closing in on your position. Take your squads and get out of here. Someone has to report to the Chapter Council.'

'I'm not leaving them the captain's body, damn it!' growled Werner. 'Not here!'

Mishina knew better than to believe he had the words to dissuade the sergeant. Instead, he said, 'Then, for Throne's sake, call in the Thunderhawks right now! If we don't get air support, none of us are going to get out of here alive!'

SIX

Arx Tyrannus, Hellblade Mountains

'AGAIN,' SAID KANTOR. 'I wish to hear it again.'

It was fifteen days since the engagement at Kruger-port. Just seven hours ago, *The Crusader* had docked at Raxa Station, the main orbital refuelling and rearm-ing station which sat halfway between Rynn's World and her closest moon, Dantienne. Once adequate fuel had been taken aboard, *The Crusader's* bay doors had opened and her two surviving Thunderhawks had dropped to the planet's surface carrying the bat-tered remnants of the expedition force. The Chapter Master had met them on the landing pads of Arx Tyrannus with the first rays of daylight breaking over the peaks to the east. He had rarely seen any of his Crimson Fists return to their beloved sanctuary in such misery.

From a force of eighty-four Space Marines, only twenty-eight returned alive. Most of these had been wounded, but the two Apothecaries attached to the force, Arvano Ruillus and Lyrus Vayne, had worked hard to patch them up on the journey back. Astartes bodies healed fast, but it would be up to the Chaplains of the Sacratium to patch up their wounded spirits.

The Thunderhawks had touched down three hours ago. Sensorium scans and verbal debriefings had started immediately. The first of a string of council sessions had been called. The Chapter had suffered a dire blow indeed. All the fortress-monastery's inhabitants, even down to the lowliest serf, soon heard about Third and Tenth Companies' losses. Many of the Chosen wept openly. Vigils were scheduled in the Reclusiam. Here in the Strategium, a dark, heavy air hung over the great crystal table, centred on Drakken's empty onyx chair.

Ashor Drakken dead! It was almost inconceivable. Kantor felt the loss like a gaping wound in his own flesh. Not only had he lost a trusted and respected warrior-brother but also many of the Third who Kantor had once led into battle. The 3rd Company captain had been a model Astartes, stoic, brave and dedicated. Proper tribute would be paid when time allowed. For now the latest ork transmission had to take priority. Several raw, uncompressed signals had been picked up by The Crusader's dorsal comms array just before the ship had escaped from the Freiya system, transiting into the warp just minutes before the ork heavy cruisers could close to firing distance.

On Kantor's command, Forgemaster Adon replayed the translation again from the start. Underneath the clipped, mechanical tones of the translator unit's synthesised voice, the grunting, snorting pseudo-language of the original ork speaker could just faintly be heard.

The translation was rough and highly interpretive. The ork tongue was extremely unrefined and employed little actual grammar. Adon's algorithms could only do so much.

'Listen Snagrod, Arch-Arsonist Charadon. Blue-shelled human dead. Ork alive. This fight, ork kill blue-shelled human. Ork stronger, tougher, bigger. Ork fight blue-shelled human again. Good fight. Ork attack world of blue-shelled human. No escape. No-shelled human also die. Many. Much fighting. Much killing. Ork grow. Waaagh! grow. World of blue-shelled human burn. Human burn. Waaagh! Snagrod not stop. Comes soon.'

As the synthesised voice went silent, Kantor looked around the table. Every last Astartes sitting there, with the exception of the metal-masked Forgemaster, was scowling furiously. Despite the rudimentary nature of the language, there was no mistaking the core of the message. The voice was Snagrod's, and his intent was all too clear.

Captain Cortez spoke before anyone else had the chance. 'We go back in with as much of the fleet as we can. We cut their ships to pieces and turn the whole planet into a ball of molten slag.' He looked over at Kantor and added, 'We should have done that in the first place.'

Drigo Alvez answered without glancing in Cortez's direction. 'And perhaps you, my invincible brother, would explain to the High Lords of Terra why a world with a breathable atmosphere and valuable raw resources was made worthless to the Imperium. I would gladly travel with you just to see their reaction.'

'I'll go anywhere you like once the killing is done,' Cortez shot back.

'Enough,' said Kantor, raising his hands to quiet both of them. 'Badlanding is no longer of strategic value as a target. The orks have had two further weeks to plunder it. They will have moved on. What I need is an assessment on the earliest this Waaagh could strike at Rynn's World, the kind of numbers we could be facing, and our current capabilities with regard to repelling a full-scale assault from space.'

'An accurate assessment is impossible at this stage, my lord,' answered Ceval Ranparre. As Master of the Fleet, such an assessment fell under his remit. 'Adon and I ran the projections you requested based on neighbouring ork populations that might have responded to the original greenskin clarion call. Given the paucity of hard data, the results are highly questionable. Still, we both believe that what we've seen so far is barely a hint of the force we are likely to face. In the time it took *The Crusader* to return here, we lost contact with eleven occupied systems, all to the far east of our sector, all with historical records of past greenskin incursion. In the days since the Badlanding incident, there has been no word from any of them, and no sign of any Imperial vessels having escaped. No communication from the Naval auspex posts at Dagoth, Cantatis III, Heliod or Gamma Precidio, either. Our entire eastern border has gone dark. Even factoring in unpredictable warp currents, I would give us no more than ten days to prepare. Depending on which systems are the next to fall, it could be as little as six.'

'Six days,' muttered Selig Torres. 'We might be able to mobilise in time, but the Rynnsguard and the System Defence Fleet won't be. Not for something like this.'

Ranparre met Torres's gaze and held it as he replied, 'Since the enemy has already expressed his plans to come to us, the warp will work to our advantage. The ork ships will have to translate back into real space relatively far from any significant gravity wells, just as our own ships must. That factor alone should give us between forty and fifty-five hours during which we can tag, track and analyse the ork fleet and configure our own high orbital response accordingly. As fleet commander, I will do everything in my power to see that no ork sets foot on this world.'

'I do not doubt that for a second,' said Kantor. 'But I'll want every last ground-based asset at full combat readiness just the same. In preparation for a ground defence, we will split our forces between the fortress-monastery and the capital.'

'What of the other provinces?' asked Olbyn Kadena, Captain of the Sixth, Master of the Watch.

Kantor faced him, eyes hard, and shook his head. 'We cannot risk spreading our forces too thin. I will send brothers from the Crusade Company to oversee their defensive preparations, but they will be called back before the fighting starts. We make our stand here and in the capital.'

Eight per cent of the Rynnite populace lived in New Rynn City and the surrounding environs – over sixteen million people. The second largest city on the planet was home to less than three million. Most of those who lived outside the cities were indentured workers serving in the tens of thousands of agri-communes that covered the arable land on three continents.

'The Rynnsguard and the Civitas authorities can deal with refugees,' Kantor continued. 'Our sole priority will be the elimination of the xenos.'

He turned to Captain Alvez, and said, 'Drigo, I'm putting you in command of the detachment that will defend New Rynn City. Occupy the Cassar. I shall assign a number of squads from Crusade Company to assist you.'

Alvez's face betrayed the hint of a frown.

'Be at ease, brother,' said Kantor, noting the captain's expression. 'They will be instructed to follow your command as if it were my own. The Cassar is well stocked and there are four-hundred Chosen already stationed there, but you should prepare an additional requisitions list for my approval.'

Now, Kantor returned his attention to the Master of the Fleet. 'Brother Ranparre, how quickly can we recall *The Prosperine* and *The Hadrius* from the N'goth-Katar trade route? The firepower they wield may be much needed before this is over.'

'Depending on the warp tides, my lord, transit would take ten weeks at best. Getting new orders to them would take half that again.'

'Fifteen weeks in total,' said Kantor sourly. 'No. It's too long. The trade routes may prove vital to us if this war becomes protracted. We shall leave those ships where they are for now. How quickly can we recall the rest of our fleet?'

'Most of the fleet is within a few days' warp travel. In a way, my lord, we are fortunate that this crisis comes so soon after the Day of Foundation. Our ships have not had time to disperse all that widely. Most can be called back in time.'

'At least that's something,' growled Cortez from across the table.

'Do so,' said Kantor. 'Call them back, and coordinate with local naval forces to establish a defensive perimeter with the highest density on the system's eastern flank. The orks will attack us directly from the space they have already conquered. As always, brother, I leave command of actual fleet operations to you. I will personally supervise our surface-to-orbit defences from here. You will have the full support of every plasma and missile battery on the planet, I promise you that. If there is anything you believe can aid you in your fight, contact me directly and I will have it seen to. Yours is the first line of defence, Ceval. Emperor willing, you are the only line we shall need.'

The Master of the Fleet smiled at that, but the smile did not reach his dark eyes. 'If the greenskins dare to enter our space, I will wreak havoc on them, lord. Be assured of that. Unless you require my presence for anything else, may I take my leave? There is much to do, and I would like to get things moving.'

Kantor stood, prompting the entire council to rise. 'Go brother,' he said, 'and may Dorn watch over you, revelling in every kill you make.'

'May he watch over us all,' said Ranparre. He saluted, fist to breastplate, turned from the table and left through the Strategium's west exit.

While they were still standing, Drigo Alvez said, 'If I am to leave soon for New Rynn City, my lord, then I too request permission to be about my preparations.'

Kantor's eyes met those of the captain, almost his equal in height. 'You may go, Drigo,' he said. 'You and I shall convene later. There is much we still need to talk about. For now, though, you had best get started. You are dismissed.'

There followed another round of salutes. A moment later, with Drigo's heavy footfalls ringing through the air of the chamber, Kantor motioned to the others and said, 'Be seated, brothers.'

The council was quiet, pensive. Even Cortez seemed unusually reluctant to speak.

Finally, Torres asked, 'How do you plan to distribute the rest of us?'

'Most of you will command your companies on the walls of our home in accordance with siege defence protocols,' said Kantor. 'I will call another session at twenty-three hundred hours this evening to discuss specifics. The moment the ork ships translate from the warp, you will bring your men to full combat readiness. I believe Brother Ranparre will stop them. He has never failed before. But I would have you all ready, regardless. Not one ork must set foot on the hallowed grounds of our home. I would consider that a great and terrible sacrilege.'

'So would we all,' spat Caldimus Ortiz, Captain of the Seventh, Master of the Gates. That no enemy should ever breach Arx Tyrannus was his responsibility above all others.

Kantor noted the fire in Ortiz's eyes at the very thought of the greenskins returning to Rynn's World. Turning his gaze from face to face, he saw the same dark determination, the cold, hard violence that lay just below the surface in all of them.

This so-called Arch-Arsonist has underestimated us, he thought. We will punish him severely for that.

'You each have preparations to make,' said Kantor. 'Tailor all training exercises accordingly. If there are no further issues to raise…'

'My lord,' said Eustace Mendoza. 'There *is* one more matter before we dissolve this session.'

Kantor turned towards the Chief Librarian. 'Speak on, my friend.'

'Forgive me, brothers,' said Mendoza, 'for diverging from our most pressing issue, but we have yet to decide the fate of the Scout, Janus Kennon.'

High Chaplain Tomasi nodded grimly. 'Brother Kennon is, at least in part, clearly responsible for the dark losses our Chapter suffered at Krugerport. Does Captain Icario have anything to say for him?'

Tomasi had removed his skull-helm on entering the Strategium, as was Chapter law. Now, he turned his coal-black eyes towards the unusually quiet 10th Company captain.

Ishmael Icario could not meet the High Chaplain's gaze. Instead, he spoke down towards the table, as if his neck was weighted by a great shame. 'Fellow sons of Dorn, I deserve no small share in Brother Kennon's culpability. In my rush to put him on the battlefield, to test the true extent of his talents, I ignored the concerns expressed by my sergeants. My own personal hopes clouded my judgement, and for that I am truly sorry. But if he is to be punished, then I too must suffer for my mistake.'

Alessio Cortez snorted and shook his head. 'If lightning strikes a tree and starts a fire, is that the fault of the forest?'

Icario looked up, surprised. 'Now *you* are quoting Traegus to *me*, brother?'

Cortez forced a grin, and Kantor saw the beaten look in Icario's eyes mellow, but only for a moment.

'No one blames you, Ishmael,' said the Chapter Master. 'How could we? I, too, had great hopes for Janus Kennon. But talent is nothing without discipline. He did not bear the tenets of the Chapter in mind. A Space Marine who disobeys orders has not fully embraced his psycho-conditioning. He cannot be called a Space Marine. If there was any failing here, it was Kennon's alone. Did you not also assign Sergeant Mishina to the mission? And did he not earn his company great honour, risking his life to retrieve Captain Drakken's body from the battle-field?'

'Aye,' rumbled High Chaplain Tomasi with a glance over at the Chapter Master. 'Ezra Mishina is a most worthy brother.'

Kantor could hardly miss the meaning behind the Chaplain's look. 'He is, indeed. It is high time he was granted the Steeping. He will join Third Company, the first of many who will be needed to bring their numbers back up over time. I hope this pleases you, Ishmael.'

Kantor threw a rare and fleeting smile at Captain Icario, and, at last, saw the beginnings of a reciprocal smile break through the Scout captain's dour expression.

'Lord Hellblade honours me and all of the Tenth,' said Icario, but he paused, and the smile fell away as he added, 'Still, there is the matter of Kennon's fate.'

'How does he bear his guilt?' asked Cortez.

'Poorly, it must be said,' admitted Icario. 'Despite everything, he stands by his decision to fire, to take the shot while this warlord, Mag-Kull, was in his sights.'

There was a grunt of derision from Kantor's left. Matteo Morrelis, Master of Blades, Captain of the 8th Company, leaned forward with his forearms on the crystal surface. 'The sensorium uploads prove his culpability beyond any doubt. We have all seen them. If he cannot respect the chain of command, no matter the circumstances, he is unfit to wear our colours and call himself kin.'

Kantor was about to respond when Cortez slammed a rough hand on the table. Every head turned sharply in his direction. 'If he had slain the ork,' Cortez growled over at Morrelis, 'we would be calling him a hero.' He turned to Kantor. 'You would be promoting *Kennon* to Third Company, not Mishina.'

'This decision can hardly rest on an *if*,' barked Caldimus Ortiz, 'particularly given that he did not *slay the ork*, brother.'

Cortez glared back Ortiz.

'High Chaplain,' said Kantor. 'Have you anything to add before I make my pronouncement?'

Tomasi sounded genuinely sorrowful as he answered. 'The loss of a captain is always a great tragedy, not just for the Chapter, but for all mankind. Those truly fit to lead are a rare commodity. Brother Kennon has, by disregarding a direct order, played a significant role in the death of one of this Chapter's finest. Ashor Drakken was a decorated hero with a record of achievement spanning more than two centuries. There *is* precedent for such a case as this. We have searched the archives.' Here, he indicated Eustace Mendoza, who nodded once with eyes closed. 'The punishment for precipitating this disaster,' Tomasi continued, 'must be the most severe available to us. As much as it pains us, there can be no other choice.'

Several of the captains bowed their heads at this proclamation.

Kantor did likewise. When he lifted his head a second later, he said, 'I have made my decision.

Judgement is passed. Janus Kennon shall undergo servitor conversion.'

Alessio Cortez loosed a string of quiet curses.

Mendoza nodded. 'The Librarius will be ready to receive him once he has been informed.' Turning to Captain Icario, he added, 'The process of mind-ripping is painful. I shall not lie to you, my brother. But it will be mercifully short. This much, I promise.'

Ishmael Icario did not answer. He rested his shaved head in his hands, allowing his elbows to support him on the crystal tabletop.

Forgemaster Adon interjected in crisp machine monotone. 'Kennon's innate skills may still be utilised. They need not be lost. As a gun-servitor, he will serve the Chapter for a thousand years, and, on his decommissioning, will perhaps have expunged the stain on his honour.'

'Whether or not his guilt shall be expunged is a matter for the Emperor alone to decide,' said Tomasi.

'Ishmael,' said Kantor. 'Take Brother Kennon to the Librarium at sunrise tomorrow. Do it quietly while the rest of your men are observing the morning combat rituals. Let them learn of it after the fact. I would have this matter seen to and put behind us as soon as possible. It must not linger to cast its shadow over the honour service for the dead.'

'Sunrise,' said Icario softly. 'I will see it done, lord.'

For a moment, silence descended over the crystal table once again. Then Kantor stood and formally ended the session, dismissing the council members. They would be back here soon enough, he knew.

He and Cortez were the last to leave.

As they walked together though the gloomy, candlelit hallways of the fortress keep, past shadowed alcoves where the stone likenesses of past heroes stood at eternal attention, Cortez asked his old friend and master a question.

'Thinking of the glory, of the blow it would strike to the enemy, and unaware of whatever technology was shielding this Mag-Kull beast, would you yourself not have taken the shot?'

The Chapter Master frowned. 'You already know my answer to that, Alessio.'

'I suppose I do,' Cortez replied heavily, 'as certainly as you know mine.'

'Indeed.'

They walked on, side-by-side, unspeaking for a few more paces, until they reached the junction in the corridor where they would part. Kantor's private chambers were high in the uppermost levels of the central keep and he had many hundreds of stairs to climb. The act of climbing them often helped to clear his mind, and he knew he needed that clarity of thought now more than he had needed it in a very long time.

Before the two friends went off in different directions, Kantor placed a hand on Cortez's shoulder and said, 'In the name of the primarch, Alessio, never put me in that position. To pass judgement over you as I just did over Brother Kennon would destroy me, brother.'

'No,' said Cortez. 'It would not destroy you, Pedro. You have the right strength for such things. It is why you were chosen to lead us.'

Kantor smiled briefly at that, but it was hollow and he knew Cortez could tell. There were no secrets between them. They knew each other far too well for that.

He dropped his hand from his friend's shoulder, turned in the direction of the great stone staircase at the end of the corridor, and walked off, hoping it would be the last they spoke of disobeying orders for a long time.

SEVEN

New Rynn Spaceport, Rynnland Province

THE CAPITAL AWOKE to the deep, window-shaking roar of sixteen Crimson Fist Thunderhawks as they swept in low over the sprawling slums that had grown up around the planet's only spaceport. Sturdy landing gear emerged from metal hulls. Powerful turbines changed pitch, from a roar to a high, throbbing whine. The Thunderhawks settled on an airstrip that had been cleared for their arrival only twenty minutes earlier.

It wasn't that the New Rynn Spaceport staff were lazy or disorganised. They simply hadn't been told until the very last moment that the Space Marines were coming. That lack of adequate warning was deliberate. Captain Alvez did not want the people of the city to know. He had no wish to drive through streets thronged with cheering civilians. They did not know what they were cheering for. He was born to wage war. Did they wish to celebrate his gift for slaughter? Did they wish to celebrate the thousands of gallons of blood he had spilled year after year? He doubted it. Most would be sickened by the things he had seen and done. If not sickened, then terrified to the point of madness.

The spaceport was about sixty kilometres south-east from the outermost of the capital city's great defensive walls, but the noise of the Thunderhawks' powerful turbines carried all the way to the city centre, a glorious fortified island surrounded on both sides by the waters of the River Rynn. This was the *Zona Regis*, often called the Silver Citadel, home of the governor and secondary residence to all the members of the Upper Rynnhouse. The Cassar lay within its towering walls, a large keep built by the Chapter after the greenskin invasion of twelve hundred years ago so that a detachment of Crimson Fists could garrison the capital if it were ever threatened again.

It seemed that time had come.

As the Thunderhawks powered down their engines, the sun crested the horizon to the east. Most of the people who had heard the roar, adults and children alike, were already dressing for another day of labour in the fields and manufactora, their sweat and toil dedicated to an Emperor none would ever see save in ancient carvings and frescoes, or rendered as figurines for sale on the stalls of the city's *zonae commercia*.

It was not uncommon for the citizens of the capital to hear ships coming and going, no matter the time of day. The spaceport often played host to far bigger, noisier craft than Thunderhawks. Aside from its many ground-level airstrips, the gargantuan structure boasted three vast, thick cylindrical towers, each topped with circular landing plates supported by anti-grav suspension. They could provide berths for even the largest trans-atmospheric craft. Most of the citizens who heard the noise of the Thunderhawks stopped what they were doing and cocked their heads to listen. There was something different about this sound. Only military aircraft ever approached together and in such numbers.

On contacting the spaceport's air traffic personnel, Captain Alvez had been adamant that his force's arrival go unannounced. He told the spaceport's chief administrator over the vox-net that, if there were any choirs or bands, fanfare of any kind, he would kill the man himself.

Alvez was naturally somewhat angry, then, when he marched down the ramp of his Thunderhawk to find himself being greeted by over a thousand individuals in immaculate cream-coloured uniforms.

The moment they laid eyes on his broad, armoured frame, they dropped to one knee and bowed their heads. A heavy-set officer with golden shoulder-boards shouted out a command, and the kneeling troopers called out as one, 'All hail the Crimson Fists, righteous sons of Rogal Dorn, hand of the Emperor, saviour of the people!'

'Dorn's blood,' cursed Alvez quietly, eyes panning across the rows of starched soldiers. 'This is just *perfect.*'

Behind him, his Astartes were beginning to disembark, marching briskly down Thunderhawk ramps, heavy boots striking metal in perfect military cadence. Serfs and servitors followed in great number, hefting ammunition cases, weapons and supplies of every possible description.

Spaceport servitors shambled forward to assist, and the airstrip was abuzz with activity.

Alvez strode forward and called out to the Rynnsguard, 'At ease, you men. On your feet. Get up!'

The unsolicited welcoming committee rose smartly. Every last one of them kept his eyes straight forward, not daring to meet the Space Marine captain's icy glare. It was patently obvious they were at anything but ease.

'Officer in charge,' bellowed Alvez. 'Make yourself known to me. Now!'

The deep, harsh, barking quality of his voice made some of the Rynnsguard jump. After a heartbeat's nervous hesitation, the overweight officer with the shoulder boards strode forward, arms swinging rigidly at his sides. His chest glittered with bronze, silver and gold starbursts, and, above the brim of his starched cap, there was a badge in the shape of a golden aquila.

Alvez noted the polished silver skulls on the man's tunic collar, and said, 'Your name, colonel.'

It was phrased as a demand. The colonel bowed at the waist, hands pressed to his chest in the standard Imperial salute. When he stood upright, he removed his cap, fixed his gaze on the centre of Alvez's gleaming breastplate, and said, 'Portius Cantrell, my lord, commanding officer of the Rynnland Second Garrisoning Regiment, Soroccan Defensive Operations Group, at your service.'

Alvez wasn't impressed.

'I am Drigo Alvez, colonel. I am the captain of the Crimson Fists' Second Company, Master of the Shield, and you will do me the courtesy of looking me in the eye when you speak to me. Your reverence has been duly noted, but I would have you address my face, not my armour.'

Cantrell, who, at one hundred and seventy-eight centimetres, came up only as high as the embossed eagle on the Astartes captain's chest, gulped and hastily lifted his eyes.

Alvez glared down at him, unsmiling. 'That is better. Now tell me what you and your men are doing here. I issued strict orders to this facility's administrator. He was warned that I would execute him for disobeying.'

Cantrell glanced down at the ferrocrete surface of the landing strip on reflex, then hurriedly returned his gaze to Alvez's face. 'Air Controller Celembra did not disobey you, my lord. He issued no request for a formal welcome. My men and I, however, were already here on a security rotation. One of my lieutenants was in the air traffic control centre when your message came through. He brought word of it to me, and I took the liberty. Forgive me, lord. I know you were most specific about fanfare, but I thought a respectful military greeting would be appropriate. I could not, in good conscience, have let your arrival pass without some show of respect.'

My orders left room enough for that, I suppose, thought Alvez.

'Though I was not advised of your coming in time to prepare properly,' continued the colonel, 'my men and I are honoured to be at your disposal. Anything you need, anything at all, and we will endeavour to provide it, in the name of the Emperor and of Lord Hellblade.'

At our disposal, thought Alvez darkly. You'll soon learn the real meaning of that, colonel, but not today. Look at you, so willing to have your men reduced to the level of servants. Fighting men should have more pride.

Alvez hated diffidence, hated the way most humans fawned and scraped in front of him, always so desperate to earn the favour and protection of the Astartes. The situation would get worse, he knew, once his forces were established in the city proper. He had been through it all a hundred times and more during the course of his life. The presence of even a single Astartes among normal people caused a range of often extreme reactions. From sickening servility to abject terror, he had seen it all.

In most cases, it was standard operating procedure to keep his forces as far from the civilian populace as possible. It didn't do for the people to get too close to their protectors. Fear and avoidance he could handle – in fact, in light of the alternatives, he welcomed them – but excesses of worship, love and attention soon became a hindrance, with hourly offerings of luxury foodstuffs, expensive silks, religious trinkets, alcohol, narcotics, even women – none of which an Astartes had any use for in the slightest.

'I do not foresee us requiring your services at the moment, colonel,' said Alvez. 'If that is to change, rest assured I will alert you. As to the reason for our presence here, you will be fully briefed when I decide it is time. For now, you will clear your men from this airstrip and return to your security duties. We have much to unload, and there may be injuries if you get in the way.'

Just for a second, Alvez saw the colonel's expression grow rock hard at the barely veiled insult. Good, he thought. Perhaps there *is* a fighting man underneath all that decoration. We shall find out for sure when he learns of the coming storm. By Terra, it's high time these people were reminded that the price of survival is paid in blood.

'A good day to you, then, my lord,' said the colonel, his tone slightly colder than before. Having been so bluntly dismissed, he saluted once more, turned and marched back to his men. When he had crossed half the distance towards them, Alvez relented and called out to him.

'Colonel Cantrell.'

The Rynnsguard officer stopped and turned. This time his eyes went straight to the towering captain's face and stayed there. 'My lord?'

Alvez paused, then, pitching his voice so that Cantrell's troopers could hear it clearly, he said,

'Perhaps you and your men *could* do me a service after all.'

The colonel's face visibly brightened, and the chests of the Rynnsguard troops seemed to inflate.

'Anything my lord requires. Anything at all.'

'Provide a cordon,' said Alvez. 'Keep the public and the rest of the spaceport personnel at arm's length while we prepare our ground transports. We shall be leaving for the Cassar as soon as possible. Have a direct route cleared for us. Set up barriers, do what you must. Co-opt local law enforcement if you feel it necessary, but I want nothing in our way between here and the Zona Regis.'

'You will have it, lord,' said Cantrell. 'Is there someone with whom I can coordinate?'

'coordinate with my personal retainer,' said Alvez. 'Keep a vox-channel clear. Beta-channel, band four will suffice. His name is Merrin, and he will tell you all you need to know.'

Cantrell accepted this information with a final bow, then turned towards his men and started snapping out orders.

Alvez watched the Rynnsguard march off at double-time, then turned to supervise the unloading of his Thunderhawks.

Had the politicians heard of his arrival by now? Almost certainly. They would be scurrying to make a great occasion of it, eager for the people to see them beside the Emperor's finest. Blasted peacocks!

There was a deep rumble and a clanking of treads from his right, and he turned to see his Land Raider armoured transport approaching to take him into the city.

He walked off towards the massive machine, silently wondering just how long he had to get this city ready for the tide of foul xenos that was coming.

Somehow, he knew it would not be long enough.

EIGHT

Zona Regis, New Rynn City

MAIA CAGLIESTRA COULDN'T recall being shaken awake since she had been a child of ten years old, but that was exactly how she met the world today. Groggy, her eyelids feeling like they had been tacked together, she struggled to get her bearings.

'What... what's going on?'

When she opened her eyes, there was a moment of bright pain. Golden sunlight was already spilling into the room from the south windows. The heavy velvet drapes had been pulled back. Outside, the sky was blue and cloudless, a clear indication that the summer was on its way.

Her chief lady-in-waiting was gently gripping Maia's shoulders. She had stopped shaking them now. 'You need to wake up, ma'am. We must get you ready at once. Secretary Mylos is already waiting for you on the grand balcony. I shall bring you breakfast there.'

'What time is it?' asked Maia. 'And why are you waking me like this? You've never done that before, Shivara.'

Shivara took her hands away now, but her expression was steely. She was a unique and formidable woman, and Maia trusted no one, not even Mylos, as much as she trusted her. Shivara was tall and beautiful, and, under her form-fitting robes of white silk, powerfully muscled, though no less feminine in appearance for all that. Few people realised that Shivara was an off-worlder, not even Mylos. The woman was a sister of the Adeptus Sororitas, trained from birth to be bodyguard and aide to those judged worthy of such protection. Planetary governors across the Imperium were protected by these deadly guardians. If something was bothering Shivara, Maia knew that she, too, had ample reason to be worried.

'Please get up, ma'am,' said Shivara. 'Something unexpected has happened. The Crimson Fists have come to the city.'

Maia sat bolt upright in her bed, dark hair tumbling down over her pale shoulders, a great smile spreading across her face. 'They have? This is wonderful. Dare I hope the Chapter Master himself is among them?'

Shivara frowned.

'What is the matter with you?' asked Maia, confused. 'Their presence bothers you?'

'Greatly, ma'am.'

Maia was getting angry now. Her smile fell away. 'I think you had better explain yourself. The sons of the

Emperor Himself are here. I cannot understand your mood.'

She threw off her sheets, swung her legs over the side for the four-poster bed, slid her feet into fine white slippers, stood and stretched her lean form.

Her eyes went automatically, as they did every morning, to the great statue in the south-west corner of the room. It was cut from the purest white marble on the planet. Aurella's *Œdonis in Death*. A masterpiece. If the Secretary of the Treasury knew how much Maia had appropriated from the palace funds for its purchase, there would be hell to pay. But she had been unable to resist when the sculptor, Ianous Aurella, had finally offered it for sale. Blackmailing the old man had been a difficult and lengthy process, but ultimately worth it.

Shivara's gaze followed that of her mistress.

The figure, Œdonis, was as big as an Astartes, and there was something about the face, some subtle nuance of expression or bone structure, that reminded Maia daily of the Chapter Master, Pedro Kantor.

'What bothers me, ma'am,' said Shivara, cutting across Maia's thoughts, 'is their numbers. They are here in company strength at least.' She hesitated a beat. 'Word from the spaceport has it that they have come prepared for war.'

Maia tore her gaze from the statue's broad sculpted shoulders. 'For war?' she said. 'Don't be preposterous. There hasn't been a war on Rynn's World for...'

'One thousand two hundred and sixty-four years, ma'am,' said Shivara heavily. 'Meaning one is long overdue.'

NINE

New Rynn City, Rynnland Province

Sᴇʀɢᴇᴀɴᴛ Hᴜʀᴏɴ Gʀɪᴍᴍ could tell that his superior was in a dark mood, or rather, a darker mood than usual. Captain Alvez rode in the left side cupola of the Land Raider, *Aegis Eternis*, refusing even to glance at the cheering crowds which lined either side of Carriageway 19. Grimm knew this because, as befit the captain's second-in-command, he rode in the vehicle's right cupola, a position of no small honour. He was a veteran sergeant, a long-serving squad leader who had proven himself in battle a great many times. When Brother Romnus had been killed in action three years ago, Alvez had chosen Grimm as his new right-hand man, elevating him to the 2nd Company's command squad, a decision generally well met by the rest of the company.

Aiding the captain directly was a duty that Grimm relished, though the relationship between the two

Space Marines remained strained at best. Their personalities were anything but similar. Grimm would do whatever his commander asked, naturally, but he found the tall Alvez to be a cold, self-isolating individual. Perhaps it had not always been so. It had occurred to Grimm more than once that Alvez might simply have lost too many good friends along the way. Such a hardening of the soul was not unknown among Astartes who outlived many of the brothers with whom they had started service.

Grimm had passed the Chapter's selection trials one hundred and three years ago. He had earned veteran status, and the honour of painting his right gauntlet red, relatively early in his career, successfully leading a squad of ten men against a push by traitor armour units on 6-Edinae. Few brothers survived to serve two whole centuries: he knew, and from these the captains were drawn. They were the truly exceptional ones: Alvez, Cortez, Kadena, Acastus and the like, not to mention the Chapter Master himself.

Unlike Alvez, who clearly found the public's adulation irritating in the extreme, Grimm accepted it. He allowed himself to feel the warmth that flowed from those smiles and tear-streaked faces. They were like children, these people; their experiences limited to shorter lives, their bodies limited by their relative fragility. Despite this, the Imperium was nothing without them. What did it stand for if not their continued survival? It was why the Emperor had made his Space Marines at all.

Young and old, the citizens of the Rynnite capital gazed up at him, waving and crying out as *Aegis Eternis* rumbled past, wide treads grinding the rockcrete surface of the wide lanes.

'Hail the Crimson Fists! Hail the protectors!'

Women on both sides of the road, weeping openly, barely held back by the cordon of struggling Rynnsguard troopers, threw great armfuls of red and blue flowers in front of the column. The sweet floral scent was strong on the air, but it quickly became mixed with the promethium fumes from the armoured vehicles' rumbling exhausts, and became altogether less pleasant.

A waste, thought Grimm, to spend hard-earned money on flowers, only to see them crushed beneath the treads of a tank. It would keep the flower-sellers in liquor for a while, he supposed.

Behind *Aegis Eternis*, the train of armoured vehicles stretched out, each painted in the blue of the Chapter, each proudly bearing the icon of a red fist in black circle. Their thunderous passage shook ornaments from sills and mantles as far as a kilometre away. Long cracks appeared in the windows and walls of the shining, white-painted hab-stacks. The people didn't notice. They might grumble later, but a force like this hadn't visited the capital in decades. It was a spectacle no one wanted to miss. The bars and inns would be filled with stories for years to come:

I was there when they rode through the city.

I saw their captain in the flesh, I did.

Then, the stories would be embellished over time:

The great captain singled me out and waved to me, I swear it.

One of them asked me my name!

Why not? thought Grimm. Why should warriors not be venerated a little now and then? The fighting men of the Imperium dedicated their lives to war in the name of the Emperor. They brought peace to others with their sacrifice. So it was with the Imperial Guard, the Navy, the clandestine but powerful forces of the Holy Inquisition. Even the Ecclesiarchy had its fighters.

Their blood was the coin by which the realm survived. War on the fringes kept the core safe. In such dark, dangerous times at these, with humanity constantly besieged by fiends on every side, people needed heroes to believe in more than ever. Grimm saw the importance of that. Could Captain Alvez not see it, too?

Of course, the Space Marines represented so much more than just a military force. They were the closest living link to the Divine Emperor that these people would see in their lifetimes. All the toil, all the worship, all the coppers they put in the collection plates; the sight of just one Astartes made the legends more real somehow. If the Astartes were real, then the Emperor was, too. And if the Emperor was real, humanity could still dare to hope for its eventual salvation. His Divine Majesty would rise again and crush the myriad foe, and, after so very long, there would at last be peace and security in the galaxy.

Holier men than Huron Grimm called it *faith*.

Eight decades ago, during a mission to hunt down eldar slave traders on Iaxus III, a young priest, slashed to ribbons and left to die in a burning Imperial church, had coughed out words to this effect as Grimm dragged him to safety. The priest hadn't lasted long, his wounds flowing copiously, but Grimm had never forgotten the zeal in the dying man's eyes.

He had been humbled by it. Even a Space Marine could still learn valuable lessons from ordinary men, he knew.

Looking down from the cupola, his gaze passed over a gaggle of well-dressed children practically screaming with delight as the ground beneath their feet shuddered and shook. Others waved frantically from the shoulders of their fathers, desperate to be acknowledged by the armoured giants they recognised from their storybooks and history lessons. Some, particularly the youngest, were terrified beyond words. Grimm saw a good many take refuge in the fabric of their mothers' skirts, leaving little smears of nasal mucus there.

A tiny malnourished girl, her orange rags marking her as an orphan from one of the city's many workhouses, gazed up at Grimm with wide blue eyes. She didn't scream, or shout. Neither did she smile or even cry. She simply gave him the smallest and shyest of waves. Grimm raised his own gauntleted hand just a fraction and returned the greeting.

Without taking his eyes from the road straight ahead, Captain Alvez barked, 'Don't encourage them.'

Nothing escaped his notice.

'My apologies, lord,' said Grimm.

Alvez grunted. 'I don't care if the twelve lords of Terra are down there. Acknowledge no one. We are not here to entertain these fools.'

'As you say, of course.'

'And they *are* fools, Huron,' Alvez went on. 'Just look at them. So blindly, happily ignorant. Not one of them, not a single blasted one, judging by the gormless smiles on their faces, has stopped for a second to question why we are here. None have considered for even a moment that the presence of so many Space Marines must surely presage some terrible danger. Dorn alone knows what they think we are doing here.'

Grimm couldn't argue with that.

They *will* think of it, sooner or later, he thought. And then we'll have a panic on our hands.

Two hundred million people on this world. Two hundred million lives in the balance. He'd seen what the orks did to the helpless. He'd seen the horrors they perpetrated.

Thinking of this, he turned his eyes to look for the workhouse orphan again, but someone had shoved her to the rear and she had disappeared behind a dense forest of adult legs.

An image appeared in his mind, and his brow furrowed in furious denial. He gritted his teeth. In the image, he saw the girl looking at him again, but her blue eyes were lifeless. Her blonde hair burned as he watched. He saw her flesh crisping and realised she had been spitted. She was being cooked over an open fire. He saw a massive ork, a black-skinned warboss of prodigious size, pull the spit from the flames and sink his tusks into the meat, devouring her as if she were little more than an snack.

It was no idle daydream. Grimm had seen the evidence of such abominable crimes all too often on other ork-blighted worlds.

'In Dorn's name,' he growled quietly, 'not here. Not while I draw breath.'

Despite the roar of the Land Raider's engine and the rattle of its wide treads, the captain had heard him.

'You wish to say something, Huron?'

Grimm shook his head.

'Not really, my lord,' he replied, but, after a heartbeat, he added, 'Only that, if the Waaagh does come to Rynn's World, I swear I will turn the Adacian red with ork blood!'

The captain absorbed this comment without turning his eyes from the road ahead. The armoured column was approaching the Ocaro Gate now, its white stone towers rising tall and proud against the deepening blue sky of mid-morning. Beyond the gate lay Zona 6 Industria, the only manufacturing zone though which the Crimson Fist convoy would have to travel to reach the Cassar. There would be fewer people on the streets there. The industrial zones were for working in, not living. Not unless you wanted to die young, riddled with toxins and disease.

'The Waaagh *will* come, Huron,' said Alvez as the massive Ocaro Gate groaned open to admit them. 'When it does, know that you and I will turn the seas red together.'

TEN

Rooftop of the Great Keep, Arx Tyrannus

KANTOR GAZED OUT over a sea of cloud through which
the black peaks of the surrounding mountains rose
like claws. The sky above was deep azure, just like his
armour, and the sibling suns were bright, but they
were not warm. Up here, on the roof of the fortress-
monastery's tallest structure, it never truly got warm.
The technical crews servicing the anti-air batteries at
each of the rooftop's corners wore their thickest
raumas-wool robes. Even so clothed, they could not
work up here for long. The air was so thin that they
required rebreather masks or they would pass out
and eventually die.

The thin air did not bother the Chapter Master, of
course. Nor did it bother the captain at his side,
Selig Torres of 5th Company. The two Astartes
could endure long periods up here with little
discomfort.

Ordinator Savales had been unable to persuade Torres to await the Chapter Master below, but Kantor didn't mind. Here above the clouds, with the freezing wind buffeting you, was as good a place as any to talk about the darkness that approached this world. Torres had sought him out because he was in opposition to the way the Chapter Master was handling the threat of the Waaagh. He had made his stance clear at the last session. Now he stood in silence at Kantor's shoulder, unsure of how to begin. That was unlike him. Kantor had known the acerbic, outspoken captain for over a century, and knew well enough when he had a point to make.

'Best speak freely, Selig. Do not change your ways now.'

Torres stepped forward and turned, angling himself towards the Chapter Master so that he could look him in the eye. Kantor saw that he was not smiling.

'How sure are we, my lord,' said Torres, 'that this will all play out as expected?'

Kantor thought about that. The council session late last night had been more heated than any other in his memory. Some of the captains, Torres foremost among them, were calling for more forces to be put into space to be used as boarding parties. What was the point of keeping the Crimson Fists on the ground, they argued, if the orks would have to fight their way past a major blockade first? Surely the best use of the Chapter's warriors was to send them to the very front line where they could assault the ships of the ork leaders and assassinate them?

The oldest and most experienced council members had sided with Kantor. No matter how effective the blockade proved, orks *would* set foot on Rynn's World. Even with ten times more ships available to the Chapter, the gaps in the defence grid would still measure many thousands of kilometres across. Such was the nature of war in space. The orks would get some of their ships through, and, when those ships landed, they would spill out their savage cargo onto land that hadn't seen such bloodshed in over a millennium. Kantor wasn't about to let the Rynnsguard fight the greenskin ground forces alone.

It was critical that the true strength of the Chapter remain planetside to meet the invader wherever it landed. Any other approach was, in Kantor's eyes at least, foolish to consider, and it bothered him that several of the captains present at the session had argued so vehemently. He could understand their desire for glory well enough. Boarding actions were some of the most intense and dangerous operations a Space Marine would ever face and success brought great honour. But this battle was less about glory and honour than it was about protecting their home. It was about preserving everything the Crimson Fists represented, both to themselves and to their people, in the face of a threat the likes of which few other Chapters had ever known.

'You will have to trust me, Selig,' said Kantor. 'You know I would not lead our brothers astray. If I tell you we must concentrate our brothers' strengths on a ground-based war, it is because I have considered all the alternatives. The orks must not gain any solid foothold here. Their spores, if left unchecked, will spread on the winds and blight our world for decades to come. By organising our squads into rapid-response units... you heard me last night. I'll not repeat myself.'

Torres nodded, but said, 'It is not that I doubt you, lord. Your word is law, and I would follow you into the mouth of oblivion, as you surely know. But I cannot shake my grave reservations about this course. It assumes a certain degree of failure from the start.'

Kantor nodded. 'I am a realist, Selig. Orks will get through. How many, we cannot say, but they will. Even if we committed every last battle-brother to boarding actions, we could not change that. So we will fight on both fronts. The decision is mine, and it has been made.'

Torres looked far from satisfied, but he knew well enough when there was no more room to manoeuvre. Changing tack, he asked, 'Have the Thunderhawks returned from New Rynn City yet?'

'They will be here soon.'

'And our brothers in the Crusade Company? When do you intend to call them back from their advisory missions?'

Kantor looked out over the vista of endless white cloud as he said, 'They will be called back as soon as we have first sign of the foe.'

He turned his eyes skywards. High above the planet's surface, he knew, the Chapter's ships, along with the System Defence Fleet – an armada of warp-incapable battleships under the auspices of the Imperial Navy – would be slowly shifting into place, forming a battle-line that measured hundreds of thousands of kilometres.

'I still cannot believe it has come to this,' said Torres. 'To have already lost Ashor Drakken... And to think that the same orks would dare to strike us here, on our own world...'

Kantor winced a little. He, too, still grieved for Drakken. Sooner or later, a successor would have to be named, someone from the Crusade Company, someone worthy of leading the 3rd Company into battle. For now, the survivors of the Krugerport fiasco had been fused with Drigo Alvez's 2nd Company and were stationed with them in the capital, but the situation was far from ideal. The 3rd Company had an identity of its own, and a proud and glorious tradition to maintain. There just hadn't been time to nominate a new captain before the men had been deployed. It would have to wait until after the orks were beaten back.

'Ashor is with us in spirit, Selig. A proper tribute will be commissioned for Monument Hall once there is adequate opportunity. As for the Waaagh penetrating so deep into this sector so quickly, I have been thinking on that myself. I believe Snagrod's forces are prioritising communications relays. It explains why no warning of the Waaagh has come from anywhere else but Badlanding, and yet we know they have overtaken a score of other systems already.'

Torres squinted. 'You are suggesting, lord, that this Snagrod is employing an isolation strategy prior to launching his attacks?'

'We've seen hints of it from ork warbands before, though never so well executed, I grant you.'

Across the Imperium, the vast Munitorum propaganda machine was relentless in presenting the orks as inferior, dull-witted, bestial foes with only the most rudimentary understanding of what it took to win a protracted war. The filthy xenos were driven by instinct, their tiny brains incapable of tactical analysis and response. For the most part, the propaganda was close to the truth. The average ork got by on muscle, resilience and raw savagery – little else. But Snagrod was clearly anything but average. He had already proved that. Centuries of fighting the greenskins had taught Kantor not to be hasty in underestimating those that climbed to the rank of warlord. The forty-first millennium had seen increasingly disturbing proof that, out there among the millions of disparate ork tribes, there were increasing numbers of individuals that represented a threat unlike anything the Imperium had faced since the dark days of the Heresy. One need only peruse recent battle-reports from Armageddon, a key Imperial hive-world located in the Segmentum Solar.

In 949.M41, an ork warlord had led an unprecedented Waaagh against Imperial forces on that world. The greenskin leader was called Ghazghkull Mag-Uruk Thraka, and such was his rare ability for strategic thinking that he failed in his conquest by only the narrowest of margins. As further testament to his unusual military intellect, he had even managed to affect a massive greenskin exodus when the tide of battle had irrevocably turned against him.

If Ghazghkull Mag-Uruk Thraka was capable of effective strategy, then the Arch-Arsonist of Charadon was, too. Snagrod was employing lighting-quick surprise assaults on every deep-space communications relay he came across. Then, and only then, did he send his forces in *en masse* to slaughter and pillage the isolated worlds.

But he would not do that on Rynn's World. Kantor would not let him. Snagrod had made a great mistake in his choice of target, and another in announcing his intentions so overtly. The orks were coming in force, and their leader *wanted* the Crimson Fists to be ready. He wanted a fight he could consider worthy, a fight that would make him a legend, a fight that would bring greenskin tribes from all over the galaxy under one banner. If the beast succeeded in that, the Waaagh would be unstoppable.

Kantor realised that Torres was staring at him, face twisted in concern.

'I have never seen you like this, lord. Never so... dour.'

Kantor did not insult his brother's intelligence by affecting a false demeanour. Torres deserved more than that, and deception was not Kantor's way. Lies rarely served honour. 'We must not under–'

A hiss of static on the comm-link cut him off mid-sentence. Kantor pressed a finger to the bead in his ear and said, 'Monitor.'

The voice on the other end was unusually frantic. Kantor's eyes went wide as he listened.

'Impossible,' he growled. 'Check your instruments. There must be some mistake.'

A moment later, he added, 'Then tell him to check *his* instruments, damn it!'

As Kantor continued to listen to the Monitor speak, he locked eyes with Torres.

When the message ended, he lowered his hand from his ear and muttered, 'Dorn's blood!'

'My lord?'

Kantor gripped Torres' armoured shoulder. 'The orks, Selig. The Waaagh! It's here. They're already in-system!'

Torres shook his head. 'Impossible, lord. They can't be. How far out are they? Forty hours? Fifty?'

'That's the worst of it,' said Kantor through gritted teeth. 'Three.'

'Three?' gasped Torres. 'That would mean...'

'It's insane. Suicidal. Their entire force just burst from the warp only a hundred and fifty thousand kilometres from the planet. Our ships are already turning to engage. Get your company brothers to combat stations. I'm putting you in charge of the Laculum Bastion. coordinate with the Technicarum. I want all missile and plasma batteries at full operational status at once. And be ready when I call you to the Strategium. There will be a final emergency session while we still have time.' He turned to the technical crews finishing up on the corner batteries. 'You Chosen,' he said. 'Finish quickly. You will be needed below.'

They bowed reverentially to him, turned and attacked their work with fresh urgency.

Torres was too stunned to salute as Kantor spun away from him and began marching at speed back towards the staircase at the edge of the north side. Already, sirens could be heard wailing from towers all across the expanse of the black fortress.

Damn it, thought Kantor as his ceramite-plated boots pounded flagstones. No Imperial fleet would exit this close to a major gravity well. It would tear half the ships apart.

Dare he hope that the same might be happening to Snagrod's ships even now? It was impossible to believe they would come through such a reckless jump unharmed. Warp exits were impossible to stabilise this close to a star.

How many would make it through intact? How many would survive to bring death and torment down on Rynn's World?

ELEVEN

New Rynn City, Rynnland Province

GRIMM HAD BEEN to New Rynn City only twice in his life and the last time had been forty-two years ago. It was rare for battle-brothers to be sent there. The Arbites and the Rynnsguard were enough to keep the peace, and there was little call for the war-mastery of the Space Marines in a capital so obsessively focussed on trade and commerce.

As the Crimson Fist convoy rolled on, through district after crowded district, he reacquainted himself with the place. Few things had changed in the outer wards. The habs were still mostly squat boxes of sandstone and corrugated steel. The middle districts through which he now travelled, boasted clusters of monolithic new towers fashioned from dark stone and steel, built to house the city's burgeoning middle class. They rose high over the streets, casting them in shadow, but never rising as high as the shimmering spires and minarets at the city's centre.

Up ahead, another of the city's many interlocking curtain walls came into view, and another vast adamantium gate, its surface etched with ancient images of the city founders. This was the Peridion Gate, and beyond it lay the Residentia Ultris, the most expensive and exclusive residential zone in the city. It was in this district that the members of the Upper and Lower Houses maintained their mansion homes. On the far side of it, at its northmost extent, the convoy would cross the Farrio Bridge, a four-lane titanium and rockcrete structure that spanned the River Rynn. Beyond the Farrio Bridge was the convoy's destination, the island on which sat the Zona Regis, also known as the Silver Citadel.

The Astartes had made reasonable time from the spaceport, though the Rynnsguard troopers providing the corridor of passage had had their hands full with the jubilant crowds. There had been moments when the convoy had been forced to stop. In fits of zeal, a number of insane citizens, seemingly indifferent to the risk of being crushed, had leapt out from the crowd to kneel and offer praise before the rumbling chassis of *Aegis Eternis*. The local troopers had run forward and wrestled them out of the way, employing judicious violence when forced to. But no one had been killed. The Rynnsguard were not typically heavy-handed. They were well practiced in dealing with their own people.

The Peridion Gate groaned loudly up ahead as its vast metal gears began turning. A gap appeared between the gate's massive titanium teeth, and a widening zigzag showed Grimm the road and the buildings beyond. The gates were huge, impenetrable things. They had been constructed after the last ork assault on the planet, and built with another such attack in mind. Likewise, the ancient curtain walls had been upgraded by varying degrees, all with the aim of ensuring that the capital never fell to an invasion of any kind.

Grimm wondered just how soon the walls and gates would be tested. The city's outermost defensive structures were simple stone affairs that wouldn't survive any kind of sustained artillery fire. But the closer one got to the city centre, the sturdier the walls became. He knew, for instance, that the walls of the Silver Citadel, within which lay the Cassar, the governor's palace, and the parliament buildings, employed void-shields like those of Arx Tyrannus. And Arx Tyrannus could never fall. It was unassailable. Perhaps the Silver Citadel was unassailable, too. No doubt Captain Alvez would order the Techmarines attached to the company to do a full assessment. One had to know the limits of endurance of the place one was meant to defend.

Aegis Eternis rumbled through the archway of the Peridion Gate and into the Residentia Ultris, and the contrast with the other zones they had driven through was immediate. On both sides of the highway, exit ramps rose to offer access to elegant structures of white marble, their walls and rooftops adorned with fine statuary and bas-reliefs. The gardens around each were so verdant. Grimm turned his head to either side, scanning the trees and bushes by habit, noting the profusion of brightly coloured blossoms, many of which were not indigenous to Rynn's World and would have been imported and cultured at very great expense. Through gaps in the foliage, he saw the shadows of armed security personnel patrolling the grounds of each estate.

Captain Alvez kept his eyes forward, utterly disinterested in these statements of wealth and prominence.

Grimm wondered how the captain would deal with the members of the Upper Rynnhouse when it came time to address them. They would want to know why the Fists had come, but, when they found out about the approaching Waaagh, they would wish they'd never asked.

Still guiding the rest of the column, *Aegis Eternis* rolled over the Farrio Bridge, leaving the gleaming white estates behind her. On the far side, the last great gate, the Regis Gate South, was fully open to welcome them. Beyond it the government buildings glistened like mercury in the bright sunlight, putting the estates of the *Residentia Ultris* to shame. It was here that the business of ruling Rynn's World was conducted. Here was the Spire, a towering, many-turreted edifice dripping with the finest architectural embellishments that the greatest artisans in Rynnite history had been able to produce.

At the top of the tower, in a dome of pure synthetic diamond, sat the council chambers of the Upper

Rynnhouse, where decisions were made that often affected commerce across the entire Peryton Cluster. Just west of it, shorter by half, and nowhere near as splendid, though many times as valuable for the weapons, ammunition and support systems it housed, was the Cassar, a sturdy keep maintained by the Chosen on the Chapter's behalf.

On the keep's broad octagonal rooftop, long-guns and missile batteries sat pointed towards the sky. Grimm had no doubt that they were already loaded. The Chosen would have seen to that by now.

He was distracted from the sight of the Cassar by Alvez. The captain loosed a string of curses, and Grimm turned his eyes back to the road ahead to see what had prompted it.

There on the shining road, blocking its entire width, was a gaggle of Rynnite politicians, diplomats, religious figures and high-ranking military officers. They gleamed like the buildings around them, as if every last piece of clothing and adornment was absolutely brand new, purchased only moments ago for the occasion of greeting the Crimson Fist detachment.

'I'll not pander to them,' growled Captain Alvez to himself.

The captain resented having to put up with anything that did not directly relate to his duties as a Space Marine. War was his business. He had no inclination to master the niceties of speech and manner that these fools thought so important.

He rapped a red gauntlet on the roof of the Land Raider and the driver, Brother Agorro, rolled it to a smooth stop, letting the engine idle rather than cut it off. Agorro knew Alvez well enough to be confident that the vehicles would be underway again within minutes.

Alvez turned to Grimm. 'With me, sergeant,' he said, and hauled himself out of the left cupola. He moved to the side of the vehicle and dropped to the ground, armoured boots clashing heavily on the surface of the road. Despite their reverence for the Space Marines, Grimm saw some of the dignitaries drop their smiles. It was impossible for them not to feel intimidated. The Astartes were so much more than human, in every way. It was not just the physiological differences, though they were, perhaps, the greater part of it. Psychological differences served to widen the gap.

Grimm doubted any human could imagine what it was like to be Astartes, save perhaps in dreams. The oaths, the sacrifice, the relentless conditioning, inuring oneself to agony in all its most brutal forms. No, these people could never understand, and what they didn't understand, they feared, though it was often all that stood between them and the final darkness.

Grimm dismounted just as his captain had done, and strode forward to stand by his side. Together, the two hulking warriors looked down at their over-dressed welcoming party.

Lady Maia Cagliestra, who was, judging by her warm, open smile, the least intimidated of the group, bowed her head before the captain and sank to one knee.

'My lord,' she said.

Drigo Alvez looked down at her, then turned his eyes to the others.

'What is this?' he demanded, his tone harsh. 'Only the governor kneels? Are the rest of you above such obeisance?'

There was a sudden rush among the nobles to drop to the ground and obey the order, but some moved quicker than others. One, a skinny, bug-eyed man, seemed particularly unwilling to do as the situation demanded. An older, chubbier individual on his right tugged at the skinny man's sleeve and hissed, 'Kneel, Eduardo, for Throne's sake!'

'I am a marquis and a cabinet minister,' this Eduardo replied churlishly, but, with everyone else kneeling, he finally relented, though his distaste was plain on his features. Despite being angered by the little fool's insolence, Grimm hoped Captain Alvez had not registered it. But, of course, the captain had.

'You,' boomed Alvez, pointing a rigid finger at the man. 'Stand and approach me.'

Eduardo suddenly looked a lot less arrogant. Paling visibly, he gulped and pointed to himself with an expression that said, 'Who, me?'

'Hesitate a second longer, vermin, and I will repaint my gauntlets with your blood,' Alvez rumbled.

The other nobles kept their eyes firmly fixed on the rockcrete as Eduardo stepped forward as commanded. A dark, wet stain spread down the left leg of his trousers. His earlier self-assuredness had vanished completely now.

'Who are you, worm?'

The man seemed genuinely surprised at the question, as if surely the captain should know who he was. Didn't everyone?

'I am Eduardo Corda, of House Corda, Marquis of Paletta, Vice Minister of Education.'

Captain Alvez loomed over him like a storm cloud about to unleash its thunder on all below. 'Education, you say? Perhaps I should educate you on the fragility of your pathetic little life. Do you think your status, or the history of your house, grants you special liberties with one of the Emperor's own Space Marines?'

Eduardo Corda now looked ready to weep.

'Answer!' snapped Alvez, the word cracking like a gunshot.

Grimm suspected that, if the foolish Corda had not already emptied his bladder, he would have done so right then. But perhaps he underestimated Corda, for the marquis licked his lips, took a steadying breath, and stuttered, 'G-great are the Astartes of the Crimson F-fists. I meant no offence to your lordship, and I apologise if any was taken. But I am a member of the Upper House of Nobles. It is not fitting for a man of my station to take a knee. I come from an old and respected line.'

Alvez thrust his head closer. 'No,' he hissed. 'You are an idiot. Perhaps your line will end with you. In fact, that sounds best all round.' He turned to Grimm and added, 'Sergeant, pick him up.'

Grimm stepped forward immediately and gripped the man's collar with one hand, lifting him easily into the air. Corda's feet now dangled a metre above the ground. It was then that Lady Maia spoke. She was still kneeling, but she raised her head to look Alvez in the eye.

'I beg you, lord. Do not kill him. He is unworthy of your forgiveness, and, in offending you, his actions bring shame on the entire Upper House, but he serves a senior member of my cabinet and will be difficult to replace.'

Alvez looked at her, silent for a moment. Then, he said, 'Do not think me so eager to kill the very people I was sent here to protect. For this transgression, he will not die. But all must bow before the Crimson Fists. There are no exceptions. I care not at all for your institutions and your notions of high status. These things are less than nothing to me. Remember that. In the coming days, you will have my protection because the Chapter Master commands it. No other reason exists. Were I commanded to kill you all, I would complete my task in a heartbeat, without a moment's remorse, and nothing in this galaxy save the word of Pedro Kantor could stop me.'

He turned back to Grimm, and said, 'The marquis has soiled himself, sergeant. He requires a bath. See to it.'

Grimm didn't need to ask what the captain meant.

'At once, lord,' he Grimm, and he began walking back towards the Farrio Bridge, holding Eduardo Corda out in front of him as if he weighed little more than a handful of trash.

When he judged he was far enough from Captain Alvez to risk murmured speech, he said to Corda,

'You must never go near him again. Do you understand, fool? It was only the governor's intervention that spared you today.'

Corda was stifling sobs as he answered, 'A mistake, my lord. I swear it. I meant no harm. I... I inhaled the smoke of the ceba-leaf an hour ago. I had no idea...'

For a moment, Grimm felt the urge to strike the man. *Ceba-leaf*. It caused disease and mutation in one's children. Why the wealthy continued to abuse it was a mystery to him. He had heard all the excuses. The universe was a dark and brutal place, they said, and it was true, but other poorer men managed fine without the self-inflicted curse of such narcotics.

'Then you are doubly a fool, and must stay out of my way, also, lest you wish to die.'

'I don't,' whined Corda. 'I don't wish to die, by Throne!'

'Can you swim?' growled Grimm.

'I... what?'

'Can you swim, oaf?'

'I... yes. I mean, I swam a little as a child. I...' Looking out beyond the bridge, it suddenly dawned on Corda what was about to happen. 'In Terra's holy name, please. Don't do this. You don't have to.'

They were approaching the wrought-iron balustrade at the side of the bridge. A few more steps and Grimm came slowly to a halt right beside it. 'I will cast you into the shallows close to the south bank. You will only have to swim a little. Unless you are as hopeless as you look, you will survive. Show proper reverence to your betters next time. If my lord believes you have not learned your lesson, he will kill you on sight.'

Corda was opening his mouth, about to reply, when Grimm leaned back, put his considerable physical power into an overhand swing, and launched the Vice Minister of Education out over the waters of the River Rynn.

As good as his word, he put the whining noble fairly close to the shallows by the bank, but in truth, not as close as he had planned.

The man immediately began coughing and splashing in a great panic, and Grimm could tell that it was no act.

Good, he thought. Let the Emperor decide whether you live or die.

He turned back towards the captain and saw that the nobles had been dismissed. As they backed away from Alvez with their heads bowed, they looked extremely dismayed.

Grimm met his captain halfway back to the Land Raider.

'You told them of the Waaagh, my lord?'

'Briefly,' said Alvez. 'There was no time to elaborate. Word has just come through from Arx Tyrannus, Huron. The ork ships are already here.'

'In-system?' asked Grimm. 'It cannot be!'

'It is.'

Alvez clambered up the side of the Land Raider and lowered himself down into his cupola again. Once Grimm had done the same, and the vehicle began to move off in the direction of The Cassar, Alvez raised his voice over the growl of the Land Raider's engine.

'Be ready, sergeant. The killing will soon begin.'

TWELVE

The Blockade, Rynn's World Local Space

'BRING US AROUND. Get me a forward firing solution. I want our prow batteries locked onto that destroyer before she fires again!'

Ceval Ranparre sat atop his massive command throne, on a dais that extended to the back wall of the ship's bridge. In the work-pits below him, his subordinates were frantic, a thousand voices talking at once, half of them in Binary, the machine-language of the Adeptus Mechanicus.

Another massive impact shook the ship, the third such blow in a minute, scattering charts and data modules all over the metal decking. Ranparre felt the artificial gravity flicker for the briefest instant, and knew from long experience that his battle-barge, *The Sabre of Scaurus*, must have been hit amidships, close to where the critical systems were located. The ship's shielding was heaviest there, but it couldn't take impacts like that for long. The void shields would give out soon. The Astartes and Imperial Naval ships were outnumbered a hundred to one, and more of the ugly, scrappy ork vessels were bleeding into the system every minute the battle raged on.

We weren't ready, thought Ranparre. The line was still forming. Of all the blasted xenos in the galaxy, only orks would try a jump as psychotic and self-destructive as this.

He had seen the worst effects of breaching real space so close to the planet already. At the beginning of the engagement, a number of neatly severed prows had tumbled past him, bleeding breathable atmosphere and lifeless alien bodies into the freezing void. Some of them would impact on the planet with the all the explosive power of a long-range, high-yield missile. There was nothing Ranparre and his crews could do about that. Blasting those wrecks to pieces would only turn one deadly mass into many. Besides, every last bit of offensive firepower at their command was needed to fight off the greater threat of the manned alien vessels that were trying to fight their way through. It was already clear to him that the blockade was pathetically inadequate. Such numbers!

Ranparre had several centuries of space battle experience behind him. Under his command, the ships of the Crimson Fists had saved over a dozen worlds without the need to drop any troops on the surface. Rebels, traitors, heretics, xenos, even warp-filth... Ranparre had beaten all kinds of enemy craft in high-orbital and deep-space combat. But he had never, in all his unnaturally long life, faced the kind of numbers that the Arch-Arsonist of Charadon was throwing at the planet now.

Even in the gaping black vastness of space, there seemed no quarter that was not under assault, filled with ork craft scything inwards on angry trails of glowing plasma.

'Order the *Aurora* and the *Verde* to close formation with us. I want the *Aurora* on our left flank, the *Verde* on our right. All forward batteries to target the command bridge of their flagship. If the beast Snagrod is aboard that vessel, we may still have a chance to end all this.'

From a row of stations sunk into the metal floor on the bridge's right, one of the weapons co-ordinators called out, 'I have your forward firing solution, my lord. Permission to fire forward lances?'

'Hold,' said Ranparre. 'We fire together with the strike cruisers. If that monstrosity has shields, we must hope to overload them at the very least.'

Seconds later, a comms-station operator on the left reported that the *Aurora* and the *Verde* had plotted their firing solutions and were awaiting Ranparre's order to engage.

'Give the signal,' barked Ranparre. 'All forward batteries... open fire!'

The central display screens in front of him crackled with blinding white energy as the massive weapons loosed their fury. Thick spears of light burned across ten thousand kilometres. A dozen small ork fighters and support craft caught between the two closing flagships were obliterated, simply wiped from existence. Then the lances stuck the ork flagship full in its gargantuan beast-like face.

'Direct hit, all batteries,' the weapons co-ordinator reported.

We could hardly miss, thought Ranparre. Just how big *is* that monster?

'Damage assessment on enemy vessel,' he demanded.

'Unclear, my lord,' replied another voice from the pit on the right. 'Our forward auspex array has been badly damaged. Operating at forty per cent efficiency. Preliminary scans suggest enemy shielding absorbed most of the impact. Enemy still advancing with full offensive capabilities.'

'How long till another charge builds up?' Ranparre demanded. 'I need our forward guns online again now!'

'Does my lord wish to issue a call for further support?' asked one of the comms-operators. 'The battle-barge *Tigurius* is only twenty thousand kilometres away. Strike cruisers *Hewson* and *Maqueda* are six and nine thousand kilometres away respectively.'

Ranparre scanned the tactical displays in front of him, focussing on those that showed the situation to port and starboard. What he saw was utter chaos. The planetary blockade was fracturing in countless places as the ork vessels ploughed in amongst the Imperial ships on a hundred different assault vectors at once. Between the battle line and the planet, space was glittering with ship debris and bright ordnance impacts.

He found the *Tigurius* quickly enough by its ident-tag. She was leaking atmosphere from her port side, listing to starboard, harried by a swarm of ork assault ships, all far smaller than she was. The ork craft buzzed around her like angry wasps, peppering her sides with explosive slugs and energy weapons. She was in no position to lend *The Sabre of Scaurus* any kind of assistance.

His eyes picked out the tags CF-166 and CF-149 – the *Hewson* and the *Maqueda*. Both were engaged in heavy fighting. Even as he watched, the *Maqueda's* hull started to rupture. Desperate to take some of the foe down with him, her captain, Darrus Gramedo, must have ordered her brought around and onto a full forward ramming course. Plasma streamed from her rear thrusters, and she ploughed headlong into the side of an ork heavy cruiser that had been launching relentless port broadsides at her from her two-o'clock position.

As Ranparre watched, the *Maqueda's* sharp prow bit deep into the side of the ork ship. The hulls merged violently. There was a ripple of bright flashes, then, as one, the ships imploded, collapsing in on themselves, every last light onboard winking out.

'We've just lost the *Maqueda*,' said a voice from one of the pits.

Ranparre turned his attention to the *Hewson* and saw that she, at least, was doing better. She rolled to her right and launched a blistering broadside just as a monstrous ork craft attempted to pass by overhead. The enemy's iron belly was punctured in a hundred places, shedding thick pieces of bulkhead into space. Critical systems overloaded. An explosive chain reaction started, ripping the entire alien craft apart seconds later. As the space around the dying ship filled with spinning fragments, the captain of the *Hewson* ordered her crew to swing about for a port-side volley against three ork light cruisers that had been flying in support.

For all these worthy kills, Ranparre saw too many gaps where the ork ships were getting through. The xenos were just too numerous to stop, and the biggest of all their ships was closing on his own, second by second, kilometre by kilometre. The *Sabre of Scaurus* would not have the advantage of range and accuracy for much longer.

'Prow batteries at maximum charge in eighty-three seconds, my lord,' reported the senior weapons co-ordinator.

'Someone get me the captain of the *Hewson*,' barked Ranparre. 'And get me a direct link to Chapter Master Kantor at once.'

'As you command, lord,' said the closest of the comms-operators.

Dorn help us, thought Ranparre as he continued to process the nightmare on his tactical screens.

Dorn help us, we are lost.

THIRTEEN

The Upper Rynnhouse, New Rynn City

'IT MUST BE a mistake,' Baron Etrando called out. 'An auspex glitch, surely. Martial law? It's... it's unheard of. Preposterous!'

Maia could barely hear him over the din the rest of the Upper Rynnhouse was making. The Speaker had called repeatedly for order, but the place was in an uproar. There were one hundred and eighteen nobles in the Upper Rynnhouse, twenty-six of whom were members of her cabinet, and every last one seemed intent on expressing his or her horror or denial at the very same moment.

Jidan Etrando was only three seats away from Maia. Any further and his words would have merged completely with the wall of noise.

'There is no mistake,' she called back. 'The lunar tracking stations on Dantienne and Syphos both confirmed it before they went dead. The entire orbital defence grid is on combat standing. They are coming. There is no doubt of that.'

'Why here?' asked a young minister in the row behind her. 'Why now?'

Maia half turned and saw that it was Bulo Dacera, Under-Secretary for Mining and Ore Processing.

'They are aliens, Bulo. We are not supposed to understand them. The fleet will stop them before they can land.'

Those close enough to hear her went quiet now, and the silence spread until the noise in the plush, vaulted chamber died off to the level of a murmur.

The Speaker, whose ancient body was as much machine as man and was permanently hard-wired into the data systems that served the Upper Rynnhouse, could at last be heard properly. 'In the name of the Emperor,' he blustered, 'you will remember yourselves. All matters, even such as this, must be handled with the decorum this noble establishment demands.' He turned his sensor-studded head towards Maia.

She felt his electronic eyes lock onto her as he added, 'If the governor wishes to take the floor, she will step to the Lectern of the aquila.'

'I will take the floor,' said Maia formally, and rose from her bench. Her steps were measured, presenting a confidence she did not really feel. The news of the Waaagh had rocked her. In her mother's time, no conflict greater than a prison breakout had ever occurred. The sharp-tongued, cold-hearted female politico from whose womb Maia had sprung had taught her many, many things, most of them the hard way. But she had not prepared Maia for the possibility of an alien invasion that threatened the lives of every man, woman and child on the planet.

Maia was clinging desperately to her faith, but a voice at the back of her mind persisted in asking how the Emperor could let this happen to people who loved and honoured him so?

She stopped behind the lectern and cleared her throat, then looked out at the nobles watching her expectantly on the benches to either side of the chamber.

They are as terrified as I am, she thought. More so, perhaps. I wonder how many believe this is punishment for their sins?

There had already been an incident with local law enforcement. Eighteen ministers had attempted to secure illegal outward passage on a fast ship. Had Captain Alvez not grounded all non-military craft already, Maia suspected she would be speaking to an empty room.

She told herself that she would not have fled. Situations like this were what the Crimson Fists trained for, what they excelled at. To turn back the enemies of man – it was the reason they existed at all. Pedro Kantor would not let her down.

For a moment, she turned her eyes heavenwards, staring up at the underside of the exquisite diamond dome. Through its panels, the sky was deep blue, the sibling suns already halfway towards the western horizon where the waters of the Medean would swallow them for the night. Painted on the inner surface of the largest and most central of the diamond panels was an image of the Emperor, looking down on the assembly with a face she had always thought stern but loving, dark locks framing his golden skin.

Lend me strength, she silently begged him.

'Fellow members of the house,' she began, her voice amplified by the vox-mic concealed in the eagle's head that decorated the lectern, 'We face something each of us has only ever read about in the archives. No one thought the greenskins foolish enough to return here. Now they have, and I understand your fears. But I do not share them.' This, of course, was something of a lie. 'We are leaders,' she continued, 'and we must act as such. It is to us that the common man will look for his example. The Crimson Fists are here in force. Surely there is no greater source of comfort than that.'

On a bench to her left, Eduardo Corda looked as if he might disagree. His hair was still a little damp.

The other faces turned towards her were pale and beaded with cold sweat. Regardless of her words, they still seemed terrified. Only Viscount Isopho looked composed. That shouldn't have surprised her. As a young man, he had bucked family tradition to remain in the Rynnsguard for a commission twice as long as any other noble, and had only left due to his father's passing. By all accounts, he had been a good officer, and the Rynnsguard still afforded him a certain respect they did not afford others.

I should keep Nilo close, Maia thought. His perspective might be useful if...

'The Rynnsguard, too,' she went on, 'assure me that they will protect us. Additional forces are even now being sent from Targis Fields. Once they arrive, they will help to secure the city. The people in the fringe settlements are being brought into the protection of the outer wall even as we speak. We do not expect a protracted siege, if indeed the orks get through at all. Nevertheless, emergency provisions are being shipped in by sea and road, and all goods for export have been recalled from the spaceport.'

Presented with these facts, the ministers seemed to calm a little, their minds latching on to details rather than vision of a hideous alien scourge undoing all they held dear. One woman, Countess Maragretto, whimpered from the back row on the right at mention of a siege, but she managed to stifle it quickly.

'Trust in our protectors,' Maia told them. 'They have taken an oath to defend this planet, and so they shall. Trust, too, in the Civitas enforcers and, by extension, the Adeptus Arbites that supervise them. They too have sworn a solemn oath before the Emperor and will not allow our society to descend into panic and self-destruction. A curfew is being put into effect to facilitate proper control. And trust, above all others save the Emperor himself, the mighty Space Marines of the Crimson Fists. Therein lies our surest hope. They will end the nightmare. Already, they are about it, and my own faith in them is absolute. Let your faith be as mine, and it will be rewarded.'

She looked out at her peers, reaching for more words that would gird them, but there was nothing more to say for now. They would simply have to watch and wait while others took the fight to the foe.

'I now offer the floor up to any member who wishes to speak.'

She stepped out from behind the lectern and, with the same measured grace, returned to her bench.

When she was seated, the Speaker rasped, 'Raise your hand, you who wish to address this noble House.'

Immediately, a hundred arms were thrust into the air, and the chamber exploded once again into the din of voices raised in abject panic.

FOURTEEN

Arx Tyrannus, Hellblade Mountains

KANTOR WAS STRIDING rapidly across the inner courtyard towards the central hall of the Strategium when he saw the first signs of battle in the sky above.

The sky was darkening. From the peaks of the Hellblade Mountains, the last remnants of the day shone as little more than a soft, lambent glow beyond the horizon in the far west, but the sunset was hidden from view by the high walls all around him, not that he would have had time to stop and appreciate it anyway. Above him, the sky was dark purple, shifting towards black, and the stars were coming out.

It was there, up among the familiar constellations, that he saw it all begin. There were more stars than normal tonight, and many of them moved restlessly towards each other. Some were short lived. Every bright flash the Chapter Master saw up there represented either the blast of powerful energy weapons, or the dying moments of a sizable craft. For every one of the latter, how many lives were lost in those ever-so-brief flares? He could only hope that each marked the violent end of ork lives, not human.

Other lights, even brighter and more distinct, appeared, following fiery arcs across the sky. They glowed with the orange heat of atmospheric entry, and he knew the worst had now begun. The line had been breached.

Orks began to rain down on the planet.

So soon, he thought to himself? Can it really be?

The Imperial blockade simply hadn't had time to organise itself. Snagrod must have known this, must have guessed his best hope lay in a full-frontal surprise attack that no human commander would dare. To translate from the warp so close to the planet... No human commander would have dared.

And that is why I should have foreseen this, Kantor thought bitterly. I should not have expected the beast to think as we do. I should have considered the alien nature of the ork mind.

This was no time to stand here and berate himself. The Chapter Council waited. He entered the Strategium's outer halls, sped along the stone corridors, reached the broad double-doors a matter of seconds later, and flung them open.

A dozen faces, all lined with deep concern, turned to regard him. The Chapter Council rose to its feet. Kantor took the carpeted steps down towards the crystal table two at a time. Above the table hovered a static-ridden hololithic image of the battle in orbit.

'My brothers,' said Kantor as he reached his onyx throne. He sat down, and the throne accepted his weight. The gears under the floor began to grind, and the mechanism wheeled him forward, stopping when his breastplate was half a metre from the edge of the table and his booted feet were underneath it. 'Sit.'

There was a clatter of ceramite on stone as they obeyed.

Catching Kantor's eye, Alessio Cortez was the first to say anything. He gestured to the hololithic image above. 'Absolute slaughter,' he managed to say between jaws clenched tight with anger.

Forgemaster Adon had opened a link into the fleet communications net so that the council members could all hear what was going on as it happened. The voices they heard were filled with desperation, every word confirming the worst.

'There was insufficient time to prepare,' grated Forgemaster Adon.

High Chaplain Tomasi did not look up at the hololith. Instead he looked at his hands, the fingers interlocked, and said, 'So many of the faithful have already made the ultimate sacrifice.'

'They have,' agreed Mateo Morrelis, 'but they made it count. The fleet's kill ratio must not be ignored. Our forces up there are fighting like cornered lions!'

'And we sit here talking,' spat Cortez. 'Give us orders, lord. Send us out there.'

Kantor glared at him. 'You'll have all the fighting you want soon enough, Alessio. They are landing their drop-ships even now, and we will greet them with bolter and blade.' He turned to Adon. 'Forge-master, I want every last enemy ship tracked to its landing coordinates. There will be an orbital bombardment soon. The void shields will protect us, but the moment it is over, we will send out purgation squads in our Thunderhawks. I want the entire effort coordinated through the Communicatus and the armoury. Those not selected to launch ground assaults will man our surface-to-orbit emplacements. While even one of our ships continues to fight in space, we will offer every last bit of support we can.'

'The Technicarum is already monitoring the trajectory of each enemy vessel, my lord. There will be no mistakes.'

Kantor nodded, and there was a brief silence, broken when he said, 'My Fists, I did not imagine that the ork warlord would risk the strength of his force in the way he has. His gamble has paid off. But, in centuries hence, when men read of this day, when analysts at war colleges across the Imperium look to their historical texts, they must see that we endured, and, ultimately, that we turned this blow aside. We are the Crimson Fists and this is our home. We will deal with the invaders as they deserve to be dealt with.'

'We might manage to hold Sorocco,' offered Raphael Acastus, 'but what of Calliona and the Magalan?'

Kantor had already considered this. 'The Monitor will liaise with local Rynnsguard forces on both those continents and keep us abreast of developments. But we must secure Sorocco first. The oceans will help in confining the foe to wherever they land. Sorocco must be cleansed first.'

'If the orks create a strong blockade of their own,' said Chief Apothecary Curien Droga, 'they will be able to land additional forces wherever and whenever they like.'

Kantor faced the old Apothecary. 'I am not giving up on our fleet yet, Curien,' he said. Gesturing up at the spectral battle taking place above the surface of the table, he continued, 'Ceval Ranparre has never lost an engagement in his life. Though he is greatly outnumbered, he *will* find a way to turn this around.'

'The elimination of Snagrod,' said Cortez, 'But we cannot even be sure he is here in person.'

'The beast is here,' said Eustace Mendoza. 'I assure you.'

'Can you pinpoint him?' asked Kantor. 'If we could guide the remainder of the fleet in on him before he makes planetfall–'

Mendoza shook his shaved head. 'The warp is in turmoil all around us, torn open so close and in so many places. It will take days, perhaps even weeks before we can read its flows and eddies again with any accuracy. I can sense Snagrod's foul aura out there among all the psychic death screams, but that is all.'

'If there's any change in what you sense, tell me at once, brother.'

Something Forgemaster Adon was listening to made him look up. He turned his optic-lenses towards the Chapter Master and said, 'The Master of the Fleet has just placed an emergency request to speak to you, my lord.'

Kantor frowned. 'Let me hear him, brother.'

The rest of the council looked to Kantor, awaiting his dismissal so that he could converse with the Master of the Fleet in private, but Kantor shook his head and told them, 'Whatever Ceval Ranparre has to say must be heard by all of us. You will stay. You will listen with me.'

So they stayed and they listened, and the news was not good.

'The situation is now desperate,' crackled the voice on the link. 'I say again, put me through to the Chapter Master at once. There is no time for delay.'

'Can he hear me?' Kantor asked Adon.

'Yes, my lord.'

'Ceval, this is your Chapter Master. Report.'

Kantor had known the Master of the Fleet a very long time, and, despite Ranparre's best efforts, he could easily detect the strain in his voice. It disturbed him far more than the words themselves. He had always believed Ranparre unflappable.

'My lord, we have lost more than fifty-six per cent of our force, and more ork vessels are still translating into real space. I no longer believe this conflict can be won in space. You must prepare for a ground offensive of significant proportions.'

Kantor imagined his own expression was reflected in the dour looks he could see on the faces of his fellow council members. 'Are you telling me, Ceval, that you can do no more up there?'

There was a pause. Ranparre seemed taken aback by the question. 'My lord? I'm not sure I understand the question. We will fight to the very last, naturally. Every ship we eliminate means less greenskins on the ground.'

'That is not what I am getting at, Ceval,' said Kantor. 'I need to know if you feel it would be wiser for our surviving ships to disengage.'

Again, a pause.

'I cannot see any circumstances, my lord,' said Ranparre in tones heavy with emphasis, 'that would cause me to consider disengaging. Every ship we have lost so far has accounted for a great many enemy craft. It would do our fallen a great disservice, and myself a great dishonour, were I to leave this fight without claiming victory in their name.'

'There is no dishonour in a tactical withdrawal,' replied Kantor, 'least of all one that I order. I cannot have the entire fleet destroyed. Things are already far worse than we anticipated. Order *The Crusader* to reposition. She is to make for Segmentum Headquarters and solicit aid. I will not let pride to be our undoing.'

'She cannot possibly jump this close to a gravity well, my lord,' said Ranparre. 'And she will not break through the ork fleet alone.'

Kantor frowned. He knew he had no choice. 'Then commit all remaining ships to getting her through. She will have to risk the jump. Many of Snagrod's ships survived it. She can, too. These are my final orders to you, brother. After *The Crusader* is away, you may fight on to a worthy end. Your legend will live on forever.'

Ranparre would never know just how hard that had been for Kantor to say. He answered, 'Thank you, lord. Fight well. May Dorn watch over you all.'

The link went to static as Ranparre broke the connection.

'Farewell, brother,' said Kantor solemnly, almost to himself. 'I will see you again at the Emperor's side.'

FIFTEEN

The Cassar, New Rynn City

ALVEZ DID NOT sit. He paced back and forth at the head of the table, armoured boots heavy on the granite floor. The others watched him wordlessly.

The Cassar boasted only a small Strategium. Unlike its equivalent at Arx Tyrannus, it was square and boasted no ceiling dome. The table, too, was different – angular, fashioned from ebonwood rather than crystal, and as old as the building itself. Around it sat twelve Crimson Fists, including Huron Grimm, Epistolary Deguerro, and squad leaders from both the Crusade, Second and Third Companies.

The captain finally stopped, turned to scan the eyes of his fellows, and said, 'Rynnsguard High Command is sending an armour and infantry column down from Targis Fields, so I want Carriageway 2 held secure at all costs. The moment that armour passes through the Umbris Gate, I want it sealed and barricaded. Orks tend to follow the lay of the land. The mountains of the Anshar Minoris protect our north-west flank, but they will also funnel the enemy down towards the northern districts. I'm expecting the Umbris Gate to come under heavy attack in the opening phases of the invasion.' His eyes settled on one of the veteran sergeants seated at the far end of the table, a narrow-faced Astartes with a sharp chin. 'Sergeant Delos, you will be responsible for that section of the wall. There are four Rynnsguard platoons already stationed there. Assume command the moment you arrive. Make sure their senior officer understands exactly who is in charge.'

Delos gave a tiny bow of his head. 'Understood, my lord.'

At last, Alvez deigned to sit. He put one gauntleted hand on the table and leaned back in his chair. 'We bear a great burden, my brothers, but we are more than equal to the task ahead. The Chapter Master is depending on us. Word has just come through that the blockade has fallen. The orks will pour down on us like monsoon rains. It has already begun. The city is to be placed under martial law. Those citizens who are able will be drafted into militias. All food stores and key resources will be pooled and distributed in accordance with emergency Munitorum protocols. These things are of peripheral concern to us, of course. Let the Rynnsguard and the Arbites deal with the civilians. Our role is much simpler. We are here to win a war. To succeed, we need only remain standing when the last xenos falls.'

A few of the others nodded at this. Others murmured their assent, or sat in silence, as Huron Grimm did, with dark looks on their faces.

'The city walls are solid,' Alvez continued. 'They are strong, and they will hold if we allow no mistakes. The gates are even stronger, and I have already assigned our heavy armour to guard them. Any breach will be met with immediate Predator and Vindicator fire. The Techmarines are on the parapets as we speak, readying the Thunderfire cannons for operation. While we have ammunition and supplies equal to the task, I have absolute confidence in our ability to resist the foe, at least on the surface. The city underworks are another matter. I have no choice but to assign all our Terminator squads, with the exception of those posted at the spaceport, to the task of holding the tunnels.' Preempting a protest from the Crusade Company sergeants seated before him, he held up an armoured hand. 'I would not issue this order if it were not absolutely necessary, brothers. Dorn knows, I would rather place you at the city gates, but the orks will try to infiltrate our lines via the tunnels, and tactical Dreadnought armour is best suited to resist them there. At least you will have your share of killing. We cannot afford to collapse the tunnels, since at least some are part of the city's anti-flooding system. Others carry power and coolant to critical defensive emplacements. They must be secured.'

'Then they shall be,' said Barrien Gallacus, the sergeant in charge of the 1st Vanguard Squad. 'We will choke them with greenskin dead.'

'See that you do,' said Alvez.

He leaned forward, eyeing each Astartes in the room, a feral grin on his scarred and weathered features.

'Rejoice in the battle to come, brothers,' he added. 'This is what we live for. This is what we were born to do. We will prove our strength in the heat of combat. We will breathe victory in like air. Trust me, legends will be made here.'

SIXTEEN

Arx Tyrannus, Hellblade Mountains

THEY CAME.

In later days, this night would come to be known as the Night of the Burning Sky, and well it deserved that name. The entire length of the Hellblades, over a thousand kilometres of jagged mountain range, shook and flashed with sharp detonations. The greenskin fleet, having swept aside the hastily prepared defensive blockade, launched a planetary bombardment that would claim the lives of millions. Snagrod's ships had come prepared to carpet the towns and cities in flame. They didn't need to be accurate, not with the sheer amount of ordnance at their disposal.

Pedro Kantor clenched his jaw as he watched the deadly rain of bombs fall around him. Behind him, the brothers in his Honour Guard were restless, uneasy. In the sky above the Sercia Bastion on which they stood, alien payloads fell without cease. None struck the fortress-monastery. Those that should have done exploded harmlessly a half a kilometre above Kantor's head, unable to penetrate the powerful void-shield defence system that protected Arx Tyrannus.

Every explosive impact on the shimmering shields caused the landscape below to flicker bright as day.

With the void-shields at full power, the air became close and clammy, almost oppressive, and there was a constant loud hum in the air, discernible in the spaces between the thunder of the relentless barrage.

Kantor called Ordinator Savales to his side. The seneschal had been following his lord at a respectful distance, braving the greenskin storm in case Kantor should need him for anything. Now the Chapter Master wanted Savales safe. The moment the bombardment ended, the void shields would be lowered to allow return fire. Keeping the shields up was safer, but it would allow the orks to land wherever they wanted with relative impunity, challenged only by the scattered plasma defence installations operated by the Rynnsguard.

At his lord's command, Savales stepped forward and stood before Kantor with his head bowed. 'What does my lord wish of me?' he said, and looked up.

Kantor searched the man's expression for fear, and was proud to find none. Savales was as composed as ever. *He should have been one of us*, thought Kantor. *He might have carved a fine legend for himself.*

'Return to the central keep, Ramir. The shields will go down soon, and I'll not have you out in the open.'

The old seneschal held his lord's gaze. 'My place is by your side, lord, whatever the danger, to see to your needs.' There was no defiance in his tone. He simply stated this as plain, inarguable fact.

'My current need is to have my seneschal return to the keep as ordered,' said Kantor. 'The dead serve no one. Gather the youngest of the Chosen in the Refectorum. They will be frightened, and you will teach them to deny their fear.'

Savales let his reluctance show, but answered, 'I will do as my lord commands, of course. Should you need anything of me, you need only call, no matter the circumstance.'

Kantor was not prone to smiling. It was not an expression that came naturally to his long, solemn features. But, he smiled now, briefly, at a memory still crystal clear. Though Savales looked far older than he, Kantor felt an almost paternal affection for the man. He remembered Savales as a dejected youth, remembered his face as he had sat in that cell so long ago, believing death the only escape from his despair at failing to become Astartes. He remembered, too, the change in that face when the boy had been offered a new and worthy purpose.

Savales bowed deeply, excused himself, turned and strode off in the direction of the main keep, his robes billowing behind him. Explosions continued to flower and boom in the air above.

On the comm-link, Kantor heard the voice of the Monitor.

'My lord, we have just lost contact with Scar Lake Airbase. I have tried all secondary and tertiary frequencies, but there is nothing. Nor can I communicate with the Rynnsguard forces stationed at Caltara, Sagarro, Mycea... I- I cannot explain it, lord.'

The Monitor's agitation was well founded. Losing contact with one of the provincial capitals would have been bad enough, but the airbase at Scar Lake was heavily defended. If the orks had already knocked out the base's communications, it would not be long until they overran the base itself. Were they even now marauding through the streets of the provincial capitals, cutting down whole families that fled before them?

'What of New Rynn City?' Kantor asked through the vox in his helmet.

'The signal is weak,' reported the Monitor. 'Sporadic. But we are still in contact. The reports are grim. Ork landers have been spotted descending on all sides, a great many in the marshes to the south, near Vardua and Porto Kalis. The city's entire defence grid is still engaging with surface-to-orbit munitions, but the density of targets...'

Yes, thought Kantor. And they will try to land here, soon.

'Do all you can to maintain links with the capital,' he told the Monitor. 'And keep me updated.'

He turned to his Honour Guard and barked, 'Our brothers have this bastion well in hand. We will proceed to the Protheo Bastion next. Follow.'

The five-man squad barked out a unified response and fell in behind him. As they walked, Kantor looked west over the battlements and saw, even through the bright rippling fire of detonating bombs, the entry glows of all too many xenos craft. All across Rynn's World, ugly, filthy, noisy ork vehicles would be rolling down ramps and racing out over the hard-packed dirt in search of slaughter.

The farming communities will be devastated, thought Kantor. The orks will descend on them like locusts, and nothing will be left alive. The beasts will have a bloodlust on them. If only the damned bombardment would cease so we can start knocking them out of the sky.

His view from the Protheo Bastion only added to his concern. Where the mountains dropped to the low hills, and the hills dropped to the steppes, bright fires studded the night. The sky boiled with descending craft, their trails cutting across the black canvas of the sky in long curving arcs. Bombs continued to fall from space, cratering the mountains where the umbrella of the void-shields ended.

A disaster, thought Kantor. In the history of the Chapter, my name will forever be linked with this night. I must do all I can to ensure that it is remembered with honour, not shame. I will not be the Chapter Master who faltered on his home ground.

When the bombardment began to slacken, as it did now, he noticed the change immediately. Soon, the fiery bursts above the fortress-monastery died off completely. It was a sign that the orks were coming.

Soon, they would try to land nearby and launch their ground assault on Arx Tyrannus. He would teach them what a mistake that was!

On the comm-link, he opened a channel to Forge-master Adon.

'Yes, my lord?' rasped the old Techmarine.

'Drop the shields,' Kantor commanded. 'It is time to unleash our fury.'

'The Sercia, Protheo and Marez batteries are ready, my lord. The Laculum batteries are powering up now.'

'Problems, Javier?'

'A momentary glitch, lord. System checks now report optimal status. We have targeting solutions already mapped. Tracking data for the missiles is being uploaded now. The Laculum batteries will be online within three minutes.'

'As soon as they are ready,' said Kantor, 'launch everything we have. I want maximum retaliation on the greenskin fleet. We'll honour Ranparre, by Terra! What is the risk of large-scale debris impacting post-contact?'

'Very small, lord. The largest of the ork ships are locked in orbit so they can deploy their landers. Any heavy impact will propel debris outwards, away from the planet. The probability margin of collateral surface destruction is within the lower tenth of a per centile.'

'Very well,' Kantor replied. 'You have my full confidence. Let the enemies of mankind know our wrath.'

'In Dorn's name,' grated Adon.

The comm-link clicked off.

Over the command channel, Kantor addressed all his squad and company commanders. 'The shields are going down, brothers. They will be coming. Bless your weapons and honour the Chapter with your kills.'

Another voice, Marqol Tomasi's, added, 'There is only the Emperor.'

Kantor's voice joined the others in the traditional response.

'He is our shield and our protector.'

Sirens began to wail and red warning lamps spun into life. From the top of a tower sixty metres to Kantor's right, a great cloud of steam billowed up into the air. A circular hatch in the tower roof, one metre thick and five metres across, hinged open with a hydraulic hiss. All around the fortress-monastery, the same was happening, hatches rising to reveal the blunted noses of surface-to-orbit ballistic missiles, each equipped with the most devastating conventional warheads available.

The sirens changed pitch now, warning of imminent launch. The Space Marines stopped checking each other's gear for a moment to turn and watch as the first flames licked up from the top of the tower-silos. The ground began to shudder, and the air filled with a rumble that drowned out all else.

Snagrod had underestimated the Crimson Fists in coming here. He was about to pay for that mistake.

The deafening roar of plasma-jet rockets intensified in pitch, and the nose of the missile nearest to Kantor slowly rose into view. Its acceleration seemed painfully slow at first. It wrestled with gravity, fighting to heave its bulk into the air.

More and more of the missile emerged from the silo, and its speed continued to increase. Gravity was losing. The missile burst clear of the silo, shooting straight up into the sky with a roar like an angry god. Its tail of flame was almost blindingly bright.

Others followed, streaking upwards on thick columns of fire and smoke.

Watching them arc towards their distant targets, Pedro Kantor never imagined, not even for an instant, that a terrible hammer was about to fall on everything he held most dear.

The Night of the Burning Sky had only just begun.

SAVALES STOPPED IN the hall just outside the Refectorum and immediately perceived the fear that hung in the air. The smooth stone benches within were crowded with the youngest of the Chosen, many of whom were hunched over, looking up at the vaulted ceiling from beneath rumpled brows. Others had their eyes shut tight. Some hugged themselves or rocked back and forth. The youngest were a mere eight years old, the oldest closer to fourteen. None had experienced anything like this before. Even Savales would have bet against the orks being so brash as to assault an Astartes home world directly.

The young Chosen had been gathered here to wait out the orbital bombardment, but also to keep them from under the feet of the Astartes and the older serfs, many of whom had duties critical to the defence of the fortress-monastery. A few adults paced between the benches, telling the boys to be strong, that the storm which was shaking the entire mountain would be over soon enough.

One of the adults, a whip-thin man named Bernis Kalisde, Master of the Refectorum, barked at some of the boys as he passed close to them, causing several to jump and one to cry out in surprise. 'You are pathetic!' he told them. 'Look at you, cowering like beaten dogs. You belong to the Chapter. In your time here, have you learned nothing from your betters? Fear is useless to you. It holds you back. Let go of it, or it will have to be beaten out of you.'

Savales watched Kalisde from the shadow of the western entrance. No one had yet noticed his presence. He did not like the man. Kalisde was quick to criticise and loath to hand out praise where it was well deserved, and he had no right to beat anyone who did not serve directly under him. Some of these boys were already marked to study for roles in the Sacratium, Apothecarion and Technicarum once they were old enough. If the Master of the Refectorum lifted a hand to them, he would find himself facing a very harsh penance.

'Look at me,' Kalisde continued. 'Do you see me shaking? Are my eyes wet with tears like yours? No. You are weak, all of you. The bombs do not scare me at all. I'd be laughing at you all if I wasn't so disgusted.'

Savales stepped fully into the Refectorum now, walking straight for the centre of the hall. His robes, bearing the personal heraldry of the Chapter Master on the back and breast, marked him out as the supreme authority among the Chosen. No other mortal man had the right to bear that sigil until Savales passed it on. On seeing the Ordinator enter, Kalisde stopped pacing and drew himself up straight. He eyed Savales with grudging respect as he approached.

'Look here, you boys. Ordinator Savales fears no greenskin bombs, is that not right, Ordinator?'

'Not so long as I have void shields over my head,' said Savales, stopping a few paces from Kalisde and smiling at the boys who looked up at him from either side. Then he fixed his eyes on the Master of the Refectorum and said, 'I will take things from here, Bernis. You and your staff are free to retire for now.'

Kalisde did not like being told what to do on territory he considered his own, but he knew the power the Ordinator wielded. His jaw worked for a moment while he considered a response, but if he found one, he thought better of voicing it. He gave a curt nod and moved off to an arch in the north wall that would take him back to the kitchens. The other adults followed in silence.

Savales looked at the boys around him. He couldn't fault Kalisde for what he had been trying to do, but there were better ways to do it than making scared children feel guilty and miserable.

'Make room,' he told two on his right. He stepped over their bench and sat down beside them. 'Gather close, the rest of you,' he called out. 'Make sure you can all hear me.'

Wordlessly, the young serfs from other tables rose and gathered around, their fellows making room for them so that the benches became closely packed. There was a certain primal comfort in this new proximity. Huddled together like this, the shuddering of the mountain lost a little of its edge.

'Now,' said Savales, 'how many of you understand what is happening outside?'

None raised a hand. They all knew that the fortress-monastery was under attack by orks, of course, but none had ever seen one. All they knew of the greenskins was the stories the older serfs sometimes told, always third hand, and whatever they could glean from the friezes that decorated many of the Chapter corridors, ancient artwork in which Crimson Fist heroes were depicted slaying thick green figures by the hundreds.

'You know that the aliens hoped to surprise Master Kantor, yes? They hoped to strike hard at the Chapter's foundations and gain a quick victory. Well, try to imagine how frustrated the foolish greenskin leader must be feeling right now. He and his troops have spent years preparing, maybe even decades. His armies have crossed great stretches of cold, dark space, intent on obliterating the single greatest threat to their species in the entire sector. They risked death by the millions, exiting the warp dangerously close to a planet, losing many of their most powerful ships in the process. It's true. And now, having finally reached their goal, they launch their payloads, only to find their weapons utterly useless. Every last bomb they drop explodes harmlessly on our shields. Afraid? Us? Throne, no! It is fine comedy.'

He saw a few faces brighten as they listened, but the walls still rumbled. The bombardment seemed endless and it was clear the youngsters needed more from him.

'When I was your age,' he told them, 'I experienced the greatest fear of my life. Do you know what that was?'

'You saw a xenos,' said a wide-eyed boy of nine from across the table.

'No,' said Savales. 'Not that.'

'A daemon, then?' said another of about the same age.

The others hissed at him and made warding signs, and he shrank back from them.

Savales frowned and shook his head, but he was not angry. 'No, not that. And we do not say that word aloud, child. Remember your lessons. Well, it seems none of you will ever guess, so I will tell you. The greatest fear of my life was that my chance to serve the Chapter was lost forever. I was not much older than you are when I discovered I would never be Astartes. I had wanted it so much. I doubted the worth of any other kind of life. I thought my life over. I was sure I would be put to death. But I've lived a better life than I ever deserved, and so will each of you. The Chapter needs us, you know, and each of us need the Chapter. Master Kantor knows all your names. He cares for all the Chosen. In fact, he once said to me, "Ramir, the Chosen are like this mountain". "How so, my lord?"'

I asked him. "They are the rock on which the Chapter stands," he told me. "It is by their labours that the battle-brothers are always ready for war. I only wish the rest of the Imperium knew how much of our glory and honour rightly belongs to the ones who serve us."'

'He really said that?' asked a boy on Savales's left.

'He did,' said Savales. 'Throughout your lives, the Chapter will ask much from each of you. Sometimes you will be tired, but you must go on. Sometimes you will feel pain, but you must overcome it. You must give everything you have to your duties. Lord Hell-blade is depending on you. The Chapter's victories are our victories, too. Do not forget it.' He pointed upwards towards the high ceiling and raised his eyes. 'When the orks finish dropping their useless bombs, our masters will begin the real fight, and they will fin-ish it, too. You will see. The Crimson Fists cannot be overcome. Even the accursed Scythians failed in the end and fled into the Great Dark to escape the Chap-ter's wrath.'

The air in the Refectorum had brightened notice-ably now. Most of the boys had straightened in their seats. Savales saw pride burning in bright eyes. Good, he thought.

'I hope you all know *Gordeau's Ninth Litany Against Fear.*'

The youngest looked nervous and guilty, but the others nodded.

'If you don't know it,' Savales said kindly, 'just listen and do your best. You will soon pick it up.'

So, he led them in the litany, their voices joining to fill the air and challenge the noise of the bombs. They hardly noticed when the bombs stopped falling. A short time later, when death came to take them all, that was how it found them; unafraid, with pride in their hearts.

Savales need not have worried about the worth of his life. He had lived it with great honour, and it ended in the only place he ever called home.

THE ORKS CAME soon after the first of the ship-killers were launched. They came in uncountable numbers, with tanks and bikes and weapons that beggared description, spewing forth from fat transports that braved the fortress-monastery's mid- and close-range defences to land and disgorge them. They swarmed up the mountainsides, heedless of the fire that spilled out to meet them.

Alessio Cortez felt no fear. It had been so long, he no longer knew what true fear felt like. When the call went up that orks had been spotted on the slopes, he felt only the familiar, welcome heat of battle-rush. His blood surged through his veins, flooding his muscles with everything they would need for the imminent combat. He felt the cardiovascular drumbeat in his gauntleted fingers where they gripped his trusty boltpistol.

Now they'll see, he thought. Now they'll pay for their arrogance.

He and his company had been charged with defending the Protheo Bastion from the lower ramparts, and, as the alien horde charged into view, they began pouring fire down onto the snorting, roaring front lines. The orks, usually disinclined towards night attacks, when their poor eyesight was rendered even poorer, carried flaming torches that made them all too easy to target. They had little chance of breaching the western wall. The chasm helped prevent that. But they had brought heavy armour with them, great lumbering artillery pieces with unbelievably wide muzzle, and, if these were brought within range, they would be able to lob their barrel-sized shells over the walls.

The 4th Company was not about to allow that.

Bolter-fire sputtered out, splitting apart the night, bright muzzle flares strobing across the walls. Lascannons cracked like lightning, ionising the air, lancing into ugly enemy tanks and cutting them apart as soon as they came into view. Explosions once again rocked the mountainside.

'For glory, brothers!' shouted Cortez as he fired again and again.

Behind him he heard another voice boom out, 'For glory, captain!'

Cortez glanced round for the briefest instant and saw a white skull. He recognised the voice, one of Tomasi's Chaplains, Brother Rhava, with two black-robed Sacratium acolytes in tow. Each acolyte silently carried a tray of extra ammunition and charge packs.

Rhava came forward and joined Cortez at the parapet, raised a glowing plasma pistol, and began firing burst after flesh-searing burst out into the crowded greenskin ranks where they were forced to halt at the chasm's lip. Many had already plunged over, struck by the fire of the Space Marines, or pushed to their deaths by overeager comrades.

'How goes the defence, brother-captain?' the Chaplain asked Cortez between rounds.

Cortez's clip ran dry. As he slid another from his belt, he answered, 'There is little sport in this, holy one. They can't gain ground here. This assault is mass suicide.'

'And yet,' said Rhava between his own shots, 'sport or not, you seem to be revelling in it.'

Cortez grinned beneath his helm. 'Tell me you find this a chore.'

'It never is,' said Rhava. Another of his blinding plasma-bolts struck an ork full in the chest. It sank to its knees, its chest little more now than a gaping crater of burned flesh. The ends of ribs poked from the side of the wound like stubby teeth.

There was a great roaring noise just to the north, and Cortez glanced that way to see another ship-killer emerging from its silo-tower, flames and smoke billowing up around it.

'I have heard,' said Rhava, also noting the missile's emergence, 'that *The Crusader* escaped successfully.'

Cortez's eyes followed the missile's burning path. The power of such weapons was astounding. Part of him wished he could fly with it, to see the raw destruction it wreaked on whichever warp-damned enemy ship it struck.

'Ranparre gave everything to make it so,' he said. 'We will turn this around in his honour. Now that we—'

He never finished that sentence.

Something was wrong. One of the missiles from the other side of the fortress-monastery had suddenly changed vector.

No one would ever know what caused that change. Was it a simple malfunction? Sabotage? The will of malicious gods? No answer would ever come forth, but the results would be remembered in the Imperial history books for all time.

Rhava followed Cortez's gaze.

'By Dorn—'

The missile corkscrewed in the air above the Arx Tyrannus for a brief moment. Time seemed to slow down for Cortez as he watched, helpless to do anything. Then the missile plunged deep into the mountainside, its powerful thrusters forcing that armour-piercing nose-cone through metre after metre of rock.

The mountain shook.

Cortez and Rhava were thrown from their feet.

Shouts of alarm replaced the stutter of gunfire on the air.

When the missile reached a depth of two-hundred metres beneath the rock on which Arx Tyrannus stood, it detonated, igniting the Chapter's ancient underground munitions stores one after another.

There was no time to shield oneself, no time to run, nor even to curse.

White fire engulfed all, and burned to embers the hopes of an entire world.

TWO

'These were days so dark they had been rivalled only once in the history of the Chapter, and darker still were yet to come. But darkness is not a thing in and of itself. It has no form, no substance. It is merely the absence of light, and where light enters, darkness always recedes.

The smallest most ephemeral spark can grow to burn like a mighty sun.

It requires naught but the right kind of fuel.

Snagrod gave us all the fuel we needed.'

– Brother-Codicier Ruthio Terraro of the Librarius,
Crimson Fists Chapter, Adeptus Astartes

ONE

The Gorrion Wall, New Rynn City

THE CONCEPT OF patience was as alien to the orks as they themselves were to the race of man. They did not hesitate, did not congregate around fires to hold war councils or to assess the success of their landing. They simply swarmed, and the outer fringes of the planetary capital, those poorest of districts that fell out with the city's grand defensive walls, were engulfed in fire and raw, rampant destruction.

Alvez and Grimm had been out on the south-western ramparts of the Gorrion Wall for hours, overseeing the deployment of Crimson Fist resources to those sections of the city's outermost defences that were judged to be weakest. The rest of the city's perimeter, in particular those sections that were expected to hold longest, were assigned to companies of nervous-looking Rynnsguard. Alvez deemed this best for now, though a stout, high-ranking officer called General Saedus Mir protested as vocally as his respect for the Astartes would allow, adamant that his men would prove the equal of any blasted aliens. The first hour of battle, Alvez knew, would separate the real fighters from the cowards. He would pay particular attention to how the Rynnsguard handled their wall sections. Only then would he have an accurate idea of just what General Mir's forces were capable of.

The night sky was criss-crossed in every direction with arcs of orange light as ork craft poured down through the atmosphere from their warp-capable cruisers and destroyers. The city's fixed defences were taxed beyond capacity, firing almost non-stop, and the concussive waves of noise from each shot shook the air all around. Alvez saw a good number of the clumsily fashioned greenskin landers fall from the sky as burning junk, but there were simply far too many of them for it to make any real difference.

Squadrons of Imperial fighters and bombers screamed in overhead to engage those that got through, but the Rynnite pilots were woefully out-numbered. Though they killed a great many with their superior flying skills and lethal weaponry, the sheer number of greenskin fighters in the sky soon overwhelmed them. They would never return to the hangars at Targis Fields, never paint those well-earned kill-signs on their fuselages.

As he watched the aerial battles turn in favour of the invaders, Alvez said a grim prayer for the souls of the doomed Rynnsguard pilots. If the infantry and tank crews were anywhere near as brave, he decided, they might yet surprise him.

'You knew it would come to this,' said Sergeant Grimm, standing at his side.

Alvez, dressed for battle in a massive suit of Tactical Dreadnought Armour – better known among the Astartes as Terminator armour – fingered the trigger of his twin-barrelled storm-bolter. The weapon was large, much larger than a standard bolter, and fitted with a heavy box magazine. They made a nasty mess of organic targets and its oversized bolts could rip through the side of a tank if they had to.

'It was always going to be this way, Huron. One rarely stops a Waaagh in space. You see all these craft? They are but the beginning of the green tide. By dawn, the land beyond these walls will be seething with alien filth and their machines.'

'I'm glad you consented to evacuating the outer boroughs, my lord. I know it was a risk with the enemy already landing, but it was… the *right* choice.'

Alvez sneered beneath his cold metal faceplate. 'You mean it was the moral choice, Huron. Do not confuse the two. I am not a wasteful man. This siege will not be over quickly. We have lost control of local space. The enemy land in droves. Sooner or later, every man, woman, and perhaps even child, will be called upon to fight for survival. If evacuation saved the people of the outer boroughs tonight, it was only to postpone their deaths to tomorrow, or the next day. Be under no illusion. A great many sacrifices will be made here. But the Crimson Fists will remain standing.'

An ork troop transport with a metal snout crafted to look like a fang-filled maw roared in low overhead, and Rynnsguard troopers on a neighbouring section of the wall instinctively ducked. The growl of its jets was deafening, and there was a wash of heat after it passed. Neither Alvez nor Grimm moved except to track the craft with their eyes.

Two powerful laser-defence towers hummed noisily as they locked onto it. Bright lances of light flashed out, ripping into the transport's hull. The stricken craft blossomed with bright bursts of orange fire and listed to starboard, but its momentum kept it soaring through the air until, seconds later, it smashed prow-first into a huddle of stocky, flat-roofed habs. The explosion lit the surrounding streets like a flare. By its light, Alvez could see thousand of orks charging along every street and alleyway, roaring insanely with battle lust and waving all manner of killing implements above their ugly, misshaped heads.

'Ready yourself,' the captain said to his second. 'They must not set foot on the ramparts, nor breach the gates.'

He ordered the rest of the Astartes on the Gorrion Wall to ready their weapons, and, all along its length, bolters were cocked, fat rounds sliding into empty chambers. He sent a short message to General Mir, authorising the Rynnsguard to begin the first Earthshaker barrage, and was rewarded seconds later with the flash and boom of mighty long-guns as they claimed the first alien casualties of the opening battle.

Two squads of Crusade Company Terminators, Squads Zarran and Valdeus, had been tasked with holding New Rynn Spaceport with a full regiment of Rynnsguard in support. Alvez checked in with them now, and learned that the fighting around the spaceport, sixty kilometres away, was already intense. Sergeant Zarran had local command. He reported to Alvez that the spaceport's anti-air defences had claimed a great many enemy ships, but that enemy armour and infantry were massing in great numbers. Despite this dark news, there was a distinctive tone in Zarran's voice. It was a tone Alvez knew well: that of a man in love with his work. Zarran was looking forward to the slaughter to come.

As he should, thought the Alvez. The purging of xenos is righteous work.

The green horde boiling through the streets below the ramparts were almost in bolter range now. The captain stepped forward to the very edge of the rampart, pistons hissing as they powered the movement of his massive form. He raised his right hand and aimed the barrels of his storm-bolter down at the charging front ranks.

'Come, sergeant,' he said to Huron Grimm. 'You spoke of turning the Adacian red. Now that work begins.'

Grimm joined him at the wall and, together with the forces stationed all along its many kilometres of length, they opened fire on the savage invaders.

In all the flashing light and smoke and noise, neither Space Marine noticed the brief, sudden brightening of the sky far to the east.

The first they knew of any catastrophe was when frenzied voices burst over the comm-link on a dozen different channels, all relaying the same information.

The Librarians were down. All of them.

The captain cursed.

'In Terra's holy name, what is going on?'

TWO

Arx Tyrannus, Hellblade Mountains

PAIN WOKE PEDRO Kantor. Something was yanking hard on his left arm, along the length of which a dozen fractures were trying to mend. His nerves sent fiery protests to his brain, demanding that he remain still while his body was about the business of healing itself. He heard a high-pitched growl of frustration, and the yanking took on a more frantic edge.

Kantor opened his eyes. There were red warning glyphs at the edges of visor display, but he ignored them, focusing instead on the cause of the tugging sensation. A short, sinewy form squatted on his left, its wrinkled green flesh naked but for a loincloth of poorly cured animal skin. Sharp teeth jutted from a mouth above which extended a long, hooked nose. Its beady red eyes burned with frustration.

It was a gretchin, and it clearly thought Kantor dead. It was trying to take Dorn's Arrow, but the relic storm-bolter was fixed tight to the back of Kantor's left gauntlet, and the ugly little xenos wasn't making any progress.

Despite the fractures, Kantor's arm moved as fast as a striking snake. He wrenched his wrist from the creature's long-fingered hands and grasped it by its scrawny throat, digging his fingers deep into its flesh.

The gretchin began to flail in panic and tried to call out to its fellows, but the vice around its throat permitted breath in or out.

Kantor squeezed harder, piercing the skin, feeling the tendons tear beneath it. Rivulets of alien blood spilled out over his hand. The gretchin's eyes rolled up into its head and its tongue flopped out. Its flailing ceased. Kantor felt vertebrae snap under his fingers and knew the creature was dead. He threw the body aside.

Where was he? What had happened?

One moment he had been firing down from the upper ramparts of the Protheo Bastion, the next, the world had turned white. He remembered Javier Adon frantically calling to him over the comm-link, but after that...

He turned and pushed himself to his feet. His suit registered elevated background radiation and several weaknesses in his cooling systems – nothing critical, but the latter would require the attention of the Techmarines eventually.

Dawn was breaking, but it was a dawn unlike any he'd seen on Rynn's World. The sky was an angry red. Rynnstar and her sister, Eloix, were hidden from view by great veils of smoke and ash. All around him, bright cinders danced and cavorted on the updrafts. Instinct told him he was facing west with the fortress-monastery at his back. He turned to look east...

...and almost dropped to his knees.

Utter devastation.

Even through the thick veils, he could see that the destruction of his beloved home was almost total. He stood on the far side of the western chasm, close to its edge, and beheld a scene his mind desperately wished to deny. Something had wiped Arx Tyrannus from the face of the planet. Whatever had done so had presumably thrown him clear across the chasm and onto the mountain's western slope.

Gusting winds momentarily drew the veils of ash aside, and Kantor saw that the walls, the gates, the bastions, tower and keeps, all were no more. Arx Tyrannus had been reduced to jagged spurs of steel and stone, jutting from the rubble like so many broken teeth. Here and there, he spotted familiar things in unfamiliar states, the remains of glorious works reduced to wreckage. He saw a great stone block standing tall among its shattered neighbours, its surface embossed with a pattern of carved skulls. It had been part of the towering north-western archway. Now it was part of nothing. To the right of it, he saw a figure in black marble, slumped awkwardly amid tumbled iron beams, its hands and head shorn off. He recognized it by the details on its chest. It was the statue of Isseus Coredo, a Crimson Fists captain who had given his life in battle two hundred years before

Kantor had been born. The statue had stood in Memorial Hall, surrounded by worthy company. Now it had none, a lonely symbol that embodied loss, a symbol, Kantor realised, of his own disgrace.

I am the Chapter Master, he thought. It was my role to prevent this. Dorn, forgive me.

Curtains of ash and smoke closed over the view, and Kantor was almost glad of it. His hearts ached, and his limbs were numb with sorrow and disbelief. What was it that had struck them so hard? Had the ork fleet held some terrible weapon in reserve, knowing that the void-shields would fall when the Fists believed the orbital bombardment over?

Such questions were quickly put aside when he heard grunting and shuffling behind him. He spun to face the source of the noise, raising Dorn's Arrow as he moved. Visibility was extremely poor, the light of the suns interacting with the ash-filled air to cast little more than a dim red glow, but Kantor knew what he faced by their silhouettes alone. Three sturdy figures advanced towards him, large hands gripping heavy pistols and blades.

He didn't wait for them to see him. At a single thought impulse, Dorn's Arrow barked, and the silhouette in the centre spun and fell, bringing a yell of surprise from the throats of the other two. They had seen Kantor's muzzle flash through the smoke, and they raced forward, weapons raised, firing rounds that buzzed past his head like furious insects.

Kantor fired again, targeting centre mass, catching the ork on the right twice in the torso. The rounds detonated and split the creature's body apart. The last of the greenskin trio put on a burst of speed, racing out of the smoke directly at Kantor, eager to engage in close combat where the prodigious strength of its race would give it greatest advantage.

Or so it thought.

Raw strength was so much less when wielded without skill. The ork's first wild swing – a lateral stroke intended to behead the Chapter Master with its large, chipped hatchet – was easy enough to duck. The blade whistled over Kantor's head. The instant it passed, he stepped forward, activating the energy field of the power fist on his right hand, and launched a lethal uppercut that cored the xenos beast like an apple.

Its hollowed form collapsed to the rocky ground, steam rising from the gaping cavity in its chest.

How many more of them were out here on the slopes?

They had been assaulting Arx Tyrannus in great number. Had the cataclysm devastated them, too?

Had any of his brothers survived?

Kantor tried to open a comm-channel, unencrypted, desperate to reach anyone at all, but his visor display reported too much interference from the residual energies of the great explosion. He removed his helmet, considering whether or not to call out. If the orks were still here in number, they would make straight for him with murder on their minds.

Let them come, he thought.

He would take whatever temporary comfort he could in dispensing death to them.

Clipping his helmet to his belt, he took a great lungful of air and was about to call out when he heard the distinctive sound of bolter-fire just off to the north. Without hesitation, he followed it. Was one of his brothers alive, or had some greenskin marauder simply salvaged a boltgun and was firing it at random into the air?

As Kantor moved north along the lip of the chasm, he saw a great many shapes on the ground. Most were orks, their heavy bodies burned black or pulverised by large blocks of stone thrown out in the blast, but there was a far sadder sight among them. With increasing frequency, Kantor came across the still forms of Crimson Fists lying among the xenos dead. They, too, had been thrown from the fortress-monastery's ramparts to land here, their bodies broken beyond their ability to heal. He wanted to stop, to check each for signs of life, but the sound of the boltgun was closer now, and he could see muzzle flare through the smoke up ahead.

Stepping over the dead, ready to join the combat, Kantor hurried towards it.

'More!' yelled a familiar voice. 'Come and meet your death, filthy scum. You've won nothing, do you hear me? As long as I live, your kind will have reason to fear.'

Kantor saw an ugly shape loom up on the speaker's left and, before the furious battle-brother could turn his boltpistol on the creature, he fired, two bolts punching wounds in the monster's side.

It sank to the ground, dead, and for a moment, the area was clear of threats. The determined battle-brother turned. 'You there!' he barked. 'Well met. Now name yourself, brother!'

Despite everything, Kantor grinned. Of all the voices he could have heard at that moment, here was the very one he would have wished for most. He stepped towards the figure, presenting himself, and answered, 'You once called me Pollux reborn, brother, but you were in error then.'

The other stood stunned, then surged forward to place his hands on Kantor's shoulders.

'Pedro! By all the worlds... You're alive!'

Kantor returned his old friend's embrace. 'Unless we have died, Alessio, and our spirits wander a nightmare... yes, I am alive.'

They released each other and stepped back, each studying the other's face. Alessio Cortez was smiling, but it was impossible to miss the pain in his eyes. Kantor knew his friend felt the loss of so much every bit as keenly as he did.

'Others?' he asked.

'None that I have found so far,' answered Cortez quietly. 'I have checked a great many bodies, brother. But, no. None, yet.'

'Do you know...?'

Cortez scowled. 'One of our own missiles, Pedro. By the blasted bones of the Scythians, it was one of our own damned missiles! Rhava and I saw it just before it hit. It hammered straight into the mountainside.'

Kantor shook his head. 'The Forgemaster said there were problems with the Laculum batteries, but the follow-up scans showed everything in order.'

'Adon would not have fired otherwise.'

It was true. The Chapter Master could not believe that Javier Adon had been at fault here. Had it simply been an accident? A billion-to-one quirk of ill fate? If not, had sabotage been the cause? Each of these explanations was equally difficult to swallow.

'A ship-killer couldn't have wreaked so much devastation on its own,' Cortez offered. 'It must have detonated our underground munitions stores. A massive chain reaction is the only thing that would explain such a... catastrophe.'

Kantor was about to respond when the report of a bolter sounded from the west, a little further down the mountain.

A look between them was all that was needed. The two Astartes turned and began racing in the direction of the noise. As they ran side-by-side past the smoking ruins of ork machines and the heaped bodies of the greenskin dead, Kantor said, 'If there are answers to be had here, brother, we will have them one day but our destiny lies elsewhere. We must gather together anyone that lives and move from here. More orks will be coming.'

FOLLOWING THE SOUNDS of bolter-fire, Kantor and Cortez were soon reunited with a sergeant by the name of Viejo. When they found him, he was standing over a body in black armour, cutting down a small mob of greenskin filth he had discovered trying to loot it.

Viejo's joy at seeing his two superiors was tempered by the horror of all that had happened. The body in black was that of Chaplain Rhava. Cortez knelt beside it and offered a short prayer. Around Rhava's neck there hung a thick gold and ruby pendant, its aura of power palpable. It was a rosarius, a protective amulet given to all Chaplains on full acceptance into the Sacratium. In these times, its ancient technology was only barely understood. Cortez removed it gently, muttering to the corpse, 'If you will permit me, holy brother, I will carry this until I might return it to another of your order. It belongs with them.'

He did not presume to hang the rosarius around his neck. Only another Chaplain might wear it in such a manner. Instead, Cortez fixed the pendant to his belt, noting a strange pricking sensation on his skin as he did so. Then he rose, swearing revenge.

Continuing the search, Kantor, Cortez and Viejo moved off, maintaining a ten-metre gap between them. Time and again, they turned over the bodies of their brothers to find the armour crumpled or split, and the flesh within cold and dead. But they did not give up, and their determination soon paid off.

Half an hour later, the three had become nine. An hour after that, sixteen. Though they continued to scour the area, killing any greenskins that stumbled onto their path, their number rose no higher.

Sixteen Crimson Fists had survived from a force of over six hundred. Of most of those who had perished, there were no remains to be found. The explosion that had destroyed their ancient home had obliterated all trace of them. So it was with the thousands of Chosen who had believed themselves relatively safe within the fortress-monastery's walls.

A few of the Chapter's serfs lay here on the slopes among the Astartes and the aliens, but not many. Their twisted, broken forms would have been hard to recognise but for the distinctive robes in which they'd died. Every last one he passed made Kantor think of his loyal Ordinator. The knowledge that the old man would never again bring him spiced fruits and fresh water in his chambers, nor stay a while to share in the joys of friendly discussion, was like a knife in his side. He would miss Savales's honest, open face and his kind ways.

It soon became clear that any further searching was futile. It was time to think about setting some objectives. There was only one place to go, Kantor knew – New Rynn City. Thank the Emperor and the primarch that a good number of the Crimson Fists had been there when the missile struck.

'Weapons,' he told the somewhat battered-looking Astartes that stood in front of him. 'We will need supplies. Grenades, ammunition, water, nutricaps, blades, anything you can find. Strap on as much as you can. We've a long and difficult path ahead of us.'

Cortez came in close, and said in an undertone, 'What of our fallen? We can't just leave them out here like carrion.'

Kantor knew exactly how the orks would treat the dead. They would strip the sacred armour from them and bastardise it to suit their own ends. Then they would defile the corpses, hacking off heads and hands to wear as sickening trophies.

He shook his head, as much to rid himself of that image as to reject what Cortez was suggesting.

'I wish we could honour our brothers properly, Alessio, but we have lingered here long enough. More orks will be coming, and in force. They will want to gloat over this. There is no time to bury anyone.'

'If I may, lord,' said a brother called Galica, a member of 5th Company, 'We could perhaps burn them. Some of the dead xenos were carrying crude flamers. A pyre would deny them their sacrilege.'

Kantor felt fifteen pairs of eyes on him, awaiting his pronouncement. He could read their faces. If he denied them this, he was sure, they *would* follow him, but none would be happy about leaving the dead this way. In his heart of hearts, he knew he wouldn't be, either.

'Very well,' he told them. 'Galica, Olvero and Teves will gather the xenos flamers. Look for fuel canisters, too. The orks may have been carrying extra ammunition for them. The rest of us will gather our dead. Work quickly.'

So they did, and soon there was a mound of figures in dark blue armour. Among them were other colour in lesser number – Chaplains in black, Rhava among them, Techmarines in red, Apothecaries in white.

Kantor particularly lamented the fact that none of the latter had survived. An Apothecary could have recovered priceless gene-seed from the dead. That gene-seed was needed now more than ever, a critical resource in bringing the Chapter back up to strength in the future… *if* the Chapter was to have a future.

The work of ensuring it did, Kantor knew, fell squarely on his shoulders.

He prayed to Pollux that he was equal to the task.

Brothers Galica, Teves and Olvero lit the pyre, white fire gushing and spitting from the nozzles of the alien weapons. Then, when the fuel canisters were spent, they threw the weapons aside and joined the others in a final salute.

As the fire claimed the bodies of the dead, Kantor found himself wishing that High Chaplain Tomasi were here, for his spiritual strength as much as for his knowledge of the appropriate rites. He offered words of his own as the flames crackled and snapped, but, though his brothers appeared moved by them, he felt them were a poor substitute.

Tomasi had been ministering to the souls of his fellow Crimson Fists since long before either Kantor or Cortez were even born – almost five hundred years of unswerving loyalty and honour. And then, in an eye-blink, he had been wiped from existence. One of the largest, most forceful personalities Kantor had ever known, snuffed out in an instant with those he tended, another legend cut short without fitting glory to punctuate it. It had been Tomasi who had overseen the Rites of Succession that saw ultimate authority pass from the late Chapter Master Visidar to Kantor. Who would oversee those rites now? Who among the Chaplains in the capital was fit to take Tomasi's place?

He reached out and put a hand on Cortez's shoulder. 'Enough,' he said. 'We have done all we can here. New Rynn City is over a thousand kilometres away, and the land that separates us from our goal will be seething with the foe. Snagrod means to obliterate us entirely. He may think it a task already accomplished, but he *will* send forces to make sure. Get the others ready to leave.'

Cortez didn't move. He stood staring into the flames. 'When I lay eyes on the vile bastard, Pedro...'

There was a shout from the other side of the fire. Kantor left Cortez where he was and strode around it, already certain it would not be good news.

He was right.

Brother Alcador was staring out over the vast expanse of the Arcalan Basin to the west, eyes fixed on a point in the sky. 'We have aircraft inbound, my lord,' he said. 'And they are not ours!'

Kantor followed the battle-brother's gaze.

He saw them now, a cluster of dark shapes in the distance, far away but moving swiftly. If they didn't change vector, they would be on top of the Fists' position in a matter of minutes.

They flew in what could only loosely be called formation. The smaller craft rolled and swooped dangerously close to a knot of larger, bulkier machines.

Their recklessness was unmistakeable.

'Damn them,' spat Kantor.

Cortez had followed him around the fire, and was now tracking the dark objects in the distance, too. 'This is a gift, brother.' He lifted his boltpistol in front of his breastplate to emphasise his point. 'We can begin our vengeance now!'

'I will not risk the lives of the Fists I have left,' snapped Kantor. 'How do you propose to fight their jets without anti-air weaponry?'

The approaching ork aircraft might be carrying high-yield bombs, air-to-ground missiles and Throne-knew-what-else. To die here, bombed from the air by the filthy savages… No. Their chance for justice, for revenge, would vanish like smoke on the wind.

'We pull out,' said Kantor. 'Now!'

Cortez glared at him as if he were mad.

'Run, Pedro? You cannot mean that. Let them land. We can ambush them. If we allow ourselves to fear death now, we are not worthy to survive. Surely you see that. Honour will only be served by taking the fight to them. It is the Astartes way. It is the *only* way.'

Kantor's eyes bored into Cortez's. 'This is not about honour or pride, damn you. This is about the survival of our Chapter. Nothing else. New Rynn City is our only hope. We must reunite with Alvez's force. Now move these battle-brothers out, captain. We will follow the Yanna Gorge. It will give us good cover until we reach the steppes.'

Cortez cursed and spat on the ground, and, just for the briefest instant, Kantor found himself furious at his insolence. They were friends, yes, and he had always afforded Cortez certain liberties because of that. But he was taking them too far now. Rank superseded all else. The captain clearly needed reminding.

Kantor's voice was dangerously quiet as he said, 'Understand me, Alessio. These are my orders. Orders, brother! You have debated them countless times before, but you have never disobeyed them. You will not do so now when I need your strength most.'

Cortez's eyes were wild. Missile malfunction or not, his soul burned with a need, a compulsion, to eviscerate those who had come to Rynn's World with the intention of doing his brothers harm. His home was gone, his proud 4th Company obliterated with he the only member left. He struggled with himself, the effort plain on his scarred face. He was torn between doing as his master ordered and doing what his heart demanded. As Kantor watched him, he saw the psycho-conditioning win through. Cortez's face became gradually less feral, the curled upper lip sliding back down over clenched teeth.

'I will do as my lord asks,' Cortez growled at last, 'but I don't have to like it.'

Kantor let that pass. Cortez would do as ordered. Despite their words in the corridor after judgement had been passed on Janus Kennon, he could not disobey. A true Astartes embraced his psychological augmentation utterly. Cortez's mood would remain foul until his armour was slick with the blood of the foe, but that moment would come soon enough of its own accord.

The black shapes in the sky were growing closer, visible in more detail.

Fighter-bombers and troop carriers, thought Kantor. The orks control our airspace. How easy it was for them. We were complacent. *I* was complacent, and it must never happen again.

Raucous jet engines could be heard clearly now, their noise echoing up from the plains below. Kantor stepped past Cortez, intent on getting his party moving quickly.

Wordlessly, Cortez fell in behind him.

Do you think I want to punish the xenos any less than you do, Alessio, Kantor silently raged? I would slaughter every last one of them. I would look into their red eyes as I twisted my blade, and steep both my hands in their blood. But I will wait until the time is right, and so will you. My orders *will* be followed. We are Astartes. Space Marines. We are the shield against the darkness, yes. But without discipline, we are nothing at all.

THREE

The Cassar, New Rynn City

DAWN AT THE capital brought no relief. In fact, with the coming of the light, it brought more horror and despair than the night could ever have. The extent of the invasion was revealed, and many who gazed out over a horizon literally filled with hostile alien monstrosities lost all hope. In that first morning, there were over four hundred suicides on the Gorrion Wall alone. Most of these were Rynnsguard, men who should have known better, men who should have been trained to sell their lives dear, who were expected to fight, no matter what, for the sake of all that depended on them. But most had joined up never expecting to see combat. They joined for the uniform, the attention of loose women, for the money to feed families.

As they gazed out over what had once been teeming suburbs built to house the city's cheap, uneducated labour force, all they saw was death.

Death was green. Death carried strange, shoddy looking weaponry and roared around in noisy, fume-spewing junk-heaps. And death was everywhere, bellowing curses, promising slaughter, and trying to get inside the gates.

Alvez had given temporary command of the Gorrion Wall to a veteran sergeant from 3rd Company, Dremir Soto, while he and Grimm sought out the most senior of the Librarians. All the reports listed the same phenomena – Librarians everywhere across the defensive line suddenly howling in pain and crashing to their knees. They had been either unable or unwilling to talk to anyone since. Alvez suspected a concentrated psychic assault of some kind, perpetrated by the ork shamans in Snagrod's army.

He was not prepared for the truth.

He and Grimm found the senior Epistolary, Delevan Deguerro, kneeling in silence before the altar in the Cassar's small but adequate Reclusiam. Images of Dorn and the Emperor gazed down impassively from the intricate stained-glass windows. Alvez could tell by the Librarian's posture that something was gravely wrong. Deguerro had always cut such a powerful, confident figure. Now he looked, not like a mighty son of the greatest primarch who had ever lived, but beaten, stricken as if by an illness that robbed him of all strength.

If Deguerro heard his two battle-brothers approach – and he could hardly have missed the floor-shuddering footfalls of the captain's Terminator armour – he showed no sign. He did not look up from the cold stone floor.

'Librarian,' said Alvez, his voice kept low out of respect for the sacred nature of the place.

Deguerro did not turn.

Alvez raised his voice further, 'Deguerro, I am talking to you!'

Again, there was no reaction. Huron Grimm stepped forward and laid a hand on the Librarian's right pauldron, with just enough pressure to turn him slightly. 'Brother,' he said. 'This is no time for silence. We must know what ails you. Our entire Librarius contingent has been struck dumb. If you cannot speak, then show us in Astartes battle-sign.'

Deguerro's voice, when it sounded, was scratchy and low. 'This is exactly the time for silence.'

He turned to face them at last, and, when Alvez looked into his eyes, his first thought was of how hollow they seemed. No light glimmered there.

'So much glory, so much nobility, bravery, pride… So much lost,' Deguerro murmured. 'Lost forever, brothers.'

Alvez and Grimm exchanged looks. 'Elaborate,' said Alvez.

'It was this tragedy,' said Deguerro, 'this that we sensed drawing near. If only the portents had been clearer…'

He turned back to the altar, apparently done with explanations, and Alvez let out a growl. Enough! How could he hope to address the problem if no one would tell him what it was? He grasped the Librarian and wrenched him back around, something few others would have dared. 'I am in command here,

235

Epistolary. The Chapter Master assigned you to my service, and you will respect that assignment. You will tell me in plain language what is wrong with you, or, so help me, Eustace Mendoza will hear of it.'

Deguerro struck Alvez's hand aside. 'Eustace Mendoza is dead, captain! Is that plain enough for you? They all are. All who stayed to defend our home have perished. Arx Tyrannus is gone!'

That made no sense. Arx Tyrannus, gone? Of course it wasn't gone. It was impregnable, unassailable. It would be there atop its mountain seat until the planet itself melted from the heat of its dying suns fifteen billion years from now.

'Not since the Siege of Barenthal have so many brothers fallen together,' muttered Deguerro. His anger melted had away again, the waters of his grief rising to submerge it.

Alvez was having great difficulty processing what he had just heard. Deguerro was no fool, no deceiver. Surely, then, he was mistaken. But there was no denying the pain he was in, the sorrow carved in the flesh of his face.

'You are confused,' Alvez insisted. 'A trick of the ork psykers.'

'I wish it were, brother,' said Deguerro without turning. 'Last night, a catastrophe struck our home. Our brothers died in searing white flames. I heard it, felt it. We all did, as if we, too, were dying. The psychic shockwave threatened to rip away our souls.'

'What stopped it?' asked Sergeant Grimm, his voice kinder than the captain's.

Deguerro looked up and snorted, but it was an empty sound, without real humour.

'The orks,' he said simply.

Alvez look at Grimm, face betraying his confusion. 'The orks?' he said dubiously.

'The ork psykers,' said Deguerro. 'They have been launching psychic assaults since they landed. Nothing we couldn't handle, though there are a great many of them with the Waaagh. Combined, their power is such that we cannot broadcast messages through the warp. Not while they are here in such force. Their unfocused thoughts create a choking psychic fog. Be glad you cannot perceive it, brothers. It is a smothering, suffocating thing.'

'I still do not understand,' said Grimm. 'You said the presence of the ork psykers saved you?'

'I did,' said Deguerro, nodding. 'We are surrounded by them. They are among the hordes on every side, enough of them to buffer us against the full blast of the psychic death-scream. You see, like energy in all its forms, psychic energy dissipates over distance, and much faster where it meets resistance. The ork shamans struggled to survive the blast. Had they not, we may have lost every last Librarian in this city. In that, if nothing else, we were lucky.'

Alvez stared up at the stylised glass image of Rogal Dorn, resplendent in armour of shimmering gold. 'It cannot be,' he muttered to himself. 'Arx Tyrannus? Pedro Kantor? I will not believe it until I see it with my own eyes. When we win this war, we will return to the Hellblades, and you will see for yourself,

Deguerro.' He stared hard at the back of the Librarian's head. 'You will see that you are wrong.'

The Librarian made no response.

'Report to the walls within the hour,' the captain commanded, his voice harsh. 'You and all your Librarius brothers. There will be no more of this. You are still a Crimson Fist, by Throne, and you will do your duty with honour, no matter the circumstances.'

So saying, he turned and thundered from the Reclusiam, his steps shaking stands of devotional candles as he went.

Grimm was left behind, looking down on a brother whose suffering he did not know how to ease. With no other choice, he turned and made his way to the doors of the small Reclusiam. Before he passed between them he turned and said, 'I believe you, brother, though I wish I did not. Still, the captain is right. This despair, this hopelessness…' He shook his head. 'You know as well as I that it is not our way. We are Astartes. Eustace Mendoza would expect you to fight.'

Then Grimm, too, left the nave, and silence returned.

A long minute later, Deguerro pushed himself to his feet. He looked up at the image of the Emperor, at His noble features cast in amber glass, and said quietly, 'I am a Space Marine. Of course I will fight.'

CAPTAIN ALVEZ WAS already beyond the walls of the Cassar when Grimm caught up to him. In fact, he had almost crossed the bridge between the Zona Regis and the Residentia Primaris. Even in his Terminator armour, the tireless captain covered ground quickly, and there was a new urgency in his stride. Grimm could see it clearly as he closed the distance. He fell into step with the captain just as they passed beneath the arch of the ornate Ocaro Gatehouse.

'It is true,' said Grimm. 'You can see it in his eyes.'

Alvez grunted something unintelligible.

'You will have to tell the others. They know something is deeply wrong here.'

The captain didn't slow. 'And if it is true?' he boomed. 'Can we do anything about it now? Can we somehow go back in time and undo it? We don't even know what happened.'

'But you *do* believe him,' said Grimm.

'I wish I did not,' replied Alvez. 'I am fighting to keep the full implications of it at bay, but I have my orders, and even this can hardly change them. We are defending a city from a siege the likes of which I have never known. If our Chapter *has* suffered this terrible blow, we must ensure that we, at least, survive. I don't know about you, Huron, but I didn't plan on dying at the hands of some cack-eating xenos anyway, so it changes nothing.'

Grim found he had no answer for that.

'Actually,' said Alvez when they had gone a dozen more metres, 'there is one thing I can do about it. I'm initiating the Ceres Protocol.'

Grimm looked up in surprise. The Ceres Protocol hadn't been employed since it had first been put to parchment all those centuries ago in the years after the blasted Scythian race had reduced the Chapter to a handful of squads. Its strictures were clear: no Crimson Fist was permitted to die in battle for any other cause than the saving of his battle-brothers. The strength of the Chapter was everything. That meant no battle-brothers lost for the sake of protecting humans or materiel of any kind.

'Are you sure that's necessary, my lord?' asked Grimm.

Alvez kept his eyes on the road ahead. 'I'm putting it in place anyway.'

Eighteen minutes later, they passed into a lower-class hab zone called the Deltoro Residentia. The streets were narrow here, and untidy, and the lopsided habs loomed over them as if they might topple at any moment. Many of the buildings looked as if they had been built in a hurry, then added to little by little over the years, so that the stonework of the upper stories was seldom the same colour or tone as that of the lower.

The contrast with the Zona Regis and the noble estates was stark. Here, the shadowed side alleys were strewn with heaps of waste and the occasional, fly-covered remains of a dead canid or felis. The air smelled strongly of chemical compounds drifting over from the nearby manufacturing zone. To live in such surroundings, or worse, was the lot of the vast majority in cities all across the Imperium. If New Rynn City was any different, it was not evident among the people of the so-called *Poor Quarters*.

What these people lacked in material riches, they clearly made up in faith. The sign of the Imperial aquila was everywhere, as were street-corner shrines to myriad saints and other assorted religious figures. In contrast to all else, these were immaculate. They bore no signs of damage or graffiti.

Grimm eyed them as he and Alvez continued their brisk march back to the ramparts of the Gorrion Wall. Not far off, he could hear the thump of artillery and the muffled crack and rattle of the city's huge gun-towers.

Though wailing sirens had, for the most part, cleared the streets of people, it didn't take long for Alvez and Grimm to be spotted. The locals peered out from behind wooden shutters at the sound of their boots on the cobbles.

'It is the Crimson Fists!' called one.

Grimm heard the shout being taken up all along the streets.

'Damn,' said Captain Alvez.

Doors were flung open and people poured out into the light of day to throw themselves onto the ground before the two Astartes. The air filled with the sound of pleading voices. Shabby women elbowed their way forward, holding their screaming babies out to be blessed. The old and the sick begged to touched on the head, believing, perhaps, that this alone might cure them of all their pains and ailments, or just bring them a little closer to the Emperor somehow. Others offered up their most prized possessions, hoping to win favour. Here, a curved knife, badly chipped, with a small red gem – almost certainly just coloured glass – set in its tarnished hilt. There, a kynid's-tooth statue of Saint Clario of the Blazing Lance with its left hand missing, broken off many years before. None of these, nor any of a hundred others, would have fetched more than a single Imperial centim at market, but they clearly meant a great deal to their possessors. These people were desperate that their district be saved from the orks. They were used to finding themselves and their neighbourhood low on the ladder of the politicians' priorities.

Alvez and Grimm found their path utterly blocked. To push through would leave many injured, perhaps even dead.

'Fools,' cursed Alvez quietly, so quiet, in fact, that only Grimm's superior hearing could pick it up. 'Do I look like a blasted Chaplain?'

A bent-backed old woman in a moth-eaten red shawl pushed herself up from her knees and shambled towards them, cradling something precious in her tiny withered hands. Grimm saw that she was weeping. He could not identify with her emotion, nor with the emotions of the people all around them, but he had seen its like enough times to know that such a potent effect on the faithful was one of the burdens of being a Space Marine. In all likelihood, these people had never been as close to a living symbol of the Emperor's light as they were now. He could see the zeal in their eyes. It was right there alongside their joy.

The old woman limped straight towards Alvez, and, mumbling something indecipherable, raised her hands, offering her personal treasure to him.

Grimm knew instinctively that things were about to take a turn for the worst.

'In Dorn's name,' the captain snarled, 'Get out of our way at once. All of you, get back to your homes. This city is under martial law. We do not have time for this.'

In anger, he batted the old woman's hands aside, and the little treasure she offered went flying from her. She collapsed to the rockcrete surface of the road, cradling her broken wrists, mewling softly. The crowd gasped and shuffled backwards, still on their knees. Some pressed their foreheads to the ground in utter submission. None spoke.

'Make way,' Alvez commanded through the vox-amp in his helmet. His voice reverberated along the street, shaking dust and grit from the sills and ledges of the buildings. 'We are at war. Do not seek blessings from any of my Astartes again. Is that understood? We are not priests, we are warriors. Move aside, damn you!'

When the people leapt to obey, clearing the road so the Astartes could pass easily, Grimm saw that fear had replaced the joy in their eyes. That was regrettable. Did Captain Alvez truly think so little of the people's love and respect? Sooner or later, Grimm believed, these very people would be called on to fight, to give their lives in a battle none of them had ever trained a single day for. They would die to hold back the foe just a little longer. Would they not fight that much harder *inspired* by their Astartes betters, rather than terrified by them?

Alvez was already thundering off down the street, not deigning to glance at the rows of people bowing and begging his forgiveness from either side of the street.

Grimm turned to the old woman on the road and, gently, lifted her to a sitting position. She gazed up at him and smiled a toothless smile. Though her bones were broken and it must have caused her great pain, she lifted a limp hand to the faceplate of his helmet and brushed it with her fingertips, mumbling something Grimm could not make out.

In her eyes he saw adoration and joy, as if Captain Alvez had not struck her down at all.

He glanced up and called out to a middle-aged couple on his left, 'You there! Will you take care of this woman? She requires a medicae. Take her to the nearest facility. I command it.'

The couple, an overweight man in bright quilted trousers and his waif-like wife, bowed excessively, and moved forward to help the old woman to her feet. Grimm lifted her into the man's arms, marvelling at how impossibly light her frail body seemed. He was glad he would never know such weakness himself. It was a cruelty that time inflicted on most living things, but, buried somewhere in the mysteries of the Astartes gene-seed was the secret to beating it. No Space Marine would ever wither away like that.

The Emperor had spared his sons that fate.

He turned, searching for something, and, after the briefest instant, his enhanced eyesight located it. He crossed to the front of a small hab, and the people in his way instantly moved aside. There beneath a filthy window, he bent over and retrieved the old woman's treasure. It was really the simplest of tokens: a small wooden aquila on a length of cord, a charm intended to be worn around the neck, though it would barely reach around an Astartes' wrist. It had once been beautifully painted, but it was very old now, the colours cracked and flaking.

When he turned back to the old woman and tried to give it back to her, she became agitated and expressed something to the fat man carrying her. He shushed her, and his wife hissed, 'Don't be foolish, old mother. The great one has no need of it.'

'Explain,' said Grimm.

The fat man gulped, his throat bobbing, and said, 'She would like you to have it, my lord. I'm afraid she is senile. She doesn't understand...' His eyes flicked briefly to the visor in Grimm's faceplate, then returned to the ground at his feet.

Grimm looked at the little aquila, so minute in the palm of his red gauntlet. He could not accept the gift personally. On acceptance into the Chapter, the Astartes of the Crimson Fists swore an unbreakable vow of non-possession. It was considered weak and unworthy to covet or collect material objects. One's armour, one's weapons, even the trophies one gathered from the battlefield – all of these and more belonged, not to the individual, but to the Chapter.

The Chapter, then, could accept her simple gift.

Grimm addressed her directly, though he was unsure she would understand him. 'I thank you for your offering, old mother, not for myself – it is against our ways – but on behalf of my Chapter. May the Emperor smile on you…' and, here, he turned his gaze to the fat man and his wife, and added pointedly, '…and on all those who do you kindness.'

There was a sudden harsh bark over the comm-link. 'Sergeant, you are wasting time.'

Captain Alvez was already a hundred metres away.

With the little wooden aquila in his left hand, Grimm strode past the old woman and the couple, and made his way towards his increasingly impatient superior. On both sides of the street, the people bowed deeply.

Grimm offered the slightest of nods in return as he passed, thinking to himself that, no matter the strength of their faith in the Emperor or in the power of the Adeptus Astartes, very soon, these people would be homeless… just like him. The Deltoro Residentia would be swallowed up by the fighting. How many of these people would be dead by season's end?

He had almost caught up with Captain Alvez when a great metallic scream sounded from the sky. A broad black shadow flitted between the street and the sun. Grimm looked up and saw the underside of an ugly ork troop-transporter bleeding black smoke and flame from a rent at its rear. The craft was out of control. It was going down fast, and it would crash in one of the wards nearby.

Captain Alvez was already making for a stone stairway that led up onto a hab roof. His heavy footfalls cracked the steps, raining dust and rocky pieces down on the ground below. Grimm followed him up and, together, they stood atop the hab and watched the ork craft cut a smoky black arc across the city.

It struck and shattered a massive stone cylinder far taller than the wall that separated the neighbouring districts, and fell from sight. Grimm knew the cylinder, or at least what it represented. It was a chimney, one of many that sprouted from the roofs of the capital's Mechanicus-controlled manufactora.

'Zona 6 Industria,' he said.

Alvez was already on the comm-link. 'All squads in zone six. This is Captain Alvez. We have a breach. An ork transport just went down. I need an immediate purge. Leave sections three and four of the Gorrion Wall to the Rynnsguard. This is a priority command. I repeat, we have a breach. Eliminate all orks in the Zona 6 Industria.'

While the captain had been issuing the order, Grimm had been checking the charge in his plasma pistol and warming up the flexors of his power fist. His own squad, which he had left under the command of Brother Santanos, was one of the squads in close proximity to the crash site. If the captain allowed it, Grimm would go to them and lead them in their elimination of the greenskin intruders. How many would have been on that craft? How many would have survived impact? If the orks got a foothold there, a critical resource would be lost all too early in the conflict. The manufactora were essential for ammunition re-supply. It would be a disaster.

With his orders given, Alvez checked his own weapons, one a master-crafted power sword, the other a massive storm-bolter, both Chapter relics awarded to him on his ascension to the captaincy, both exquisitely decorated with fine golden scroll-work and detailed chasings. Weapon checks and a brief prayer completed, the captain turned his head towards Grimm and said, 'We are near enough to offer assistance, sergeant. Follow me.'

Alvez did bother with the staircase for his descent. He stepped straight off the roof and plunged to the pavement, a drop of four metres, landing so hard that his boots shattered the flagstones. Grimm followed, the impact of his own boots markedly less. Then the two Crimson Fists were off, powering down the street towards the gate that linked the residential zone to the industrial.

Grimm hoped at least a few of the greenskins had survived. If what Epistolary Deguerro had said was true, he would revel in extracting payback. His armour, he swore, would be caked in xenos gore by the end of the day.

FOUR

The Western Slopes, The Hellblade Mountains

KANTOR AND HIS fifteen battle-brothers moved at speed down a sloping defile, loose stones skittering out in front of them. The Chapter Master was confident that the ork pilots hadn't spotted them. None of the ugly, heavy-looking fighters had peeled off from the main group, not yet, but the noise of their engines was louder by the second.

Kantor hoped the site of the ruined fortress-monastery, all that body-strewn rubble, would hold the orks' attention away from Yanna Gorge. But he wasn't taking any chances. He pressed his Space Marines hard. Sergeant Segala's makeshift squad were out in front, providing forward eyes. Viejo's squad were at the rear, alert as they moved, ready to warn of ork pursuit. Cortez and his squad moved with Kantor.

Communication was brief and infrequent as they pushed on. That suited Kantor fine. There was little to say. Better that each man be left to his own private thoughts for now, each remembering the brothers that had meant most to him. He still wrestled with his own grief, of course, but, as the leader, he didn't have the luxury of letting it dominate his mind. He had to get his Fists away from here. Soon, they would reach the foothills. There would be less cover there. Trees were sparse. Only hardy dry-grasses and thorny shrubs flourished. If the ork pilots opted to sweep the region looking for fresh targets, it would be on the foothills that Kantor and his men would be seen, out in the open with nowhere to run.

Cortez moved up beside him, fell into step, and, after a moment, said, 'No time to cover our tracks. They will follow us sooner or later.'

Cortez's helm hid his expression, but Kantor could hear his old friend's inner thoughts clear enough in his voice: *I want them to find us.*

'It cannot be helped, Alessio,' said Kantor. 'The best we can do is to hide our numbers. Keep to the tracks of our forward squad.'

Cortez looked north-west, eyes following the line of the gorge. Up ahead, Segala's squad were moving quickly, eyes scanning the land for signs of any ground-based foe. He turned back to Kantor and said, 'You have us scurrying away like mice, Pedro, when I would have us turn and fight like lions.'

Kantor frowned under his faceplate. 'The ways of the mouse suit our purpose, brother. He is a survivor. The time for battle will come, but we will reunite with our brothers in the capital before that. It is the only logical path.'

'Logic,' repeated Cortez, but he spoke it like a curse word. 'Ask the orks what they think of–'

Kantor raised a hand to hush him, his ears picking up a new sound on the air. Cortez listened, and heard it, too. Beneath the splutter and throb of the ork engines, something else was rising, faint but growing steadily stronger. It was a smoother sound, more rhythmic, more finely tuned.

'Lightnings,' said Kantor, his Lyman's ear implant filtering and enhancing the noise. 'They're coming in from the south-west. Three of them. It must be a fighter wing out of Scar Lake.'

Cortez tilted his head. 'Closing fast. They must've seen the orks.' He looked to the rocky slope on his left, then back at Kantor.

'Go,' said Kantor. 'Report what you see.'

Around him, the other Astartes stopped to await his command, bolters rising to the ready position by force of habit.

'All squads, hold position,' Kantor ordered over the link.

Cortez sprinted up the slope, his heavy boots crushing small rocks to powder beneath him and causing a miniature landslide of dirt and pebbles. Just below the ridgeline, mindful of his silhouette, he stopped, crouched, and peered over.

'You were right, lord,' he reported. 'Three Lightnings vectoring in towards the mountains. The orks have seen them. Their fighters are breaking off to engage. I don't like the look of it. Those Lightnings are out-numbered three to one.'

Ork flying machines might look clumsy, nose-heavy, and just about as aerodynamic as a Dreadnought, but therein lay the trick. Despite appearances, they were often lethally effective. No Rynnsguard air unit in active service had ever faced orks before. Imperial Lightnings, armed with auto-cannon and lascannon as standard, were crafted for performance, not durability. And ork pilots were as liable to ram them head-on as to fire on them.

'They must have been sent here to investigate the explosion,' said Kantor.

It made sense. The blast that had obliterated Arx Tyrannus would have been visible across almost the entire continent. Contact with Scar Lake Airbase had been lost hours ago, during the first ork strikes on the planet, but the appearance of the Lightnings sug-gested a slim possibility the airbase itself was still under Rynnsguard control. Kantor hoped so, but there was little he could do about it either way.

To Cortez, he said, 'We cannot aid them from here, Alessio. Not with the weapons we have. Keep moving. Their arrival will buy us time to put more ground under our feet. Hurry.'

Though reluctant to turn his eyes from the immi-nent dogfight, Cortez left the ridge and half-skidded, half-strode back to Kantor's position.

'All squads, move out,' ordered the Chapter Master.

'Emperor be with them,' said Cortez as he fell into step.

FIVE

Three thousand Metres above the Hellblade Mountains

'FALCON ONE, THIS is Falcon Three,' said Lieutenant Keanos over the vox. 'I have a lock.'

'Falcon Three, you are clear to fire,' came the reply. 'Falcon squadron, engage, engage!'

Keanos flipped the red toggle on his stick and thumbed the fire button. From a pylon under his right wing, white fire flashed and raced off, painting an arc of smoke that curved in towards his still-distant target.

Two second later, a little ball of fire bloomed in the distance. Black trails fell from it towards the ground.

'That's a kill,' said the voice on the vox. 'First blood to Falcon Three.'

Keanos felt a surge of elation. He had just destroyed an alien aircraft. In all his ten years as a Rynnsguard pilot, he had never actually imagined he would see real combat. Most of the flight time he had logged was routine patrol or war games. He couldn't wait to tell his wife, Azela, and their son, Oric, about this. It would have to wait until after the war, of course, when they could be together again.

He would have to embellish the telling a little, mind you. It was the AF-9 Airstrike missile that had done most of the real work. He had one left, slung under his left wing, and he hoped to gain another kill with it before the skirmish was over. The orks hadn't opened fire yet, so it looked like they didn't have missiles with the kind of range the Airstrikes had. But there were still eight of them left according to his forward auspex. Even if he and the rest of Falcon squad made a kill with every missile at their disposal, there would still be three ork fighters which they would have to eliminate in gun range, and that was another kind of combat altogether.

Up ahead, the ork fighters were banking to face him now. The numbers on his auspex's rangefinder display were dropping fast, far too fast for comfort. The ork were making a beeline directly for the Imperial Fighters. A familiar alarm sounded in Keanos's cockpit. Keanos spoke over the vox. 'Falcon One, I have another lock. Alpha-Six. I repeat, I have a lock on target Alpha-Six.'

As he spoke, he saw two white trails streak out towards the orks, one from each of the Lightnings on either side of him. Keanos hoped they hadn't fired at Alpha-Six. He wanted the kill for himself.

One of the missile trails started corkscrewing a second before it plunged towards the ground. A frustrated voice announced, 'This is Falcon One. Missile malfunction. No hit. No hit. Falcon Three, cleared to fire. Light him up.'

Keanos hit the button on his stick and felt the last Airstrike drop away from below his left wing. The white trail curved off ahead, and, a second later, a churning ball of red fire and black smoke started dropping from the sky.

'That's two for two, Falcon Three,' said the squadron leader.

Keanos wanted to jump up and down. Second only to Oric's birth, this was turning into one of the best days of his life. Two kills! How many more would he make by the end of the war?

With his main ordnance spent, he switched his targeting systems over to manual. Looking at his display, he saw that both his autocannon and lascannon were primed and ready, ammo counters at max. Up ahead, the rest of the ork fighters were almost in gun-range.

Come on, you alien bastards, he thought. I'll be an ace for sure.

SIX

Zona 6 Industria, New Rynn City

THE FIGHTING IN the streets around the damaged manufactorum was already heavy when Alvez and Grimm arrived behind the hastily erected barricades. The moment the captain arrived, those not engaged in direct fire turned and threw him short, sharp salutes. He nodded, but did not salute back. Though he was a rigid traditionalist, he knew, too, that there was a time and a place to reinforce proper conduct and discipline, and here, under heavy fire from a large, confident warband, was not that time.

Solid slugs whined over his head as he strode across to Squad Anto where they were hunkered down behind thick sections of Aegis pre-fabricated walls.

A fellow Blackwaterite, Faradis Anto had served under Alvez for more than a century. He was relatively short for a Crimson Fist, but he had a quick mind, and was known for being decisive. Alvez had once considered Anto for Grimm's position, but Anto and the captain were too similar in many ways. Huron Grimm was a contrast, and Alvez had opted for the balance that their dynamic allowed, though he had never said so to Grimm. So far, he'd had no cause to regret that choice.

As he approached Anto, he told Grimm, 'Go, sergeant. Command your squad, but keep this channel open should I need you.'

'My lord,' said Grimm. He turned from Alvez, and crossed to greet his squad brothers where they sheltered behind the concrete corner of a processing mill that was being peppered by ork stubber-fire.

Anto saluted Alvez. 'It is good to see you, lord.'

'Status report, Faradis.'

'The transport was large and very full. A great deal of damage was done to the manufactorum, but the superstructure remains intact. There are orks are holed up inside. We estimate their number to be between sixty and eighty. Others are using the wreckage of their craft as cover. Still more are moving through the streets, killing all they find. They have attempted to flank us on this side of the district twice, but we have turned them back both times. If we are to dislodge them, we will need to storm their positions with a full frontal assault.'

Here, Anto paused, before adding, 'It could be costly, my lord. The orks taking cover in the wreckage and the manufactorum have significant firepower. Scouts from Squad Bariax are acting as our forward eyes. They have reported signs of las and plasma analogues, and a number of xenos weapon types. The orks are highly alert, too. Sergeant Bariax and his men attempted to infiltrate the manufactorum eleven minutes ago. It was hoped he and his squad might be able to eliminate the warboss and throw the entrenched forces into confusion. I'm afraid it did not work, my lord.'

'Losses?' asked Alvez.

'Two Scouts, good men I'm told.'

Not good enough, thought Alvez. We can't afford to lose anyone, not if we are all that is left of the Chapter.

He still hadn't made Deguerro's dark revelation common knowledge, partly because he hoped it could still prove to be false, partly because there had been no time.

'Do we have schematics for the area?' he asked. 'We need an access plan.'

There was a tremendous pounding from behind them, like a god hammering on a vast door, and Alvez and Anto turned to look for the source. They could hardly have missed it. There before them stood a gargantuan figure, his every angular surface etched with the deeds and glories of his past. On the right side of his massive armoured carapace, he bore the Chapter icon set within the stone cross of a Crux Terminatus, a symbol permitted only to those who had earned their place in the Crusade Company. Between his piston-like legs, a white tabard rippled in the breeze, decorated with an aquila embroidered in gold thread. And on his left leg, he wore a sculpted arc of silver laurels leaves surrounding a golden skull, yet another of the great honours he had gained throughout his six centuries as a member of the Crimson Fists.

He was a Dreadnought. His name was Brother Jerian, and, when he spoke, his modulated voice was so deep, like the bellow of a massive bull brachiodont, that the air around him trembled. 'You need no access plans, honoured captain.'

He raised his left arm into the air and spun his monstrous metal power fist through three hundred and sixty degrees.

'Where you require a doorway, I shall make one.'

Now, he raised his right arm, and the air filled with a mechanical whine as he cycled the clustered barrels of his auto-cannon.

'Where you require death, I shall dispense it.'

Alvez looked up at the ancient warrior. Inside the walking metal sarcophagus, there was a battle-brother much like himself. Or rather, he had been once. Jerian had been a hero of the Chapter before Alvez had known life. But the hero had fallen in the Battle for Emerald Sands, his body eaten away almost to nothing by the concentrated bio-acids of the despicable tyranid race. It was a slow, painful death, no death for a Space Marine. The Apothecaries had saved what they could of him, and the Techmarines had interred him in this venerable and ancient apparatus. If death ever tried to claim him again, it would find him a hard target. Alvez was sure of that.

Every brother in the Chapter knew the tales of Jerian's victories and heroics. Clearly, the Dreadnought sought to add to that list now.

Alvez walked towards the boxy metal giant, stopping five metres in front of him and fixing his eyes on the rectangular vision slit cut high on the hulking frame.

'Very well, Brother Jerian,' he said. 'You will provide our heavy support. We will push in directly and slaughter the foe where they stand. Obey my orders. This will unfold as I command it. No other way.'

Alvez felt wrong addressing such a legendary figure in this manner, but he had to be sure that all, even Jerian, recognised his authority here as absolute.

If Pedro Kantor *is* gone, he told himself, the future of the Chapter is in my hands.

The thought was sour. It gave him no pride.

'You understand, Old One?' he said to the Dreadnought. 'We will do this my way.'

'We may do this any way you please,' rumbled Jerian, 'so long as I get to kill orks.'

SEVEN

The Western Foothills, Hellblade Mountains

KANTOR AND HIS Fists emerged from Yanna Gorge onto a shallow slope that wound its way between the last of the foothills. The Eastern Steppes spread out before them, bright and glaring in the midday sunlight. To the west, smoke from a thousand fires rose into the air. The roiling black pillars were so large, the Astartes could see them from a hundred kilometres away, rising just beyond the curve of the horizon. They did now know if the smoke represented crashed ork craft or burning townships. Kantor hoped it was the former.

As he ordered his Astartes to continue north-west across the steppes, he heard explosions behind him. He turned, but his view was blocked by the bent backs of the hills. He hoped the explosion was not the death rattle of a Lightning fighter.

To the east, back the way they had come, the Hell-blades rose up like a wall of jagged tusks, their sharp peaks bone white, their roots and ridges almost black. He had known these mountains almost all his life. Why did he feel that he was saying goodbye to them? Arx Tyrannus was gone, but the mountains would endure. He couldn't explain the feeling.

Cortez's squad had moved up, a kilometre ahead, to take its turn as the party's forward eyes. Sergeant Segala and his squad had fallen back to march beside Kantor, but the men kept a respectful distance. They did not want to bother their Chapter Master, perhaps recognising the burden he now bore.

They knew he would call them to him when and if he needed them.

There was a sudden scream of rocket engines as one of the Lightnings streaked by barely a hundred metres above Kantor's head. Sixteen pairs of visored eyes whipped up to follow it. A heavy-looking ork fighter roared past just a second later, spewing a hail of lead and las-fire from a bristle of forward guns. Kantor saw the Lightning dance from right to left, trying to shake its pursuer, but the ork was stuck to its tail. The Lightning pilot tried to swerve left, following the gradient of the land downwards, but the ork must have anticipated the move. The Lightning turned directly into a stream of shells that ripped its metal body apart.

It hit the ground north of Cortez's position.

The ork fighter peeled off. In the heat of battle, its pilot failed to notice the line of Space Marines on the ground below, or so Kantor hoped.

'Pedro,' said Cortez over the comm-link. He didn't need to say anymore.

'Go, Alessio,' said the Chapter Master. 'The rest of us will follow.'

THE LAND WAS strewn with shining pieces of metal. The Lightning had cut a great furrow in the ground and had come to rest with its nose half-buried.

Cortez crouched by the body of the pilot and read the name tag under the winged skull patch on his chest.

'Keanos,' he said. 'That's your name? I am Captain Cortez of the Crimson Fists. If you can hear me, Keanos, speak your first name.'

The wounded man stirred. His flight-suit was soaked with blood. The smell of it was thick on the air, mixing with the acrid stink of burnt metal. 'Galen,' he said at last. 'My name is… Galen… K-Keanos.'

Cortez lifted a canteen to the man's lips. 'Can you drink, Galen Keanos? It is water.'

Keanos managed a sip, but a second started him coughing, and the coughing was agony to him, so Cortez removed the canteen, stoppered it, and stowed it on his belt.

Heavy footsteps crunched the dirt and rock behind him, and he knew instinctively that the Chapter Master was there. Without turning, Cortez said, 'He is in a bad way, Pedro. He will not last long. Let me give him final mercy.'

Kantor lowered into a crouch beside the Rynnite pilot and gestured for Cortez to move back a little. 'We must have information first.'

'His name is Galen Keanos,' said Cortez.

'Galen,' said the Chapter Master with a nod. Then he turned his eyes to the dying man and said, 'Galen, can you hear me?'

Keanos looked up in the direction of the voice, but his eyes were unfocussed.

'I am Pedro Kantor, Lord Hellblade, Chapter Master of the Crimson Fists.'

'My… my lord,' gasped Keanos. He struggled, as if trying to rise.

'No, Galen,' said Kantor, placing his right hand gently on Keanos's shoulder. 'Lie back. You must not move. Your pain will end soon, but if you honour me, and if you honour the Emperor, you must bear it a little longer. We need information.'

'I will try to… answer, lord.'

'Did you fly from Scar Lake?'

'Yes. My… my squadron was sent to investigate a light in the mountains. We thought it was over Arx Tyrannus, but long-range comms were down. The orks hit our… our vox-masts in the first wave. We needed help, but there was no way to… My wife and child… were evacuated south. Oric. My Oric.'

'He's fading,' said Cortez.

'There will be a medical pack in the cockpit, Alessio. Get it quickly.'

Cortez shook his head. 'I checked after I pulled him out. It was shredded. The whole cockpit was shot to pieces.'

'Galen,' said Kantor, 'Is Scar Lake still operational? Is it still resisting?'

Keanos coughed, and blood flecked the corners of his mouth. 'The… orks attacked the perimeter but… we… we turned them back twice. Then General Mazius was… killed.'

'What about the cities? What word from the capital? From Caltara, or Sagarro?'

They waited for Keanos's answer, but the man's face was slack now. His eyes no longer blinked.

'He is gone,' said Cortez. 'Scar Lake must have fallen by now.'

'Almost certainly,' said Kantor, still looking down at the dead man. 'Nothing Snagrod has done so far seems to be random. It's almost… systematic.'

'We can't know that yet,' protested Cortez.

Kantor locked eyes with him. 'No, Alessio? The deep-space relay station strikes, the concentrated assaults on our surface communications arrays, the immediate targeting of military installations. This one isn't waging war like an ork. He is fighting like the Imperium. This Snagrod has learned from *us*.'

Cortez narrowed his eyes, unsure whether to believe that or not. Long experience had taught him that what the orks boasted in strength, they more than lacked in brains. Their low intelligence was what really kept them in check, not the forces arrayed against them. Smart orks – the kind of smart that Kantor was suggesting – were a foe of a different order altogether, a foe that perhaps no one could hope to stop.

'We must push on,' said the Chapter Master. 'That ork pilot missed us the first time, but it might not miss us on another pass. There will be a scavenger party on its way to salvage scrap from the kill.' Anticipating his friend's next words, he added, 'No, Alessio. We will not wait to ambush them.'

The Chapter Master turned and began to walk away, calling for the battle-brothers guarding the perimeter of the downed Lightning to fall in behind him. He was five metres from Cortez when he half-turned and said over his shoulder, 'You may rig the wreckage with some of our melta charges, brother. I'm sure the orks will appreciate the surprise.'

That, at least, made Cortez grin. Minutes later, it was done. He and his squad hurried to rejoin the rest of the group, taking their place now as rearguard.

They marched hard. The land underfoot changed, becoming greener by degrees until, hours later, they found themselves crossing lush grassy plains. They had descended thousands of metres since leaving the ruin of their home. So much closer to sea level, the land seemed to be enjoying a different season altogether from the wintry heights of the mountains. The air was warmer, its pressure and humidity higher.

As the sibling suns began to set in the west, casting everything in hues of red and gold, there came a great boom that echoed off the mountains and out over the plains.

Looking back the way he had come, Cortez squinted, and made out a column of smoke rising from the final resting place of Galen Keanos.

He resumed his march, wondering how many stinking xenos he had just killed and swearing to himself that he was just getting started.

EIGHT

Zona 6 Industria, New Rynn City

BROTHER JERIAN WAS death incarnate, and there was little the orks could do against the fury of his weapons. Not at first. The roving ork units that had attempted to flank the Crimson Fists position made a third attempt just minutes after Jerian had shown up behind the barricade, and they soon found themselves faced with an enemy utterly invulnerable to their stubbers and bladed weapons. Jerian did not need cover. He *was* cover. He stomped out in full view of the roaring alien filth and began cycling his assault cannon.

When he fired, the torrent of shells was so intense, so destructive, that it cut the orks in half. Even the greenskins at the very back of the charging mass could not avoid the hail of sharp-nosed slugs as they punched through body after body until the street was awash with blood and steaming viscera.

Jerian let out a battle cry that resonated over the whole south-eastern quarter, audible even above the distant boom of Basilisk SPGs and Earthshaker batteries. Few alien battle cries could have matched it.

As the sound faded, Alvez suspected some of the orks nearby would be turning to flee. The larger greenskins were not typically fearful of anything, but they were highly superstitious, wary of the unknown, and they were not above breaking from a fight in the face of obvious defeat. It was the clearest sign of intelligence they typically showed.

'To me!' Jerian roared as he thundered down the street in the direction of the manufactorum and the crashed ork lander. Strong-smelling smoke wafted from the barrels of his assault cannon. The massive hydraulic pistons that powered his legs hissed and clanked as he moved, and oily black smoke poured from two large exhaust stacks on his broad metal back.

'Squads Rectris and Gualan,' said Alvez over the comm-link, 'move up behind Brother Jerian. Cover his blind spots. Squads Grimm and Ulias flank left. Squads Anto and Haleos, you have the right flank. Move!'

Alvez marched with Maurillo Rectris and his squad. Greenskins rushed out from corners to intercept them, but they were cut down the moment they showed their ugly flat faces. Within minutes, Jerian had led the others close to the manufactorum, and a hail of stubber and pistol-fire began pouring out of shattered black windows high in the building's side wall.

RYNN'S WORLD BATTLE MAPS

ZCALAN BELT

THE HELLBLADE
MOUNTAINS
Ref. 932/MNT

Ref. 223

Ref. 462

ARX
TYRANNUS

Ref. 543

Ref. 445

THE EASTERN STEPPES

Ref. 082/00N

THE GREAT SCARP

SOROCCO
❖ MAP KEY ❖

Light forest		Roads
Thick forest		Vox-masts
Rock and Scrub		Agri-settlements, Urban and Industrial
Grassy plains		Bridge
Grassland		Ruins
Marshland		Rynnsguard Outpost
Rivers and Sea		Hills and Mountains
Weapon Batteries		Railway

Ref. 87635/UnderoT/24356

LAN

Ref. 435

Ref. 342

SCAR LAKE
AIRBASE (PDF)

9.624

9.265

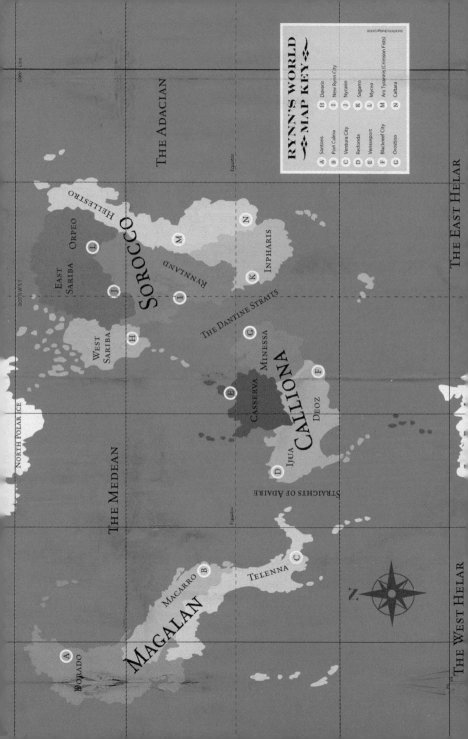

The Crimson Fists did not hesitate. They raised their bolters, took aim, and loosed a deadly torrent of rounds at the windows. Jerian added his own fire, the raw destructive power of it quickly making the well-aimed bursts of his battle-brothers superfluous. The manufactorum's upper walls were being ripped apart. A rain of brass shell casings fell around his sturdy metal feet.

The orks pulled back from the windows rather than face such a lethal fusillade.

'Jerian,' called Alvez, but the Dreadnought either didn't hear him, or didn't wish to.

'Brother Jerian,' Alvez barked again, this time with more force. 'Cease fire, now. Move up. Secure the north wall. We will blow our way in.'

Jerian stopped firing, and his assault cannon cycled down with a whine that sounded almost disappointed. He lurched forward as ordered. Squads Rectris and Gualan moved up quickly to take position along the north wall of the building. On the other side, the south side, the spiked hull of the ork transport still lay half-buried in tumbled brick, pouring trails of thick black smoke into the air.

Alvez opened a link to Huron Grimm. 'Are you in position, sergeant?'

'We are, my lord,' replied Grimm. 'We encountered some resistance on the south access, but we have cover with a clear view of the downed ship. Significant enemy activity to the north-west and west of us.'

'Hold for further orders,' Alvez commanded. Then, he opened a link to Sergeant Anto. 'Report your status, brother.'

'Both squads in position, my lord, awaiting your command to attack. There is no breach here, but there are four large loading bays through which we are observing the orks. They are Deathskulls.'

Alvez thought about this. The Deathskull clan were notorious looters and took their obsession with scavenging machines to murderous levels. 'If they are Deathskulls,' he told Anto, 'all the better. Their attentions will be split between us and the machines inside. As soon as Rectris and Gualan breach the north wall, I want all flanking squads to give suppressing fire. Confirm.'

'Affirmative, lord. We await the signal.'

Closing the comm-link, Alvez turned to Maurillo Rectris, who stood on his left, backpack pressed tight to the manufactorum's brick wall. 'Have your men plant the charges, sergeant. Twenty seconds should be enough.'

'My lord,' said Rectris. He stepped out from the wall, called two members of his squad to him, and began issuing orders of his own.

Just a few metres away from Alvez, Brother Jerian growled. 'You should let me rip the wall open, captain.' He flexed his power fist restlessly.

'I need a good clean breach, brother,' said Alvez. 'It must be wide and instantaneous. I'm sure you could rip this entire place apart single-handed, given time, but I would prefer you focussed on smashing orks, not walls. Just be ready to go in. You will be the first.'

Jerian stopped flexing his fist. 'In that, at least, you show great wisdom.'

Alvez did not miss the barb in the comment. He felt a flash of anger, just briefly, but it soon subsided. The Chapter's Old Ones, as the Dreadnoughts were collectively known, were widely understood to be a gruff, cantankerous lot. One did not try to change a personality forged in battle over six hundred years. Not unless one enjoyed courting failure. Besides, Jerian and his machine-entombed fellows had, by their long history of heroic endeavour, earned a level of tolerance Alvez accorded few others.

There was a hiss of static on the comm-link, followed by the voice of Sergeant Salvador Ulias. 'Lord captain,' he said. 'We have orks moving around the perimeter of the building. They are heading your way. Twenty of them with heavy-stubbers and blades. They'll be on you soon. Permission to engage?'

'Rectris?' said Alvez.

'Ten seconds. Setting the last of the charges now.'

Judging by the report from Ulias, ten seconds was too long. Alvez raised his storm-bolter.

'All squads, fire at will!'

'For Dorn and the Emperor,' replied Anto over the comm.

The sharp crack and rattle of gunfire erupted on the other three sides of the structure, immediately answered from inside by the deep drumbeat of ork heavy weaponry.

'Charges set,' Rectris announced. 'Back away!'

Squads Rectris and Gualan pressed themselves flat against the wall. Brother Jerian merely took two steps backwards and waited for the blast. Watching him,

Alvez noted how fearless he was. Any normal Space Marine would have risked serious injury, perhaps even death, standing so close to so much high explosive. Not so Jerian.

There was a deep, ear-splitting bang and a gush of dust and stone. Jerian was obscured from Alvez's vision, but the captain could hear the rain of stone chips bouncing off the Dreadnought's armour plate.

'Forward,' Jerian boomed. 'We are their death!'

The dust cloud swirled and Alvez knew that Jerian had charged inside. He heard the distinctive whine of an assault cannon as it strafed the interior.

'Kill them all,' Alvez roared over the comm-link before he, too, charged through the gaping wound in the brick surface. His battle-brothers followed him in without hesitation.

Inside the manufactorum, the orks retaliated at once, pouring fire down on the Space Marines from raised gantries of metal mesh, or from behind the conveyors of the huge automated assembly lines. Gretchin skittered from shadow to shadow, terrified for their lives, turning to fire their large-bore pistols only when they found the safety of good cover. Their oversized kin fought without any such fear. Scores of them charged madly forward, their chainaxes whirring, only to be blown apart by mass-reactive explosive rounds from the boltguns of the Crimson Fists.

Brother Jerian ran out of ammunition soon after entering, but it did not slow him. He stormed forward, smashing idle machinery aside in his eagerness to spill the blood of the Chapter's foes. Then he was right in among them, an awesome sight to behold. With every whistling arc of his mighty metal fist, he smashed ork bodies aside. Moving deeper into the mass of aliens that flowed out of the shadows to surround him, his heavy feet pulped and crunched the bodies of the fallen.

Alvez heard the Dreadnought's mechanical laughter, and the sound was as far from human as it could possibly be.

Three orks dropped from an upper walkway right in front of Alvez, no more than three metres from him, close enough to lash out at once. But Alvez was fast, even in Terminator armour. His finger squeezed the trigger of his ancient gun, and the largest of the three orks reeled backwards, struck directly in the forehead before it could take its opening swing. The bolt detonated, blowing brain and skull outwards in all directions, and the creature collapsed to the floor as limp as a sack of meat.

The others did not wait to meet the same fate. The closest of the two lunged with a large, chipped blade, more cleaver than sword or knife. The blow struck Alvez's storm-bolter aside, but did not knock it from his grip. The creature raised its other weapon, a spiked club of solid iron, and brought it down with blinding speed, but the blow bounced from Alvez's ceramite-plated shoulder with a clang.

'Die,' spat the captain. The power sword in his left hand was a glowing blur. It crackled and hummed as it slid through the beast's belly, cutting the ork in two.

Each half slapped wetly to the floor as Alvez turned to face the third of his attackers. But there *was* no third. Sergeant Gualan had gunned the creature down, firing into its back at point-blank range. Its chest cavity lay open to the air, blown out by a triple burst of explosive bolt rounds. Gualan, like the rest of his squad, was already moving on to other prey.

'Huron,' said Alvez over the link, 'report status.'

'Thirty-eight targets confirmed dead on the south side, my lord,' said Grimm. 'The orks taking refuge in the crashed ship are severely depleted. Suggest squads Grimm and Ulias move in and finish the job.'

Alvez could hear bolter fire over the link as the sergeant spoke, but it sounded sporadic, as if foes were getting harder to come by.

'Do it,' Alvez ordered. Then, switching channels, he said, 'Faradis, status.'

Sergeant Anto's report was likewise given against a background of lessening gunfire. He, too, reported a significant reduction in live targets in his sector and, like Grimm, requested permission to move in. It came as no surprise. What true Crimson Fist could stand to hold back when there were orks in close proximity? There would be little sport for either Grimm or Anto. The fight inside the manufactorum was well in hand, due in no small part to the unstoppable fury of Brother Jerian.

'Request denied, Faradis,' said Alvez, making a quick assessment. 'I need you and Haleos to hold the outer perimeter. There may yet be ork cells in this district. Squads Grimm and Ulias are purging the ork wreck.

Rectris and Gualan have the facility under control. This is over. I am coming outside.'

And that was what he did. He handed command of the mop-up operation to Maurillo Rectris, then emerged back into the last of the fading daylight.

In the sky above, ork ships were still painting dirty black trails across the darkening blue. Pillars of dense smoke rose hundreds of metres into the air. He could see them towering above the city walls like vast ghosts slowly clawing their way towards the heavens. He did not know if they represented dead orks or dead men, but death, certainly.

He caught sight of Sergeant Anto and his squad sweeping a row of ore silos to the east and began striding towards him. He was about to hail him over the comm-link when the ground under his feet trembled. He heard the sound of a great explosion out beyond the districts defensive walls. Anto looked up at the same time. An insistent voice sounded in his ear, overriding all other channels on the emergency band. 'This is Squad Thanator to Captain Alvez,' said the voice. 'I repeat, this is Squad Thanator to Captain Alvez. Please respond.'

'Alvez, here. What is it, sergeant?'

'My lord,' said Sergeant Thanator, 'another ork ship just struck the city. The damage is severe.'

'Where?' Alvez demanded. 'Can we contain them?'

'There will be no containing this one, my lord,' said Thanator, and Alvez could tell by the sergeant's tone that this was more than just another crash. 'They just took out an entire section of the Pavelis Wall!'

Dorn's blood, cursed Alvez.

'I need to know which section, sergeant.'

'Zona 4 Commercia, section two, my lord. They're pouring in like locusts. We need reinforcements. The sheer number of them…'

'How many Astartes did we lose?' he demanded.

'None, lord. Our forces were massed around the gate itself. The breach is a kilometre west of it. But the Rynnsguard losses… I can only guess they number in the high hundreds. There are over a million citizens in this district, my lord. We are doing everything we can, but we are few. This place is a charnel pit!'

Alvez had already begun striding in the direction of the industrial zone's eastern gate. 'Hold fast, Thanator,' he commanded. 'You will have your reinforcements. I swear it. I'm sending Predators and Vindicators to your position.'

Alvez's strides became longer, faster. His footfalls shook the buildings and the streetlamps as he passed. He called to Squad Anto as he went, and they joined him, marching with bolters ready.

A dark thought had taken hold of him and it wouldn't let go.

It was deliberate! It had to be. The orks had started using their ships as battering rams. What in Terra's holy name had the Rynnsguard anti-air crews been doing?

Had he and his Fists held Zona 6 Industria, only to lose Zona 4 Commercia?

If the orks kept this up – and he knew they would –
just how long would New Rynn City survive?

NINE

The Eastern Steppes, Hellestro Province

FEW NORMAL MEN ever realised just how much information was all around them. The air they breathed was filled with it, but their noses were not attuned to it in the way a canid's was, or the olfactory senses of a million other kinds of creature.

Space Marines knew. Within their bodies, each of Kantor's survivors carried an organ called the neuroglottis, or *The Devourer*, grown from the gene-seed of their fellow Astartes and implanted during the painful process that forever physically separated them from their fellow men. The primary function of the neuroglottis was to allow instant analysis of a substance by taste. Toxins could be easily detected. Organic compounds could be tested for nutritional content. And a single scent molecule on a breeze could give away a hidden foe or tell the direction in which it had travelled.

Cortez and his squad were once again on point, ranging a kilometre ahead of the rest of the group.

The captain breathed, and smelled death on the wind.

Night had fallen three hours ago, and the Chapter Master had ordered everyone to increase their pace. He hoped to cross as much distance in the dark as possible. Too slow and the daylight would find his party in the open with the sun glaring off their armour and weapons. Ork aircrews would be able to spot them from as far as the horizon.

They had to make the most of the darkness. Kantor was guiding them north-west to the place where the Eastern Steppes ended and the Azcalan, the Soroccan continent's massive rainforest, began.

Once the Crimson Fists were in the cover of the trees, night and day would become irrelevant. They would move without rest, and make the capital that much sooner. Right now, all Cortez could think about was the familiar smell he had detected.

Every breath he took spoke to him of spilled blood, of wet viscera exposed to the air. There were other scents, too. One of the strongest was dung, neither human, nor ork.

Cattle, he thought. Kine. That's what I'm smelling.

The planet's closest moon, Dantienne, was high and almost full. Her surface rock contained cobalt, and the dim light she threw down on the plains was distinctly blue. To Cortez and the rest of the Fists, everything had a greenish tinge. Their helmet visors were set to low-light mode, further brightening the gloom.

As he marched his squad onwards, Cortez now noticed large dark objects slumped on the grassy plains. They were shapeless black things. As he and his battle-brothers drew closer to them, the smell became stronger and stronger.

Cortez opened a link to the Chapter Master.

'Orks have been here, and recently.'

'They killed all the kine,' replied Kantor, pre-empting Cortez's next words. 'I can smell the blood.'

Cortez trod over to the nearest of the bodies. Danti-enne's light glistened on the piles of looping wet entrails that had spilled from a wound in its stomach.

Why didn't they take the meat, he wondered?

If there was one thing orks were not, it was wasteful. Everything was scavenged. But not here.

Then he saw deep furrows in the dirt and had his answer.

'War bikes,' he told the Chapter Master over the link. 'I have tyre tracks here. Ork riders did this.'

'Right,' said Kantor. 'They wouldn't stop to strip the carcasses. They must have ridden through here slaughtering everything in sight, leaving the bodies for a follow up party to process.'

Cortez found other tracks now. 'It looks like they rode off in the same direction we're moving.'

He tested the air again with his nose. There were definite traces of the ork stink on the breeze from the north-east. It was an acrid smell. Even the foulest of unwashed, disease-ridden human beggars couldn't hope to smell so offensive as the xenos. Cortez detected other scents, too. One was definitely promethium. Liquid fuel. He could tell it wasn't from a local source. There was more carbon that the refined fuels the Imperium used.

The breeze changed direction then, coming to him not from the north-west, but from the north, where a gradual rise blocked his view of the land ahead.

What he smelled on it stopped him in his tracks.

'Human blood,' he told Kantor over the comm-link. 'Fresh. It's coming from the side of a ridge just north of my position.'

'There is only one small settlement in the area. The Zar-Menenda agri-commune. Can you hear anything?'

Cortez strained his ears but the night was quiet. If there were sounds, the rise was blocking them. 'I need to cross the ridge.'

'Do it,' said Kantor. 'Reconnaissance protocols, brother. Understand? Keep me apprised. The rest of us will catch up to you once you have established an observation point.'

'Understood,' replied Cortez. 'Moving out.'

FIELD OPERATIONS WITH an entirely new squad were never ideal. Cortez tried not to think about the fine brothers he had lost. Was it really only weeks ago that he had looked across the nave of the Reclusiam and felt his chest swell with pride? Was Silesi really dead? Would he truly never hear Iamad's sharp laughter again? He was the last survivor of 4th Company. Why was he always the last? It had been the same at Kalaphax and again and Gamma VI Monserrat, whole squads lost, and always

Alessio Cortez returned from the battlefield alone, wounded and weary, but inexplicably alive.

Now Kantor had assigned him four new faces, new to Cortez anyway. He had seen them before, of course. They were not new in that sense. In a brotherhood of approximately one thousand warriors, there were few real strangers, and though the brothers of each company mostly kept to their own, a certain amount of cross-company interaction was inevitable and actively encouraged.

Two members of Cortez's new squad – Brothers Rapala and Benizar – had belonged to Caldimus Ortiz's 7th Company, though they had served in different squads. Cortez remembered both of them from a winter combat exercise he and Ortiz had run about twelve years ago in the mountains north of Arx Tyrannus. Rapala and Benizar had performed solidly. Their scores had been unremarkable, but they were reliable with good skills across the board.

The other two battle-brothers assigned to Cortez's command were less well known to him. One was Brother Fenestra, a quiet, thin-faced Blackwaterite from Selig Torres's 5th Company. He had cold, dark eyes that never seemed to blink. Cortez had the feeling Fenestra didn't like him much, though they had never really crossed paths before the cataclysm. It hardly mattered. He didn't need people to like him, just to do as he said when he said it, and to show the right initiative when forced to act alone.

The last of the four was also the youngest. Brother Delgahn had served with the Chapter just eighteen years, only graduating from 10th Company to 8th Company a decade ago. Like Fenestra, he seemed wary of Cortez, never speaking unless spoken to, holding back on the periphery unless called forward.

'Stay low,' Cortez told them over the comm-link as he led them up the rise. He didn't need to whisper for the sake of stealth. His helmet's external vox-amp was switched off, and, without it, no sound leaked from beneath his ceramite faceplate, but his voice was clear and sharp on the link.

It was hard to stay low in full battle-plate, almost as hard as it was to stay quiet. Even in a well oiled and treated suit of armour, ceramite plates often rasped or clanged against each other. There was the constant low buzz of the atomic power-supply, too. After spending centuries in power armour, one tended to block it out, but it was always there, always present, and it could give you away if you forgot about it entirely.

Within seconds, Cortez and his squad made the top of the rise and peered over. The night-time land-scape stretched out before them, a broad patchwork of fields and pastures. In daylight, each would have been a different shade of green or yellow depending on the crops and grasses that grew there. Right now, viewed through the Astartes' helmet visors, they were all varying shades of muddy green. Wire fences and stone walls separated each, and, from the west and the north-east, two wide dirt roads snaked towards a cluster of buildings some eight hundred metres away.

This was the Zar-Menenda farming commune and, in the middle of it, hidden from Cortez's direct view by a row of large metal grain silos, a huge fire burned, throwing its telltale orange glow on the shell-pocked walls.

There had been fighting here, or perhaps not fighting, but slaughter. What kind of resistance could the farmers and their families have offered the brutish bloodthirsty invaders who had massacred all their cattle?

The greenskin stink was sharper and stronger now. So was the scent of human blood. Listening hard, Cortez began to catch sounds of activity from the commune, too.

His primary heart quickened.

They're still here, he told himself with a grin. Automatically, his fingers tightened on the grip of his bolt pistol.

THERE WERE THIRTY of them, thick-set and green, none weighing less than two hundred kilogrammes. Cortez cursed under his helm. On one hand, he was glad they hadn't posted any sentries. It had made the final approach to the agri-commune all too easy. On the other hand, their arrogance rankled. Were they so complacent because they believed they had already won this war?

He would teach them the folly of that assumption soon enough.

His squad hung back, cloaked in the shadows between two vast octagonal grain silos. The light from the massive fire the orks had lit didn't reach all the way back here. It was as good an observation point as any.

Peering out from those shadows, Cortez scanned the scene in front of him. On the very far side of the flames, a row of ugly vehicles, barely recognisable as bikes and buggies, sat with their engines switched off. Each was painted red. He could see that by the light of the fire. Each was lightly armour-plated and fitted with forward-pointing heavy-stubbers. From the front armour, cruel metal spikes and blades protruded.

Cortez had seen such machines in action before, other conflicts, other worlds. He knew how much ork bikers revelled in running down their prey, shearing them to pieces by ramming them head on. Despite their appearance, the ork machines could move fast. Their hit-and-run tactics made them hard to counter with just infantry. It was imperative that these orks did not get back on their bikes before he had a chance to put them down.

Of the civilian workers who had occupied the farm, there was little sign. Cortez zoomed in on a black shape in the fire, and scowled. It was clearly a human foot. How many living souls had these orks already burned to death?

There was a scream, and Cortez turned his eyes left. It seemed the orks were not quite done with having fun yet.

The sound had come from the throat of a woman, perhaps thirty years old, lying in the dirt. She was sur-rounded by children, five of them, of varying ages, and she was hugging them to her hard. 'Don't look, my babies! Don't look!' she cried at them.

Now Cortez saw why. From the other side of the fire, a man emerged into view, walking backwards towards the woman and her children, his arms shaking as he tried to wield an ork blade that was obviously far too heavy for him. Reflected firelight shone on the tear tracks that marked his cheeks.

He was obviously retreating from something, and that something now appeared.

It was the ork boss, a towering, yellow-tusked giant in a long sleeveless coat fashioned from some kind of thick, scaly reptoid skin. On the beast's head there was a helmet boasting two straight horns, each over a metre in length. From its nose hung a gold ring, and from the belt at its waist hung four human skulls, seemingly tiny in contrast to its tree-thick legs.

The ork boss moved slowly forward following the terrified man around the fire. It was unarmed, but that hardly mattered. Even though the farmer bore a blade, he was outmatched in every way. This was a game to the orks, a sickening cruel game with only one possible outcome.

The other orks sat in the dirt hooting and howling with bestial laughter, watching their boss torment the last of the humans. They, like their boss, had rings through their noses. Their waistcoats were made of the same kind of reptoid skin as their bosses. It hadn't come from any creature on Rynn's World. Cortez was sure of that.

The woman was screaming directly at the man now. 'Just run, Aldren,' she begged. 'Just leave us and run!'

If the man, Aldren, heard her, he showed no sign of it. His wide, unblinking eyes were locked on those of the monster as it closed the gap with him. He lifted the blade as high as he could, grunting with the effort. The ork boss stopped for a second and watched him, red eyes gleaming with cold, cruel amusement. Then it stepped forward.

Aldren lunged and brought the ork blade down as hard and as fast as he could, but it was a pathetically inadequate stroke. The ork boss batted the blade aside, and it flew from Aldren's hands.

'We're going in,' Cortez told his squad. 'Weapons ready.'

'I thought we were on reconnaissance protocols only, my lord,' said Brother Fenestra uncertainly.

'We were. Now I'm putting you on combat protocols. Lock out all other comm channels except this one and encrypt it with an alpha-three key. The only voice you need to hear is mine until I tell you otherwise.'

He sensed their hesitation. They knew what he was doing. By locking out communication from the Chapter Master, Cortez was denying Pedro Kantor the chance to issue orders, orders that would most certainly have him falling back without dispensing the kind of righteous vengeance his soul demanded. Unreachable over the link, Cortez could thus avoidance any charges of direct disobedience. It was a strategy he had used before, and not just a few times.

'Did you hear me?' he snapped at his squad. 'I said alpha-three. Do it now.'

His Astartes did as they were told. He had known they would. He was still Alessio Cortez after all. Despite everything that had happened, his legend still loomed large over the Chapter. Sometimes, his fame and reputation were useful after all.

When each of his Astartes confirmed the comms lock, he told them what he wanted them to do, and, in pairs, they moved off. Benizar and Delgahn went left. Rapala and Fenestra went right.

There was little Cortez could do until they were in position. It wouldn't take them long. The commune was small, and the deep shadows thrown out by the fire hitting the buildings and silos offered superb cover.

Cortez turned his attention back to the fate of Aldren, the woman and her children.

The ork boss had reached out its right hand, gripped Aldren by the head, and lifted him into the air. With the man dangling, his arms flailing uselessly at the ork's arm, his legs kicking and flailing, the ork boss turned towards the fire and began walking, a deep, throaty chuckle emerging from its throat as it did so.

The woman's screams took on fresh urgency now. 'Throne, no!' she wailed. 'Aldren!'

To her children, she yelled, 'Close your eyes, my babies. Close your eyes and don't listen!'

Cortez tightened his grip on his boltpistol. The fingers of his power fist flexed and clenched hard. They could have crushed steel. 'Damn it,' he muttered. 'Hurry up.'

But he knew his Space Marines would not be in place in time to save Aldren, and, if he moved prematurely, he would jeopardise the first part of his plan. There was nothing he could do.

The ork boss reached the edge of the blaze now and bellowed something to its fellows. Cortez scowled at the sound of the ork language. It was as ugly as the beasts were themselves. Whatever the creature said, a fresh round of hooting and laughing began, which seemed to satisfy the ork boss. It stretched out its arm and held Aldren out over the fire.

Yellow flames licked his legs greedily.

The air filled with the skin-crawling sound of agonised, high-pitched screams.

'Where are you?' Cortez demanded of his Fists, speaking through gritted teeth. 'Why aren't you in position?'

It was Brother Benizar that replied. 'We're at the vehicles my lord. We're cutting their fuel lines now.'

'Work faster,' Cortez snapped back.

The flesh of Aldren's legs was blistering. He kicked and screamed for all he was worth, but he was helpless against the strength of the ork boss. Soon, the flesh had turned black, and the flames crept higher, moving towards his torso.

The orks were still enjoying the show. The woman had turned away. She was holding the heads of her children down so they couldn't watch the final, tortuous moments of their father's life.

'Done,' reported Benizar over the link. 'The bikes aren't going anywhere.'

'Get into firing positions, now!' Cortez barked. 'It's time.'

So saying, he stepped out from the shadow of the silos and into full view of the enemy. He raised his bolt pistol, knocked the safety off, and braced it on the back of his power fist, almost as if he were about to take a competition shot in some tournament.

He lined his sights up on the ork boss, zeroing in on its oversized skull. The orks still hadn't noticed him. They were too wrapped up in the torment of the human.

Cortez took a deep breath. With a single thought, he activated the vox-amp set into his helmet. His voice boomed like thunder, drowning out the last of Aldren's screams.

'You! Xenos scum!'

There was a moment when none of the orks moved, then, as one, thirty hideous, red-eyed faces turned to regard him.

Cortez fired a single shot.

It caught the ork boss in the throat and exploded, popping his helmeted head clean off his shoulders with a spray of blood so thick it was almost black.

The creature dropped Aldren straight into the flames. It didn't matter. Aldren was already dead. The pain had killed him before the flames had climbed above his waist.

The headless body of the boss fell to the ground like a dead tree. The moment it crashed on the dirt, the other orks leapt to their feet and swept up their weapons. Cortez angled his pistol's muzzle left towards the orks closest to the woman and her children. He put three rounds in three more snarling xenos faces. More bodies crashed to the ground.

'Space Marines!' he roared. 'Engage!'

Bolter-fire sounded from multiple directions at once. Brother Delgahn lit the river of fuel that leaked from the ork bikes and buggies, and a wall of fire leapt into the air, penning the orks in just where Cortez wanted them. He would not let a single one survive this night.

Kantor would have heard the gunfire the moment it begun. He would have seen the blaze. If he was trying to raise Cortez on the comm-link, then he already knew the captain had locked him out. There would be hell to pay later, but Cortez could live with that. Right now, all he cared about was blood and fury.

Ork dead carpeted the ground. Hate had been served.

'Take your helmet off, Alessio,' said Kantor. His tone was as hard as iron and as cold as the polar seas.

He and Cortez stood off to the side, by the east wall of one of the agri-commune's raumas meat processing blocks. Dead xenos lay around them. The other Crimson Fists went among the bodies, attending to the grisly business of ensuring that none of their fallen foes were merely wounded. The quickest way to guarantee the xenos wouldn't rise to fight again was to crush their skulls under an armoured boot, but ork skulls were incredibly dense. Even for an Astartes in full plate, it often took a number of impacts to properly shatter the thick bone and pulp the pinkish grey tissue beneath.

Cortez lifted his right hand to the clasps and cables at his neck and did as his lord commanded. He pulled his helmet up over his head and placed it in the crook of his left arm.

Kantor's eyes burned into him.

'We spoke of this once,' said Kantor. 'After the judgement was passed on Janus Kennon, we spoke of this.'

Cortez nodded. 'And I was honest with you then. You know me better than anyone. Did you really expect me to quell my rage until we reached the capital?'

'I expected you to honour the ways of the Chapter, *captain*. I expected you to honour me. If not as your Chapter Master, then as your friend and brother.'

'Of course I–'

'Quiet, damn you! You will hear me out. I cannot have you taking liberties like this. We both know how many battle-brothers look to you for their example. Would you have them disrespect my command as you have done tonight? I am your lord and leader. You think our losses at Arx Tyrannus change anything? They change *nothing*. The Chapter is mine to lead. You are mine to command. You, me, all of us... we will live or die by the decisions *I* make, and, in Dorn's name, you will abide by them, Alessio. Remember your place. Be the Space Marine I need you to be, or so help me, things will change forever between us.'

Cortez did not want that. He had always thought their friendship a constant in an uncertain universe.

How many times had each saved the other's life? How many times during those first two centuries of service had they stood back-to-back, protecting each other as foes assailed them from all sides? Cortez missed those simpler days. Part of him envied his lower ranking battle-brothers. Command was a great honour, but it was a burden, too, and it had changed things between them. He and Kantor were no longer equals. In fact, they hadn't been equals for more than a century, but Cortez had never felt the gap as keenly as he did now. Naturally, he felt no remorse for the killing of the greenskins, but now he would pay the price for the satisfaction of cutting them down.

'Tonight, I put vengeance before my duty to you,' he said. 'I have angered you, and for that, I am sorry, brother. I will accept whatever punishment you deem fit. But I do not regret the killing of the xenos. I stand by my actions.' He gestured at the nearest of the meaty green corpses. 'This filth had to die. The souls of our fallen demanded it.'

Kantor glared back in silence for a moment, then said, 'The demands of the living outweigh the demands of the dead. You led four of my Crimson Fists into a battle we could have avoided. I'm initiating the Ceres Protocol. There are not enough of us left to risk losing any more in satisfying your damned rage. You will accept a penance from the Chaplains at the capital once all this is over. Perhaps they will help you understand your error, since it seems I cannot.'

He turned away from Cortez.

The other Fists, having satisfied themselves that all the orks were dead, now began carrying the heavy alien bodies to the fire where they threw them into the crackling flames. It was standard practice to burn greenskin bodies after combat, and it had to be done quickly. Orks multiplied by shedding spores. Within hours, the air would be filled with them, tiny cellular capsules dispersing on the breeze. Most would not find suitable ground, but a percentage would land in dark, damp places and take root. Fungal protrusions would sprout from the ground, and below, a new life, born to hack a bloody path across the galaxy, would begin to take form.

Slumped against the white plaster wall of one of the farm's hab-blocks, the woman and her five children huddled together, still weeping, still unable to break free of the terror that had gripped them, unsure of what would happen next. They did not watch the burning of the foe. They had seen more than enough of burning bodies tonight.

'Daybreak is but three hours away,' said Kantor. 'I had hoped to be much closer to the Azcalan by now. Tell the others we leave as soon as the last of the bodies is on the fire.'

With this, he left Cortez and strode towards the woman and her children.

Cortez watched him go.

WITH THE ORK dead now crisping on the blaze, there was only one more matter to attend.

'The woman's name,' reported broad-faced Brother Galica as the Chapter Master stopped beside him, 'is Jilenne.'

'Jilenne,' Kantor repeated with a nod. 'Thank you, brother. Make ready to leave.'

Galica saluted, turned and strode off towards his squad who were running quick armour and weapons checks in preparation for moving out. Kantor looked down at the cowering civilians. They were huddled together in a knot. Galica had given the woman a canteen of water and she was trying to coax her still-shaking children into taking small sips.

How wretched they looked. No child should see what they had seen. No Rynnite civilian was supposed to endure this. It was the responsibility of the Crimson Fists to protect mankind. How did this woman judge him? He had failed in that task. Her husband had been burned alive not five metres in front of her. The man's own children had heard his screams. It seemed impossible to Kantor that any of this, any of it at all, was really happening. War had come to his world despite everything, despite the fact that his very presence should have prevented it. How much had his own decisions precipitated this?

The woman looked so small and fragile, and yet she held her arms round her children as if she might somehow spare them further horrors by her own meagre power. She did not look up at him, but whether that was out of fear or respect, he could only guess. Was she as terrified of the Astartes as she was of the orks?

He had removed his battle helm before speaking with Cortez, and had left it off deliberately so as to make the woman feel more at ease while they spoke, but he wasn't sure now that it would make any difference. With a conscious effort to soften his voice, he said to her, 'Have you or your children suffered any wounds?'

The question sounded foolish to him the moment he said it. Of course they were wounded, though perhaps not physically. In their eyes, the universe had changed forever. No night would ever again bring peaceful, restful sleep. Vision of green horrors would torment every last one of them until the day they died. The Imperial records spoke for themselves. Many who encountered alien races went mad, no longer able to believe there was any safe place in a galaxy that tolerated such abominations. Others committed suicide rather than face the grim truth.

'We will be leaving you soon,' he told her. 'My Astartes and I have far to go. Is there anything you need before we depart?'

The woman murmured to her children, and slowly, reluctantly, they untangled their arms from around her.

Kantor watched.

When her children had drawn back, the woman crawled forward on her knees and, sobbing quietly, pressed her forehead to Kantor's right boot.

'You saved us, lord. By the Golden Throne, by the God-Emperor's light, you saved us. I beg you, in the name of Holy Terra, don't abandon us now. The beasts will come back, won't they?'

I did not save you, thought Kantor. Alessio did.

She was right about the orks. More would come. Many more. It was as inevitable as the sunrise. The ork bikers often rode at the head of a much larger contingent. When that contingent arrived, there would be no saviours a second time. The woman and her little ones would provide a brief moment of entertainment before they were butchered like the livestock they had once depended on.

But if we take responsibility for these people, Kantor thought bitterly, where does it end? Are we to save every other man, woman and child we happen across? They will slow us down when our greatest need is to move quickly.

He grappled with the most human part of himself, fighting to lock it away behind walls of resolve. He needed to crush these feelings of pity. They would do him no good now.

The Chapter must endure, he told himself, repeating it like a mantra. The Chapter must endure. Nothing else comes close. Good intentions will undo us. They will lead to our destruction. If that happens, we might as well have died with the others when the missile hit.

It was hard to do, but he stepped back and pulled his boot from under the woman's head. Only now did she look up at him, and her large brown eyes, wet with tears, sought his.

'Please, lord!' she cried out. 'What hope do we have alone?'

What hope, indeed, thought Kantor. I could say the same for my brothers and I. What hope do sixteen have against a Waaagh?

He turned from her and called out to his men to make ready for their departure, then he marched towards the fire where his three squads had finished their checks. The sound of her weeping followed him, clawing at his resolve.

He heard his inner voice say, 'Turn from those who need you, and you will lose everything that defines you.'

Master Visidar had spoken those words to him just a decade before his death.

Kantor cursed, knowing them for truth.

When he was ten metres from Jilenne, he turned and looked over his shoulder. He felt himself speak to her, heard the words in his ears as if they were someone else's. They seemed to pass from his lips automatically.

'I will not stop you from trying to follow us,' he told her. 'But you will not be able to keep up. Not for long. While you can, however, no greenskin will take you, nor any of your children.'

He turned his eyes forward again, adding, 'This is the best I can do for you.'

To Jilenne, it was enough. The timbre of her sobs changed from sorrow and fear to gratitude.

Kantor heard her urge her children to stand and follow as she fell into step behind him. He continued towards the fire, not slowing his pace, but not increasing it, either.

All the same, as he and his Crimson Fists left the farming settlement with their gaggle of refugees in tow, Kantor couldn't escape a feeling of deep foreboding. He had crossed a line. The woman would soon realise he had given her false hope. She and her children would tire quickly and the Astartes would begin to pull ahead until they disappeared from view altogether.

What would she think of her saviours then?

And what would he think of himself?

THE SKY TURNED from blue to purple to red in the east. The Hellblade Mountains looked like black saw-teeth against the backdrop of the lambent dawn. Small puffs of pink cloud scudded overhead on a light westerly wind, but the season was changing and the clouds would be boiled off by mid-morning.

The Azcalan rainforest had been but a dark smear on the far north-western horizon when Cortez and the rest of the survivors from the fortress-monastery had set off on their journey towards the capital. Now they were closing on its south-eastern edge. The land was far greener here. There were crowns-of-gold and snap-thistles everywhere, and spiny cyclacore trees stood in groups of twos and threes, already starting to turn their blood-red plates towards the glow of the new day.

Cortez led the rearguard, following five hundred metres behind Kantor and Squad Segala, eyes alert for any sign of pursuit. Throughout the night, flaming streaks had continued to cut across the sky, a clear sign that the orks were still landing more of their number with impunity. It seemed there was nothing left to stop them. The global defence batteries were either spent or overcome. There was no further sign of Rynnsguard aircraft. Even if Scar Lake had been overtaken, surely there should have been something from the spaceport at the capital... unless that too had been overcome.

The thought of it chilled Cortez. If New Rynn Spaceport was lost, the orks would be landing forces directly on the outskirts of the capital without challenge. He couldn't imagine Drigo Alvez allowing that, but, if the spaceport was still in friendly hands, where in blazes was their air support? Where were the reconnaissance flights? Surely Alvez would have sent someone to discover why he had lost all communication with Arx Tyrannus?

Brother Fenestra's voice broke over the link. 'They are flagging badly, captain. We should abandon them now.'

Cortez turned and looked back the way he had come. Tired figures staggered after him. The woman and her children were falling further and further behind.

Damn it, Pedro, he thought. You should have left them at the farm.

But he could hardly absolve himself. It was his actions that had denied them a quicker death in the first place. Perhaps Pedro had been mistaken in giving the woman permission to follow, but it was he, Cortez, who had drawn out her suffering in the first place. Might it not have been more merciful to let the ork warboss kill her before he had intervened? She could have followed her husband into the Emperor's light. It would have spared her the torment she was going through now.

He watched her for a moment, stumbling on weak legs while she desperately tried to carry her two youngest ones. The other three, between the ages of nine and thirteen, traipsed along in a line abreast of her, heads bowed with exhaustion, eyes fixed on the ground. None of them spoke. They had no energy for that. In the hours they had tried to keep up with the Crimson Fists, they had been forced to run for short periods to make up ground, and still they fell behind bit by bit.

Cortez was sure the woman would collapse soon. The children she carried were small, but even a small weight took its toll on a long hard march. It was a pity. He found that he respected her a great deal. Her arms and shoulders must have been burning with lactic acid, not to mention her legs and the muscles of her lower back. But she kept putting one step out in front of the other.

Then, just as he was about to turn around, he saw her left leg crumple under her and she went down, turning to protect her little ones from impact with the ground even as she fell. It looked like her foot had snagged in a clump of grass. Her other children shuffled to her side and crouched there, urging her to stand.

Fenestra had seen it, too. 'It is over, then,' he said. 'About time. We can move at speed.'

Cortez opened a link to the Chapter Master. 'Pedro, it's me. The woman has fallen. I don't think she'll be getting up. I just wanted to let you know.'

There was a moment before Kantor replied. 'She fought hard to hang on. Impressive that she lasted as long as she did, is it not?'

'It is,' said Cortez after a beat. 'But it ends here. Her burden is too great to continue.' Again he paused. 'I… I should not have saved her, Pedro. I merely postponed the inevitable and prolonged her torment. Perhaps I should…'

'…grant her the final mercy?' said Kantor, finishing Cortez's sentence for him.

'Yes.'

There was such a long pause this time that Cortez started to think the Chapter Master had cleared the link. Then, finally, Kantor said, 'Hold position and wait for me, but tell the rest of your men to keep moving towards the tree line. I want our squads in cover before the suns are visible.'

Cortez was unsure what his old friend was up to, but he said, 'As you wish,' and, a second later, cleared the link. He relayed the Chapter Master's orders to his men, and they pushed ahead, Fenestra striding away faster than the others. He watched them for a moment until they disappeared down a shallow decline. Close to where they vanished, the tall figure of Pedro Kantor appeared, walking back towards him.

Even though Kantor's armour was scratched, chipped, dented and burned black in places, he still looked like a figure of legend, still everything a Chapter Master should be. His golden halo shone in the growing light.

When he was three metres from Cortez, he stopped and looked east. 'The suns will be up very soon, Alessio. We should have been in the cover of the forest by now. We run great risk of being spotted from the air.'

Cortez nodded. He knew the habits of the orks, knew they seldom flew at night. Their eyesight was poor compared to their sense of smell, and darkness brought a kind of malaise down on them without which they might have butchered each other in the dark, so violent were their tendencies. They only ever launched night attacks by the light of flaming torches or searchlights, which was doubly fortuitous because such lights made convenient markers for Imperial artillery fire. As soon as the suns were up, the sky would fill with noisy, ugly flying machines. Kantor was right. They had to get to the cover of the forest within the next ten minutes.

'Come,' said the Chapter Master, and he strode in the direction of the children where they hovered over their mother's unmoving form.

The children heard the two massive Space Marines approaching, and, with fear apparent on their faces, took a few nervous steps back, conflicted between feelings of concern for their mother and concern for their own lives. Cortez saw them eyeing his weapons, especially his power fist. He wondered what they were thinking. Did they really believe he would crush them with it? In a universe as cruel as this, perhaps they did.

Come to think of it, what exactly were Pedro's intentions? Did he plan to put the entire brood out of its misery?

Kantor crouched at the woman's side and removed his helmet.

Cortez tried to read his face, but it betrayed no emotion.

'Jilenne,' said the Chapter Master. 'Can you hear me?'

The woman's eyes were closed, but her lips parted. Weakly, quietly, she said, 'They were so heavy. So heavy…'

Kantor nodded. 'Yes,' he said, 'but you did well to bring them this far.'

Reaching out, he lifted the two smallest children away from her and gestured to the older children to take them. They did so, and Kantor turned back to the woman.

The Emperor's mercy, thought Cortez. You should not have to do this, Pedro. It is my fault. It is my soul that should bear the stain.

Before he could communicate this, Kantor spoke.

'It is time,' he said, and he reached down to the woman with his gauntleted hands. 'Time that someone carried you now.'

As Cortez watched, the Chapter Master lifted the woman and stood to his full height, cradling her exhausted form in his arms. She looked so small and fragile against his sculpted ceramite chest, little more than a rag-doll.

Then the Chapter Master turned to Cortez and said over the link, 'Once we are among the trees, they will have a better chance. They are charges of the Chapter now, and we cannot abandon them.'

Carrying the woman as if she weighed nothing at all, Kantor began striding for the distant tree line. Over the link, he added, 'Help the children, Alessio. Help them get to cover quickly. The suns will be up within moments.'

Cortez looked down at the children. Their clothes were torn and stained with the dirt of their night-time trek, but, in eyes of the three eldest at least, he could see a fierce spark and recognised it as the will to live.

Very well, he thought.

His own childhood had been brutal, a daily struggle to survive in the swamps and marshes of Blackwater, where even the smallest creature represented a deadly threat, and children often killed other children over matters of hunting territory and material possessions. These children were not like him. They had been raised as farmers, not killers. At least they were healthy from working the land. They would not need to be carried. They would make the tree line in time if they moved off now.

'Do not be afraid,' he said as he stepped forward, bent, and scooped up the two smallest children. 'Your mother will be fine, but we must hurry and follow her. You must be hungry, all of you. There will be fruit in the forest, and water. You can eat as much as you can find, but only if you keep pace with me. Is that clear?'

The oldest, a boy of thirteen, stammered a little and couldn't bring himself to look up at the hard, emotionless mask of Cortez's helmet, but he managed to say, 'We can rest and eat there, in the forest?'

'You can,' said Cortez and he turned in the direction of the tree line. 'But, as I said, you must keep up.'

He began walking at a fair clip. The two small children he carried were both crying loudly, a particularly grating sound.

Behind him, he heard the others panting hard as they jogged to keep up as well as they could. The trees loomed closer and closer, and reached out cool shadowy arms to gather them in, embracing them just as the larger of Rynn's World's two suns poked its head above the knife-like peaks of the Hellblades.

A new day had begun, and, all across the continent, the savage hordes were stirring.

TEN

Zona Regis, New Rynn City

'EGGS ARGALATTO,' SAID a petite servant, 'sliced marsh-melon, and pickled valphid hearts.' She placed three dishes on the table. With a bow, she retreated from the balcony, moved back into the shadows of the main chamber and stayed there, out of sight but close enough to swiftly answer any requests her ladyship or her two guests might make.

Shivara, the governor's bodyguard, stood there, too.

The suns were up, and the air on the balcony was warming quickly. The sounds of heavy artillery from the city perimeter had started an hour ago, shocking and unwelcome at first, but so constant, so unrelenting, that they quickly became background noise.

No screams or battle cries could be heard at this distance. Maia was thankful for that. Despite the booming of the guns, she smiled across the table at her breakfast guests, Viscount Isopho and General Mir, and gestured at the food. 'Please, enjoy.'

Isopho smiled back, but Mir glanced at his food without expression.

'I'm sure it's divine, my lady,' he said without much conviction. Perhaps it was too rich for his tastes, Maia thought. He picked up his fork, but he didn't take a mouthful until Maia herself had done so. Among the Rynnite upper classes, no man ate before a lady seated at the same table took her first bite.

Maia lifted a small forkful of the eggs and swallowed, breaking the spell. The others began to eat.

'I asked you to join me, gentlemen,' she said, 'because there is much to discuss, and I would do it here where the constant interruptions of the Upper Rynnhouse will not bother us. I want you to speak frankly about our situation.'

'What do you wish to know, lady?' said Mir, lifting a goblet of chilled water. 'The essentials were already covered in yesterday's final session.'

'True,' said Maia, 'but you've had a night to reassess. I'd like to hear your current thoughts.'

'It is as the Astartes said it would be,' said Mir. 'The greenskin assaults eased off during the hours of darkness. Captain Alvez had our artillery targeting enemy light sources close to the walls. We dim our own lights, naturally. Without a visible target, the orks are unfocussed and have nothing to attack. If last night was anything to go by, our forces will have ample time for re-arming and recovery before each dawn. That will be crucial if we're to hold long enough for aid to arrive. And we *will* hold, but there is no room for complacency. The Space Marine Scouts maintain a constant vigil, no matter the hour. Our own Scouts do likewise, though at shorter range. I've heard that a subset of the greenskin horde utilise night-vision equipment and stealth tactics, but they are a tiny minority. If they seek to infiltrate the city, we will respond with lethal force.'

Maia nodded. 'Then it is the hours of daylight we must worry about. Has our anti-air defence been strengthened in accordance with the captain's decree?'

'To the best of our ability, yes,' said Mir, gulping down a mouthful of valphid heart before continuing. 'Our Hydras and missile batteries have been repositioned to counter the greatest areas of threat, but it leaves certain other sections of the wall at risk, mostly to the east, west and north-west. Of course, the Shield Range offers us a measure of cover on the latter. The mountains are relatively free of the foe.'

'Surely we can't afford any weak points at all?' said Isopho.

Mir turned to him. 'I'm afraid our tactical choices are rather limited, viscount. We face greatest pressure from the south and south-east. Most of the ork ships in this region landed there. Given the size of the capital, our defence has to be somewhat reactive. The Crimson Fists have organised their Land Speeders, bikes and transports into rapid response units. I've done the same with our Sentinels and Chimeras. They will move to hold any gaps the orks try to exploit. Together with our infantry and artillery regiments, the main bulk of the Space Marine force will hold the walls and gates where we face the most continuous pressure. We shall do everything we can to maintain the territory we have. I only wish we'd had time to organise a trenchworks on the outskirts of the city before the xenos landed. We might have held far more ground that way than we did.'

Maia raised her goblet in Mir's direction. 'You did exceptionally well under the circumstances, general. But it's imperative we lose no more ground. Bishop Galenda visited me personally after yesterday's session to demand extra protection for the Zona Sanctum and the churches in the other districts.'

'He shouldn't be bringing that to you, my lady,' said Isopho with a scowl.

Mir nodded. 'If the bishop wishes to discuss the defence of the Great Basilica, send him my way.'

Maia looked out from the balcony across the city. *Her* city. In the distance, where the fighting was, columns of smoke stood like dark towers against the sky.

'He plans to petition the Astartes,' she said. 'But I doubt he will find Captain Alvez a willing ear.'

Isopho and Mir shared a look. 'The Crimson Fists are not as people think them to be,' said Isopho. 'Our protectors are as cold and hard as the armour they wear. I sometimes wonder if there is a human being inside at all.'

'They are not human,' said Maia, returning her eyes to her plate and spearing another slice of marsh-melon.

'They are something greater, and it makes them distant, yes, but we should love them all the more for that. Perhaps loss of humanity is the price of such strength.'

There was an unmistakeable sadness in her tone.

Isopho shifted in his seat as if suddenly uncomfortable. He had heard the rumours about the statue in Maia's room. He had heard whispers of her infatuation with the Chapter Master. He had hoped it was just talk, but now he felt certain it was more than that.

'I doubt we will ever understand them,' Maia continued, somewhat wistfully, 'but I know I'm glad they're here.'

General Mir voiced his agreement. As they ate, the fighting continued all along the defensive line. Out there on the walls, men and Astartes alike fought and died to hold back the xenos hordes.

It was still early, but already many had begun to pray for night to return.

ELEVEN

The Azcalan Rainforest, Rynnland Province

'SOMETHING IS WRONG here, lord,' said Sergeant Viejo to the Chapter Master.

Upon reaching the forest, the Crimson Fists had pushed inwards a few hundred metres and spread out, establishing a small perimeter, making sure that no surprises lurked in the dense shadows under the thickly clustered trees.

Now they stood in a circle, weapons held ready, eyes outward, their light-boosting visors helping to pierce the shade beneath the dense canopy.

The forest was deathly quiet, as if there were no animals of any kind. With winter over, the thin shafts of light that penetrated the canopy and dappled the forest floor should have been alive with clouds of needlewings and scallopbacks, the predators that feasted on them, and all the other forms of life that flourished here.

But there were none.

No ornithids cried out from the treetops. No brachiodonts brayed from the banks of the River Rynn that cut through the forest deeps. No kynids growled and spat from their burrow entrances among the tangled roots and vines.

Kantor drew a deep lungful of the cool air and focussed his mind on processing the molecular messages within it. Some of the scents were his own: metal, ceramite, the hot ionised air which constantly vented from the exhaust ports of his back-mounted generator.

On his armour, Kantor also smelled traces of the skin and sweat of the woman, Jilenne, whom he had set down against the bole of a thick tree once it was clear that there was no immediate danger in the area. She was resting now, sleeping with her children after consuming some of the forest fruit that Brother Alcador had found for them.

The scent of vegetation dominated, of course. Kantor could smell the thick spongy bark of the trees, the leaves overhead, the weeds and shoots underfoot. The soil was rich with nutrients and minerals.

And there was something else, faint but familiar. He had last smelled it just three hours ago.

Ork.

The other Crimson Fists detected it at almost the exact same moment Kantor did, their fingers ready on triggers as they scanned the foliage for the source. Though their faces were covered by their helmets, Kantor could read the sudden tension in their moments easily enough.

'There is no breeze here,' said Sergeant Segala. 'Hard to track them by scent alone.'

Sergeant Viejo concurred. 'Difficult to pinpoint. There's no sign that they have passed this way. No footprints. No blade-marks on the trees.'

Orks would not have passed through here without hacking at the tree-trunks with their blades. Such mindless displays of aggression were as natural to them as breathing. Their tiny minds constantly drove them to express their violent natures.

'West,' said Cortez, removing his helmet to take a deeper draught of the air. 'I cannot be sure, but it seems slightly stronger from the west.'

'The Tecala River is that way,' said Kantor. 'So is the bridge we must cross.'

Brother Delgahn spoke up, the first time anyone had heard him do so since they had left the ruins of Arx Tyrannus behind.

'My lord, permit me the honour of reconnaissance. If there are orks west of here, I will find them.'

Now another of Cortez's squad added his voice. It was Brother Fenestra. 'Perhaps my lord will consent to send both of us.'

What is this, thought Kantor? Do they think I hold them responsible for the battle at the farm? I displayed no anger towards them. They were merely following Alessio.

Even so, Kantor decided he would send someone else. Let them think what they would of that.

'Denied,' he said flatly. 'Sergeant Viejo, pick two members of your squad. They will scout ahead. I want them to secure the bridge first, then move out from there. Have them report back to me within the hour. Captain Cortez, your squad has not rested since seeing combat. They will clean their armour and weapons, then enter a full sleep state for one hour. Sergeant Segala's squad will patrol our perimeter. That is all.'

'Teves, Galica,' barked Viejo. 'Forward eyes. The rest of you are on overwatch.'

The two battle-brothers chosen by the sergeant saluted Kantor, turned, and melted into the shadows to the west, moving a few metres apart, weapons held ready, fat muzzles sweeping left to right, each covering the angles outside the arc of the other.

Kantor watched them go, then turned and glanced at Jilenne and her children where they lay sleeping against the tree. Their muscles would be stiff and painful when they woke. That would not help their speed.

I have turned my peerless warriors into child minders, he thought bitterly. And the enemy is somewhere nearby, somewhere in this forest. Unburdened and unchallenged, we might have made the capital within three, maybe four, days. How long will it take us now?

Looking at the sleeping family, he felt a mix of emotions. Could he leave them here? It was the smart move, he knew, the right move. There was food in the forest. Water was abundant. They could make their own way to the capital by following the waters of the River Rynn. There was a chance they would survive, so long as the orks didn't stumble across them.

He remembered words spoken to him by High Chaplain Tomasi after the Battle of Braxa Gorge, frank words, but well-meaning, spoken with a rare half smile some two-hundred-and-forty-seven years ago.

'I applaud your unbending sense of honour, Pedro,' the High Chaplain had told him. Kantor had been a sergeant back then. He had risked his life and the lives of his squad brothers in holding the gorge open for a final convoy of refugee vehicles. Thousands had been saved. 'But sometimes honourable men must do dishonourable things. What is morally right must bow before what is tactically sound. I fear the standards you impose on yourself are impossibly high. Unless you give them up, they will be the death of you one day.'

Kantor was glad those words had come from the High Chaplain and not from the Chief Librarian. From Eustace Mendoza, he would have taken them as dark prophecy. From Tomasi, they were advice.

Advice I never learned to follow, he thought.

FROM THE TREE line, Kantor could now see what Galica and Teves had reported and then, at his request, had drawn in the dirt with their knives. There, about two hundred metres north-west of his position, was the crumpled hull of an ork transport. The craft had plunged from the sky, smashing a great hole in the forest, creating a clearing that was now filled with the greenskins that had survived the crash. The treetop canopy had been ripped wide open. The ruined ship lay belly up with the Rynnite suns blazing down on it. Smashed tree trunks lay at all angles on the ground. Some had been hacked up to fuel the fires that dotted the clearing. It was around these fires that knots of big, powerful orks sat gorging themselves on hunks of roasted meat.

Kantor sniffed the air. At least the meat was not human. He tracked its scent north and found its source, the corpse of a bull brachiodont, its pale body ripped open, thick sections of muscle cut away, its wounds black with clouds of feasting flies.

Despite measuring over twelve metres in length, the creature hadn't stood a chance against armed orks. Neither had the people stuffed into crude cages on the south-western edge of the camp. These were no Rynnsguard soldiers. Judging by the colour of their stained and torn attire, they were simple pilgrims. Most likely they had been on the road to Ivestra's Shrine in the north-east when they had run into the ork invaders. Now they huddled together in the tight confines of their cages, whimpering and soiling themselves, each praying he or she wouldn't be the next one picked.

What happened to those that *were* picked was all too clear. From the lower branches of nearby trees, lifeless bodies hung, their flesh covered in deep red gashes, their clothes reduced to blood-soaked tatters. These wounds were not the worst of it. Each of the dead had suffered a further, greater cruelty. Their faces had been entirely removed. Not messily, not brutally, but with chilling surgical precision. The dead swayed and turned in the occasional light breeze, their rictus grins taunting those that had yet to follow.

'All squads in position,' Captain Cortez reported over the link.

'Good,' said Kantor. 'We go on my command.'

He knew he couldn't avoid this. At first, he had wished for another way, but then he had seen the slave cages, and his mind had been made up.

Besides, he rationalised, there are close to a hundred orks here. We couldn't press on simply hoping they wouldn't give chase. They would have hit us from behind the moment they picked up our trail.

Still, he was anxious about pitting all the Astartes he had against so numerous a foe when ammunition and supplies were running dangerously low. His assault plan called for only the minimum expenditure of bolter rounds, but it would also put his Fists in close range with the orks, something he would have preferred to avoid given the choice.

He had hoped to identify the mob's leader, too, before launching the attack, but so far none of the orks in view seemed to be in charge. None were that much larger or darker than the others, and it was these two signs, above any other, that usually indicated which greenskin dominated.

Kantor's eyed flicked back to the twisted wreckage of the ork craft.

The leader must be inside, he thought, but the fighting will bring it out.

He keyed an open comm-channel and addressed the three squads at his disposal. 'Crimson Fists,' he told them. 'Give vent to your rage. Do me proud. Open fire!'

From the tree line all around the ork camp, the bark of bolter-fire sounded in short, sharp, tightly-controlled bursts. Each of the Crimson Fists had already picked his target and lined it up before the order was given. On Kantor's command, the first lives were taken. Explosive headshots sent a dozen carcasses slumping to the ground, blood pumping out in great fountains.

The other orks, seeing their kin slaughtered in front of them, swept their weapons up and cocked them. They had seen the muzzle flashes from the inky shadows beneath the trees. Now they swung their broad stubber muzzles around to open fire.

'Smoke!' Kantor commanded over the link.

Small metal canisters glinted in the Rynnite sunlight as they arced out from the trees and in towards the densest knots of orks. Some of the orks stared at them dumbly as they landed by their feet. Others opened fire at the trees with typically poor aim. The canisters began hissing and spewing out a thick, choking blanket of grey smoke that soon clogged the air over the entire clearing. It was impossible to see anything but the bright muzzle flashes of the ork guns as they fired madly at nothing.

'Switch to thermal sight,' said Kantor over the link, simultaneously sending the thought along the neuro-connectors that linked his brain to the systems of his armour. His helmet's vision mode flickered to the appropriate filter, showing him a noisy grey image with fat white silhouettes firing wildly in all direction. 'Move in!' he ordered.

It went exactly as he had planned. The orks could see nothing at all, and cut down a good many of their own number with torrents of lethal, undisciplined fire, while the Astartes pressed into to the smoke-filled clearing, killing as they went. Bestial roars of frustration and anger echoed back from the tree trunks on all sides, merging with the deep rattle of so many guns.

Kantor strode forward with Dorn's Arrow raised at shoulder height. Every bellowing xenos shape that loomed out of the smoke received two lethal storm-bolter rounds in the head. Huge bodies dropped to the forest floor, their weapons clattering on rocks and fallen trees. The greenskins were blind, and the Astartes were not, and it was more a massacre than a true fight.

Kantor lowered Dorn's Arrow and flicked on the energy field of his power fist, feeling its lethal aura prick the skin of his arm as it crackled to life. All over the clearing, his Astartes were doing the same in a bid to conserve rounds. Cortez, Viejo and Segala each bore power fists of their own, and they employed them to deadly effect now, punching and ripping at anything that came within range. The other Fists carried long combat blades with monomolecular edges and cruel serrations. These they wielded with the cold efficiency that many decades of daily practice had given them. They slashed and stabbed at the arteries and vital organs of enemies who still could not see them.

The cover of the smoke wouldn't last much longer. There was a slight breeze from the north-east and the veils of grey began to dissipate. How many of the orks had already fallen? Sixty? Seventy? Kantor didn't know.

The nature of the battle changed. The smoke no longer offered adequate cover. Kantor cycled his visor back to standard vision mode and saw a huge, battle-scarred beast surging straight towards him with iron axes in both meaty hands. The beast roared as it came, mad red eyes burning with bloodlust. Kantor felt his centuries-honed combat instincts take over, moving him into position without conscious thought. He slipped the ork's first whistling slash easily, stepped in, and caught the second on his left vambrace before it fell. For just an instant, he and the monster stood locked in that position, the creature's breath sour and hot and utterly foul, reaching Kantor's nose through the ducts in his faceplate. There were thick gobbets of brachiodont flesh lodged between the monster's teeth, rotting remnants of its last meal.

'Eat this instead,' growled Kantor.

He threw his weight behind a deadly right uppercut, and heard the energy field of his power fist crack like a bolt of lightning. The blow caught the ork in the sternum and blew the entire contents of its torso out a massive exit wound in its back. Red eyes rolled back in their sockets. Cored like an apple, the suddenly limp creature fell away from its killer, collapsing to the ground in a splash of wet gore.

Kantor stepped back and looked up. Close to the centre of the clearing, his battle-brothers were working together to exterminate the last of the ork fighters, cutting them down two- or three-to-one. Movement close to the jagged rent in the hull of the crashed ship caught Kantor's eye. One squad, he saw, was about to go inside.

He didn't have to check to know who was leading that squad.

'Alessio,' he said over the link.

The figure at the front of the squad turned for a moment. 'Let me do this,' said Cortez.

Kantor nodded. 'Go.'

The squad disappeared inside the downed ship, and the Chapter Master turned to survey the rest of the camp. Many of the ork fires had been kicked over in the fighting. A few still burned. Two of those snapped and popped as they consumed the flesh of orks that had fallen on top of them.

Kantor turned his eyes to the cages in which the captured pilgrims were huddled. Some of those closest to the bars, he saw, had been caught in the firefight, their bodies perforated by stray shells from the ork stubbers. He heard the sound of sobbed denials as those close to them hugged the bodies close, desperately pleading with their fallen kin or spouses to hold on to life despite their wounds.

Kantor walked over to the nearest of the cages. The people inside shrunk back in fear, despite the fact that he had saved them and they surely knew what he was.

'Stand back,' he told them, though he hardly needed to.

He reached forward with his power fist, grabbed a hold of the spiked and rusty iron bars, and ripped the cage open.

This done, he looked down at the people he and his Astartes had just saved.

'Exit the cage and gather in the centre of the clearing,' he boomed at them. 'I am Pedro Kantor, Lord Hellblade, Chapter Master of the Crimson Fists. Do as I say. You are safe now. I will free the others.'

THE CRASHED ORK craft was not all that large, but its corridors and chambers had been built to accommodate beings taller and broader than Alessio Cortez, and he and his squad moved easily along them, bolters up, clearing room after dimly lit room. Mostly, they found only gretchin working busily with wrenches and hammers on pieces of weird and inexplicable machinery. These they dispatched with knives or gauntleted hands, running them through or twisting their heads from their necks before they could scramble for shelter.

They found only a few full-grown orks. Most of the larger brutes had been outside when the assault took place. Those left within were strapped to gurneys, apparently recovering from some kind of bizarre surgery. It explained why they hadn't rushed out to join the battle. One of these had a second grotesque head grafted to its left shoulder, the crude stitching clearly visible even in the low light. It appeared to be unconscious. Cortez jammed his knife between its vertebrae, severing the critical nerves, making sure it

never woke up. Another of the orks, not quite unconscious but still groggy, had an extra pair of thick,
muscular arms grafted onto its hips. The appearance
of the Crimson Fists roused it, and it struggled against
its bonds to rise and engage them. Brother Benizar
stepped in and plunged his knife into its throat.
Brother Rapala joined him and, together, they cut the
beast to pieces.

Soon, the corridor they were following ended in a
broad archway through which bright light could be
seen. Cortez, out in front as usual, held up a hand,
and his squad halted. 'Listen,' he told them over the
link.

There was a strange sound coming from the well-lit
chamber up ahead. It was a sound that didn't belong
here, almost a human sound, but issuing from inhuman lips. There was something else, too – the sound
of muffled crying, as if someone was sobbing through
a gag. Cortez crept forward as quietly as possible and,
from the cover of the archway, peered into the chamber beyond.

Cables and pipes hung from overhead in great tan-
gles. The floor, which had been the ceiling before the
craft landed on its back, was littered with broken sections of pipe, metal plates, snapped stanchions and a
collection of instruments the purpose of which
Cortez couldn't begin to guess at. And there, in the
centre of all this, he saw a bizarre and terrible scene.

There was a single ork in the middle of the room,
and it was humming a tuneless melody to itself as it
sharpened a large scalpel on a whetstone. It wore a

long tunic which had perhaps once been white, but which was now so soaked and stained with blood that it wasn't easy to be sure anymore.

The beast looked like a twisted parody of an Imperial medicae. Perhaps it had seen members of the medicae on its travels through the galaxy and had realised that their attire symbolised their profession. Had it sought to emulate them? Perhaps it had simply picked the tunic up somewhere and had donned it arbitrarily. Whatever the reason, it was clear that this monster was responsible for the two-headed ork Cortez and his squad had found earlier, not to mention the other monstrosities.

It was also clear that this beast was responsible for the faceless human corpses that hung from the branches of the trees outside. Cortez could tell this immediately from looking at the ork's face. Where an Imperial medicae would have worn a surgical mask to do his work, this creature wore the facial flesh of its last victim. The effect was horrifying. The fleshy mask was still wet with the victim's blood.

The muffled whimper sounded again, and Cortez turned his eyes to the source. Strapped tight to a table in front of the strange ork surgeon, a human male of about twenty years old struggled against his restraints. His mouth was indeed gagged, but his eyes were wide as the ork turned, scalpel in hand, and approached him.

Cortez turned from the scene and handed his bolt pistol to the battle-brother behind him. It was Fenestra. 'Hold this,' he said. 'I won't be needing it for now.'

Fenestra took the pistol and looked back at Cortez. 'What are you going to do?'

Cortez moved out from the shadow of the archway and stepped into the chamber, letting the bright electric light show him in all his lethal glory.

The ork had been about to make its first incision in the trapped human's face. But, with Cortez making his presence known, it looked up from its work and gave a snarl of fury. It abandoned the scalpel for a nasty looking buzzsaw and moved around the operating table towards Cortez, its intentions clear.

Cortez dropped into a combat stance.

'I'm going to rip this filth limb from limb,' he told Fenestra.

And that was exactly what he did.

CORTEZ EMERGED FROM the hull of the ork transport and strode over to Kantor's side where he stood talking to the leader of the pilgrims they had rescued from the cages.

The haggard refugees looked up at Cortez in horror. Drenched as he was in the blood of his enemies, he looked like some kind of death god fresh from the pit, and he would have terrified almost anyone.

'The craft has been cleared,' he reported to the Chapter Master coolly.

Kantor glanced over at his old friend, noting the state of his armour, then merely nodded.

Brother Benizar brought the man Cortez had rescued from the operating table forward, and a woman rose from the ground and raced towards him to embrace him, calling his name between great sobs of relief.

The Space Marines ignored the joyful reunion, but the grateful woman insisted on throwing herself before Benizar and kissing the back of his right gauntlet. Fenestra and Rapala, who were just behind him, laughed out loud, and Benizar pulled his hand from the woman's grasp, saying, 'It is the captain you should thank, woman.'

He gestured at Cortez, and the woman turned eagerly to lavish her gratitude on the one who had saved her husband. But, when she saw the gore-splashed figure to which Benizar was referring, she balked and knelt where she was, muttering her thanks over and over, not daring to lift her eyes.

Cortez paid her no heed whatsoever.

'This,' said Kantor, addressing him, 'is Menaleos Dasat, the leader of this group.' The Chapter Master gestured to a skinny old man in stained brown robes. Despite all the man had clearly been through, there was something strong about his bearing, if not his body. 'Dasat was guiding them to the shrine of Saint Ivestra,' continued Kantor, 'following the old path on foot, when the orks ambushed them. Dasat, this is Captain Alessio Cortez, Master of the Charge, commander of the Crimson Fists Fourth Company.'

Dasat pressed his forehead to the ground, then sat back on his calves and said, 'I am unworthy even to kneel before you, my lord.'

Cortez gave only the briefest of nods by way of greeting, then turned his eyes back to Kantor. 'We should be away from here. There is still a long way to go.'

At that moment, Sergeant Viejo appeared from the clearing's eastern edge leading Jilenne with her children in tow. Prior to the assault on the camp, Kantor had ordered the woman to remain behind, sheltering beneath the roots of an ebonwood tree. He hadn't needed to tell her twice. She knew the moment she saw the Astartes readying their weapons that there were orks in the vicinity. She and her children had waited, scarcely daring to breath until someone came back to fetch them. Viejo carried the two smallest children in his arms.

The Chapter Master turned Dasat's attention towards them and said, 'This woman and her children were also rescued from the xenos. They are not pilgrims, but you will show them the depths of your kindness. They have suffered much as you have.'

Dasat bowed again. 'All the faithful are one under the Imperial creed,' he said. 'We will embrace them as if they were our own, my lord. To think that children so young...'

He let the words hang.

'How long will it take your people to get ready, Dasat?' Kantor asked. 'We can waste no time. Other ork parties may have heard the gunfire.'

The mention of this possibility seemed to put fresh energy into the tired looking refugees. 'We have nothing, lord,' said Dasat. 'We are ready to follow at your command. But we have not eaten since our capture, and the water they gave us was foul with their waste. We could not drink it. I'm afraid we are very weak.'

Kantor called Sergeant Segala over to his side.

'Sergeant, how long would it take you to find something these people could eat?'

Segala barely thought about it for an instant. 'There are fruiting trees nearby. Ground pears and aberloc.'

'Good,' said Kantor. 'Dasat, send some of your people with Sergeant Segala here. He will lead them to food. They must bring back enough for everyone, and extra for the journey ahead.'

To Segala he said, 'We can spare only minutes for this, sergeant. Make haste.'

Segala clashed a fist on his breastplate. 'By your command, lord.' Then he turned and began striding towards the edge of the clearing. Dasat called out several names, and figures hurried from the group to follow the massive Space Marine.

Jilenne and her children had joined the group now, and the female pilgrims were making a great fuss over them. Dasat smiled as he watched.

'I will leave you to become acquainted,' said Kantor, turning from the little man. He gestured for Cortez to walk with him.

Behind them, Dasat pressed his head to the ground again, then turned and rose to introduce himself to Jilenne.

'Did you see it?' Kantor asked Cortez. 'It is quite remarkable, yes?'

Cortez detected unexpected pain in the Chapter Master's voice. 'I'm sorry, Pedro,' he said. 'Did I see what?'

Kantor angled his head to look at him while they walked. 'The resemblance, Alessio. The resemblance. This man, this Dasat... he reminds me so much of Ramir that I had to look twice to be sure I wasn't seeing things.'

Now Cortez understood the pain in his old friend's voice.

'I'm sorry, brother,' he said, 'but I don't see it. The Ordinator was easily twice that man's size.' He paused. 'And Ramir Savales would have died fighting with his bare hands rather than let the orks take him alive.'

Kantor was taken aback at the anger he detected in that last sentence. He stopped and faced the captain.

'Do you detest them, Alessio?' he asked. 'Do you hate them because they cling to life so desperately?'

'I do not hate them,' said Cortez. 'But they are another burden on us now. I admit that the woman and the children were my doing, Pedro. I wish it were otherwise. But now we are shepherding almost thirty people, none of whom are even armed. Where will you draw the line?'

Kantor answered through lips drawn tight. 'There *was* a line, Alessio. Remember that. There was a line, and it was *you* who crossed it. Now we are responsible for these people, and you will protect them. You will honour the name Rogal Dorn, and you will honour me.'

As he turned and strode away from Cortez, he had one last thing to say.

'Get your squad ready, captain. You are on point.'

MENALEOS DASAT WAS awed and terrified at the same time, but he dared not show the latter for fear of insulting his saviours. All his life, he had preached the Imperial creed to any who would listen. He was no Ecclesiarch, just the son of a simple farmer, but his faith in the Emperor of Mankind was a powerful thing, and over the years he had drawn others about him, others who needed more in their lives, needed something to believe in, something to give their labours a grander purpose.

Dasat had grown up in a crop-harvesting settlement just north of Sagarro, on the provincial border between Inpharis and Rynnland. In his early years, he had often travelled to the towns and cities with his father. The trips were usually for the purpose of negotiating with buyers and exporters, but his father had always made time to give praise in the Imperial temples while they were there. In those days, it seemed that images and statuary of the Crimson Fists were everywhere, and the young Dasat had marvelled at them, finding it difficult to imagine what such beings would be like in life. Now he knew.

He had never imagined, not once in all his sixty-eight years, that he would speak to the Chapter Master, Lord Hellblade himself. He hoped he had covered the tremors he had felt on addressing that grim, austere giant. Perhaps the Chapter Master had taken it as the palsied shudders of old age, rather than fear.

Such a face that one had! So hard and angular. And those deep-set, hard and cold like a mountain winter.

Dasat was unused to fear. He had always lived secure in the knowledge that the Emperor had a plan, and all men were a part of it. He had believed his part was to live and die as a farmer who, in his spare evenings, took the good word wherever it might be received. When he had been approached by a group of the faithful who wanted him to lead a pilgrimage to Ivesta's Shrine, he had been flattered and had even seen the honour as his due in a way. The group looked up to him with such respect. No man could have walked away from that. It was the greatest feeling of his life... for a time.

Then the nightmare began. Beyond the treetops, the pilgrims had glimpsed snatches of the fires in the sky. They had heard the roar from the Hellblade Mountains, and had seen night turned to day by the flash in the east. The others had turned to Dasat for answers, their fear all too plain. But he had had no answers, so he told them they should continue. Had he been wrong? No. The pilgrimage had been a worthy endeavour. He could not have lived with himself to have come so far only to turn back for causes unknown. It was shortly after that, an hour before the party was due to strike camp, that the monsters had exploded from the forest, swarming on the group, butchering a score before anyone even realised what was going on.

Dasat had heard of orks, but his knowledge was limited to the content of the traditional cautionary tales his father had told him as a boy. Small children heard such tales and were afraid, and their parents would tell them, 'Pray to the Emperor every night, work hard in His name, and he will protect you.' As he had grown older, Dasat had made the mistake of taking such stories less seriously. No one he knew had ever seen a xenos of any kind. Without experience to contradict him, he had started to think man's dominion over the galaxy absolute.

Being thrown in a cage and forced to watch members of his flock endure hideous, sickening torture had quickly divested him of that misconception. And, if even Rynn's World was not safe, then surely nowhere was.

By a miracle alone, by the intervention of the Emperor, who had sent his warrior sons to deliver them from evil, Dasat and the rest of the party lived. But for how long?

He walked silently, deep in thought, and the other survivors followed behind him. They, too, were quiet, cowed by the figures up ahead who hacked and slashed their way through the dense forest without ever resting or talking. In fact, their silence unsettled Dasat. It seemed almost as if these blue giants communicated mind-to-mind, but more likely they were just using some kind of communication system installed in their helmets. They never took those helmets off. In fact, only the Chapter Master did so, and only when addressing Dasat and the rest of the pilgrims, as if it were important they see his human features. Then there was the woman, Jilenne, and her young. The Crimson Fists had rescued her from a farming commune somewhere to the south-east, or so she said. Dasat was pleased to see his flock fussing over her children. Even in the face of all they had seen, their humanity endured. His heart sank as he remembered the children who had set out from Vardua with his group. There had been nine of them. All had been trampled to death in the ork attack. At least they had been spared the horrors to which the survivors had been subjected. Surely they were with the Emperor now.

Glancing again at the broad backs of the Crimson Fists up ahead, Dasat wondered that they allowed he and his party to tag along at all. Surely they would make better time by abandoning their tired charges. He knew they were pushing for New Rynn City. At first he had thought his party would never be able to keep up. He had even considered suggesting to the Chapter Master that he leave them all behind, for surely nothing was more important than for the Crimson Fists to reach their goal and begin the task of repelling the invaders. But the idea of addressing the Chapter Master, or indeed any of these massive, stony warriors, filled him with cold dread. They were not like the murals or the statues. Those images had been warm, glorious things wrought by the hands of normal men.

These beings were living breathing myths come to life. They were angels of death, bred to kill. He could not begin to imagine what went on in their minds, though he suspected he knew what a few of them were thinking. The body language of two of them seemed downright hostile. Had they not been wearing helmets, Dasat could imagine them spitting on the ground in disgust whenever they looked at the helpless refugees. He made a special effort to keep his followers away from those two. He did not want to give them any excuse to express their impatience. One of them had been introduced by name, the famous Captain Cortez. He did not know the name of the other.

If Dasat had imagined his people would slow the Crimson Fists down, he was wrong. The Azcalan was managing that quite well enough and, in fact, by presenting such a troublesome obstacle to their progress west, it allowed the pilgrims to keep up. The Chapter Master hadn't explained himself, and Dasat didn't expect him to, but he steered his Space Marines away from the few beaten paths that led through the forest. These paths followed the course of the River Rynn for the most part, and Dasat wondered if the reason the Crimson Fists avoided them was because the orks might be making use of the river and the paths to move troops. It made sense.

As Dasat was thinking about this, Molbas Megra, a cattle-hand in his thirties and one of the most outspoken members of the group, hurried his pace until he was walking by Dasat's side.

'They are not as I had imagined them,' he said to Dasat in hushed tones. 'Most of the women are terrified of them, even though they saved us. They are so… different from us.'

You mean *you* are terrified, thought Dasat. And of course they are different. They are the Space Marines, the Emperor's sons.

Megra had always thought himself brave and strong, and had never been shy about telling others so, but he had wept openly when the aliens caged him. Dasat did not judge him too harshly for that. He had wept himself when the cage door had closed on them, believing a long, painful death was his imminent fate.

'There is a highway just south of here,' said Megra. 'It runs all the way to the capital. Why do they not lead us down on to the road? Surely it would be faster than this. Safer, too, I imagine. I don't think we should stay in the forest. Do you?'

Dasat resisted the urge to turn and scowl at Megra. 'You would have us all exposed to the invaders? Trust in our lords. They did not save us only to have us die on the journey toward sanctuary.'

Dasat could feel Megra's eyes on him, staring hard, a sharp retort forming on his lips. But the retort never came. From the thick greenery up ahead, a deep voice called back, 'Danger will find us sooner or later, farmhand. Pray only that we see it before it sees you.'

Now Dasat *did* turn to look at Megra, and saw that he had gone utterly pale. The voice from the trees ahead did not sound friendly. It was the voice of Captain Cortez.

'H-he heard me?' stammered Megra in disbelief.

Dasat scowled. Of course he heard you, he thought. Do the legends not tell of how their senses are far beyond our own?

No doubt they could see farther and with much greater acuity, too. What other feats were they capable of? Could they read minds after all? He had heard that some of them could. Did they realise, then, how afraid his people were, stumbling through the thick jungle in the wake of demigods dedicated to war? Megra was foolish enough to voice his thoughts, but none of the others were. They limited their sporadic talk to the comforting of Jilenne's children.

Perhaps time will remedy our fear, thought Dasat. As they say, familiarity with a thing removes the fear of it.

It was something he had read in an old book a long time ago and he had taken it as great wisdom back then. Now the lesson seemed pathetically naïve, utterly false.

After all, he was more familiar with greenskins now. And his fear of them had increased a hundredfold.

TWELVE

Zona 3 Commercia, New Rynn City

Captain Alvez stood on the upper gallery and looked down at the ground floor of the Menzilon arcade. The arcade was a massive structure, a great open space, the arched glass ceiling of which rose some fifty metres above the colourful mosaic of the marble floor. Before the arrival of the alien horde, it had been an enclosed market, a place where the burgeoning Rynnite middle-classes came to spend their time and spare centims. Now, it was an emergency refugee centre, serving as such since the outer districts had first been evacuated. The mosaic on the grand marble floor was bloodstained in places. Elsewhere, it was covered with dirty white sheets beneath which lay the wounded and the desperate. Not all those who sought shelter here had suffered injuries. Many simply had nowhere else to go. Their homes had been burned or blasted to rubble. Beside them, Alvez saw bags of possessions, usually not very large. These people had had only moments to grab what they could before the Rynnsguard herded them from the unprotected, unwalled outer settlements. Judging by their wretched attire, they probably hadn't owned all that much anyway. There were children among them. Those young enough to remain ignorant of the true threat chased each other around the thick stone pillars that supported the ceiling and the galleries.

Alvez could smell human blood, lots of it. His hyper-sharpened hearing could make out every moan, every plea for water, for food, for something to dull the pain. He heard women weeping, crying out the names of their lost sons and daughters. Men wept, too, calling out to the Emperor, asking what they had done to offend him, why he had removed his protection from his faithful servants.

Fools, thought Alvez. The Emperor helps those who help themselves. He has not forsaken anyone. He created Rogal Dorn, and the primarch created us. No ork will overcome us. Whatever the odds, the Crimson Fists will win out in the end, even if we are the only living things left standing on this planet. We will triumph, and we will reclaim this world.

He heard the sound of heavy footsteps to his right. An Astartes was ascending the marble stairway. As Alvez watched, the laurelled helmet of a sergeant came into view. Alvez knew the chips and scrapes on that helmet well enough to recognise its wearer, though there were a few new ones, it seemed.

'Huron,' he said. 'What kept you?'

'The greenskins, naturally, my lord,' said the sergeant. He stepped up onto the landing and crossed to Alvez's side.

'And your squad?'

'Awaiting us on the Verano wall to the north, as per your orders. The trucks have arrived to evacuate these people.'

'Good,' said Alvez.

Grimm looked down towards the lower floor, and said, 'A pitiful sight, this.'

'Indeed,' said Alvez. 'Look to the south-east corner where no lights are lit. From there, the worst of the stench emanates. That is the dying place, for those beyond help.'

Grimm nodded. 'Can the medicae do nothing for them?'

'Short of euthanising them,' said Alvez, 'no.'

'Then that is what they should do, and spare their attentions for those that can be saved.'

Alvez snorted. 'You know the medicae healers as well as I, Huron. Even when the obvious is right in front of them, they do not give up, not even on a single soul. Our Apothecaries are much the same.'

'I wish the Rynnsguard and the civilian militias were as stoic.'

Alvez frowned. 'The commissars will keep them in line. There were more executions this morning. Desertion rates will fall for another few days, though I doubt it will affect the suicide rate.'

'Their fear of the orks is so great that they take their own lives.' Grimm shook his head. 'It bewilders me. If they will not grit their teeth and stand strong…'

He let his sentence hang unfinished. Stepping forward, he placed his hands on the sculpted baluster, and leaned out over the edge. Beneath him, he saw minor ecclesiarchs, their beige cassocks trimmed with black and white check, moving among the displaced and the desperate, offering words of consolation from the Imperial creed and its innumerable supplementary tomes.

'Are they ready to evacuate, my lord? There is no telling how long we will have.'

'Now that the trucks are here,' said Alvez, 'the senior medicae will start the process. Those with the best chance of survival will be moved first.'

Outside, gunfire was constant. The closest section of defensive wall had fallen less than thirty minutes ago. Two regiments of Rynnsguard infantry and a company of Leman Russ tanks were punishing the orks that were pouring through the breach, but the Crimson Fist captain knew it was only a matter of time before the defenders were forced into a retreat. The orks would keep coming, a ceaseless tide that gained ground little by little, until the entire district fell. One section of the city at a time, the orks were slowly, inexorably pressing the Imperial forces back towards the Silver Citadel. All the Crimson Fists and the Rynnsguard could do at this stage was slow them down as much as possible. Retaking lost territory was beyond them. The cost in life and materiel would be far too high.

As movement increased on the floor down below, and the first of the wounded were taken to the north exit to board the waiting trucks, Captain Alvez found himself thinking of Ceval Ranparre, the Master of the Fleet. Had he been able to get a ship out in time? Had any of the Crimson Fists' spacecraft escaped into the warp? He hoped so. Though his pride protested bitterly against such thoughts, the reality was this: without significant outside intervention, all he and his Crimson Fist brothers could hope to do was to hold the line, to last out as long as they could. Beyond that...

From somewhere outside the arcade, a battle-brother transmitted an update on the situation at the breach. Alvez listened. It was a Devastator Squad sergeant called Lician. The sergeant's squad had been charged with providing heavy fire support to the Rynnsguard 12th Infantry Regiment. Judging by Lician's tone, things were not going well.

'My lord, Colonel Cantrell has ordered his men into a staggered retreat. The wall is lost. Xenos are spilling into the streets now.' Almost as an afterthought, he added, 'These men fought hard, brother-captain. We gave them all the support we could, but I'm afraid their eventual loss was inevitable. The greenskins are pouring through like floodwaters.'

'Were the habs evacuated in time?' Alvez asked.

'Many were,' answered Lician, 'but just as many were not. The orks are torching everything in their path.' His voice took on a bitter tone. 'I have never heard such screams.'

'What is the position of your squad now, brother?'

'We are moving back with the Twelfth Regiment. Currently, we are three kilometres east of–'

Lician stopped mid-sentence. Alvez could hear him conferring with another battle-brother. Then, addressing the captain again, Lician said urgently, 'My lord. You need to get out of the arcade! There's a–'

Alvez never heard the rest. The far wall of the arcade exploded inwards in a great cloud of stone, steel and glass. Deadly debris flew in all directions, and those closest to the south wall were crushed to death. Something huge and dark rumbled in the great cloud of dust that shrouded half the arcade now.

Grimm, still standing at the stone baluster, bellowed down to the floor beneath him. 'Get everyone out of here!'

Even though his helmet's vox-amp was set to full volume, no one heard him over the roar and splutter of whatever had just demolished half the building.

As the cloud of dust thinned a little, the shadow within took on clearer form.

'Move!' barked Captain Alvez, and he shoved Grimm violently aside just in time.

There was the sound of a cannon firing, and the baluster where Grimm had been standing only a second ago exploded in fire and shrapnel.

Alvez raised his storm-bolter and fired at the black behemoth now emerging from the dust, but his storm-bolts rattled off its armour. Engines spluttered and rumbled, and the thing lurched out of the cloud, its great treads crushing wounded men and women who were unable to roll clear.

It was a massive ork battlewagon, a mishmash of looted tanks and APCs welded together on a vast track-mounted chassis. Twisted black spikes covered its armour, and fat cannon swivelled from a cluster of armoured mantlets.

Those guns swung towards Alvez now, and, with a stutter of thunder, launched a volley of explosive shells his way.

Had Alvez not been wearing Terminator armour, the proximity of the detonating shells would have blasted him apart, but it would take nothing less than a direct hit to fell him.

Under the cover of the smoke and debris that the exploding rounds had kicked up, Alvez retreated, ordering Grimm, who had narrowly missed being blasted apart himself, out of the arcade in front of him.

Outside, all but one of the trucks had left at speed, carrying the Rynnites who had made it out alive. No one else would emerge from the building now. In the driver's cabin of the last truck, a terrified man in Rynnsguard fatigues waved frantically at them.

'My lord,' he yelled over the sound of the arcade's destruction. 'Please, hurry. Get in the back.'

The truck was military issue, a big, tough six-wheel drive affair capable of handling three tonnes of cargo. The back was unshielded. Alvez looked at it dubiously. Grimm jumped up into the rear, and the suspension compressed with a groan. Alvez followed quickly, and the driver put the truck in gear. It struggled to accelerate at first, but soon they were roaring away from the arcade, abandoned shops and hab-blocks whipping by them.

Alvez and Grimm watched from the back as the Menzilon arcade finally collapsed in a great mushrooming cloud of dust and smoke.

'Do you think, perhaps…?' Grimm asked.

'No,' said Alvez. 'It'll take more than that to stop it.'

A new sound was intruding on his thoughts, just audible above the rumble of the truck. It was a distant angry buzzing noise, and it came from the south-east. Actually, it was several noises merging together.

'Damn it,' cursed the captain. 'We've got ork copters coming in!'

He was right. The copters swung out of the sky, guns blazing, the insane greenskin pilots laughing with delight. Stubber-fire stitched the back of the truck and rattled off the armour of the two Space Marines. Alvez targeted the lead copter and fired a quick burst from his storm-bolter. The machine dipped for a moment, but stayed in the air. A second later, when the pilot's torso blew outwards, the shells inside him detonating, the buzzing one-man craft went into a wild spin and exploded on contact with the corner of a tall hab.

There were still two copters. Grimm fired his bolter and blew out the gas tank of the second, turning the whole machine into a blinding yellow fireball that crashed onto the road behind them.

'Keep moving,' Alvez roared at the driver. Turning to look ahead, he could see the Verano wall looming into view. The other trucks from the arcade were already well beyond its great gates.

'Almost there,' said the Rynnsguard driver.

He spoke too soon, of course. The last of the ork copters dived towards them and, before either Grimm or Alvez could open fire, launched a volley of rockets right at them.

Most of the rockets went wide, but one screamed straight in under the vehicle and struck the ground. The explosion tossed the truck into the air, its back end spinning over its cabin. Grimm and Alvez were thrown out and hit the ground hard, but, saved from grievous injury by the armour, they were soon up and moving towards the Verano Gate.

The Rynnsguard driver was not so lucky. His broken body lay still, soaked in blood, half in, half out of the crumpled cabin.

Grimm was at Alvez's side now, pacing him, slowing his own steps to match those of the far heavier Terminator suit.

'Damn them,' spat Alvez, looking to his left and right.

From the streets on either side, a tide of orks was boiling towards them, weapons firing, blades raised, a wall of green flesh and sharpened metal. The two Crimson Fists immediately opened fire, cutting down dozens in the front ranks.

'Get moving,' growled Alvez. 'Get to the gate, Huron. You have to close it before they get through. I won't lose another district today.'

'And I won't leave your side,' Grimm argued, voice shaking with the recoil from his bolter as he fired burst after burst at the horde. His left hand flashed to his belt and pulled a krak grenade free. He primed it with his thumb and tossed it at the closest knot of greenskins.

There was a deep boom, and the luckless orks at the front exploded in a shower of red flesh and bright bone. Grimm tossed another, killed a dozen more of the savages, and that was it. His grenades were spent.

The roar of the ork horde was joined by the sound of engines now. Buggies and bikes revved noisily, eager to get through, but there was no room for them, the streets were so thick with greenskin infantry.

'Don't you disobey me, sergeant,' Alvez barked between shots. 'Don't you start that now. I need those gates closed before the orks push through. You can get there a lot faster than I can. Start the mechanism. I will slip through just before they shut. We're operating under the Ceres Protocol, remember. I'm not about to die at the hands of this filth.'

He strafed the orks to his left with storm-bolter fire and cut several apart, but there were so many of them, and they kept coming, stampeding over their dead.

Grimm had his orders. He didn't have to like them, but they were orders just the same. Firing a last burst from his bolter, he turned and sprinted for the Verano Gate. As he ran, he told his captain over the link, 'I'm not letting them close until you're through.'

Alvez ignored that. He was busy picking his targets, walking backwards, his storm-bolter keeping the orks at bay. In his left hand was a glowing power sword, a relic blade called *Riad*. Its blade, forged with technology long-forgotten, could cut through tank armour with ease. If, no, *when* the orks got within range, Alvez would cut through them like they weren't even there.

He did not feel even the slightest fear as the horde closed on him. Glancing back, he saw that Huron Grimm was through the gate now, and he had only fifty metres to go. But the damned gate was still wide open.

'Grimm?' he bellowed over the link. 'What in Dorn's name is going on?'

'The mechanism, my lord,' Grimm answered. 'It's jammed. We'll have to close the gates manually.'

'Then do it,' Alvez snapped. The orks were almost on him now. He hefted *Riad* in his hand, ready to swing. 'And hurry up!'

Grimm could hardly believe this. He wanted someone to blame, someone to rip apart with his bare hands. The Rynnsguard troopers manning the walls were firing down into the ork horde that was closing around his captain, but their lasguns were pathetically inadequate. Only their heavy weapons – the autocannon, lascannon and heavy bolters they employed – had anything but a negligible effect on the xenos mob, and there weren't nearly enough of those to turn the orks back.

Grimm's squadmates were on the walls, too, and had been firing in support of him, but the moment he discovered the gate mechanism was malfunctioning, he had called them down from the walls to help him. Closing the gate manually meant pushing each of the two gate sections together. Thick metal bars stuck out from the rear of each section to make this possible, but it would have taken the Rynnsguard many men far too much time even to budge the gate a centimetre. Instead, Grimm's squad went to work, even while, on the other side of the gate, their brave captain cut a path of gory destruction through his enemies.

Grimm heard him on the link, breathing hard despite the capabilities of his gene-boosted body.

'Progress report, sergeant!'

Grimm answered through gritted teeth as he pushed with all his strength against the handle in front of him, desperate to get the gate moving. 'Doing our best, captain.' He managed, but that was all.

'Not good enough,' Alvez answered. 'Work faster!'

Grimm grunted and put everything he had into pushing the gates closed. Beside him, two of his brothers also pushed. The other two worked the opposite section. The sound of gunfire was loud and constant from atop the wall.

'We can't keep them off him!' shouted a Rynns-guard officer. 'There's too damned many!'

Grimm howled with rage. He wanted to be out there beside his captain. What in the blasted warp was he doing here, about to lock Drigo Alvez out there with the enemy?

Orders, said a voice in his head. You can never disobey your orders.

'Captain,' Grimm grunted. 'How close to the gate are you? It's almost shut. We've only three metres to go!'

It was true. The Rynnsguard would later tell of the Space Marines' incredible strength that day. It shouldn't have been possible. The gate's sections weighed several tonnes each and were only ever meant to be manually closed with the aid of powerful trucks that could shunt them together.

'Close the gates,' ordered Alvez.

Grimm stopped pushing immediately, his squad brothers following suit.

'My lord–'

'I said close the damned gates, sergeant. Are you deaf? They're all around me now. There's far too many of them, and, if they get through, Dorn help me, you'll have disobeyed a direct order. You'll no longer be Astartes, I promise you. I am commanding you to save that district, and you will do it. How many hundreds of thousands of people are sheltering behind those walls? Do it, Huron!'

The conscious part of Grimm's mind railed against it, but his psycho-conditioning was incredibly deep, and, through a strange numbness, he felt his body once more put all its strength into the effort of sealing the gate.

Again, his squad brothers took their cue from his example.

Before he knew it, the task was done, and he stood gasping, helmet pressed to thick metal surface.

He ordered his squad brothers back onto the ramparts to lend their Rynnsguard their firepower, but he knew it was too late. He felt the loss inside him already.

A moment later, Brother Kifa hailed him on the link, and his tone was enough to tell Grimm everything. Even Terminator armour had its limits. Against such overwhelming numbers, the captain could not have fought longer than he did.

He was gone.

Grimm allowed himself to fall to his knees. He had never felt like this in all his life. He hoped he never would again.

His left hand sought something on his belt and he tugged it free with a snap, raised his hand in front of his visor and looked at it.

It was a tiny wooden aquila, the charm that the old Rynnite woman had tried to give Captain Alvez as they marched through her street.

Grimm stared at it, the relentless noise of battle all around him dimming to mere background static. This pathetic little trinket was supposed to protect people. It was supposed to have some power, yes? The woman, filled with reverence for the Crimson Fists, had wanted the charm to protect Drigo Alvez. But it was he, Huron Grimm, that had carried it with him. And it was he who lived.

What did that mean, he wondered?

Nothing, answered a voice in Grimm's mind.

It sounded so much like the captain's.

It *means nothing at all, Huron*, the voice repeated. *It is just a piece of wood. Destroy it!*

Numbly, automatically, Grimm closed his armoured fist over the tiny icon, and crushed it to splinters.

Now get up, said the voice. *Get back in the fight. Honour me. Honour the Chapter as you were taught to do.*

Grimm got up as the voice commanded, slammed a fresh magazine in his bolter, climbed to the top of the ramparts, and went back to war.

THIRTEEN

The Azcalan Rainforest, Rynnland Province

Cortez's pistol clicked empty, and there wasn't time to change the magazine. Rearing up in front of him was a huge ork with skin the colour of coal. In each clawed hand, the slavering beast held a cleaver over a metre long, each blade viciously serrated like the jaws of a Medean killfish. There was a blur of motion. Cortez's reflexes shifted him a step to the left before his conscious mind even had time to register the angle of the blow, his response time the product of centuries of diligent training.

The greenskin berserker's blades bit deep into the soil where Cortez had been standing. In the half-second that the creature took to reverse its momentum and wrench its weapons up again, Cortez's power fist flashed forward in an arcing blur. It was a body shot, a thunderous strike to the monster's exposed side, and the crack of lethal

361

energies ionised the air, giving it a sharp metallic smell. The ork howled and crumpled to its knees, a great spherical section of its torso utterly destroyed. Gore poured forth, and it sank forward, but Cortez wasn't finished. One did not leave a wounded ork breathing on the battlefield. These were hardy creatures, far hardier than any living thing had a right to be. Wounds that would have killed even a Space Marine might only cripple an ork until its incredibly resilient algae-infused system could put it back together. He had seen it happen before.

The moment the creature's head struck the dirt, Cortez raised his booted foot and hammered it down on the beast's ugly head. Once, twice, three times. At first, the skull resisted the massive impact of the blows, but, by the third stomp, it gave way, the bone shattering at last, the brain turning to a jelly-like smear.

There was no time to glory in the victory. All around Cortez, his battle-brothers were engaged at close quarters. It was here the orks were most dangerous. It was here they excelled. Their raw animal power and savagery were incomparable among all the alien races, save perhaps the disgusting tyranids. Individual combat would favour the Astartes, of course. No living being trained as relentlessly, nor mastered war to the same degree. But the orks were not fighting as individuals. Their strength was in their numbers. Hundreds poured forth, as if the forest was vomiting them out, like something poisonous eaten by mistake and rejected. 'Stand fast!' Cortez bellowed, drawing his combat knife. Its blade was long and keen, sharpened to the monomolecular level, treated with a coating of synthetic diamond, as were the knives of all the Crimson Fists. They cut through the flesh of the orks, carving great hunks of bleeding meat from the densely muscled bodies.

Days had passed since the rescue of Dasat and his pilgrims from the slaver camp, and this was the third time since then that the contingent from Arx Tyrannus had run into wandering ork mobs. The two previous times, whichever squad was on point had quickly eliminated the problem. Those mobs had been relatively small. This one was far larger, and there had been no going around it. A pitched battle had been inevitable.

Cortez heard Kantor on the link ordering Squad Viejo to break north with the refugees, to get them away from the edge skirmish as quickly as possible. Then the Chapter Master was in among the orks, a whirlwind of violence, felling all that tried to swarm on him.

Cortez would have enjoyed watching his friend's martial prowess in action, but two snarling orks, marginally smaller and lighter-skinned than the monster Cortez had just slain, lunged at him from both sides. Cortez slid backwards a single step, and the aliens' crude blades cut empty air. He did not give them time to recover. Every blow they missed was an opening he was conditioned to exploit. Lunging to the right, he rammed his combat blade deep into the belly of one, so deep he felt its point catch on the inner surface of the beast's vertebrae. Instantly, he yanked back on the knife's grip. The serrations on the back of the blade caught on the creature's innards, and ripped them out through the gaping hole in its skin. For an instant, the creature stood looking down at its own looped intestines, a look of dumb curiosity on its idiot face. Cortez had already turned to the other, kicking at its leading knee, hard enough to smash the kneecap to pieces. The ork went down on its other knee with a roar of anger and pain. Again, Cortez's power fist flashed out. There was a sharp electrical crack, and the creature's head vanished in a red mist.

The lifeless, headless body fell forward on its chest, twitching and gushing hot blood.

Cortez spun and caught the other ork, the one his knife had just gutted, on the side of its head with a backhand blow. It, too, collapsed headless to the soil, falling to rest atop its own slick viscera.

Over the comm-link, Cortez heard himself addressed. 'Alessio, try to draw them west. Crush them between your squad and Segala's.'

Easier said than done, thought Cortez as his power fist felled another green wretch.

From the corner of his eye, he saw the Chapter Master fighting only a dozen metres from his side. Fenestra and Benizar were beside him, giving their all. Cortez threw himself into the fight even harder, and became a blur of blue motion, slaughtering the brutish foe as quickly as they could emerge from the dark green shadows.

Cortez relayed the Chapter Master's orders to his squad between blows and, together, they began moving west even as they fought. Kantor moved with them, growling over the link, 'That's it. Keep them coming. North a little. Draw them on.'

Cortez's squad let the orks come to them, giving ground metre by metre as they backed away. The foliage thinned a little, cover for the orks began to lessen. Targeting the beasts became easier, and they went down in increasing numbers, their heads detonating in bright sprays as perfectly placed bolter rounds exploded inside their skulls.

Any moment now, thought Cortez.

And the moment was right. The orks took the bait, and Kantor ordered Squad Segala to swing in from the west flank and cut them down. Caught in a deadly crossfire, the greenskins were shredded to fleshy tatters. Those that survived fled back into the undergrowth, their green backs merging with the jungle.

For the moment, at least, the Space Marines had held them off.

'North,' said Kantor. 'We'll be closing on the capital soon. From here on in, we follow the River Rynn.'

Squads Cortez and Segala followed him.

Cortez gauged his remaining ammunition as he moved. He was running extremely low now. He would have to ask the others for extra rounds.

They had better reach New Rynn City soon.

* * *

KANTOR HAD NEVER intended for them to come this way. He had suspected from the beginning that the orks might use the River Rynn as a quick route to the capital from wherever their ships crash-landed. He re-assessed that decision now. He and his survivors looked out over the fast, cool waters and saw no sign of ork boats or rafts. They did see human corpses drifting by, floating spread-eagle, the wounded flesh of their backs just breaking the surface of the water. They were people who had been killed up-river, per-haps men and women from the small settlements in the foothills and mountain slopes where the river began its journey.

Of the pilgrims Kantor had wished so desperately to save, three more had been killed, though not through wounds inflicted directly, but by all they had suffered in the camp. That and the march through the jungle were just too much. Somehow, old Dasat held on, though he looked weaker by the day. Kantor guessed the pilgrim's leader still felt responsible for the safety of his people. He would see them to the capital, no matter what.

This latest battle with the orks was something Kan-tor had desperately wished to avoid. Every encounter cost them time, valuable ammunition, and risked alerting even greater enemy forces to their presence. But he was proud of the three makeshift squads who travelled with him. With their backs to the proverbial wall since the destruction of their home, they had fought like swamp-tigers, leaving countless dead xenos in their wake.

After an hour's march, Kantor and the two squads with him finally caught up to Squad Viejo and the refugees who had already reached the riverbank. Viejo saluted when he saw the Chapter Master and gave him a quick update. No one had been injured, but some of the pilgrims were in shock, terrified by the fighting.

Dasat waited behind Viejo until the sergeant had finished his report, then, when the sergeant moved off, he bowed deep and made the sign of the aquila on his chest. 'Praise the Emperor, my lord,' said the old man, 'that the foe didn't harm you.'

Kantor took off his helmet and looked down at the man. 'I've faced far worse,' he said. 'And I will again.'

Tears began to course down the old man's cheeks. 'You and your warriors continually risk your lives for ours. I can hardly tell you the shame I feel. I've never seen such selfless bravery, lord. Our worthless lives are not worth the burden we place on you. You have so much else to cope with.'

Sobs of sorrow and guilt shook the man's bony shoulders.

Kantor reached out a massive hand and steadied him.

'Enough, Dasat,' he rumbled quietly. 'No life lived in dedication to the Emperor should be cut short by filthy, mindless xenos. Besides, we are almost at the capital. Another day will see us there, if I have it right. The bank of this river will take us to Jadeberry Hill. Be strong a while longer. A battle awaits us there. My brothers will try their best to protect you, but you will need your strength. Drink from the river. Find food. Sleep till we wake you. It is your last chance to do so. By the Emperor's grace, this journey ends soon.'

Dasat nodded. 'I'll pray it ends well, lord. For all of us.'

Kantor decided that he, too, would pray, not on his knees like those who followed the Imperial creed, but in the act of caring for his armour and his weapons. He would quietly chant the holy litanies of the Chapter, litanies to keep him strong, litanies to invoke the spirits of the wargear he relied on. He thought of the Emperor. The Crimson Fists, like many Astartes Chapters, did not revere the Master of Mankind as a god, per se, but as a father. Still, the gifted brothers of the Librarius had, since the dawn of the Chapter's existence, always maintained that the Emperor was ever-present somehow, a shining psychic light, a beacon of hope that did indeed seem strengthened by the devotion of all those who laboured in His name.

Kantor hoped He would hear Dasat's prayers.

He moved off towards the riverbank where Cortez and some of the others were cleaning xenos gore from their armour.

Kantor waded into the shallows beside them and scooped water into his hands with which to clean his ancient suit.

We are sixteen against a world swarming with the foe, he thought. And yet, we sixteen have survived this far. There is meaning somewhere in all this. May I live long enough to discover it.

FOURTEEN

The Cassar, New Rynn City

'Sergeant Grimm was the captain's second-in-command,' said Faradis Anto. 'I can see no reason for your objection but simple pride, brother.'

Grimm hated this. How did it serve the memory of Drigo Alvez bickering over who was to command the forces that remained? Did the brothers assembled here around the ebonwood table of the Strategium think he *wanted* this? Coveted it? If he could have given his own life, right then and there, to have the brother-captain back, he would have taken his own blade and pierced both his hearts without hesitation.

He considered telling them this.

'You seek to offend me, Anto?' snarled Barrien Gallacus defensively, dangerously. 'Pride is no factor in this. Drigo Alvez was a captain and a former brother of the Crusade Company. It is the latter that is important here. There is a hierarchy that must be adhered to. A Crusade Company sergeant is the obvious choice.'

'And that would be you?' asked Erdys Phrenotas.

Phrenotas led the Crusade Company's Fourth Stern-guard Squad. Gallacus led the First Vanguard Squad. Grimm shook his head in despair the moment Phrenotas opened his mouth. The old rivalry between the two elements would now dominate the debate. Any hope of a swift resolution had just vanished.

Or had it?

Gallacus was about to begin verbally sparring with Phrenotas when the doors of the Strategium swept open and three more Astartes strode into the room.

'What is going on here?' demanded the figure in the centre of the trio. 'Why are you wasting time? You should be on the walls, marshalling our forces. What is the meaning of this?'

Despite the harsh tone of the voice and a sudden dark change in the air, Grimm found himself sup-pressing a half-smile. Here was a swift resolution after all. The figure in the middle was Epistolary Deguerro. He was flanked by Codiciers Terraro and Corda.

'We are in the process of selecting a temporary com-mander,' explained a Vanguard Squad sergeant by the name of Hurien Thanator. He thrust his chin at Sergeant Anto, and added, 'But our brothers in Sec-ond Company seem incapable of respecting the proper chain of command.'

Deguerro stopped beside Thanator's chair and glared down at him. 'Just as well, then, that I am here to simplify matters for you all.'

He looked over at Grimm, meeting his eyes, and said, 'I will be taking temporary command of our forces. No!' – he held up a hand towards Sergeant Gallacus, palm out – 'Do not waste your breath attempting to debate it. There is clear precedent. You may check the archives in the Librarium downstairs. Sergeant Gallacus, I am placing you in charge of all Crusade Company assets. Sergeant Grimm, you will be responsible for Second and Third Company assets. Both of you will follow my orders to the letter. Is that clear?'

Gallacus worked the muscles in his jaw angrily, but he knew well enough that Deguerro was right. In the absence of a captain, a senior member of the Librarius ultimately held highest rank. After a moment, he nodded.

'Clear, brother.'

'Sergeant Grimm?' said Deguerro.

'As you command, brother,' said Grimm, and he meant it.

'Excellent, then there is no more call for you to linger here. Your brothers need you on the walls. Gallacus, Brother-Codicier Terraro will accompany you. My liaison, if you will. Likewise, Brother-Codicier Cordo will assist Sergeant Grimm.'

The Astartes seated around the table rose from their chairs and saluted with fist on breastplate, some begrudgingly, others with sincerity.

Deguerro saluted back. 'Thank you, my brothers. May the primarch go with you.'

The sergeants filed out the broad ebonwood doors in silence.

Grimm was about to join them, the last to leave, when a hand on his upper arm stopped him. He turned.

'A moment, brother-sergeant,' said Deguerro, and Grimm noted the anxious look that had appeared in his eyes.

'Do you wish me to leave, brother?' asked Codicier Corda.

'No,' said Deguerro without taking his eyes from Grimm. 'You already know what I wish to say to the sergeant.'

Corda nodded and stood patiently.

Grimm raised an eyebrow in silent query.

'Huron Grimm,' said Deguerro. 'There are two things I must ask you to do. The first is to trust me. The second is perhaps the harder of the two. It will be dangerous, and your success or failure may well affect the lives of all who have survived thus far.'

'Go on, brother,' said Grimm, not bothering to cover his sudden sense of apprehension. The psyker would see through any mask.

Deguerro's eyes were intense. 'We of the Librarius have divined certain possibilities. Potentialities, if you will. We believe a number of strong... presences... are coming to New Rynn City. If they survive the final stages of their journey, their arrival may have a most significant impact on the outcome of this war.'

'You don't sound very sure,' said Grimm.

Deguerro smiled humourlessly. 'That is the way of witch-sight. It is frustratingly vague at times. We know something is about to change. We are approaching a major branching point, a juncture in time where the paths to the future diverge in very different directions. We must do everything we can to guide this reality, our reality, along the correct path.'

Grimm squinted back at the Librarian and, after a moment, shook his head. 'Matters of the empyrean are best left in your hands, brother. I need no explanations, only your orders. Tell me what you require of me, and I promise you, it will be done.'

FIFTEEN

The Azcalan Rainforest, Rynnland Province

THE RIVER CURVED, and, following its slippery bank, Kantor and his battered fellow survivors saw Jade-berry Hill rising over the treetops in the near distance. The Hill was symbolic, representing, to Kantor's mind at least, the coming end of a journey that should never have taken place. How different would things now be had the fortress-monastery not been sundered? How hard might the Chapter have been able to strike back at the xenos? He would never know, just as he would never know exactly how a single missile from the Laculum battery had managed to wreak such raw devastation on all he held dear.

Cortez, too, noted the profile of the hill as it became visible around the curve of the river and the trees on its bank. Opening a channel to Kantor, he said, 'We are closing at last, Pedro. But I'll wager the hardest part still lies ahead of us.'

'I'm sure you're right,' replied Kantor. 'The lack of communications bothers me. At this range, we should at least be able to hear some kind of traffic, even if it is weak and fragmented.'

'Viejo reports nothing yet,' said Cortez. Squad Viejo were on point, ranging ahead of the rest by half a kilometre. 'It's as if every wide-area transmitter on the planet was taken out of commission. Either that, or the orks are employing some kind of communications suppressor. We *have* encountered the like before.'

Kantor looked up at the sky over the wide expanse of the river. It was a mix of bright gold and dark grey. The Season of Rains would be here soon. How would the orks respond to it? Would it alter their behaviour somehow? He realised there was a gap in his knowledge. Documentation on the effects of weather patterns on the greenskin race was practically non-existent. If he lived through this, he would commission such a study by the Adeptus Mechanicus' biologis arm. Such science was their exclusive domain, and forces throughout the Imperium would surely benefit by it.

Across the grey-gold sky, ork craft still occasionally roared, leaving smoky black trails like banners proclaiming this world as theirs. The very sight of them sent waves of anger and disgust through him. The thick forest canopy of the Azcalan had, until now, kept such things from plain view.

Jadeberry Hill loomed closer by the minute, its summit topped with clusters of grey mausoleums and white marble angels. They would reach its base within the hour. Peering at it, Kantor realised that there was movement on its summit. Even at full magnification, it was not yet clear what was going on, but he knew signs of a firefight when he saw them, no matter the distance.

He opened a general channel and said, 'We must hurry, brothers. Conflict rages up ahead. Our brothers have need of us. Be ready.'

All along the muddy bank, the marching Astartes prepared their weapons for battle once again, locking the last of their magazines into their trusty bolters and cocking them. Their pace increased, and the refugees behind them had to hurry to keep up.

Whatever lay ahead, Kantor and his battle-brothers would overcome it, or die trying.

It was the only way they knew.

SIXTEEN

Jadeberry Hill, New Rynn City

GRIMM HAD ONLY four squads with which to hold the Jadeberry Underpass. It was here, to the mouth of the underpass, that Epistolary Duegerro had sent him, adamant that those approaching, whoever they were, would enter the city through it, or not at all. Even through the psychic haze, the roiling clouds of alien thought that billowed out from the minds of the ork psykers, the Crimson Fists Librarians had read this much clearly in the currents of the immaterial realm. Deguerro had not said who he believed the approaching presences to be, perhaps so as not to raise anyone's hopes, but Grimm couldn't suppress his own fervent hopes. Surely it was a group of survivors from Arx Tyrannus. Some of the Crimson Fists *had* to have survived. Dare he hope that the Chapter Master was among them?

From the underpass, the base of Jadeberry Hill was only two hundred metres away, just north, a pale, stony path snaking up its dark southern flank leading to the cemetery at the top. To the north-west of the hill, the waters of the Pakomac River split from those of the River Rynn. They meandered south then south-west, feeding a network of canals within the city limits before spreading out towards the farmlands where they followed countless irrigation ditches. Finally, the Pakomac split into a thousand smaller tributaries before it met the mighty Medean Sea.

The orks had not let the rivers and canals stop them from spreading into the region in force. In fact, they thrived with such an abundance of water. They used it in the massive steam-driven machines which filled the foundries they had hastily established, taking their cue from the manufactora they had already overrun. Their position was strong. They had encircled the city as completely as they could.

As Grimm looked out from behind the barricades he and his squads had erected around this, the mouth of the last Imperial-held underpass this side of the river, he cursed at all the greenskins had accomplished so far.

They were every bit as savage and violent as they had always been, but he couldn't deny a certain brutal intelligence behind all they had achieved. Their elimination of Imperial communications at the very earliest had been a masterstroke, a strategy clearly learned over their countless clashes with the Emperor's forces. The storm-trooper units of the Imperial Guard were regularly deployed early in war to achieve exactly such an objective. Astartes strike forces executed such operations as a matter of course. Someone should have realised that, sooner or later, the orks would learn from the tactics of their enemies. Such knowledge may have taken a long time to permeate the greenskins' limited minds, but it had finally dawned on them, and here were the results.

The barricades – mostly Aegis prefab shield-walls, concrete-filled steel drums, razorwire and sandbags – were the best he and his men could manage in the time they'd had. So far, they had held against the last four attack waves, but that was as much to do with the gridwork of anti-vehicle and anti-personnel mines Grimm had ordered placed on the main access road as it was the strength of the Aegis plating.

The minefield was largely depleted now. How close would the next wave get?

If there were Astartes coming in from the east, they would soon discover the challenge they faced entering the city. The towering columns of black smoke and the endless drumbeat of heavy artillery would make it clear, long before they were within striking distance, that the orks controlled everything outside the walls. Everything, that is, except this last way in.

But how long do I wait, Grimm wondered?

He knew the enemy were already mustering for another run on his position. If his brothers from Arx Tyrannus *were* out there, they would have to hurry.

He turned his eyes left and up to the top of Jadeberry Hill. He had positioned a Devastator squad there, the only one he'd been assigned. It was a good spot for heavy fire support, as the last two hours had proven. The Devastators were fielding two las-cannons, two missile launchers and a plasma cannon. Already, they had taken a staggering toll on the foe, ripping their vehicles to burning pieces from long range and atomising hundreds of alien infantry. But their ammunition was finite. If the attacks continued to intensify, they would soon run out.

The Ceres Protocol was still in effect. Deguerro hadn't reversed it, knowing Alvez's original decision was the right one. Grimm knew he would have to make a choice soon: risk the lives of all those under his temporary command for the sake of a mere psychic trace, or fall back when it became clear the barricades would no longer hold. He desperately wanted to hold the underpass to the last, giving whoever was out there every chance they could of making it back to the fold, but paying for it with the blood of his brothers was something he could not do.

No. Perhaps, if Deguerro had been sure, had named Pedro Kantor or one of his captains among the approaching party, it would have been an easier choice. Grimm would have stayed despite everything. The forces in New Rynn City needed a sign, needed one of their leaders, a member of the Chapter Council, to return to them. What might that do for morale?

But without a name, without certainty, could he really justify the death of any Crimson Fist? Such thoughts resolved the issue for him. If no prodigal Fists showed themselves by the end of the next attack wave, he would pull his brothers back and destroy the underpass. He could not risk the orks gaining access to the city that way. Librarians were not infallible. They were known to err from time to time, and Deguerro himself admitted that they were forced to constantly wrestle against the psychic fog that emanated from the undisciplined minds of the ork psykers.

Still looking at the summit of Jadeberry Hill, Grimm noticed sudden agitated movement there. Static crackled in his ear, broken by a voice that said, 'Sergeant Grimm, the xenos are massing for another run on the barricades. They are behind the ruins to the south-east.' He paused. 'There are many of them, brother. More than before.'

Of course there are, thought Grimm sourly.

The voice belonged to Sergeant Tirius, formerly of the late Captain Drakken's 3rd Company. The hard-faced Tirius and his squad had survived the debacle at Badlanding only to find themselves here, appended to the 2nd Company, and in a far greater mess than any had expected. Grimm was glad to have them. Tirius was strong and true, with little ego to get in his way.

'Armour?' Grimm asked over the link, hoping the answer would be *none*.

'I count five tanks,' said Tirius. 'Looted Leman Russ. The turrets have been modified. I can't begin to guess at their range or power now, but if they get within range of our lascannon and missile launchers, we will render them into scrap. You have my word.'

Grimm was reassured, but the mere presence of the tanks meant that the orks were escalating their efforts to take this area. It was the greenskin way. They would throw progressively heavier concentrations of forces at a problem until they overcame it by virtue of brute force. Eventually they would overcome the Astartes defenders. Grimm was no defeatist. He merely had to be realistic. Lives depended on it.

'Ready your weapons, brothers,' he called out over the comm-link. 'Dorn watch over us all. They are no match for the sons of the Chapter. Nor shall they ever be.'

Further words came unbidden into his mind, words he had heard on a score of battlefields out there among the stars, the words so favoured by the Chaplains of the Crimson Fists.

There is only the Emperor, the Chaplains would intone before battle was joined.

He is our shield and our protector, the ranks would reply.

Grimm spoke that first line to his battle-brothers now, spoke it with feeling, and received an equally impassioned response. On his left and right, weapons were cocked and readied.

Hulking figures appeared over the mounds of rubble to the south-east, great dark shapes with horned helms and flapping banners of flayed human skin. Severed heads bobbed and swung from their belts and from the poles that supported those crudely painted banners. Some were boxy, angular figures, weighed down by thick armour, but so impossibly strong that they were still fast enough to lead the charge.

One, Grimm saw, was by far the largest. The horns that sprouted from either side of his helm curved outwards, then inwards with a twist, like those of a bull raumas, but plated in sharpened steel.

The horned warboss raised a massive growling chainaxe into the air and roared long and deep, a battle cry that was taken up by its thousands of followers.

They looked fearless standing there, all those orks, and well they might, for they faced only forty. But did they realise how much fight was left in that forty? Every Crimson Fist at the barricade was ready to fight like it was the last hour of his life.

Perhaps it would be.

The looted tanks rumbled into view now, clanking between the skeletons of fire-gutted buildings, turning their stout ugly modified turrets towards the Astartes. One fired a shot, a great gout of fire and smoke erupted from its barrel.

The shell landed a hundred metres short, packed with so much explosive that it blew a crater in the rockcrete road two metres deep.

This was the beginning, the sign the orks were waiting for. They charged forward, filling the air with war cries. They surged around the tanks, mindful not to be crushed by the grinding treads.

'Steady!' Grimm ordered. 'Make every bolt count!'

From the top of Jadeberry Hill, something streaked towards the leading tank on a trail of white and yellow fire. It struck the tank right on the gun mantlet, punching deep into the metal. The tank jerked to a stop. A second later, red fire erupted from its hatches. Burning bodies tumbled out, thrashing and screaming.

One down, thought Grimm.

The ork footsoldiers were almost in range. Grimm could see the gleam of bloodlust in the eyes of the massive warboss.

All right, you foul bastard, cursed the sergeant. You've got my attention. It's time you tasted the fury of the Crimson Fists.

'Open fire!' he yelled over the link. The sudden rattle of bolters drowned out all else.

Battle was joined.

If you are out there, brothers, thought Grimm as he loosed shot after flesh-searing shot from his plasma pistol, then in Dorn's name, hurry up. Because it looks like this is your very last chance.

THE SIGHT THAT greeted Alessio Cortez as he exited from the trees of the Azcalan rainforest was one of absolute mayhem. The city burned. He could see ork ships half-buried in the outer sections of collapsed city walls. Artillery flashed and boomed all along the remaining ramparts, but far more answered back from the ground, the shells exploding on the walls, weakening them little by little, piece by piece.

The mad beasts had even breached the city walls in places by ramming them with aircraft!

Kantor and the others joined him at the forest edge, and froze.

'In Dorn's name...' gasped the Chapter Master.

'There!' exclaimed Brother Fenestra. 'Look to the base of the hill.'

Cortez saw it at once. Up ahead, a great ork horde was racing straight towards a row of Imperial barricades. Azure figures leaned out from behind Aegis armour plating to fire tight bursts at the enemy swarming all around them. Five tanks lay just to the south-east of the barricaded position, each reduced to little more than a burning black husk. Even as Cortez registered all this, a bright burst of plasma streaked down from the top of Jadeberry Hill and turned a great knot of orks to so much bubbling black flesh.

'To their aid!' barked Kantor, and he broke into a run.

Cortez was only a second behind him. 'Charge!' he bellowed at his battle-brothers.

'Our charges, my lord?' asked Sergeant Viejo, even as he too burst from the cover of the trees.

Damn our charges, cursed Cortez. Our brothers need us.

'Jadeberry Hill,' Kantor snapped between breaths. 'They'll be safe at the top.'

Kantor was almost on the orks now, but they had yet to notice the imminent attack from their rear. Tending towards tunnel-vision in a fight, they rarely noticed anything but the foe in front of them. It was a weakness the Crimson Fists had exploited many times throughout their history of violent encounters with them.

Kantor reached striking range and plunged in amongst them, a living storm of violence and revenge. His power fist smashed his enemies aside, pulping organs and flesh wherever it connected, shattering bone.

Pressed together by their sheer weight of numbers, the orks hardly knew what hit them. They were still reeling from the sudden attack of the Chapter Master when Cortez and the others joined the fray. Again, Cortez felt centuries of relentless training take over. Time seemed to slow down around him, as if he existed in some kind of bubble in which his synapses operated that much faster than everything else. Surprised orks turned to engage him, and were rendered headless before they could even raise their blades and guns in his direction. Others, just beyond these first, did manage to slash out at him, but the blows seemed absurdly slow to his super-charged senses, and he almost laughed aloud as he parried them on his ceramite vambraces. His pistol barked at point-blank range, killing almost as messily as his power fist.

Cortez did not turn to check on his brothers. He trusted that they fought as he did, and he was right, but none save Kantor himself could match the lethal speed and prowess of the 4th Company captain.

Before Cortez realised what had happened, he found himself on the other side of the ork horde. The barricades were right there in front of him. He had carved an avenue of death straight through the aliens.

He raced forward and leapt over the wall of armour plate and razorwire, then turned back to face the orks and resumed firing his pistol, every shot a kill, eliminating close range targets with a speed he could never duplicate on a mere training range. It needed the energy of real battle, the flow of adrenaline that only truly life-threatening danger brought forth.

As he fired again and again, he saw Pedro Kantor whirling among the ranks of the enemy, severing arteries with his long, gold-hilted blade, spraying the air with crimson drops. Where his sword did not cut, his power fist obliterated everything it touched. Its power was incredible. It was master-crafted, as beautiful as it was deadly and, to Cortez's eyes, it had never been as beautiful as it was at that moment, employed in the slaughter of those that had so gravely wounded his Chapter.

Cortez heard a voice over the comm-link. It was a new voice – new in that it was not one of the sixteen other Astartes voices he had become so accustomed to over the last ten terrible days.

'Captain Cortez!' exclaimed the voice. 'And the Chapter Master, by Dorn! Bless you, Deguerro.'

'Identify yourself, brother,' barked Cortez as he picked off a massive one-armed ork that was loping in to engage the Chapter Master from behind.

'I am Huron Grimm,' said the voice, 'Sergeant of the Second Company's First Tactical Squad. We… we have been waiting for you, captain.'

Squads Viejo and Segala fought their way through the horde now, rallying around Kantor and cutting him some room to move. Cortez wondered where the rest of his own squad were until, through a gap, he saw them guarding the Chapter Master's rear.

Las- and plasma-fire streaked down from the top of Jadeberry Hill and ripped into the ork ranks, killing scores at a time.

'Get behind the barricades,' Kantor yelled, and he charged forward and leapt clean over them, landing on his feet just beside Cortez.

The moment he landed, he spun, and twin muzzle flares licked out from the barrels of Dorn's Arrow. Massively muscled green bodies broke apart, erupting from the inside out as each mass-reactive shell detonated in quick succession.

Something was bothering Cortez even as he fought. 'Where is Benizar?' he demanded over the link.

'Where are Teves, Secco and Olvero?' asked another. It sounded like Viejo.

No, thought Cortez. Do not let it be! They did not come this far to fall now.

But they had.

More plasma-fire streaked down into the middle of the orks, killings so many, burning and maiming others, and a space cleared in the churning ranks. Through it, Cortez saw an armoured monstrosity with a great horned helm lift one of his brothers into the air, one massive, blood-slick power claw grasping the Astartes by the neck.

It was the leader of the ork assault. Did the creature feel Cortez's eyes on him? Did it feel the captain's hate stabbing out at it through all the noise and the killing? Perhaps it did. It turned its wicked red eyes towards Cortez and a sickening alien grin split its massive, tusk-filled maw. With Cortez's eyes locked to it, the ork snapped shut the blades of its power claw.

Snikkt!

A blue-armoured body fell lifeless to the blood-soaked ground. For a moment, the Space Marine's helmet, his severed head still inside, remained balanced on the huge claw. Then the ork boss flicked it away, as if it were mere garbage.

'Bastard!' roared Cortez, and he leaped over the barricade once more, barrelling into the orks, heading straight for the murderous abomination in the middle.

'Alessio!' shouted Kantor over the link, but there was no reaching him. Instead, his fellow Fists concentrated their fire around him, helping to cut him a path.

Dimly, Cortez registered their aid. The orks on either side of him fell with great melon-sized wounds that exploded in their flesh. From somewhere high on his left, there was a great flash of light, and howls of agony burst from alien throats. He heard the distinctive shriek of a missile, and felt the ground under him shake as it struck thirty metres away. The explosion sent a fountain of blood and cooked flesh into the air to rain down a moment later.

The Crimson Fists on the hilltop, he realised, were still giving their support.

Then he was in front of the black-armoured beast with the horned helm. His target. The focus of his rage. He noticed the black and white checks on the monster's battle-scarred armour. He noticed the icon on its banner of human skin, a red skull shaped like that of a bull auroch. And he noticed the size difference between them. The ork boss towered over him. Even hunched, the beast was at least a metre taller than he.

'Keep the others off me,' snarled Cortez over the link. But he needn't have bothered. The ork boss bellowed something in what was just barely a language, and the closest orks pressed aside, making space.

'That's right,' said Cortez, a lupine grin twisting his features. 'One-on-one.' He fingered the grip of his knife, flexed the thick digits of his power fist. 'Let's have it, monster!'

The words blared from his helmet's vox-amp at maximum volume.

The ork growled back, recognising a challenge by its tone, though the words themselves were meaningless noise to its ragged ears. Its long metal claws snapped open and shut, as if its whole right arm had a mind of its own, and a beastlike appetite for raw, bloody flesh.

In the other arm, it held a chainaxe no mere man could have hefted into the air. The weapon's teeth were an angry blur, whirring too fast to see. It was this weapon the creature raised first, opening the combat with a blistering lateral swipe that Cortez avoided by millimetres, leaning back on his rear foot as the blade swept by.

For all that armour, all that bulk, the monster was fast.

But Cortez knew he was faster.

The fight was on. There was little any of the others could do save to continue taking their own deadly toll on the rest of the ork band. They knew better than to interfere directly. Honour forbade it. One-on-one, Cortez had said, and that was how it would be.

To the 4th Company captain, the universe seemed to shrink. There was nothing else, only he and his opponent locked in struggle of life and death, the definition of existence.

Soon, there would be only one.

DEATH SURROUNDED THEM as their weapons clashed again and again, but they paid it no heed. They were well-matched, and the sound of blow after clashing blow resounded in the damp air. Cortez snarled as his power fist was, once again, deflected. The ork boss's great snapping claw was sheathed in a power field of its own. Every time the deadly claw met the Space Marine's huge red fist, there were arcs of lethal, crackling energy.

Against the monster's chainaxe, the captain's combat blade looked pathetically small, but it was the skill with which the knife was wielded that truly mattered. Every time the monster ripped through the air with its axe, Cortez shifted just enough to avoid the blow, and, little by little, his slashing, stabbing counterattacks began to take their toll. Thick ork blood started to stream from the gaps in the beast's armour, and Cortez was sure the monster's blistering swipes were beginning to slow, just fractionally, perhaps, but enough to offer him the opening he would need for a killing stroke.

The ork boss now seemed to sense the fight was not going its way. It changed tactics, feinting with a wide claw-swipe and bull-rushing Cortez when the captain moved to parry.

It worked. Cortez found himself grappling, wrestling desperately to stay on his feet. If he went to the ground under the bulk of all that armour and green muscle, he knew he would not be getting back up. He knew it would be the end of him.

Was this the moment? Were all the stories, all the legends of his immortality, to end here? He had not thought a creature like this would claim that victory, but then again, even as he struggled, he conceded a grudging respect for the ork's raw combat prowess. The creature had successfully executed a feint, something no other ork had ever done in combat with Cortez. There was more going on inside that thick skull than he had given the beast credit for.

Cortez fought force with force, but only for a moment. He knew he would not win this fight on those terms. He had dropped his knife in order to free his right hand for grappling. It was locked around the beast's left wrist, though it couldn't close entirely over it. That wrist was as thick as Cortez's knee. His power fist was, likewise locked around the armoured housing of the monster's great metal claw, but the energy fields were reacting, making the contact slippery, like two magnets of opposite charge repelling each other.

The ork had dropped its chainaxe to lunge forward and grab its enemy. It knew it had only to fall on Cortez for the battle to be won. It pressed all its weight forward, and tossed its head from side to side, trying to pierce Cortez's visor with its sharp steel horns.

A deep, wet laugh began in the creature's throat. It sensed victory was close. Soon, it would crush the Space Marine to the ground, sit astride him, and snip off his limbs, one after another. It knew that humans were soft beneath their shells. Their flesh parted as easily as the flesh of a fruit. The ork liked the parting of that flesh. It liked the hot sprays of red that accompanied it. It liked the noises the humans made, the high screams and agonised roars they vented in their final moments.

Now was that moment. The ork thrust forward one more time with all its strength, piston-boosted legs lending it irresistible power.

Cortez's legs started to buckle under him, but this was what he had been waiting for, the ork abomination's final forward push. This was the moment the ork was most vulnerable.

Cortez twisted hard, shifting the direction of his own energy, not forward against the creature as it expected, but backwards and to the left, moving with it, adding his own momentum to his enemy's.

It happened. The ork found its massive bulk off-balance, with no hope of recovery. It teetered forward on one tree-thick leg, desperate to regain its equilibrium.

Cortez was already behind it. He kicked out at the monster's supporting leg, his ceramite boot connecting sharply with the back of its knee.

The creature went down hard, its armour cracking the rockcrete underneath it. It flailed, its claw slashing back and forth, frantic swipes intended to sever the Space Marine's legs. But Cortez didn't stay still long enough to get caught. He stamped down on the ork's lower back with his left boot, raised his power fist over his head, and punched straight down into the metal plate, his knuckles passing through into the hot, bloody meat beneath.

The ork howled in pain.

Cortez found what he was looking for. He closed his metal digits around it and yanked hard, then raised his prize above his head and roared in triumph.

In his oversized, blood-drenched gauntlet, he held a large section of the monster's spine.

Other orks turned away from the barricades, sensing something had changed. They saw Cortez standing over their fallen leader, the strongest of their tribe. They saw the massive body beneath his boot and the gleaming white bone in his upraised hand. Of all things, orks recognised strength most of all, and here it stood before them, a strength they could not overcome. Not here. Not now.

The mob split, turning from the Imperial barricades and racing back towards the cover of the ruined buildings nearby. Bolter-fire chased them and a score more went down with wounds in their backs the size of grapefruit.

Cortez watched them go and, finally, lowered his arm.

He cast the ork vertebrae to the ground.

Someone was calling him over the link. The voice eased him out of the battle-rush, soothing him, slowing his primary heart back to a steady beat and sending his secondary heart back into its sleeping state.

It was Pedro Kantor. 'Well fought,' he said simply.

Cortez could hear tension, not pride, in the Chapter Master's voice. He was about to reply when another voice beat him to it.

'Armour!' It was Sergeant Tirius. The Devastator Squad leader was still on top of Jadeberry Hill. 'Sergeant Grimm, ork tanks are pressing towards us from the streets to the south. I see twenty. We'll not be able to hold this time. Our ammunition is almost out. Will you give my squad permission to descend?'

Grimm turned to the Chapter Master, immediately deferring to him.

'We had human refugees with us,' Kantor said to Tirius. 'They were ordered to high ground during the fight. Are they with you?'

'They are, lord,' replied Tirius. 'One died on the ascent. An old man. His heart gave out.'

Cortez winced. Surely it was Dasat. Kantor would take that hard, no doubt.

The Chapter Master paused only briefly, before ordering Squad Tirius to shepherd the refugees down the side of the hill at once. Then he addressed Sergeant Grimm. 'I cannot tell you, sergeant, what it means that you held this passage open for us. I swear to you that you will be honoured properly when there is time.'

Grimm answered without hesitation. 'Your words are honour enough for a dozen lifetimes, my lord. And seeing you alive is a reward even greater. We so hoped it would be you.'

'How did you know anyone was coming this way?'

'The Librarians, my lord. They felt it. Epistolary Deguerro ordered us to hold the underpass for as long as we could.'

Cortez was climbing over the barricades for a final time. 'Deguerro?' he said.

Sergeant Grimm faced him. His voice was heavy with grief as he replied, 'Captain Alvez no longer leads us.'

'You cannot mean...' said the Chapter Master.

'My lord,' said Grimm, 'the captain gave his life in battle two days ago. More than anything, I wish he could have lived to see you return. I don't think he ever really believed you had perished at Arx Tyrannus.'

The link went silent. Cortez pushed a coil of razor-wire aside and climbed over a cluster of concrete-filled drums before coming to a stop at Kantor's side.

'Drigo,' said Kantor softly. 'Dorn's blood. Not him, too.'

Cortez could hear the aching sadness in his friend's voice.

No one said another word until Squad Tirius and the refugees joined them at the mouth of the underpass a moment later.

A woman with matted blonde hair crossed to the Chapter Master and knelt at his feet.

The Space Marines looked down at her. The dirt on her face was streaked with tear tracks. 'My lord,' she sobbed. 'Dasat is dead.' She glanced fearfully in the direction of Sergeant Tirius. 'He would not let us bring the body down from the hill.'

Tirius nodded to confirm this.

'That is Jadeberry Hill,' Kantor told the woman, bending to lift her to her feet. She was as fragile as a doll, her bones showing sharply beneath her mal-nourished flesh. 'It has been a special place since the days Rynn himself claimed this world for the Imperium. Let Dasat lie there, at peace. When this war is over, his passing will be marked more appropri-ately, his and that of so many others. For now, though, we press on. Our journey is not quite over. You are not safe yet.'

Nodding obediently, stifling her sobs, the woman moved off to instruct the refugees.

Cortez detected the first sign of the approaching tanks, a tremor in the ground beneath his feet. Kantor must have felt it to, because he gestured to the cav-ernous mouth of the underpass and said, 'Lead the way, Sergeant Grimm. We should hurry.'

'This way, my lord,' said the sergeant, and began his descent down into the tunnel.

The others followed. Behind them, the rubble-strewn streets began to shake.

SEVENTEEN

Jadeberry Underpass, New Rynn City

PEDRO KANTOR WAS bone-weary, but, as he marched behind the men of Squad Grimm, he was determined not to let it show. He sensed they were all weary, the brothers that surrounded him, but he, more than any other, had to keep his exhaustion at bay a while longer. He was back among his own now. They would be looking to him for guidance, for answers, for a path into the future that would ensure the survival of their ancient brotherhood. It was up to him to provide all these things and more, no matter how impossible that seemed right now.

The tunnel was pitch-black. There were lights at regular intervals along the walls and ceilings, but their power came from a station outside the city limits, and it had fallen to the orks early in the conflict. The Crimson Fists moved easily enough in the dark, of course, their visors and gene-boosted eyes revealing every last detail to them, but the refugees needed light if they were to keep up. Thus, Brother Galica travelled at the rear, holding a lit flare for them to follow. Now and then, when their pace became too slow, he offered words of encouragement, or reminded them of the greenskins at their backs. The latter never failed to spur them on.

The underpass was broad, perhaps forty metres across with a ceiling twelve metres above the surface of the road. Pillars supported all that rock and earth, some of them sculpted in the likeness of hooded figures, the forty-two acolytes who had assisted the famed Imperial Reclamator, Saldano Malverro Rynn. The eerie red light from Galica's flare cast sharp black shadows along the folds of their stone robes.

Kantor's eyes picked out the boxy forms of two large trucks in the gloom up ahead. 'Might we not travel faster in those?' he asked Grimm.

'They have another purpose, lord,' Grimm replied. 'Their carriages are packed with high-explosive. Once we have passed at a safe distance, I will arm them. The first orks to reach them will trigger a detonation that will bring the ceiling, and the Pakomac River, crashing down on their heads.'

Kantor nodded. 'Let's hope the orks give chase in staggering numbers.'

Cortez gave an amused snort.

'I don't doubt they will,' said Grimm, 'but Snagrod has numbers to spare. It shames me to admit it, but we've lost so much ground to the enemy already.'

'Shame be damned,' replied Kantor. 'You have fought more bravely than anyone could have asked. Who else could have stood this long against such a Waaagh? I'll not hear you speak of shame again.'

'As my lord wishes,' Grimm replied. Turning back to the original subject, he continued, saying, 'This underpass is the last open path into Imperial-held territory. With the destruction of this tunnel, we are effectively sealing ourselves in.'

'Help will come,' said Kantor. '*The Crusader* got away.'

'That is something. I hope they bring aid soon. Captain Alvez placed our forces under the Ceres Protocol. Epistolary Deguerro also felt it wise.'

Grimm's question was implied. Would Kantor's famous sense of honour and his compassion for normal humans cause him to overturn Alvez's decree?

'The Ceres Protocol stays in place,' said Kantor. 'Drigo was right to put the survival of the Chapter first.'

He thought Cortez threw a glance his way as he said this.

'Ironically,' Grimm continued, 'the captain gave his own life in violation of it. Thousands of Rynnsguard troopers and civilians would have died had he not made that final sacrifice.'

'He surprised you,' said Kantor perceptively.

Something in Sergeant Grimm's tone suggested he was smiling as he answered, 'Truly, he did.'

The Fists had come abreast of the two trucks now, and Kantor could see that they were very deliberately placed in the gaps between three thick pillars. The destruction of those pillars would undermine the integrity of the whole midsection. The weight of all that rock above would pulverise and bury even the toughest ork machine. The crashing waters that followed, the ice-cold Pakomac, would pound the xenos footsoldiers to a pulp against the walls, or drown them. Either way, they were dead.

The xenos needed oxygen just as much as humans did.

A part of Pedro Kantor wished he could see it, wished his consciousness could hover here to witness the deadly reprisal as a psyker's might do. But it was only a small part. The powers of the witch-kin were as much a curse as a blessing. He knew all too well how Eustace Mendoza had wrestled with the daemons of the warp, the efforts he had made to deflect their malign intentions every single day of his long life. Such a thing was a burden Kantor's broad shoulders, already weighed down with so much, did not need.

The Fists pressed on, Grimm apprising his Chapter Master and the others of all that had occurred in the days since the first alien ships made planetfall here. In turn, Kantor spoke of the tragedy at Arx Tyrannus. His psychological wounds were no better for the telling of the tale, but the brave 2nd Company sergeant and his men deserved to hear the truth from their leader.

The survival of the Chapter was gravely uncertain. There was so little of it left on which to rebuild.

Up ahead, the light changed. Dull daylight seeped into the darkness at a shallow angle, finally announcing the end of their journey through the underpass. It had taken almost two hours. Some of the refugees had slowed so much that Kantor had ordered the Fists in the rearguard to carry those on the verge of collapse.

He had no sooner set his left foot on the shallow ramp that led out of the tunnel than he heard a great rumbling noise behind him. Air began whooshing past, escaping upwards through the tunnel mouth.

'They have triggered the explosives!' called Huron Grimm over the rising noise.

The refugees began whimpering in fear.

'Run!' ordered Kantor. 'Bring those people!'

The Astartes scooped up the civilians and began pounding up the ramp towards the rectangle of daylight. The rumble behind them grew exponentially louder.

Kantor heard Alessio Cortez roaring over the comm-link at his battle-brothers.

'Move, brothers! Dorn detests the slow!'

The noise behind them was deafening now. Any other words were lost in the cacophony. At the front of the group, Sergeant Grimm put on a great burst of speed, inspiring the others to do likewise.

They burst from the mouth of the underpass just as a great spume of water and loose rock exploded upwards from below, drenching them. The force of it knocked some of them from their feet. In seconds the momentum of the water was spent.

Kantor turned to see his Crimson Fists rising, many cradling the soaked, shivering forms of the refugees.

'Is everyone all right?' he asked, scanning them for signs of injury.

Only a few of the refugees were a little the worse for wear.

Kantor saw Alessio Cortez gesturing at a point beyond him, signalling for his Chapter Master to turn around.

He turned…

…and saw a squad of battle-brothers in heavy Terminator armour stomping mechanically towards him from the street up ahead.

A deep, dry voice hailed him on the comm-link.

It was Rogo Victurix.

'Welcome to New Rynn City!'

There was no mistaking the uncharacteristic jubilation in his tone. He was almost laughing with joy as he beheld his leader here before him, alive and well despite everything.

Victurix gestured down at his bulky armour. 'I would take a knee if I could, lord. And I see Captain Cortez continues to live up to his reputation as unkillable. Heartfelt greetings, brother.'

Cortez nodded once and clashed a fist on his chest in salute.

Beneath his faceplate, Kantor found himself grinning. Victurix and his squad were the first living members of his Crusade Company that he had seen since the cataclysm in the Hellblades. And, by Terra, what a sight they were!

'What are you doing here, Rogo? Surely you are needed on the walls?'

Victurix halted his squad about four metres in front of the others. The refugees had never seen Terminator armour before. They had thought the Chapter Master and his three squads of survivors massive, but they were not nearly as massive as these others.

They gaped unblinking at the great blue behemoths while the other Crimson Fists, those that had carried them from the underpass, set them down on their feet. None dared move.

Sergeant Victurix cast an eye over them, then returned his gaze to the Chapter Master. His tone became a shade heavier. 'The walls we *can* hold are being held, my lord, but this very section will be lost to us presently, so we cannot dally here. I have four transports waiting in a square just to the west. It is only a few minutes away.

'We,' he said, spreading his arms, 'are your escort.'

THREE

'*Before such theories were labelled heresy by the Ecclesiarchy and made punishable by death, some men once believed in parallel universes, an infinity of them, physical places like our own universe where all possibilities were played out.*

Though I consider myself a pragmatic man, it is not difficult to see the attraction inherent in such beliefs. Were those parallel universes to exist, after all, in many of them, the orks would never have come to Rynn's World.

Every day, I wish I lived in such a universe.'

– Extract: *Writings from the Ramparts: A Memoir*
Colonel (ret.) Portius Cantrell (948.M41-)

ONE

New Rynn City, Rynnland Province

IMPERIAL LIBRARIES WOULD, one day, come to be filled with great volumes covering the events on Rynn's World. Millions of parchment pages would record the feats of great heroism and self-sacrifice that took place. The suicidal charge of the 16th Rynnite Women's Militia against the orks that breached the Baradon Gate would come to be remembered, as would the further acts of bravery it inspired. Likewise, the brave but costly counterattack prosecuted by the Rynnsguard 3rd Garrison Regiment against ork armoured elements which shelled the Zona 2 Residentia to rubble.

Day by day, the last free citizens of Rynn's World clung on, proving their mettle, holding always to the desperate hope that, maybe today, a great Imperial fleet would sweep down from the skies and decimate the alien besiegers. Every hour they held out against the uncountable hordes of the Arch-Arsonist, Sna-grod, was testament to their strength and faith, their courage and passion. Each hour of life was earned with blood and sweat.

For all the feats that went recorded, how many more were not? No Imperial document would ever tell of the noble death of Sergeant Pacalis Filian, a middle-aged infantry squad leader born on the island of Calliona. He led a night assault against ork forces camped outside his section of the wall, knowing they would overcome his section the following day. None of his men returned alive, but they took more than their share of the enemy down with them.

Nor would any living man or woman retell the last hours of Captain Golrid Prinas of the Ninth Rynns-guard Artillery Regiment's 2nd Company. Prinas and his loyal gunnery crews fought to the last man against a tide of ork abominations before finally calling in an artillery strike from another company, guiding the shells in on their own heads when it was clear they were overrun. As death rained down, Prinas uttered the words, 'My life for Rynn's World, gem of the Imperium, second only to Terra herself.'

No one who heard these words lived to record them.

These brave fighters and millions more died for their world, their loved ones, and for the honour of the Emperor. But none fought as hard, nor as tirelessly, selflessly, as the last two hundred and eighteen battle-brothers of the Crimson Fists.

Though the greenskins pushed closer and closer to the Silver Citadel and its last neighbouring districts, the Crimson Fists extracted a high and bloody price for every centimetre given. The greenskin advance slowed to a crawl. Wherever their armour appeared, defensive batteries blasted it apart. Wherever the orks attempted to rig the walls with explosives, or cut their way through the gates with high-powered las and melta analogues, they were shredded in a hail of bolt and plasma fire.

For every blow the orks sought to strike, the Crimson Fists martialled everything at their disposal and launched a counter blow. And, slowly, the siege settled into a pattern, a deadly routine where attrition looked set to decide the future of the world.

Even the cycle of seasons, unchanged since long before Rynn's World had known the footsteps of man, were not immune to the effects of the Waaagh.

Barely a week after Chapter Master Kantor arrived at the capital, Matiluvia, the Month of Hammering Rains, began in earnest, and it was unlike any such season in living memory. Both the Pakomac and the River Rynn broke their banks, flooding the surrounding lands, turning the ork-held outer districts into filthy, smelly, fly-infested mires. Ork excrement mixed with the floodwaters, coating everything. When the rains finally subsided and the hot weather came, a stinking yellow-brown haze cut visibility down to only five or six kilometres, confounding the Rynnsguard artillery spotters and those manning the forwards observation posts.

Summer brought other problems for the beleaguered defenders. Though the River Rynn flowed through the centre of the city and rendered fresh drinking water a matter of little concern, the burning sun took its toll on many. Guardsmen serving high on the walls day after day were battered with relentless heat and glare. Many reported to medicae facilities with maladies caused by the intensity of the Rynnstar system's twin suns. Others simply collapsed where they stood. How many of those were shot by their commissars for sleeping on the job? How many, dizzy from exhaustion, driven to carelessness by the protests of their own bodies, fell to ork fire when they might have lived had they only been allowed adequate rest?

Only the Space Marines were immune to such things. The rains did not bother them. The blazing suns did not affect them. Rumours spread. Fresh legends grew. Some said they did not eat. Some said they did not sleep. Others said that they could not be killed, that they would fight on for a thousand years if need be, even if there were no civilians left to protect.

Maybe such talk was comforting to some, but the reality was altogether darker. Not even the Adeptus Astartes could hold indefinitely. Snagrod's Waaagh was getting stronger all the time. That each individual battle-brother was far deadlier than a typical ork, none could argue but the Crimson Fists themselves knew the truth. They saw that they were losing, and the knowledge burned.

Summer turned to autumn. Perhaps the orks favoured the milder seasons. Perhaps they too had been hampered by the hard heat of the Rynnite summer. Who could know? They were alien, and seeking to comprehend their ways was forbidden by Imperial edict to all those without the proper dispensation. Certainly, the autumn seemed to rouse them. They strengthened their assaults. Their numbers seemed to increase, despite their daily losses. More and more of them swarmed and flowed along the ruined streets each day, pillaging the bodies of their fallen kin for equipment and pulling the teeth from dead mouths to use as a kind of currency.

It was in late autumn that the aliens began constructing the first of their massive iron ziggurats. A yellow pall still hung in the air, and it was not easy to see their activities in detail, but it was clear they worked with purpose. The structure was quickly completed, and work began on numerous others. Fires still burned throughout the xenos-occupied territories, but those of destruction were soon outnumbered by those of industry.

Pessimists murmured that this was a sign of the coming end. The orks built their foul constructs beyond the range of the Basilisks and Earthshaker batteries, and the defenders could only watch. The sight of the greenskins' massive new fume stacks and construction blocks had an immediate demoralising effect. Suicides increased among Rynnite civilians and soldiers alike, despite the warnings and threats of the commissars. *Dare to insult the Emperor by killing yourself*, the black-clad zealots warned everyone, *and those you hold dearest will suffer a longer, more painful death as punishment.*

At first, this merely prompted hopeless men to slaughter their own families with merciful swiftness before turning their weapons on themselves. It was an intolerable situation. Every last individual capable of firing a lasgun had to be drafted onto the walls.

From the ramparts, they saw their planet burn. The forces of the Arch-Arsonist set light to everything within reach. Fields blazed. Forests flared and crackled. Nothing was untouched by the hungry flames. It was now, with many losing their last vestiges of hope, that Lady Maia Cagliestra made a decision. Much of the Upper Rynnhouse railed against it, but the governor would not be swayed. Together, she and a cadre of noble ladies would take to the walls themselves, bringing light and comfort, she hoped, to the tired men who defended them. Viscount Isopho made an impassioned personal protest against this. Maia planned to visit those sections of the perimeter where the fighting was heaviest, since it was these men, she judged, who needed her support most. The viscount's pleas achieved little at first, but Maia finally conceded to visit the walls only at night, since the fighting usually died off then. With the troopers at rest, she would have greater opportunity to speak with them and dispense food and water.

It became her regular routine. As twilight came each day, she and her party of ladies would make themselves as beautiful as possible – 'To give the men something to fight for,' she told the others whenever they asked – before heading out under armed escort to yet another section of the wall. Their visits soon became highly anticipated events for the Rynnsguard troopers and the militias, though more than a few men were executed by the commissars for making inappropriate comments. Maia tried to ignore that. She felt, for the first time since the war had started, that she was not hiding like a coward in the Silver Citadel, doing nothing while her people died.

Two weeks after she began her visits to the wall, Viscount Isopho announced that he was leaving his seat in the Upper Rynnhouse to rejoin the Rynnsguard as a commissioned officer. He would, he said, fight on the walls with the men, like a true Rynnite should. If, by his words, he hoped to shame other members of the government into following his example, he was fooling himself. Maia spoke privately with General Mir and made sure that Isopho was posted to one of the safer sections of the wall, even while she praised the viscount for his courage.

Despite all the measures to combat it, the death toll among the Rynnsguard, and the lack of any sign whatsoever that aid was coming, continued to eat away at the defenders' morale. Individual Crimson Fists began patrolling sections of the wall on which they had, so far, not been seen. This was done at the suggestion of a young Astartes Chaplain called Argo, and it worked. The sight of the glorious armoured giants, radiant and splendid despite all they had endured, still exerted a powerful effect on the ordinary people. The Astartes inspired faith and dedication wherever they walked. They spoke encouragement to the troopers, and fought shoulder-to-shoulder with them. The number of suicides dropped. The walls held. Snagrod and his forces found themselves at a temporary impasse, but they had already begun work on the weapons that would end this war.

When winter came, the warlord and his savage lieutenants had committed even greater numbers to the construction of their forts and war factories. The human forces could only watch with mounting fear and apprehension as, slowly and inexorably, the mightiest engines of war they had ever seen began to take shape.

Most had never heard of a gargant. Few men on Rynn's World had the kind of clearance that would grant them access to the Munitorum archives in which accounts of such near-indestructible metal monstrosities could be found. But the surviving Rynnsguard commanders knew what was coming, and so did the Crimson Fists.

They considered the viability of launching surgical strikes on the massive engines of doom before they were completed, before they could bring their unstoppable weapons to bear on the gates and walls. Considered then rejected.

Such a strike would risk everything. Many battle-brothers would be lost. Forces critical to the continued deadlock would be fatally diminished. The orks would only begin construction again. With the rest of the planet being, to all extents and purposes, dominated by the greenskin race, their resources were near limitless.

Exchanging Astartes lives for a little more time?

Chapter Master Kantor could not sanction it. Whichever way he looked at it, the losses outweighed the gains.

Deep winter came. Snow was a thing unheard of in the capital. New Rynn City lay close to the equator, and did not suffer winter like the mountain regions did.

When the first snows came, the emaciated children of the capital shuffled out into the streets to gaze up at the sky in wonder. Few remembered such a beautiful sight. Beautiful, yes, but deadly, too. Within days, the first casualties of the freak winter were reported. This season, in its own way, was as harsh as the brutal heat of summer had been, and took just as many lives. The weakest children died in droves, leaving grief-wracked parents who were barely capable of standing, let alone firing on the foe. Many of the elderly perished, too. Again, the commissars and Ecclesiarchs went out among the grieving people, threatening or consoling them, whichever was their way.

Again, it was the presence of the Space Marines that made the greater difference. It was now, with things darkest of all, that Pedro Kantor turned his eyes from the daily casualty reports and tactical hololiths, and went out among the ordinary people.

He saw a populace beaten to nothing, both mentally and physically, and felt their grief as if it were his own. He could not help but recall the tragedy that had struck Arx Tyrannus. It had haunted him every day since. It also gave him a keen sense of empathy with those who gathered around him, all those who had lost the things they loved most.

He stood before them, gleaming helmet under his left arm, and swore to them that the fight was far from over. He told them of *The Crusader* and of her escape the previous year. Warp travel was unpredictable, but help would come, he assured them. *The Crusader* would not fail.

They listened. They looked up from where they knelt in front of him, and he saw the hope in their eyes. They wanted to believe, and he let them. Somewhere deep down, he still believed it himself.

Spring came. The snows melted. The morning air became crisp, then eventually warm. The hope that Kantor spread was sustained as the climate became gentle again.

But, beyond the walls, things were different. A new wave of excitement whipped the orks to violent frenzy.

Soon, the gargants would be complete.

Soon the planet would shudder under their massive feet. Gods of death and destruction would wade towards the final Imperial stronghold, crushing everything to powder beneath them.

For almost eighteen months, the defenders of New Rynn City had endured everything Snagrod's foul orks had thrown at them.

But they would not survive the march of the gargants.

TWO

The Cassar, Zona Regis, New Rynn City

Within the void-shielded walls of the Silver Citadel, the Cassar, last fortress stronghold of the Crimson Fists, stood so far unmarked by the ravages of war. Atop its roofs and towers, great gun batteries stood, whirring smoothly on their cogged mounts as they tracked left and right, scanning the sky for aerial threats. Below them, on a broad balcony facing south, Pedro Kantor stood looking out at the haze-shrouded horizon. Black smoke billowed into the air from a score of sites in ork-held land. Noxious green and brown fumes poured upwards from towering cylindrical stacks. Far out, beyond the reach of the Imperial guns and missile batteries, greenskin transports and aerial war machines buzzed and rumbled, always audible, even this far away.

Alessio Cortez grumbled something from Kantor's left where he, too, stood surveying the horizon in the light of the morning.

'Again, brother,' said Kantor. 'I'm afraid I was not paying attention.'

'I said they've even turned the blasted air against us.'

Kantor nodded. Among his reports, he had seen those of the medicae. Allergic reactions, breathing disorders, cancers, deaths by airborne toxins, all had increased since the end of winter. This had once been such a beautiful world, so green and fertile, so rich and diverse in its animal and plant life.

The orks had raped it. They had poisoned and burned and scarred its face. Even if, by some miracle, the xenos were at last fully purged, the likelihood that Rynn's World could ever be restored to its former glory was a thing beyond even his ability to hope for.

The planet's scars, like the battle scars on his own body, would always remain.

'The next session of the Upper Rynnhouse will begin in an hour,' said Cortez. 'Have you thought about what you will tell them?'

'I have considered your proposal, Alessio, but I'll not send the last of my Crimson Fists out to die. As I grow weary of telling you, the Chapter must endure, no matter what. I will not be remembered as the last master of the Crimson Fists. Our order must survive this.'

Cortez snorted derisively. 'Nothing will survive the gargants, and we both know it. They'll march soon. Once the last few districts fall, they'll turn their guns on the Silver Citadel, and, when the void shields finally fail, we will be cornered and killed.' He raised a hand. 'Please, Pedro. I know you think aid is coming, but how long are we to sit and wait? Grant me the fight I want, for the sake of all we've been through together.'

Kantor looked away to the east, but the haze was thick today. He could see the river where it flowed towards the waters of the Medean, but he could not see the ocean itself.

'You ask to overturn the Ceres Protocol so you can lead a suicide charge,' he said, his voice low and angry. 'You ask me to throw away my best fighters for the sake of a moment's glory. Did you hit your head, Alessio?'

Cortez scowled and stepped forward, gripping the stonework lip of the balcony wall. 'Do you know how many of our brothers have expressed to me their support for a last glorious charge?' he asked.

Kantor nodded. 'Almost half,' he said. 'And they are wrong, all of them. There is more to consider here than an honourable death.'

Cortez spun, his eyes blazing. 'We are Crimson Fists! Honour is everything!'

Kantor met his friend's harsh stare with his own.

Fire and ice, he thought. We were always so different. Fire and ice.

'I tell you our honour is served best in protecting the people. Would you have history remember us as the Chapter that left them to die?'

'They will die anyway,' hissed Cortez.

Kantor flashed forward. As fast as Cortez was, the speed of the Chapter Master surprised him, and he found himself gripped tight by his upper arms.

For a moment, they stood that way, frozen, the tension crackling like static electricity between them. Kantor's eyes held the fury of a winter blizzard, but no words came from his lips. He could not deny that his hope was fading fast. He knew only too well what the first steps of the gargants would mean, and he knew it would start the moment the metal leviathans were complete. Snagrod would not wait. He had waited long enough for this. Perhaps he was even bored, already hungering for fresh battles on new worlds.

Perhaps he had only stayed this long at all because the Crimson Fists fought on, refusing to die.

At last, Kantor released his grip. Sorrow stole over his face. 'Such a wedge between us, Alessio,' he said. 'In all our centuries, we never fought quite like this. What happened, I wonder?'

Hearing these words, Cortez's fury cooled fast, like a glowing, fresh-forged blade suddenly thrust into cold water. 'You are the Chapter Master,' he replied. 'Before the coming of the orks, we had not served together on the field of battle since I took command of Fourth Company. You gave me that honour, Pedro, and the latitude I needed to execute your will in your absence. The battles I won for you were fought my way. And I never lost. Now, I want Snagrod's head… my way. I want vengeance for all the Fists he has killed. If it costs me my own life, it is a small price to pay for the honour of our dead. Every brother who wishes to go with me has asked the same question of himself, and has found the same answer in his heart.

His life for vengeance. We await only your blessing. Let us all go out as warriors should. Lead us out yourself. The future be damned!'

Kantor's features darkened again. He turned to go from the balcony.

Cortez gripped him by the right vambrace, stopping him momentarily.

Kantor looked down at his old friend's hand, then slowly turned his eyes upwards with a warning glare.

Cortez released his grip.

'I am the Chapter,' said Kantor coldly as he turned away again. 'The honour of the Crimson Fists is served only by serving me.'

He passed beyond the balcony's arched doors and into the shadowy chamber beyond. At the back of his mind was the urge to pray for guidance in the Reclusiam before the session of the Upper Rynnhouse began. And there was something else he wanted to pray for, too.

The very thought of Alessio Cortez's death chilled him far deeper than the thought of his own. Cortez the Immortal, the Chapter's greatest living legend. Without him, how could there be hope for any of them?

As the Chapter Master's footsteps echoed along the torch-lit stone corridor ahead of him, he looked back on his life, and saw it defined, not by his status or martial achievements, but by the centuries-long bond of brotherhood with the 4th Company captain. Ever since the fall of Arx Tyrannus, that bond was the rock he had clung hardest to, the only certainty he had in this never-ending storm of death and loss, and the breaking of that bond was something he knew his hearts would not be able to bear.

As he entered the quiet, sanctified space of the Cassar's Reclusiam, he thought of the final trials ahead, and knew there were many prayers he must offer today.

EPISTOLARY DEGUERRO'S PERSONAL serf, Ufrien Kofax, waited anxiously outside the Reclusiam for the Chapter Master to emerge. Every second seemed like an hour, but Kofax would wait as long as he had to. He could not enter, of course. That would mean death. Instead, he turned his eyes to the portal's etched surfaces and saw images of Chapter heroes overcoming all manner of foes. Disgusting alien and daemonic forms lay in heaps at the feet of armoured giants. The giants stood with weapons aloft, holy light blazing in stylised sunbursts from the halos encircling their helmeted heads.

Heavy footsteps announced the approach of one such giant now. The Chapter Master's prayers had ended.

Kofax straightened his robes and prepared to give his message.

Minutes later, Pedro Kantor found himself seated on a great stone chair in the speaking chamber of the Librarium, listening to Deguerro and his brothers as they updated him with everything they had gleaned from the warp so far. The words were so unexpected, so uplifting, that the Chapter Master's body actually went numb.

Hope, he thought. Slim, granted, but hope nonetheless. Praise Dorn that we stood against them this long.

'A great many, my lord,' said Deguerro, a rare grin brightening his typically dour features. 'We detected the psychic bow waves of over two thousand ships.'

'Two thousand?' echoed Kantor. 'And you are certain these are Imperial ships?'

'We were not certain at first,' said a Librarius Codicier. It was Ruthio Terraro. 'At first we thought it might be another ork wave, and a big one at that, though an increasing number of their smaller long-range ships have been detected leaving the system in the last few months.'

Why this might be the case hardly needed voicing aloud. The orks believed they had won here. Snagrod would be sending advance scouts out into the warp to search for other challenges now. That he was so assured of his victory here was further insult to the Chapter and all it stood for.

'But they are not orks,' said Kantor. Despite the burgeoning hope in his chest, he knew he had to be absolutely sure. 'You are sure you are not mistaken? Could they be other xenos? The eldar perhaps? Those capricious cowards have been known to observe the battles of other races from the edge of the combat zone.'

'It is not the eldar, lord,' said Deguerro. 'The ships are indeed human, and, in the minutes before you arrived, we received confirmation that they are loyalists. *The Crusader* is among them. Dorn and the

Emperor have answered our prayers. The Imperium has come at last.'

'How did you detect them?' Kantor asked, craning forward. 'I was under the impression that the ork psykers were so numerous that their presence somehow smothered your... gifts.'

'True, my lord,' said Deguerro. 'They are perhaps even more numerous now than before. But there are powerful psykers aboard these Imperial ships, several dozen of them registered as alpha-class, and they are doing all they can to hold the psychic channels open. There are Space Marine Librarians with them, too, from half a dozen Chapters. They have come with their battle-brothers, all swearing oaths of succour in our time of need. Even the psychic noise of the orks cannot entirely drown out our communication with them. We have been able to engage in limited two-way communication.'

'And what have they told you?' Kantor asked.

Deguerro nodded to a Codicier named Thracio, whose fingers activated a series of runes set in the armrest of his own stone chair. In the air above them, a shimmering, ghostly solar system appeared. Its two suns, one large and yellow, one tiny and white, spun slowly in the centre. Kantor recognised Rynn's World and her two moons, Dantienne and Eloix. She was the third planet out, situated perfectly in the middle of her star's life zone, much like Holy Terra Herself.

Hololithic green triangles appeared above her cloud-masked surface. These were the orks' ships at anchor in high orbit. There were still thousands of them.

Deguerro directed Kantor's attention to the orbital plane of the Rynnstar system's outermost planet, Phraecos, a barren, moonless world with a surface of frozen methane. Just within the hololithic ring of the planet's orbital path, a formation of glowing blue triangles flickered into existence, attendant streams of digital data spooling through the air beside them.

'Two thousand two hundred and sixteen warp-capable ships,' said Deguerro, 'and nothing smaller than a Dauntless-class light cruiser. There are several Space Marine battle-barges, but the main bulk of the fleet's firepower is comprised of that aboard the Imperial Navy's Emperor- and Retribution-class battleships. There are four each of these, a significant commitment from Segmentum Headquarters.'

Kantor looked again at the swarm of triangles representing the orks fleet around Rynn's World. He thought for a moment, then said, 'This Imperial force is enough to break through and land troops, but it is not enough to eliminate the enemy fleet outright.'

'True,' said Deguerro. 'But we have been assured that further support is on the way.'

'To arrive when, exactly?' Kantor asked.

There was an uncomfortable pause before Codicier Thracio answered, 'We cannot be sure. Best estimates say two days from now, but the warp...'

Deguerro gestured again at the cluster of blue triangles above. 'This fleet is under the command of Lord Admiral Prioce Galtaire the Fourth. His combat record is exemplary.'

'I know of him,' said Kantor, lifting a hand in interruption. 'What I *wish* to know is whether he intends to keep his fleet at anchor outside ork striking range until the other elements arrive. Our need for support here on the ground is desperate.'

'He knows this,' said Deguerro. 'The fleet is moving in-system as we speak. Naturally, we wished to consult with you before co-ordinating further action.'

Kantor rose from his stone chair, and stood eyeing his psychic brothers.

He thought of Eustace Mendoza, and of how much he missed him, of how comforting the presence of the Master of the Librarius would have been in recent days. Tomasi, too, should have been here.

'I regret how short we must cut this,' said Kantor, 'but I must attend a session of the Upper Rynnhouse, and I am already late. The ministers will be overjoyed when I share your news. Spread word among our brothers. Let them know the pendulum of fate is, at last, on the verge of swinging our way once more.'

The Librarians stood as one and saluted.

'By your command, lord,' said Deguerro.

Kantor smiled briefly at him, then turned and left, his pace quick, his boots ringing on stone.

THREE

The Upper Rynnhouse, Zona Regis, New Rynn City

THE CHAMBER ERUPTED into cheers and applause. One watching all the congratulatory backslapping, hand-shaking and even hugging could easily have imagined that the siege was over and the war was won.

It was far from it.

Kantor watched them behind the golden lectern. The ministers did not seem to register that the fleet would still have to fight its way through the green-skins' orbital blockade. Neither did they seem to care that it was still many hours out from the planet. He let them revel in the moment, knowing reality would come down hard on them soon enough. He had seen them eroded over the last eighteen months, proud nobility turned to lifeless husks convinced of their impending deaths. It was he who had ordered them to release their servants so that they might be con-scripted into the Defence Force. It was he who had ordered the nobles' personal stores and stockhouses raided, and the foodstuffs pooled with those of the rest of the city, to be rationed out in accordance with emergency Munitorum law.

Fighters eat first.

How they had railed against that! The commissars had been forced to make a few examples. Those who had most openly and vocally challenged martial law had been publicly flogged. It was the first time any noble had received capital punishment in over six hundred years.

Kantor had not attended the flogging, but he approved. These were times of war. Those who did not adapt were destined to die.

He thought of his own efforts to adapt to all that had happened. From leading a force of over a thousand glorious warriors, he had been left with only three hundred and eighteen. Surviving the trek from the Hellblade Mountains all the way across the continent to the planetary capital, he had been reunited with much of his First and Second Companies, not to mention squads from the Ninth and Tenth Companies present in support. The whole Chapter had gone from being a lethal interstellar strike-force to a desperate remnant under constant siege. How had he adapted? Had he, in fact, changed at all?

He was sure he had, but his line of thought was abruptly broken when a voice burst through on his comm-link's emergency channel. It was Cortez.

'Damn it, Pedro,' he rasped. 'Are you there? Can you hear me?'

Kantor turned away from the jubilant politicians and pressed a finger to the vox-bead in his ear. He always wore the tiny mechanism while his helmet was removed.

'I can hear you, brother,' he said.

'I heard word of the approaching fleet,' said Cortez. His voice crackled with static, the transmission hampered by the thick walls of the chamber. 'But the universe is cruel. Aid comes too late for us, old friend.'

Kantor was about to demand an explanation when he felt a shudder travel up through the chamber floor. Then another. And another, slow and rhythmic like the groggy footsteps of a newly-awakened god.

'No,' he breathed.

'I'm afraid so,' said Cortez. 'The gargants walk!'

'Meet me in the Strategium,' Kantor snapped, then he cut the link and strode out from behind the podium, crossing the thick red carpet of the central aisle at speed. Some of the lords and ladies moved to intercept him, their faces still glowing with joy.

Kantor scowled at them, the snarl on his features making them recoil.

'Move!' he barked. 'Get out of my way.'

He did not stop to explain himself. He left them to stare, stunned into silence, eyes following his armoured back as he passed beyond the wide gold and ebonwood doors.

Only now did the members of the Upper Rynnhouse notice the shivering and shaking of the chandeliers above them. They felt growing vibrations travel up through the floor, up through their legs.

They looked at each other, joy giving way to dark apprehension. No one remembered the Silver Citadel shaking like this. Not ever.

They streamed through the doors in a brightly coloured tide, making for the closest antechambers which boasted balconies. Deep down, they already knew what they would see, or at least they suspected, though none wanted to believe it.

Through the pall of smoke and airborne pollutants, vast figures moved in the distance, figures with great angular shoulders and arms of clustered weaponry, figures with horned heads and great skirts of impenetrable armour. Their huge round eyes glowed a baleful red, piercing the airborne murk that still veiled them. The air shook with the noise of their sputtering, fume-spewing engines.

There were six of them in all, and the whole planet seemed to tremble with every crushing step they took.

Ministers fainted, both men and women, falling to the balcony floor among the legs of their fellows. Others sank to their knees, crying out in despair. Others were too numb to react. They stood frozen, their unblinking eyes locked to the gargantuan waddling figures in the distance.

Maia Cagliestra was one of these. She saw that the end had come. The Imperial Fleet would find only ruins, if they made it through the blockade at all. Not even her beloved Crimson Fists, in whom she had never lost faith, could do anything to change that now.

She stood with the others looking out at their doom, weeping silently, nothing left to hold on to.

FOUR

The Cassar, Zona Regis, New Rynn City

KANTOR ENTERED THE Cassar only minutes after leaving the Upper Rynnhouse chambers, but he did not go straight to the Strategium. First, he made a detour to the Librarius and ordered them to put him in contact with Lord Admiral Galtaire's fleet at once.

Some minutes later, a fragile psychic link was established and updates were given in both directions. Kantor reported the movement of the gargants, impressing the increased desperation of their situation on the lord admiral. If the fleet didn't get here soon, there would be no one left alive to assist. Brother Deguerro, locked into a trance, features twisted painfully with the effort, transmitted the Chapter Master's words while the other Librarians lent their own power to maintaining and securing the connection. There could be no doubt that the orks, too, had detected the Imperial fleet. The enemy ships were already moving to intercept. If the Imperial fleet could outflank them, could just get around them somehow, they might still be able to make a difference.

Lord Admiral Galtaire, speaking through his most powerful astropath, expressed grave reservations, but he was not about to let a Chapter like the Crimson Fists become extinct while his pride and joy, the flagship *Septimus Astra*, was so close. He swore an oath, then and there, that he would succeed or die trying.

It wouldn't be as simple as slipping around the ork blockade, of course. Galtaire needed those already on the ground to do something for him, and Kantor's blood ran cold as he heard what it was.

The Crimson Fists would need to retake New Rynn Spaceport.

Securing that facility was the only chance they had. It was large enough on which to land heavy craft, including carrier-shuttles belonging to the Legio Titanicus, close enough to facilitate the immediate launch of Marauder bombers which would fly to the aid of the Silver Citadel, and armed with a defence grid capable of protecting the reinforcements as they flew in... if the orks hadn't dismantled it already.

After almost eighteen months of protecting the city walls, of guarding the gates to an ever-dwindling stronghold, Kantor and his Crimson Fists would have to go out and face the horde after all. They would have to cross ork territory filled with impossible numbers of enemy troops and all the weaponry at their disposal.

They would have to infiltrate and secure the space-port.

The odds of success were laughable, but, if they didn't try, they were dead already.

Of that, there was no doubt in Pedro Kantor's mind.

THE ATMOSPHERE INSIDE the Strategium was charged and tense. Cortez had done as ordered. He had gathered as many senior members of the Chapter as were left within the walls that protected them. Techmarines, Apothecaries, Librarians, Chaplains, Crusade Company veterans, all were represented. Kantor laid the situation out before them.

Cortez felt his blood surge in his veins as he listened.

At last, he thought. The moment has come. Blade against blade, fist against fist, armour splashed with the blood of our enemies – if we're to die, by Dorn, let it be a worthy one. I've waited for this. I've wanted this since the day we got here. Static defence be damned. Finally, it is time to do what we do best.

With supporting information and tactical hololiths provided by Brother Anais, the most senior Techmarine present, Kantor briefed them on exactly what was needed of them.

'It must be done as quickly as we can manage it,' he said. 'The first objective, naturally, will be to cover the ground between here and the spaceport limits. It is well that the city underworks were never collapsed, because they are our only hope of getting to the spaceport alive. Our Terminator squads have held them for months, choking them with ork dead that sought to sneak under our guard. We will need flamer and melta units up front to clear the tunnels of the xenos dead. Almost sixty kilometres of tunnel between us and the spaceport... We may find ourselves engaged along the way. Again, it is our Terminator squads that are best suited to lead us through. Rogo Victurix will coordinate this phase of the operation.'

Kantor nodded to the senior Techmarine, Brother Anais, and, a second later, the air over the table flickered to show an angular network of long, glowing tubes. These were the underworks, and every Fist in the room committed them to memory while the Chapter Master looked over the ebonwood table at Rogo, whose eyes were bright with enthusiasm for the task. 'Speed is key, my brother,' said Kantor. 'Push fast and push hard. The gargants will take between four and six hours to reach the Silver Citadel, and the void-shields will hold the people safe for some time after that, but we have no idea exactly how long. We have to retake the spaceport fast.'

'Our Terminator squads know the underworks back to front, lord,' said Victurix, his voice a gravelly rasp. 'Trust in us.'

Kantor did.

Again he nodded to Anais, and the Techmarine's fingers flickered over a hololith control panel. There was a burst of green static above the table, and schematics of the spaceport appeared.

It was the largest single facility on the planet, capable of accommodating three massive trans-orbital cargo lifters at a time, one on each of its specially constructed grav-suspended landing plates. Sub-orbital craft, both military and civilian, were served by several dozen airfields within the spaceports outer walls.

It was a curious structure unlike any other building in the capital. Shrunk down to tabletop hololith size, it resembled three upturned bowls clustered together around a triad of slim spikes. These spikes housed the spaceport control towers, including the control rooms for the communication and defence systems. It was these, more than any other part of the spaceport, that Kantor and his Fists needed to secure.

'Every able-bodied battle-brother we have will be going in,' said the Chapter Master, 'with the exception of our Dreadnought brothers, who are simply too big to negotiate the tunnels. Instead, they will stay here to protect the Silver Citadel, fighting from the walls alongside the Rynnsguard and the militias. The people will draw great strength and comfort from their presence, I'm sure of it.'

There were no Dreadnoughts in the room to argue the point, and Kantor was glad of that. He would go to them himself and explain all before he left.

'Most of our squads,' Kantor continued, 'will exit the tunnels close to the inner perimeter of the spaceport grounds. They will retake the facilities defensive walls and hold them against ork retaliation from outside. The rest of us will fight to secure each of the landing towers. Captain Cortez and I will be leading a further contingent into the control towers to reactivate the defence and comms networks. Dorn willing, we will have our reinforcements shortly after that. Lord Admiral Galtaire is confident in the forces he brings to our aid. There are entire companies of Astartes from our brother Chapters waiting to join us in battle. The Adeptus Mechanicus have brought their mighty Titans to rip apart the gargant abominations. And the Navy has enough Marauders to bomb the xenos back to the Age of Strife.'

He eyed them all as he spoke, one by one. 'But it all depends on us.'

Serious faces nodded back at him.

'Are you ready to take our world back, brothers?' he asked them.

'For the Chapter!' they roared. Some pounded on the table, those standing clashed a clenched fist on their chests.

Kantor smiled a hard smile at them and stood.

'Then get ready to move out. Take every bit of ammunition you can carry. Have the Chaplains bless your amour and weapons. I go now to give orders to the Dreadnoughts, and to tell the governor and General Mir that we are leaving.'

His Fists saluted him as he turned and left, then they turned to each other and clapped those nearest to them on the shoulders. Rough laughter sounded from some. Others grinned. They were going back on the offensive after so long. It felt right.

And none believed that more so than Alessio Cortez.

FIVE

The Underworks, New Rynn City

THE TUNNEL ALONG which Kantor's assault group moved was dark and damp, the concrete walls covered with slick algae and thick ceramic pipes that had been broken open in places. Even in the glare of the lights mounted on the Terminators' armour, the tunnel floor was invisible beneath a soupy black liquid some ten centimetres deep. It was impossible to move quietly, so the Crimson Fists didn't try. They moved fast instead, or at least as fast as the Terminators on point.

It was a relatively smooth journey at first, not just for Kantor's group, but for all the assault parties he had formed for the operation. Right now, there were more than twenty detachments of Crimson Fists making for the spaceport along the tunnel networks, each with their very own Terminator out in front, clearing the way with flamer and melta when the xenos bodies were heaped too thick to pass. The orks had been held back quite far out from the Silver Citadel. Over the months of the siege, they had slowly learned that any efforts to infiltrate via underground routes led to their immediate slaughter. Victurix and the other squads from Crusade Company had not relaxed for a moment. The role may have seemed inglorious to others, but the Terminator squads knew it was critical all along. They had never complained about spending days on end down here in the dark. They killed thousands of the foe down here.

Throughout the entire journey, the tunnels shook with the footfalls of the gargants overhead, but it was only after two hours that this became a danger. Victurix himself, who had been charged with guiding Kantor's assault group, called back to the Chapter Master when the tunnel's shaking was at its worst.

'We must be directly underneath one of them, my lord,' he bellowed over the comm-link. 'There are cracks in the tunnel ceiling, and they are getting wider.'

Kantor judged the sergeant's words accurate. Step after massive step was knocking dust and small chunks of stone down onto his helmet and pauldrons.

'Press on as fast as you can,' he told Victurix.

Dorn forgive us if we're buried down here without even a chance to fight, he thought.

But they were not buried.

Another two hours passed. The earthshaking power of the footfalls dissipated as the Fists pushed on, further and further away from them, and soon Kantor judged that he and his brothers would soon be within the outer perimeter of the spaceport grounds.

Communication was impossible with the other assault groups while everyone was underground, but they had their orders. They had synchronised their visor-chronometers. They would do exactly as he had asked of them.

Another hour brought Kantor and his group to the final junction before they must return aboveground. Where two tunnels met, there was a little more room to move, and Kantor stepped to the fore to look ahead between the shoulders of the Terminators. There was a dark archway set into the left of the tunnel about thirty metres from him. Cortez came up and stood by his side.

'Through that archway,' said Kantor, 'is the stone stair that will take us up into the basement level of the Coronado Tower.'

'I'm ready,' said Cortez.

Behind him, four squads of Crimson Fists readied their weapons.

'You want to be first in, Alessio.'

It wasn't a question.

Beneath his helm, Cortez grinned wickedly. 'You know I do.'

Kantor checked the chronometer display on his visor. The other assault groups would be in position within four minutes, explosives fixed to the access hatches and manhole covers they would rush from, bolters cocked and ready to rip their hated enemies apart. All across the spaceport grounds, the orks wouldn't know what hit them.

'Let's get everyone onto the stairs,' said Kantor.

His visor now told him he had thirty seconds to go before the assault began.

Behind him, his battle-brothers were coiled, ready to strike. He had brought three squads in standard MkVII aquila-pattern power armour, one in Terminator armour, and two Techmarines – Brothers Anais and Ruzco. He knew their blood was up, all of them, knew they were anxious to be in among the foe, tearing them to pieces.

Twenty seconds... ten seconds...

He looked at Cortez and said, 'When you go in, brother, go in hard!'

The captain barked out a laugh.

'I always do!'

The explosive charges they had placed on the inner surface of the access hatch exploded with a bang, and stone chips and smoke blew back over the Astartes.

They didn't wait for the smoke to clear.

'Charge,' roared Cortez as he burst forward.

The assault had begun.

ALL ACROSS THE spaceport grounds – in the lower levels of the defence towers, in basements and hangars and fuel storage buildings and more – the Crimson Fists exploded up from the tunnels with armour shimmering and weapons stuttering.

The spaceport had become a base of operations for the orks since the day they had overcome the small Crimson Fist and Rynnsguard contingent charged with defending it. Now, the tables were turned. The orks were the defenders, and, in their confidence that this war was already won, they were completely unprepared.

Thousands of greenskins died as the Space Marines swarmed the inner walls and retook the defence towers. Outside those walls, the orks were unaware that anything was wrong. Most of the alien horde had their eyes locked to the gargants and were following them as close as they dared. They did not want to miss the spectacle of their mighty metal monstrosities obliterating the final Imperial stronghold.

The groups assaulting the spaceport's main buildings – the landing towers and control spires – had it harder, but not at first.

Cortez had burst into the basement of the Coronado tower to find scores of sickly-looking gretchin facing him, frozen in fear and confusion by the sudden explosion that had just interrupted their work. They had been hauling crates of ammunition onto elevators to be taken to the loading bays above. Now, most of that ammunition lay spilled on the ground, the shells rolling and clinking together.

Cortez started picking them off with his boltpistol immediately. The first grisly death sent the others scurrying for cover, whimpering and shrieking as they scrambled, but a good number were too slow.

Squads Lician and Segala, two of the four squads
Kantor had chosen to go with him, were right behind
Cortez, and their bolters began chewing the diminu-
tive aliens apart.

The basement level was a single broad, high-
ceilinged room littered with boxes and heaps of metal
junk. The roof-space was thick with cable-bundles
and pipes that snaked between steel girders. Hanging
underneath the metal supports, large arc lights threw
out a harsh white glare. It was clear the gretchin didn't
like those lights much. They had smashed more than
half of them.

Still, the shadows offered no sanctuary. More Crimson Fists poured through the access hatch now until,
finally, Victurix and four of his Terminator brothers
stepped through, shaking the floor underneath their
booted feet.

'Clear and hold,' barked Kantor, but he was glad to
see his Space Marines already about the task.

More gretchin screamed as mass-reactive bolts
punched into their bodies and blew them open a
heartbeat later.

If there are gretchin here, thought Cortez as he
killed, then there will be an overseer nearby, too.

Gretchin were disinclined to do anything for the
good of their race without a particularly sadistic and
violent brute standing over them with a prod or whip.

Sure enough, alerted by the sound of gunfire, a
massive leathery brown-skinned ork with one eye
burst through a metal door at the top of the stairway
that led to the next floor up. Seeing the Space Marines

surrounded by dead gretchin, the beast charged into the fray bellowing at the top of its voice. It hadn't gone three metres down the stairs when an Astartes bolt detonated in its brain, spraying the metal steps dark red and causing the heavy body to tumble down them.

Brother Gaban of Squad Lician found the last of the gretchin hiding between two tall stacks of metal crates. A short burst of bright fire from Gaban's flamer turned the creature into a blazing puppet that danced frantically on the spot as its flesh was consumed.

'Up,' shouted Kantor to the others. 'They know we're here!'

Cortez raced for the metal stair and pounded up it. Squad Daecor followed right behind him, boots ringing on the metal steps. At the top, Cortez and Sergeant Daecor took position on either side of the open door. The other four members of Daecor's squad prepared themselves to rush through it, guns held ready, safeties off.

Cortez nodded to Daecor, and the sergeant ordered his squad in.

They rushed forward through the doorway, weapons firing on every target they saw as they moved. Once through the doorway, they immediately moved to the sides, two left, two right, and lay down a steady covering fire for all those that followed.

'Go!' Kantor ordered, and Squad Lician charged through next, adding their own lethal rattle of explosive rounds.

Cortez was firing into the loading bay from his position by the frame of the door. He heard Brother Ramos's plasma cannon, its steady low hum now increased to a threatening whine. The weapon's glowing coils channelled powerful electromagnetic energies in preparation for a shot. Moments later, there was a roar like fire as a blast of superheated plasma streaked from the weapon. Cortez didn't see it, nor did he see the result of the blast, but he heard an explosion and the deep howling of full-grown orks in pain.

'Moving in,' said Daecor, 'keep to cover brothers. Oro, watch the gantry above you. Greenskins! Padilla, give him some support, damn it!'

Cortez flexed his muscles and prepared to follow Daecor in. He felt his armour respond to every twitch and stretch he made. Beneath the thick ceramite plates lay a skin of synthetic fibres that acted much like human muscle, reacting to electrical impulses, to the motor commands sent by his brain. The response time was almost exactly that of his own body, making his armour feel like part of him, and he was part of it.

His power armour responded no less swiftly now as he surged out from the cover of the doorway with his boltpistol kicking in his hand. Kantor was right behind him, Dorn's Arrow spewing a torrent of death towards a trio of big orks firing down on them from a metal gallery above.

'Segala and Lician, flank and eliminate,' commanded the Chapter Master. 'Anais and Ruzco stay by me. The rest of you, suppressing fire.'

This was Loading Bay Epsilon, the main loading areas serving Coronado Tower. It was here that incoming shipments of Imperial goods had once been loaded onto trucks and driven out for distribution. There were orks and gretchin all over the place. The Crimson Fists' assault had caught in the middle of loading their ugly armoured trucks. Like the basement, the ceiling here was high and girdered. The huge metal shutters in the curving north wall were up, and beyond them lay a vast rockcrete expanse of road and runway. The ork trucks sat idling noisily, but even their spluttering engines couldn't compete with the noise of battle.

Cortez saw movement to his left. Four barrel-chested greenskins were arming themselves from the back of one of the trucks. Inside, Cortez could make out ammunition crates stacked one on top of the other. He turned with his boltpistol raised and loosed a tight, three-round cluster of bolts, firing, not at the orks, but at the crates just behind them.

For half-a-second, his rounds had no effect.

Then the truck exploded in a blaze of light and flame. The orks were blasted onto their bellies, backs studded with massive shards of hot shrapnel. Secondary explosions lifted the truck into the air before it slammed back down, nose first, into rockcrete.

Cortez didn't stop to enjoy his handiwork. All around him, the Crimson Fists slaughtered anything green and animate. He continued adding his own fire, making every shot a kill shot. This was what he trained for. He never missed.

He saw a wretched-looking ork with a mechanical hand dash towards a doorway on the metal platform twenty metres above Squad Daecor. No doubt the ugly brute was racing to raise some kind of general alarm, but the Crimson Fists could not afford to get bogged down in a heavy firefight here. Their whole plan depended on their ability to stay mobile, and on the ork inability to coordinate a proper reaction. The spaceport control tower and defence grid control room were many floors above. Terminator Squad Victurix, slower than the other lighter-armoured squads, would stay here and hold this zone. Chapter Master Kantor was counting on them to keep the orks on the ground occupied while he, Cortez and the others climbed higher towards their two main objectives.

Cortez was about to fire on the running ork when a burst of fire from his right ripped the creature to wet red pieces. Cortez glanced towards the shooter.

'Sorry, brother,' said Brother Talazar, one of Victurix's Terminators. 'My kill.'

Cortez just laughed.

Kantor was ordering Squad Lician, Daecor and Segala up onto the gantries overhead. From there, they would proceed towards the next room, where they would gain access to the upper floors.

'Stand strong, brother,' said Cortez to Talazar as he left his side.

'And you,' Talazar boomed after him.

Barely two minutes later, Kantor and the rest of his force, minus the Terminators, were running along a black metal gantry twelve metres above the floor, moving towards an archway at the far end. Squad Daecor had point, and they mustered on either side of the opening, ready to go in strong. Ferragamos Daecor had once served a term as a member of a Deathwatch kill-team. Cortez could see it in the sergeant's movements, in the cool surety with which he guided his team.

After all this, thought Cortez, when we rebuild everything we have lost, I'll wager that one makes captain.

The fighting in the loading bay below was over for now, the rattle of the Terminators' storm-bolters temporarily ended, but Cortez could hear a great commotion up ahead. The brothers of Squad Daecor gripped their weapons tight and readied themselves to surge forward.

'There should be a large elevator cage in the centre of the next room,' Kantor told everyone. 'Entry points are south and east. Make sure you cover them. Do not damage the mechanism of the elevator. We need it. Are we clear?'

Affirmative responses sounded over the comm-link.

'Good,' said Kantor, checking the bolt-feed for Dorn's Arrow, then returning his attention to the opening ahead. 'Squad Daecor, enter and clear. Lician and Segala, follow on my command. Daecor, go!'

The battle-brothers of Daecor's squad swung out from the cover of the arched entryway and sprinted forward. They slid back into the cover of a dozen metal crates just as a great hail of stubber-fire came their way. 'Heavy-stubbers!' Daecor reported as shells whined past him on either side. More shells smacked into the face of the crate he was crouched behind. 'Keep to cover,' he barked at his squad. 'Suppressing fire front and centre. Brother Cassaves, you and I will flank them. Do not move until their attention is locked on the others.'

'Clear, brother-sergeant,' replied the gruff Cassaves.

Kantor turned to Cortez and said, 'You and I take cover on either side of the doorway. Supporting fire. Understood?'

Cortez nodded. Kantor dashed for the right side of the doorway, Cortez for the left. Their pauldrons hit the wall at the same time. Cortez leaned out briefly and surveyed the scene before him. It only took an instant.

The elevator cage was in the centre of the chamber, just as Kantor had said it would be. The orks beyond it were heavily armed and dressed in plate armour. Cortez did not see any powered suits among them, but the iron plate would be thick enough to stop a direct hit with a bolt. He saw Daecor and Cassaves moving around, following the line of the walls left and right while the other members of the squad kept the orks busy, but the torrent of shells the orks were pouring out presented a real problem. The greenskin heavy-stubbers were spitting out spent brass like water from a fountain. The floor around them was ankle deep in shell casings already and the cover behind which the rest of Squad Daecor was sheltering was rapidly being chewed away.

Cortez knew the Fists giving Daecor and Cassaves suppressing fire needed support, some kind of respite, a break in the fighting they could use to move into fresh cover. They had to do it now, before it was too late.

Cortez pulled a krak grenade from the belt around his middle and primed it. 'Squad Daecor,' he barked over the link, 'be ready to move to better cover. Krak grenade coming in.'

Without waiting for confirmation, he leaned out from the side of the door, locked his eyes on the ork firing position, and hurled his grenade. He did not stay there with his head sticking out to see what happened. He knew the explosive would go off exactly where he wanted it to. He simply listened for the sharp boom he knew was coming.

Three…

Two…

The floor beneath his boots shook with the blast. One of the orks, wounded but not killed began roaring in agony. Cortez heard Sergeant Daecor shouting, 'Close in!'

The orks that survived the blast quickly opened fire again, but Cortez could hear the difference in the rattle of their guns. There were two less of them now. He heard stutter of only six greenskin guns.

From the other side of the doorway, Kantor leaned out to fire a short burst from Dorn's Arrow. The weapon's fire-rate was incredibly high. Kantor had to be careful to fire in extremely short bursts, otherwise he would burn through his back-mounted store of ammunition in less than a minute, despite the vast amount of shells he carried.

Daecor's voice was on the link. 'I have their left flank. Cassaves, are you in position?'

'Almost there, brother-sergeant.'

There was a brief pause, then Cassaves spoke again. 'I have their flank. Give the word, brother.'

Cortez leaned out and fired a round from his boltpistol. It scored a black line in the top of a crate and ricocheted, missing the hideous snarling face of one ork by scant centimetres. The ork angled the heavy barrel of its weapon towards Cortez's position and, with a growl, loosed a flood of shells his way.

Cortez both heard and felt the shells peppering the other side of the wall.

'Now,' said Daecor.

In the chamber, bolter-fire sounded from two new directions, and deep ork screams filled the air. Cortez heard heavy, armoured bodies fall to the ground with the sound of metal impacting on rockcrete. Then he heard the sound of metal clashing against metal. He leaned out and saw Brother Cassaves wrestling desperately against a black-armoured monster, trying to free his bolter from the beast's grip so that he could fire into its face at point-blank range. Daecor was on the other side of the chamber, forced to take cover again now that other surviving orks had spotted him and opened fire.

Kantor saw it, too.

'Lician and Segala, move in and support Daecor,' he snapped. Then, with a nod at Cortez, he surged into the chamber himself, Dorn's Arrow held straight out in front of him, the folds of his crimson cloak snapping behind him as he moved.

Cortez moved, too, barely half a second behind his leader. The moment he entered the chamber, he centred his pistol's iron sights on the helmeted head of the ork wrestling with Cassaves and fired off a single bolt.

It struck the ork dead centre in the side of its head, but the creature's helmet was solid, at least two centimetres thick, and the round detonated on contact, snapping the ork's head to the side, stunning it for a moment, but failing to wound it. Of course, that had never been Cortez's intent. He knew what he was doing. He was buying Cassaves the momentary advantage he needed.

As Cortez had known he would, Cassaves seized on the distraction. The ork had instinctively closed its eyes at the moment of the blast, desperate to protect them. The moment its gaze was removed from Cassaves, the Space Marine let his bolter drop from his right hand, drew his combat blade in a flash, and thrust it straight forward into the ork's throat where the beast's helmet offered no protection.

The tip of the blade slid in, severing the critical nerve bundle at the back. Any normal creature would have dropped dead right then, but, although the ork was technically dead already, its body continued to wrestle for another eight seconds. Its grip was incredibly powerful. Even when it sank to the ground in a heap, Brother Cassaves had to pry its thick, clawed fingers off one by one.

With only one ork left, the three squads swept straight in and cleared the room. Sergeant Lician slew the ork that was keeping Daecor's head down, and soon the chamber was silent. Smoke curled from gun barrels and spent cartridges. Some of the ork bodies, each of which was easily three hundred kilogrammes in weight, twitched while their thick blood pooled around them. The air was cloying with smells; cordite, blood, ionised air, the pungent stink of unwashed alien dead.

Kantor ordered his battle-brothers into the elevator cage, large enough for all three five-man squads, and stood at the control panel inside.

Cortez drew the cage's gate closed.

The elevator floor shuddered and there was a sound of powered gears grinding into motion. The elevator rose past the ceiling and into vertical shaft above it.

Cortez watched yellow lights flicker past. They were set into the smooth steel walls at regular intervals, each marking another few metres that he moved closer to victory or death.

SIX

The Coronado Tower, New Rynn Spaceport

An hour and forty-seven minutes had passed since they had blasted their way out of the work tunnel beneath the spaceport. The fighting had been almost constant since then, but, as Kantor had predicted, the sheer size of the spaceport and the maze of its halls, rooms, loading bays and elevator shafts had prevented the orks from launching any kind of coordinated purge against the Crimson Fists assault force.

Contact with Squad Victurix was difficult now, the voice of the Terminator sergeant faint on the comm-link. That, too, had been expected. Kantor, Cortez and the brothers accompanying them were hundreds of metres above the point where they had entered the spaceport. Beneath them were many floors of thick metal girders and steel-reinforced rockcrete and ferro-crete. Sooner or later, contact with the Terminators holding the lower floors would be lost altogether. Victurix had already reported further contact with the enemy. He also relayed word from the other assault groups. The battle for the rest of the spaceport grounds was ongoing. At least it seemed that most of the toughest orks were out there among the hordes surrounded the Silver Citadel. They thought that was where the action was.

To some extent, they were right. Even here, in the upper levels of the spaceport some forty kilometres south of the position of the nearest marching gargant, those thunderous, planet-trembling footfalls could still be felt, at least to senses as highly trained as those of a Space Marine.

Silently, Kantor prayed that the citadel's void-shields would hold out long enough for the Legio Titanicus to land some of their Titans. The famed god-machines would make short work of their poorer ork-built rivals. But a lot had to happen before that was even a remote possibility. The spaceport had to be utterly secure.

He looked around.

Moments ago, he and his brothers had emerged from a narrow hallway filled with scrap and ork excrement, into this, a broad, semi-circular room that had once been a passenger lounge. Large windows ran the entire length of the curving outer wall, but every last one had been smashed, and a warm wind howled through them, lifting scraps of crumpled paper from the floor and tugging at the torn edges of posters still half-stuck to the walls.

Squads Daecor and Lician were covering two sets of double doors that led out of the room. Squad Segala was covering the rear, the door through which they had just come. The Techmarines, just as Kantor had commanded, were at his side. Their survival was everything. Without them, this was a lost cause.

Kantor turned his head, surveying the room. Behind him stood his old friend, weapons holstered for the moment as he, too, looked around.

'Damned mess,' said Cortez quietly.

The captain had not left Kantor's side since they had entered the underworks back in the Silver Citadel. Kantor knew full well that Cortez had sought, perhaps even expected, command of the mission. He knew Cortez had wanted this all along, a chance to throw all caution to the wind and march out to meet the foe head on. It was his way. He wasn't interested in the bigger picture. He was focussed on the here and now, on the enemy in front of him, and he gave his all in fighting that foe. It was both his strength and his weakness.

Kantor had momentarily considered giving Cortez command, but what would he have achieved by staying back there? Against the gargants, there was nothing he could do from the citadel walls to make a difference. Here, he could make a significant difference.

'We're getting closer,' Kantor said over the link. 'Above this lounge is another for high-ranking dignitaries. It leads out into a large atrium, and, from there, we can access the landing plate itself. Once we cross it, we'll enter the central spires. The air traffic control and defence control centres are inside.'

'There are three landing plates,' said Cortez. 'What about the other two?'

'First things first,' replied Kantor. 'I am not interested in the landing plates until the air defence grid has been secured. We can think about everything else once we have airspace control.'

Cortez suddenly held up a hand. 'Listen!'

Kantor heard it now. The ceiling was thick, but, alerted by Cortez, he could now hear movement above. There was something very heavy moving above them.

Cortez sounded eager. Did he hope it was Snagrod himself?

'That's no gretchin,' he said, half to himself.

'We move,' said Kantor. 'Daecor has point. Beyond the doors, the atrium should have plenty of cover. If there are targets, do not let them dig in. The atrium is dominated by a staircase it its centre. The landing at the top goes east to west. I want that landing secured, Daecor on the east doors, Lician on the west. Squad Segala continues to protect the rear. Anais and Ruzco with Segala. All squads, confirm.'

'By your command,' said Sergeant Daecor.

'Your will, my lord,' said Lodric Lician, shortly followed with a similar affirmation from Segala and the Techmarines.

Kantor moved closer to the door Squad Daecor were covering, Cortez moving with him on his left, just a few metres behind. When they were in position, Kantor gave the order.

'Go!'

Daecor kicked open the door, splintering the finely carved wood with his ceramite boot. In a flash, he was through it, leading the charge into the Coronado atrium. Immediately, stubber-fire and the bright burst of discharging energy weapons poured down on him from a gallery overhead.

Daecor and his squad sidestepped into cover on either side of the hall, taking shelter in the lee of defaced statues that had once represented Rynn and his acolytes.

'Dorn's blood!' spat Daecor over the link.

Kantor barked out orders to Squad Lician, and the Devastator squad moved up to give covering fire. The gallery overhead was so packed with orks that they were almost spilling over the marble baluster. There were more on the floor of the atrium, too, half-sheltering behind the bases of the ruined statues at the far end. Others stood on the wide sweep of the marble central stair, spraying fire at the Astartes, brass casings falling to the thick red carpet and rolling from the steps.

Brother Morai was carrying a heavy bolter. Of all the heavy weapons the Devastators had brought, it was this that had the longest lethal range. Stepping out from cover, Morai hefted the massive barrel of his gun in the direction of the orks on the gallery and tightened his grip on the firing lever. The weapon began to shudder with incredible recoil as it poured a blistering torrent of bolter-shells on the clustered knot of xenos fiends. The marble baluster was chewed apart. With nothing left to resist the push of their fellows at the back, the brutish aliens in the front rows found themselves tumbling forward into space, falling fifteen metres to the hard marble flagstones below. Scores of them fell, hitting hard, sustaining serious injuries. But these were orks, perhaps the most resilient species in the galaxy when it came to pain. They scrambled to their feet, discarding the dented and twisted ruins of their guns, and drew cleavers, swords, axes and hammers from the loops on their thick squiggoth-hide belts.

With a unified roar, they surged forward towards the Astartes.

Morai stepped forward to meet them, strafing the muzzle of his weapon left and right in a tight arc as he moved. The muzzle flare of his weapon lit everything around him in bright strobing light. A shower of brass poured from the heavy bolter's cartridge ejection port.

The orks at the front were almost cut in half as dozens of mass-reactive shells exploded inside their guts. They went down screaming, spittle flying from their razor-toothed mouths. Gore spattered the floor, the walls, the fixtures.

The ruined statues of Rynn and his fellows were dripping with blood, the deep red stark against the flawless white marble.

The orks at the back of the charge kept coming, iron-booted feet stomping on the bodies of their fallen kin, slipping occasionally on the spilled blood and intestines.

Sergeant Lician ordered Morai to fall back, to save his ammunition. His fusillade had been enough to buy Daecor and his squad a moment to prepare. They now leaned out from cover and poured bolter and plasma fire into the rest of the charging xenos, cutting them down in the middle of the hall. The orks on the stair and those behind cover at the far end of the hall continued to pour large-calibre metal slugs at the Crimson Fists. And then Kantor heard a new noise.

It was the stomping of huge armoured feet and, just before every footfall, the distinctive hiss and clank of piston-powered legs. The landing at the top of the stair shook. One of the hanging lights fixed to the underside came loose and fell to the floor, shattering into myriad pieces.

The orks on the stair stopped firing for long enough to look up, and Kantor thought he saw hints of fear on their slack-jawed faces.

A battle-roar so deep it shook the walls sounded, and lasted so long that, for a moment, the Chapter Master wondered if it would ever end.

The moment it did, the orks on the stair gave up their positions, bolting down to the bottom and dashing for the cover of the ruined statues at the far end, the same place from which their fellows were firing.

Daecor and his men did not stop to find out who or what had decided to join the battle. They kept pouring fire out at the orks, killing a dozen of them as they crossed the open hallway at a run. Then, with a temporary lessening of enemy fire, they moved out and raced to forward positions that would offer them better line of sight on their targets. Kantor and Cortez moved a second later, leading Squad Lician into the cover that Daecor and his brothers had just abandoned.

From here, Kantor brought Dorn's Arrow to bear. He had a good arc of fire on the orks still shooting from the second-floor gallery. He raised his left hand, turned Dorn's Arrow level with the floor, and fired, ripping his targets to pieces.

The relic weapon's rate of fire was almost as great as that of Morai's heavy bolter, and it cut deep into the mob of orks, its bolts detonating messily in their bellies. Eviscerated bodies began tumbling from the edge of the gallery, smacking loudly, wetly, on the flagstones.

From the edge of his vision, Kantor saw Cortez and the men of Squad Lician giving suppressing fire to allow Squad Daecor to move from cover to cover once again. The sergeant was attempting to go around behind the great stair in the centre of the hall. He hoped to flank the enemy from the left.

Just as Daecor and his brothers had begun to move there was another deafening roar, this time from the very top of the stair. Kantor saw Daecor dive for cover, but the other four battle-brothers in his squad were just fractionally slower.

Kantor watched in horror as they were chewed apart before his eyes. Their armour should have protected them against greenskin slugs, even large-calibre ones, but this was different. Whatever stood at the top of the stairs was spewing so much firepower in their direction that there was simply no hope. Ceramite plates cracked and shattered under the deadly hail. Great gouts of blood fountained into the air. To Kantor's eyes, it seemed to happen in slow motion. He knew this feeling. He had felt it before, many times. Why did time always grind to a halt like this when he was forced to watch good brothers die?

Four brave Crimson Fists fell to the floor like so much dead meat.

If the Chapter had a future, they would not see it now.

Then their killer, still blocked from Kantor's view by the curve of the landing above, turned its lead-spewing heavy weapon on the statue behind which Daecor was now trapped. The shells began reducing the statue to rubble with terrible speed.

'Shell-breakers,' said Sergeant Lician on the link.

Kantor knew the sergeant was right. Only armour-piercing rounds could have done damage like that. It was fortunate, in some respects, that only the highest ranking orks ever seemed to have access to them.

Kantor heard Cortez roaring in rage from just behind him. He, too, had witnessed the deaths of his brother Astartes and it was too much.

Kantor instinctively knew what was going to happen next. He put out a hand to stop his old friend, but perhaps he should have known better. Nothing could stop Alessio Cortez when he had committed himself to a kill. Cortez raced forward, moving with incredible speed, boltpistol in his right hand, his other, gloved in its massive power fist, pumping the air as he sprinted.

Ork fire from three directions pocked the marble flagstones at his feet, just a fraction of a second too late to hit him. As Cortez slid into cover beside Daecor, he raised his bolt pistol in the direction of the beast that had killed his brother Astartes... and froze.

Kantor heard his words as clear as gunshots over the comm-link.

'I know you!' shouted Cortez. 'You killed Drigo Alvez!'

Footsteps shook the marble stairs now, and Kantor saw a huge armoured form come into view. As he had suspected from the noise of the piston-powered legs, the creature was covered head-to-toe in a blocky, massively-thick suit of ork power armour. One arm ended in a huge multi-barrelled stubber with twin ammunition feeds. The other arm ended in the long glittering, snapping pincers of an ork power claw sheathed in deadly energies.

Kantor realised that Cortez was right. He recognised this monster from the sensorium uploads of the Krugerport survivors. This was the beast that had ended Captain Alvez's life. It was right here, right now, right in front of them, glaring straight at Alessio Cortez.

Urzog Mag Kull!

The beast laughed and clashed its pincers.

It had already killed one Crimson Fists captain. Now it wanted another.

SEVEN

The Upper Levels, Coronado Tower

CORTEZ WATCHED MAG Kull take step after stair-shuddering step, its massive feet, encased in iron, almost too big for the broad stairs to support. The stone cracked. For a moment, it even looked like the whole stairway might collapse, but it did not.

Beside him, he heard Daecor.

'This one is going to be a handful.'

An understatement, thought Cortez.

The beast turned and roared at its smaller kin. They were still firing in the direction of the Space Marines. When they heard the monster roar, they stopped.

To Cortez, the message couldn't have been clearer. Like the ork in front of the Jadeberry Hill barricade, this one was laying down a personal challenge. Deciding to test his theory, he stepped slowly, carefully, out from behind the cover of the statue's base.

A few stubber shells whined in his direction, and the massive ork roared again.

No other fire came his way.

'What are you doing?' hissed Daecor. 'Have you lost your damned mind, brother?'

Maybe I have, thought Cortez, but it didn't change the course of his actions.

The ork monstrosity was at the bottom of the stairs now, and it turned to face him.

Cortez spoke to the others. 'This is between me and the beast. Do you hear? Just get yourselves up to the roof. Time is running out. Get to the damned control centres and do what needs doing.'

The others looked to Kantor for guidance, for a sign of confirmation. They knew what honour demanded, but surely not here, not now.

'You kill it, brother,' Kantor told Cortez, 'Do you understand? You kill it, and you catch up. That's an order.'

Cortez nodded once, eyes never moving from his new greenskin nemesis.

Kantor addressed the others. 'On the captain's signal,' he said, 'we break for the stair and the landing above.'

'My lord...' protested Sergeant Lician.

'By my command, brother-sergeant,' snapped Kantor. 'The captain wants this, and we need to break through.'

'Then get ready to move now,' said Cortez. 'Because I'm going to rip this one's head off!'

Whether Urzog Mag Kull understood the actual words or not, the beast recognised the aggression in Cortez's tone. It spun and splayed its arms, once again giving vent to a blood-chilling battle cry. Great gobs of spit flew from its mouth.

Cortez holstered his boltpistol and drew his combat knife. He knew the blade wouldn't pierce the beast's bright yellow armour, but he had already identified several areas where the blade might slip in to pierce flesh or sever the suit's control cables.

Having issued its final challenge, the monster began sidestepping to the left, circling Cortez on the open floor at the base of the stair. It gnashed the pincers of its power claw, and Cortez caught a glimmer of light. Not only was the thing crackling with an energy field, it looked like it might have been treated with synthetic diamond, much like the blade of his own knife. If so, those pincers would be able to cut through his ceramite armour like it was wet paper.

This should be interesting, Cortez told himself.

With a battle cry of his own, he charged forward, and the air rang with the clash of blades and armoured fists.

IT WAS NOT easy to leave his old friend there, locked in combat with a beast twice his size, but Kantor knew he would receive no thanks for interfering. Individual combat was a sacred thing, a thing that had to be respected. It seemed even orks could agree on that. So, while blows rang out again and again in the air of the atrium, and sparks flashed from ork and Astartes armour alike, Kantor made the best of the opening his friend's life-and-death struggle had bought him. He and the others dashed onto the stairs and up to the landing above.

Stubber-fire from the orks on the gallery chased them as they moved, and shells struck ceramite, but they were standard ork shells and didn't penetrate.

'Keep moving,' Kantor snapped as Squads Lician and Segala pounded up the marble steps behind him. Ferragamos Daecor ran at Kantor's side, the two Tech-marines just behind him. Without his squadmates, all of which lay dead, he no longer held a command. Instead, he had taken Cortez's place as the Chapter Master's second, at least while Cortez was otherwise engaged.

Together, Kantor, Daecor, Anais, Ruzco, and the two five-man squads from 2nd Company reached the top of the landing and immediately sprinted to the right. At the end of the hall, there was a large archway and, beyond it, the slope of a ramp that would take them up to the floor above. A grunting mob of ork footsoldiers gave chase, surging out from cover and up the stairs behind the Astartes. Squad Segala stopped, each battle-brother dropping to one knee in a tight line, and returned fire, putting a number of well-placed rounds into the skulls of the fastest pursuers. Sergeant Segala barked out an order and the squad was up again, running to catch up with Kantor and the others.

Kantor had reached the ramp now, and was racing up it towards a rectangle of open sky. Seconds later, he and the others emerged into the open air, and found themselves standing on the vast Coronado Plate.

It was a flat disk, six hundred and forty metres in diameter, capable of berthing ships up to five hundred and fifty metres across. Like all of the landing plates at the New Rynn Spaceport, it employed anti-gravitic suspension systems related to the grav-plates used on most space-faring vessels. Such powerful suspension allowed the plate to accept burdens of millions of tonnes without compromising the integrity of the structure below. And there was a lot of structure below. The Coronado Plate was three hundred metres tall and from its edge, the view of the surrounding lands was astounding. Kantor didn't have time to appreciate the view now, though. As he and his Astartes emerged onto the plate, there were shouts and grunts from a dozen alien throats.

Kantor spun in the direction of the sound. To his left, in a rough line that circled around all the way behind him, he saw a score of bright red ork fighter-bombers. There were ork and gretchin ground-crews fitting fresh munitions to their under-wing pylons. In front of the ugly, blunt-nosed craft, he saw a knot of big greenskins orks in leather caps and coats, flight goggles dangling around their necks. The moment he locked eyes with them, they started forward, drawing large-bore pistols from holsters at their sides.

'Kill them!' Kantor shouted, and the air filled with the bark of bolters.

Lodric Lician spotted a trolley stacked high with bombs and missiles, and immediately ordered Brother Ramos to bring his plasma cannon to bear.

Kantor heard the roar of blazing plasma just before he blinked in the blinding flash of light. The ork munitions exploded with such force that they sent two of the fighter-bombers plummeting over the edge of the plate. Others burst into flames and, shortly after that, their exploding fuel tanks ripped them apart, showering the Space Marines with burning junk.

The ork pilots which had not yet been killed by Squad Segala turned to look at their beloved machines reduced to wrecks. Great rolls of black smoke swept across the plate. Orange fires danced and crackled. The gretchin scattered, desperately looking for any kind of cover at all, but there was nothing they could reach before the Space Marines cut them down. Daecor and the men of Squad Segala picked off the last of the ork pilots as they charged straight at the Astartes with their pistols blazing.

The fight lasted only seconds.

'Clear, lord,' said Daecor.

Kantor scanned the landing plate. 'Reload and follow me.'

He directed their attention to a tight cluster of three slim, black towers linked to the Coronado Plate by a covered bridge.

'Both our objectives are in there,' he told them.

Lights could be seen in the tower windows, shining out from rooms on a hundred floors that may or may not have been occupied by the greenskins. Kantor knew exactly where he and his men had to go. He hoped resistance would be minimal. Despite the extra magazines and charge-packs he and his assault force had brought with them, he knew their ammunition must be starting to run low. He checked a readout on his visor and saw that Dorn's Arrow still had exactly four hundred and eighteen rounds left to fire before the belt feeds ran dry. After that, he would be down to his sword and power fist. Close-quarters would be the only option, and the orks were far more formidable at that range.

As he led his Fists towards the bridge that linked the Coronado Plate to the central towers, he tried not to worry about Cortez. The 4th Company Captain hadn't joined them yet, but it had barely been two minutes. Kantor glanced back to check the access ramp. No. There was no sign of him. Either he was still locked in combat, or he had shrugged off the legend of his immortality at last.

By the Holy Throne, thought Kantor, do not let it be the latter.

Short of returning to the atrium and interfering in the fight, there was nothing he could do for his old friend. He needed the spaceport. He needed the Imperial fleet.

The air traffic control tower, he told himself. The defence grid. If you die, Alessio, I promise you, it will not be in vain.

As Kantor ran for the covered bridge at the edge of the landing plate, he looked up at the triple towers. The outer stonework of each was studded with gargoyles which held pulsating red lights, the kind of lights that all tall buildings employed to warn incoming air traffic of their presence. They pulsed in sequence, creating a kind of wave effect that travelled to the summit, then started from the bottom again.

Kantor's eyes followed the waves for a moment as he ran, and he found himself looking up at a sky filled with stars. Night had fallen fast, as it always did so near the equator. Here, three hundred metres above ground level, the air was clearer, less dominated by the haze of ork pollution and clouds of flies attracted by their open cesspits. The stars were sharp and bright.

And some of them were moving.

Kantor stopped and held out a hand.

'Wait,' he told the others. 'Look up.'

As they looked, some of the moving star flashed brightly and disappeared. Other shot out hair-thin beams of white and blue light. Some seemed to travel in formation, others in random patterns.

'I hope we're winning,' said Sergeant Daecor.

Kantor hoped so, too.

He began to lead them in a run again, and soon they reached the covered bridge.

ACCESS TO THE central towers had to be fought for. No sooner had Kantor and his men reached its near edge than a stream of orks began pouring out of the doors on its far side. The bridge was narrow, only eight metres across. It forced the orks to bunch together, a fact that favoured the employment of Squad Lician's heavy weapons once again. Brother Morai stepped forward onto the bridge, heavy bolter in hand, and began cutting the orks down six at a time with tight scything sprays of fire. Anything he missed was picked off by the brothers of Squad Segala, some of whom soon reported that they were down to their last full magazine.

Even as Morai continued to clear the way ahead, Kantor hear bestial shouts from behind him. The ork footsoldiers from the atrium began pouring up onto the surface of the landing plate via the access ramp he and his men had used. They charged, and the Crimson Fists found themselves assaulted from two sides with no cover to speak of.

For all the orks' lack of accuracy, they managed to pepper the Astartes armour with fat metal slugs simply by virtue of firing so many. Kantor felt his armour struck again and again, each impact sending brief sparks up around him. His armour had once been beautiful, etched, engraved and chased with gems and gold detailing like no other. Now, it was spattered with alien gore, and chipped and blackened in places by the impact of their bullets.

'Daecor,' shouted the Chapter Master. 'You and I will cover the rear.'

Daecor spun and opened fire with his bolter, sending the lead ork stumbling to the ground, headless, a great red river spilling out from its neck. Kantor brought Dorn's Arrow level with his shoulder and willed the weapon to fire, controlling it by neural command. The command flashed down through his nervous system, through the sockets in his flesh, along the cables that made his body and armour one.

Muzzle fire leapt out from the relic's twin barrels and a stream of brass casings began to pour to the ground. Kantor watched the ammunition counter on his visor fall, cursing as it reached three hundred and fifty rounds, then three hundred. Orks crumpled before him. Every time they rushed upwards from the access ramp, he angled his left fist towards them, and Dorn's Arrow, mounted on the back of it, cut them into lifeless, blood-sodden chunks.

More were still coming when he heard Sergeant Segala on the link.

'The bridge is clear, for now.'

'Segala,' said Kantor. 'Get your men across and secure the first room on the other side. Lician, have Brother Morai and Brother Ramos take position on either side of the bridge and cover Segala's men. Send Brothers Oro and Padilla to me. Do it now. Move.'

'As you command, lord,' said Lician. 'You heard him, brothers. Get moving!'

Brothers Morai and Ramos moved to the left and right respectively, and zeroed their heavy bolter and plasma cannon on the doors at the far end of the bridge. Ork bodies littered the smooth metal surface there. Slicks of blood reflected the light of the room beyond, its interior just visible through tinted armaplas windows.

Brothers Oro and Padilla, both wielding heavy multi-meltas, jogged up to Kantor's side. Oro, the taller and older of the two, said, 'You wish us to cover the rear, my lord?'

The orks, never particularly quick to learn, had finally grown cautious in their pursuit of the Crimson Fists. Rather than racing headlong from the ramp with guns blazing, they emerged slowly and carefully, poking their heads up first to find the opening surrounded by the fallen bodies of their xenos kin. Keeping to cover now, they fired their stubbers in short burst before ducking back down. A triple-burst of shells rattled off Kantor's right pauldron as he addressed Oro and Padilla.

'You will have to hold the plate alone, brothers,' he said, 'but the ramp is a bottleneck, a perfect choke-point, well-suited to your weapons. How much power do your meltas have left?'

'I have half a charge left on this module, my lord, and two spare,' said Padilla.

'And you?' the Chapter Master said to Oro.

At his side, Sergeant Daecor's boltgun barked. Another ork slumped dead at the top of the ramp.

'Almost a full charge left on this one,' said Oro, patting the power module currently fixed in place under the weapon's thick metal frame. 'I have no spares though.'

Kantor turned to Padilla and said, 'Then you know what to do.'

Padilla nodded, unclipped one of the heavy modules from his belt, and handed it to Oro, who took it with a grunt of thanks.

'With respect, my lord,' said Oro, turning to face the Chapter Master again. 'I can cover the ramp well enough alone. Take Brother Padilla with you.' He thrust his chin in the direction of the winking towers on the other side of the bridge. 'I have a feeling you will need all the firepower you can muster in there.'

Kantor hoped not, but, in fact, he had the same feeling. 'Very well, but if they manage to break out of there, you fall back and rejoin us.'

Daecor's bolter barked again. 'With respect, my lord,' said the sergeant, 'the more time we spend here, the more time the orks in the tower have to prepare a defence. One multi-melta should indeed be enough.'

Kantor had already left Cortez to fight alone, and did not relish the idea of another of his brothers being left to do so now. There were so few left as it was. But both Oro and Daecor were right. He couldn't spare two bodies here. Oro would hold the plate.

'Padilla,' he said, 'you are with us. Brother Oro, may Dorn watch over you. If Captain Cortez survives his battle with the beast below, do not cook him by mistake on his way up.'

Kantor had wanted to say *when*, not *if*, but, as the minutes went by, he could not deny his growing doubts. The only thing good sign so far was that the monstrous warboss, Mag Kull, had not yet emerged from the top of the ramp.

On the link, they heard the voice of Sergeant Segala. 'We have secured the lobby on the other side of the bridge. Access points are covered. Awaiting your orders, lord.'

Kantor saluted Brother Oro, fist to breastplate, received a sharp salute in return, and turned to lead Daecor and Padilla towards the bridge. 'Hold the room, sergeant,' he told Segala. 'Lician, start moving your men across now.'

'My lord,' said Lician.

Kantor half-turned and looked back at Oro. A group of orks waving large black cleavers tried to rush him from below. At the top of the ramp, Oro met them calmly, setting his feet shoulder-width apart and levelling the multi-melta at them. There was a crack and whoosh of ionised air as the weapon cooked the aliens' bodies, turning everything black, bone and muscle alike. The orks barely had time to scream. Their armour and weapons dropped to the ground, losing their shape, forming little heaps of hot slag. The stench of cooked flesh became strong on the air, then gusting winds tugged it away.

Kantor turned and kept moving. He had faith in all of his Astartes. The training programmes and psycho-conditioning they had endured were second to none. Oro would hold the plate. He would hold it until Alessio emerged, bloody perhaps, but alive. He had to believe that. As his feet took him across the titanium-alloy plates of the bridge, he kept telling himself that Alessio would survive.

He was Cortez the Immortal.

EIGHT

The Central Towers, New Rynn Spaceport

THE CHAPTER MASTER and what remained of his assault group finally gained access to the triple towers, within which their primary and secondary objectives waited. But there was bad news awaiting him, too.

Kantor had hoped that the towers would be of little real interest to the orks. There were no portable weapons inside, no vehicles to salvage or customise. In each of the rooms they carefully swept for threats, abundant signs of ork presence were everywhere. The air stank of ork filth, almost drowning out other smells. Excrement stained the walls and floors. Many corners were heaped with piles of dung, armies of flies buzzing noisily, greedily, around them. White bones protruded from the mess, some recognisably human, either the bones of people brought here as food, or those of the defending Rynnsguard troopers who had been overwhelmed early in the alien invasion.

That thought led him to another he liked even less.

Kantor considered the Crusade Company battle-brothers who had died here supporting the PDF.

Crusade Company.

His company.

Two squads, Phrenotas and Grylinus, had been charged with holding this place. What kind of fight had they put up? He had seen the signs of battle, the pockmarked walls, the telltale craters in cement and ferrocrete that told of bolter-rounds fired in anger. Even now, so many months after they had fallen, there were traces of their presence that he could not fail to see. But there were no Astartes bodies. There was no sign of the Terminator armour with which the two Sternguard squads had been issued. Where had they fallen? Where had they made their final stand?

There were plenty of other bodies around. From the moment he had stepped onto the bridge that linked the core towers to the Coronado Plate, Kantor had been aware of the severed squig limbs and the twisted forms of murdered gretchin that littered the floor. These were not kills made by Rynnsguard soldiers or Astartes. This was the detritus of the orks. Gretchin, he knew, were often simply murdered on a whim by the larger orks. And the bulbous, brightly coloured squigs formed a major part of the greenskin diet far more often than they were used for tracking or waging war.

As he led his men closer towards the central elevators that would carry them up to the air traffic control tower, they passed rooms where machines had been ripped from the walls and their mechanical innards stripped as salvage. Silently, he prayed that the orks had not interfered with the spaceport's critical systems. He wondered, too, how Squad Victurix and the others were faring.

Up ahead of him, halfway down a narrow hall in which arc lights flickered from the ceiling, Sergeant Segala halted and raised a hand. On the link, the sergeant whispered, 'Occupied rooms on either side. The doors are closed, but I can hear greenskins inside them.'

Kantor considered their options. He could order his Astartes to stack up outside the doors, then breach and clear, room by room. But the sound of fighting from the first room they assaulted would almost certainly bring the others out.

Was Snagrod in one of these rooms?

It seemed unlikely the ork warlord was here. Unlike typical ork warlords, he had not shown his face, not taken his rightful place at the frontline. During the eighteen months of the siege, numerous greenskin lieutenants had been identified and killed, though still more had survived to continue fighting, but Snagrod continued to broadcast his gloating messages in that foul orkish tongue. Kantor had started to suspect that the ork warlord had never even set foot on Rynn's World. Some orks, for whatever reason, felt an attachment to space and the type of combat they could enjoy there. Such orks were rare, freaks perhaps, but they existed. Was Snagrod up there with his fleet right now, engaging the Imperial ships that fought even now for the chance to land vital ground support at this very facility?

'Move quietly,' Kantor ordered. 'If we can avoid a firefight, we can get to the next elevator all the sooner. Sergeant Segala, continue on point.'

'Aye, lord,' said Segala, and the Fists began to move again, careful not to generate unnecessary noise.

It was no easy matter, Astartes battle-plate being what it was, and ork hearing was known to be acute, perhaps to compensate for their eyesight. But with great effort, Kantor and his Fists managed to pass from this hall into another without gaining unwanted attention.

The next hall ran perpendicular to the previous one. At its far end, Kantor saw broad wooden double-doors, one of which was partly smashed and lying at an angle against the wall. Beyond the double doors, there was a broad, well-lit chamber, and, in the centre of that chamber, he saw the elevator he had been looking for.

'Keep moving,' he told the others. 'Straight ahead, as quietly as you can.'

Keeping quiet was hardest, of course, for the brothers of Squad Lician. Morai, Ramos and Padilla carried weaponry far heavier than anyone else. Though it did not slow them enough to be a problem, it did make their passage more difficult than that of their lighter-armed fellows.

The hall was filled with pieces of scrap and refuse, and each step had to be placed carefully. There were rooms off to either side of the hall and, as before, the sound of ork occupants could be heard through some of the doors. Kantor was grateful those doors did not boast windows.

As Brother Ramos, third from the rear, passed a waist-high jumble of twisted metal and wires, the power cabling of his plasma cannon got snagged. Before Ramos knew what was happening, there was a sudden clatter as the junk lurched with his next step, striking and dislodging other debris from a nearby heap.

Immediately, the other Fists brought their bolters to bear on the doors at either side. The ork voices within those rooms had gone quiet, as if the aliens were straining to hear further noise that might warrant the effort of investigation.

Kantor was right next to a door of slightly dented black metal. He heard clumsy footsteps on the other side of it, footsteps that sounded as if they were getting closer. He flexed the fingers of his power fist and activated its deadly energy field. Seconds later, the door was yanked hard. A massive xenos with a black eye-patch and earlobes pierced with lengths of bone stood staring out at him, its brain taking a moment to process the message sent by its one red eye.

That moment was enough for Kantor. He darted straight towards the creature and brought his power fist down in a blistering hammer blow. The energy field cracked sharply, blue arcs of light flashed. One moment, the beast had a head, the next, it was erased. Twitching, the corpse fell backwards. A pistol fell from its meaty right hand.

The moment the weapon struck the ground, a shot rang out. The fat bullet struck the ceiling. The sound of the shot seemed deafening in the silence.

'Dorn's blood!' cursed Kantor.

All along the hall, doors were flung open, disgorging greenskin warriors that roared as they came. They clashed with Squad Segala first, attacking with furious force, bringing their huge axes and cleavers down again and again. Segala and his men were far faster, far better trained, and they parried or slipped the orks' blows again and again, driving the xenos to fight even harder, fuelled by anger and frustration.

'Lician,' barked Kantor, 'cover the rear. Daecor, you and I move up in support. Anais, Ruzco, stay by me.'

The Techmarines, of course, were by no means helpless. They wielded massive power axes that could cleave an ork in two. Anything that came within range of them would die, but Kantor wanted them close so he could personally protect them. He had already decided to give his life if it would buy their survival in place of his own. One way or another, they had to reach the two control centres.

Sergeant Daecor was already moving, boltpistol high, firing in tight controlled bursts wherever his eyes found a viable target.

Kantor surged forward to join the battle and found himself next to one of Segala's men, Brother Bacar, who faced an ork easily twice his weight. The beast had an iron grip on both Bacar's wrists and was yanking him forward, trying to draw him into a crushing bear-hug from which he could bite at the Space Marine's less-protected throat.

Kantor's hand flashed out, power fist connecting solidly with another sharp crack of energy. The far wall was sprayed red. Brother Bacar twisted out of the dead ork's grip and kicked its body to the ground. 'My thanks, lord,' he gasped.

'Do better,' said Kantor.

He saw Segala surrounded by three orks wielding a mixture of hammers and axes. Another closed in hefting a huge spiked mace. 'Damn it,' cursed Kantor as he ran, already knowing he would arrive too late.

Segala was fighting hard, flowing from defence to counter-attack with all the speed and power one could rightly expect of a veteran Astartes. But, in the close confines of the hall, and with others fighting so close behind him, he did not have the space he needed. Kantor saw the sergeant was trying to use each ork's mass against the others, trying to angle himself so that he need only face them one at a time, but it was too late. He was surrounded. Even as Kantor lifted Dorn's Arrow to fire in support, he heard the ork with the mace grunt something. The orks on Segala's left and right dropped their weapons and grabbed Segala's arms tight. The sergeant was extremely strong – all Astartes were – but an ork was stronger, and the strength of two was impossible to resist. They bound his arms and held him in place while the mace-wielding ork hauled his weapon into the air.

Kantor fired, and a stutter of storm-bolter rounds took the left-side ork in the head, killing it instantly. But its headless body maintained its grip, its powerful hands obeying the last message from its tiny simple brain.

The mace crashed down on Segala's head with helmet-splintering force. A great splash of blood painted the sergeant's breastplate and pauldrons.

Kantor roared with rage and fired again, taking the right-side ork in the shoulder and back, but the ork with the mace had already raised its weapon for another swing. Even as the orks on either side of the sergeant finally toppled, the spiked head of the mace made contact again, battering what was left of the helmet down to the gorget. Segala's legs buckled and he fell to the floor, very definitely dead.

Kantor strode forward with Dorn's Arrow blazing, shells ripping into the ork warrior's body in a hate-filled fusillade. The mace dropped with a heavy clang, and the broad, muscular body danced on the spot for a moment as the rounds detonating inside it ripped it apart.

Kantor growled and spun to find a new target. He was spoiled for choice. Fires of hate and anger burning within him, he waded into the melee, drawing his blade from the sheath at the base of his spine. 'Tear them apart, my brothers,' he yelled. 'Blood for blood. Vengeance for the fallen. Let none survive.'

He let his emotions run through him unchecked now, drawing from them, allowing them to take control. He moved too fast, too surely, for conscious thought to play any role. His movements were the purest expression of all his training, his way of life, of all the enhancements and procedures he had endured. Here was three hundred and fifty years of martial mastery unleashed on those who had almost taken everything from him, those he now hated most in all the galaxy.

He killed without hesitation, twin hearts pumping, muscles moving in absolute unity. Anyone who had seen him then would have realised something important about him. They would have realised that Pedro Kantor was not Chapter Master by virtue of his intelligence and demeanour alone. He was once of the finest warriors the Chapter had known in ten thousand years.

Alessio Cortez would have been proud of him, but not surprised.

He had always known it to be so.

SQUAD SEGALA NOW became Squad Daecor. Kantor had little choice but to place Feraggamos Daecor in command. Segala's squad-brothers accepted it. The mission was all that mattered right now. Though their hearts were torn in two at the loss of their sergeant, they would mourn him later, if they did not join him in death.

Despite their losses, what was left of the assault force manage to overcome the orks in the hall. By the time they reached the air traffic control centre, they numbered only nine, and one of those was the Chapter Master. Sergeant Segala had fallen in the hallway.

So, too, had Brothers Gaban, Ramos and Morai, their heavy weapons impairing their combat skills in the maelstrom of close-quarters combat. Brother Oro remained on the Coronado Plate, or so Kantor hoped. He could not raise Oro on the link.

And Cortez?

Well, Alessio had always said he would meet his match one day. Kantor was trying not to think about it, but the possibility that the same creature had now killed both Drigo Alvez *and* Alessio Cortez was like a fire in him. He had to fight himself not to turn back and track the murderous beast down while there was still far more critical work to do.

The air traffic control centre dominated an entire floor of the northmost of the three narrow spires. It was a wide circular room with long curving windows that ran along its entire circumference. There had been orks in the room when the elevator arrived, twenty-three in all, but it seemed they had not been expecting any kind of attack, or at least had not prepared for it. Perhaps they were too busy to pay attention to any kind of alarm or warning the others had raised.

When the elevator doors slid open, Kantor had seen them seated in high-backed chairs, massive shoulders hunched forward, each wearing a set of headphones linked by coiled cables to the machinery of their consoles. They jabbered into microphones in that harsh, guttural tongue of theirs, barely a language at all. There were gretchin, too, dashing back and forth with various tools and inscrutable gadgets. They saw the

Astartes first, and froze for a second, fear rooting them to the floor.

Kantor ordered his men to open fire, and the control centre became a bloodbath. The orks with the headphones barely had time to turn around in their chairs before Daecor and his men fired, punching wet red holes in each misshapen head.

The bodies slumped in their chairs. Some slid forward to collapse heavily on the floor.

'Clear,' said Daecor. Black smoke coiled upwards from the muzzle of his bolter.

Kantor crossed to the windows facing north, all smashed. The wind howled and pulled at him as if trying to drag him out into a deadly freefall. He looked down at the Coronado Plate about three hundred metres below. It was pitch-dark outside. He cycled the vision modes of his helmet. Visor-based infrared was unreliable at this range. He settled on low-light enhancement. He could make out the ruins of the ork fighter-bombers down there. The fires had burned themselves out now. Panning his vision a little to the right of them, he saw the access ramp which led to the atrium. He saw greenskin bodies lying in heaps.

There was no sign of Brother Oro.

Kantor knew what that meant. The Devastator would not have left his post.

Alessio must be dead, too.

He felt something inside him come dangerously close to breaking, something important, something that had to hold for just a little longer. Alessio's memory would not be served by succumbing to it now. The survival of the Chapter had to be assured. There was still a chance, a slim chance, that a future remained, a future in which the Imperium could still call on the Crimson Fists as it had done so often in the past.

He looked further north, beyond the Coronado Plate, and saw the flash and flicker of artillery-fire far off beneath the horizon. There were bright pulses of green and purple energy, too. He strained his ears and thought he could just faintly detect the sounds of the battle for the citadel, but he was not sure. Sixty kilometres was a long way for those sounds to travel, and the wind howling through the shattered windows did not make it any easier for him.

How close were the gargants to the walls? The oddly-coloured flashes of light he had glimpsed suggested they had already started to employ the great clusters of energy weapons that bristled in place of their arms. The last few districts around the citadel had almost certainly fallen by now. Kantor had left orders for them to be evacuated by all but the defenders, but there were literally millions of civilians to be moved, and the Silver Citadel could barely contain them all.

It was impossible to predict how long the citadel's void-shields would last. That all depended on the force the orks brought to bear. Kantor had seen gargants in action before. He had even helped to bring two down, each of those more than a century apart, by leading boarding parties that managed to destroy critical elements in their power cores. Such boarding actions hadn't been feasible this time. When it came right down to it, securing the spaceport and hoping that the reinforcements were enough was the only chance they had, and it was pathetically slim, depending in large part on factors beyond his control.

Perhaps, he thought, but the things I *can* control, I *will*.

He looked down at the console in front of him. Clearly, the orks had recognised the value of not tampering with what they had here. Some of the equipment looked as if it had been taken apart, perhaps to see what made it work, but most of it looked unaltered, if not a little filthier than it normally would have.

Brothers Anais and Ruzco didn't wait for any commands. They immediately lay down their weapons and began a critical systems assessment.

Kantor let them work without interruption. A moment later, Ruzco came to his side, lifted a black cable with a golden jack at its end, and asked if he might plug it into the Chapter Master's gorget. There was an uplink socket concealed there. Kantor conceded at once, and Ruzco pressed the golden jack home with a click. Immediately, Kantor heard static inside his helmet. Ruzco turned a dial on the console in front of him, and began cycling through channels. There was nothing at first, and Kantor began to suspect the comms array on top of the tower had been damaged after all. But, if so, then why had the orks been sitting jabbering into their microphones?

Then he heard it, a snuffling, grunting transmission in the ork tongue. He recognised the voice. He had heard it many times since *The Crusader* had returned from Badlanding with news of Ashor Drakken's death. It was the Arch-Arsonist, Snagrod, broadcasting his boasts and taunts, as always. As Kantor listened, the message ended, then began again. It was being played on a loop. The moronic warlord continued to broadcast in the orkish language, despite his messages being clearly meant for the ears of the loyalist forces. It would almost have been funny had the alien fiend not been personally responsible for the sickening pain, torture and deaths of so many.

Ruzco continued adjusting the dials comms station. He was in the higher frequency range now, and Kantor was close to losing hope, when he finally heard a human voice, or rather, the voice of a being that had once been human, that may still have been partly human.

It was the voice of a comms-servitor on one of the Imperial ships fighting above the planet. Kantor lifted a hand to halt Ruzco's adjustments, and listened, but the stream of words from the servitor was intended for the ears of other servitors. It was a constant babble of systems status reports and energy readings. He waved Ruzco on, and the Techmarine turned the dial to the right a little more. Finally, they found what they were looking for.

'I want all portside batteries on that ship,' said a cultured voice in High Gothic. 'And prime the lance batteries for when we come around. We shall want to lend assistance to the *Manzarion* and the *Virago* as soon as we're clear of their fighters. See it done!'

Kantor waited until there was a pause, then he cut in, saying, 'In the name of the Emperor, identify yourself.'

The well-spoken man spluttered. 'What the bloody hell are you doing on this frequency? Do you know the punishment for interfering with Imperial Naval communications? Who is this?'

'Standby,' said Kantor, 'broadcasting identicode now.'

There was a runeboard on the console in front of Ruzco. The Techmarine's fingers beat a rapid tattoo on the runes.

The response was immediate.

'That's... that's an Astartes code!' stammered the Imperial commander.

'It is,' said Kantor. 'This is Pedro Kantor, Lord Hellblade, Chapter Master of the Crimson Fists Space Marines. Now identify yourself at once.'

The naval commander paused to steel himself, then said, 'My name is Arvol Dahan, Lord Commander of the Imperial Naval destroyer *Adaemus*. Forgive me, my lord Astartes, for–'

'There is nothing to forgive, commander,' said Kantor. 'But you will assist me in contacting Lord Admiral Galtaire.'

'At... at once, my lord. Galtaire maintains an open channel at all times, monitored by his senior commsman. Let me give you the frequency...'

Ruzco turned the dial as soon as he had the numbers. Kantor waited for him to finish, then identified himself to the commsman on the other end, adding, 'I must speak with Lord Admiral Galtaire at once.'

There was the briefest pause, during which Kantor assumed his message was being relayed to the lord admiral. Seconds later, a gruff voice said, 'This is Galtaire. I'm glad someone is still alive down there. Even gladder that it's you, my lord. What's your status? I can't help you worth a damn without a secure air corridor and landing zone.'

'I am working on that, lord admiral,' said Kantor. 'But time is running out. The gargants are assaulting the citadel. The void-shields will hold for a while, but no one can be sure how long.'

'gargants,' echoed the lord admiral. 'We'd best get the Martian priests and their machines down to you in the first wave. I've got Astartes here who are most eager to demonstrate their skills, too. I see by the header on your transmission that you're broadcasting from inside New Rynn Spaceport. May I assume that the facility is now firmly back under Imperial control?'

'We have air traffic control and comms now. The spaceport defence grid is next. I'm leaving three of my Astartes here to hold communications open and keep this place secure. Your contact is Brother Ruzco. Keep him apprised of any changes. He will relay critical updates to me directly.'

'Very well, lord Astartes,' said Galtaire. 'May the Emperor watch over you and keep you safe.'

'And you,' said Kantor brusquely. 'We shall speak again soon.'

He plucked the golden jack from the socket in his gorget and handed it to Ruzco. Turning from the shattered windows, he marched towards the elevator. His fellow Crimson Fists eyed him anxiously, curious to know what was going on.

'Two of you will stay with Brother Ruzco and hold this room at all costs,' he told them. 'Nothing, absolutely nothing, must be allowed to compromise our communications with the Imperial Fleet.'

'Are you asking for volunteers, my lord?' said Daecor.

'No,' said Kantor. 'I'm not.' His finger stabbed towards two brothers, one of which, Brother Lucevo of Squad Segala, had been wounded in the hallway battle, his side bitten by an ork axe. The other was the Brother Padilla of Squad Lician.

'Lucevo, Padilla,' said Kantor, 'make oaths to me now that you will defend this place, though your very lives may be forfeit. Swear it on your left hands and on the blood of the primarch.'

Immediately, both men dropped to their right knee and clenched their left fists over their breastplates. Lucevo sucked in a hissing breath as his wound sang.

'For the honour of the Crimson Fists, the primarch and the Golden Throne,' they said together.

Kantor asked Ruzco if he needed anything else, and was told that he didn't. He then ordered the others – Anais, Daecor, Lician, Verna and Bacar – into the elevator in which they had arrived. He entered last and closed the metal gate. Lucevo and Padilla watched the Chapter Master and the others descend out of sight.

As the elevator lowered them, Kantor told his Astartes, 'The air defence control room is in the tower east of this one. There is a walkway linking the towers on the forty-eighth floor. We cross that gantry, take another elevator sixteen floors up, and secure that room. After that... well, all else is in the Emperor's hands.'

'We should destroy this elevator once we get off,' said Daecor. 'We should cut the cables.'

Lodric Lician turned to look at him. 'We have three battle-brothers up there. You think we should trap them? Trust me. Brother Padilla will not let the orks retake that room.'

'It is not a question of trust,' said Daecor.

Orange lights flashed past them, marking the rapid progress of their descent.

'It is a matter of practicality,' Daecor continued. 'Once the reinforcements arrive, there will be time to extract Ruzco, Padilla and Lucevo. But for now, all of us are best served by cutting off the orks' only route into that room. Yes?'

Lician grunted in disapproval, but he could not argue against Daecor's logic.

'We cut the cables,' said Kantor, ending further debate. 'Our brothers will be safer, and so will our ability to communicate with the fleet.'

He looked at numbers changing on the elevator's small green data-screen, and added, 'Check your ammunition, all of you. Bless your weapons. This ride is almost over.'

THEY EMERGED INTO the same large circular chamber where they had gotten on the elevator for the journey up. Kantor stepped out first, cautiously, quietly. His eyes passed over the dim hallway in which Segala had fallen. He could just make out the edge of a dark blue pauldron among the xenos corpses, could just see the uppermost red knuckles of the icon of his Chapter.

Then pain exploded in his arm and the world flipped over. He found himself flying through the air and landed hard, sliding to a stop against a pillar of white stone decorated with fine gold-leaf filigree.

The chamber filled with the most deafening inhuman roar, so loud it shook dead leaves from the plants and trees that had once decorated the place, but now only testified further to its state of ruin and decay.

Kantor looked up and something hard and heavy hit him directly in the face, ringing against his helmet. It fell into his lap, and he looked down.

He knew this thing, ancient and so familiar.

It was polished red, chased with gold, inlaid with the finest gems and black pearls.

Skulls decorated its knuckles. The crest on the back was a single fist formed from rubies set between feathered wings of shining gold. Beneath it, a laurel wreath encircled a grinning skull, the brow of which was decorated with the two-headed eagle, the aquila of the Imperium of Man.

It was Alessio Cortez's personal crest, and this was his power fist.

Cortez's severed arm was still inside it, edges raw and bloody, white bone poking up through the meat, the cut almost surgically clean.

Kantor was frozen for a moment, reeling, desperately trying to rally himself, to steer his mind away from what this meant.

He looked up and saw the massive yellow-armoured warboss, Urzog Mag Kull, roaring at him in triumph, its left side absolutely drenched in blood. He saw that one of its eyes had been gouged out. A great flap of green flesh hung from its head, showing the bright bone beneath. Sparks flashed and spat from ruptured power-cables in its right leg. Cortez had punished the beast before he had succumbed to its superior strength. It roared again, raised its twin-linked heavy-stubbers, pointed the barrels at Kantor and fired.

There was a loud click and the whine of cycling ammo-feeds, but no armour-piercing rounds leapt out, no deadly hail. Kantor glanced at the weapon and saw that its barrels were badly crushed and mangled. Somehow, during the fight, Cortez had put the weapon out of commission. Had he not, Pedro Kantor might have been torn apart right then.

'Xenos filth!' spat the Chapter Master, pushing his old friend's arm from his lap and rising to his feet. 'You will *pay*!'

He broke into a run, racing directly for the towering two-tonne creature, peppering its armoured bulk with torrents of fire from his storm-bolter as he moved. In just over a second, he crossed the gap, and found himself mere metres from it, scowling up into that terrible fang-toothed face, power fist crackling with electrical arcs, diamond-edged combat blade held ready in his left hand.

'Let's have you, wretch!' he hissed, drawing a last howl of threat from the beast before it lunged straight at him with its blood-splashed power claw.

Despite the creature's speed, the blow was telegraphed, the ork taking a fraction of a second to shift its weight forward into the lunge. It was enough. Kantor slid aside just as the claw slashed towards his abdominal plates. He struck at the extended arm with his power fist. Had he connected properly, he might well have sheared straight through the arm, but the ork was blisteringly fast. It did not leave its arm extended long after the blow, but recoiled it as quickly as a striking snake recoils its head.

Kantor's fist passed through thin air, putting him ever so slightly off-balance for an instant. That was when the ork whipped its battered twin stubbers at him. There was no evading the blow. Instead, Kantor raised his left arm, couched his head against his inner forearm, and tried to absorb the impact.

The force was stunning, slamming into him, hurling him from his feet despite his best efforts to resist. He landed hard on his right side and slid six metres across the floor.

He cursed as he pushed himself up and tried to shake off a momentary dizziness.

He saw Sergeant Daecor, Brother Verna and Brother Bacar try to surround the beast, Daecor taunting it from the front while the other two each took a flank. It looked like it was working. The monster hurled itself at Daecor, its massive claw hammering into the marble flooring as the sergeant leapt backwards. Verna and Bacar moved the instant the blow missed their new squad leader. Verna thrust his combat blade into the workings of the left leg and yanked back hard, ripping cables from their housings and spraying himself with oil and hydraulic fluids. Bacar tried to lever his knife up underneath the monster's armpit where mobility demanded there be a gap in its armour.

The monster's remaining eye was its right one, and it saw Bacar move in its peripheral vision. In a flash, it spun on him, striking his helmeted head with the battered barrels of its twin stubbers. With Bacar momentarily stunned, hands thrown out to stop himself from toppling, the creature torqued the left side of its body and hacked him into three with a great diagonal slash of its power claw.

Bacar's body, power armour and all, slid into three parts. His head and left arm flopped to the floor. Great gouts of blood geysered upwards from his open torso.

That was when brothers Lician and Anais tried to enter the fray.

'No!' bellowed Kantor. 'Brother Anais, get back in the elevator. Lician, defend him with your life. We cannot lose him!' The Chapter Master raced towards the beast that had just killed another of his beloved Crimson Fists.

How many more did he have to lose before Urzog Mag Kull would die?

Daecor had Mag Kull's left flank now, but, as he lunged, the beast turned and clipped his breastplate with a savage backhand blow. The upwards angle of the blow sent the sergeant metres into the air. He crashed down on his back, bolter skittering away from him.

Verna, finding himself behind the beast, threw himself at the back of its piston-powered knees and tried to take it to the floor, but it was hopeless. Even in full Astartes plate, he weighed a fraction of what Mag Kull did.

He managed to confuse the creature for a second, allowing Kantor to launch himself into the air, power fisted right hand held high for a deadly downwards blow.

For a moment, the Chapter Master literally flew, all his prodigious power and strength, all his athletic ability, invested into the attack.

Mag Kull managed to kick Verna away, shattering the armour of the Crimson Fist's left arm in the process and breaking the bone beneath. It turned in time to see Kantor's attack, but not quickly enough to avoid it. Instead, it could only try to minimise the damage from the blistering overhand strike.

It rolled its massive metal shoulder in front of its face at the last instant. There was a massive crack, like sharp thunder, as Kantor's fist struck the beast's armoured plate, shearing straight through the metal and pulverising the dense bone and muscle beneath. The force of the impact launched the beast backwards and sent Kantor crashing to the ground.

The ork raged. The sparks from its malfunctioning legs ignited the oil leaking from its cables, and fire engulfed its lower body. But it was not finished with the Crimson Fists. Its right arm, the one bearing the useless heavy stubber, now hung from its shoulder by little more than a thin bundle of nerves and sinew. It slapped uselessly against the burning monster's side as it struggled forward in Kantor's direction. Irritated, the beast raised its huge power claw across its body and, with one motion, snipped the useless arm away completely.

The severed arm fell to the ground with a clatter of metal.

Verna lay groaning, fighting to rally himself. Daecor, too, was struggling to get to his feet. Kantor rose, his whole body aching, damned if he was going to let the monster get the better of him. But the creature was unnaturally tough, tougher than any Astartes. It was not just the armour, it was the nature of the ork race. Pain hardly slowed them, fear rarely stopped them in their tracks, they were addicted to war, addicted to slaughter, and they would never stop coming.

On burning metal legs, the creature staggered towards him, gnashing the blades of its only remaining weapon, its deadly power claw, as if they were a second set of jaws.

Kantor loosed a burst of bolt rounds at it, aiming for the beast's head, but the massive metal gorget of long tusk-like spikes protected the creature's face. The bolts detonated on the armour without penetrating, though they certainly angered the beast.

Four metres away from him now, it raised its massive claw into the air, and he readied to try to block or slip the blow. His entire awareness was focussed on that gleaming razor-edged weapon, as if it were the only thing in the universe right now. So, at first, he did not understand what happened next. Though his eyes saw it all, he was not sure he could believe it.

A harsh voice barked out, 'We are not finished, xenos!'

An armoured figure leapt up from behind, throwing itself on the creature's back, gripping with only its blue, ceramite-plated legs. The figure's left hand, its only hand, raised a small metal object.

The monster tried to turn to face its new attacker, but, no matter how it tried to twist and turn, the blue figure was always behind it, holding fast to its back by leg power alone.

The beast bellowed in frustration, and, the moment its mouth was open as wide as it could surely go, the attacker leaned forward and placed the metal object deep inside the creature's mouth.

On reflex, the ork swallowed, confused, not realising what had just happened.

It thrashed again, and, finally, the blue figure released its grip and was flung backwards, crashing to the ground and skidding away.

The monster turned to pursue, but it only managed two steps. It was about to take a third then the krak grenade detonated inside it. Where its head had poked out of its armoured shell, a fountain of blood and shattered bone erupted. For a second, the armour stayed upright, apparently undamaged by the explosion in the creature's body. Then, slowly, like a falling ebonwood tree, it tumbled forwards and smashed to the floor.

Kantor realised he was breathing hard and consciously tried to relax his body. He was still not entirely sure what had just happened. Then he heard dry laughter somewhere off to his right. A figure in battered Crimson Fist armour sat up, still chuckling, covered in blood, beaten almost beyond recognition.

Almost, but not quite.

'Alessio,' breathed Kantor, numb with relief. 'Alessio.'

It was Cortez, though he was in a worse state of repair than Kantor could remember seeing him for at least a century.

'You're alive! By Dorn, you're alive!'

'I've a legend to live up to,' said Cortez. He coughed, and his face betrayed a hint of his pain. 'Damn, but that bastard was tough.'

Kantor crossed the floor to help his friend rise. Lician and Anais had emerged to help Daecor and Verna to their feet.

Reaching down and offering his hand to Cortez, the Chapter Master grimaced, noting the blood-crusted stump which was all that remained of his friend's right arm. Cortez reached up with his left, gripped Kantor's hand, and hauled himself to his feet. Throughout the movement, Kantor could see just how badly injured his old friend was. He grunted in pain as he moved, and his speed was gone.

'What's next?' said Cortez once he was on his feet. He turned his head to look at across at the others.

'Nothing for you,' said Kantor. 'You'll rest until we can get an Apothecary here.'

'Not likely,' protested Cortez. 'I'm still in this. I'm fine.'

'No,' Kantor boomed. 'You lost an arm, Alessio. By the mercy of the Emperor alone, you're lucky you didn't lose your life.'

Cortez gestured over Kantor's shoulder. 'I haven't lost an arm, brother. It's right over there.'

It was. His severed arm, still wearing the glorious power fist that bore his personal arms, was exactly where Kantor had left it, close to the pillar against which the creature had thrown him.

Kantor shook his head, bewildered than his friend could consider this a time for levity.

Daecor, Verna and the others stopped beside them. 'Your legend grows, Fourth captain,' said Daecor with a salute.

Cortez kept glaring at Kantor, but the Chapter Master turned to the others and said, 'Daecor, Lician, Anais… we proceed to the air defence control centre. Brother-Captain Cortez and Brother Verna will take the elevator up to the air traffic control room and wait with Lucevo, Padilla and Ruzco.'

'With respect, lord,' said Cortez angrily, 'I told you I can still fight.'

Kantor shook his head. 'Three brothers are holding the air traffic control room alone. It is critical to our success that it remains held. I am giving you an order, and you will obey it.'

I have granted you far too many liberties already, Alessio, Kantor thought, and the last was nearly the end of you. It is enough for today.

Cortez's body language managed to convey his deep dissatisfaction and resentment without the need for words, but he did as commanded. He turned and led the limping Verna to the elevator.

'I thought we were going to cut the cables,' said Daecor to the Chapter Master.

'It is just as well we did not,' replied Kantor. 'Neither of them are in any shape to fight now.'

'Incredible,' murmured Daecor. 'Incredible that Cortez survived at all.'

Just as Cortez was about to close the elevator gate behind him, Kantor shouted after him. 'What of Brother Oro? Did you see him?'

The doors had begun to close, but Cortez thrust out his hand and stopped them. He leaned out of the elevator and said, 'He came back into the atrium and tried to aid me in my fight. I told him not to interfere, but he wouldn't listen.' He paused, then added, 'For what it's worth, he died bravely.'

Silence reigned for a moment.

Cortez let the door of the elevator slide shut. Seconds later, the winches whined and it began to ascend.

'Gather up your weapons,' said Kantor. He looked at the remains of Bacar, nothing more than three grisly parts clustered together on the floor to his right. 'Take his ammunition. We may need it.'

Saying this, he turned and began walking towards a grand archway on the chamber's south-eastern side. 'Hurry,' he told the Fists following behind him. 'The gargants may even now have broken through.'

NINE

Air Defence Tower, New Rynn Spaceport

NOTHING ELSE THEY encountered was quite as deadly as the ork boss Cortez had finally killed. Though Kantor moved with so few of his battle-brothers in support, they moved fast, killing the orks they came across with cold, ruthless efficiency. Inside, the southeast tower was much like the one they had just come from. Once they had crossed the connecting walkway, and had navigated their way through a series of filthy rooms and ruined hallways, they found themselves in a large chamber dominated by a central elevator shaft. The only difference between this chamber and the other seemed to be the absence of dead foliage here.

The air defence control centre was close to the very top of the tower, almost a full kilometre above ground level. Like the air traffic control room, it was occupied by orks and gretchin. Like those in the air traffic control room, they were unprepared for a sudden and decisive assault. Moments after they emerged from the elevator, Kantor and his makeshift squad found themselves pulling ruined bodies from the tops of the consoles.

The layout of the room was similar to that of the air traffic control centre, though fewer of the windows were smashed. Despite the season, it was cold up here. Night leached the heat away. Kantor ignored the temperature. Inside his power armour, it was well-regulated, almost constant. Some of the gretchin bodies on the floor wore raumas-wool coats and hats, spoils taken from the bodies of the Rynnite dead which must once have littered this place just as the gretchin themselves did now. Their larger ork brethren wore no such items. Their great swollen musculatures made the wearing of human clothes impossible.

Once the consoles were free of dead aliens, Brother Anais began his systems checks. Moments later, he crossed to the Chapter Master's side. 'The news is good, lord. They seem to have done little in the way of irreparable damage.'

'How long until we have full control over the surface-to-orbit batteries?'

Anais tapped runes in front of him. Figures spooled across a green screen. 'A number of weapons are out of commission. We shall need time to bring them back online. We can begin firing the others within the hour, perhaps even less.'

'And the sub-orbital anti-air batteries?' Kantor asked.

'Much the same, lord,' said Anais. 'Some appear to have been dismantled. Power readouts are favourable, however. The orks did not dismantle or disconnect the on-site plasma generators.'

'Get these systems up and running as soon as you can,' said Kantor. 'Then open a link to our brothers in the air traffic control centre. I want you to coordinate everything with them. The moment we are ready, I want a message sent to Lord Admiral Galtaire. The sooner he starts ferrying support down to us, the better. And tell Ruzco to keep trying to raise our forces at the citadel. We need information. Those void shields had better be holding.'

Kantor had barely drawn breath after finishing his sentence when there was a deep rumble from outside, getting louder. It was the unmistakable sound of high-power turbines and they were very close.

Kantor just had time to shout 'Down!' at the others before something strafed the windows of the defence control centre, blasting in those that were not already shattered. Shells ripped into the room, not stubber shells, but something far heavier. Autocannon rounds. The orks must have salvaged the guns from a looted Chimera or Hydra.

Broken glass blasted inwards. Consoles and cogitator banks against the far wall disintegrated. Anais, Daecor and Lician had thrown themselves to the floor the moment Kantor had warned them, and it had saved their lives. But Kantor himself was right in the line of fire. The heavy armour-piercing shells battered at him, rattling off him, sparks showering outwards with every impact, but they did no damage.

He'd had only a fraction of a second to activate the power-field device embedded in the golden halo that jutted up from the top of his back-mounted generator, but that fraction of a second had been enough. All it took was a single neural command, a thought, and the so-called Iron Halo, actually made of adamantium and coated with gold, shielded him in its powerful energy field, turning aside the lethal hail of shells.

The device was a last resort, but he'd had no choice. Activating the device was a huge energy drain, and the power levels of his armour dropped dramatically while it protected him. The temperature inside his suit went up. Alarm runes glowed red in his visor, but it saved his life. It was the first time he'd allowed himself to rely on the halo in half a century.

The hail of shells stopped, and Kantor flicked off the energy shield with a thought. The warning runes blinked off. Internal temperature evened out. He looked beyond the edge of the jagged window frames.

Hovering drunkenly in the air outside the defence control room, swaying back and forth on roaring jets of blue flame, an ungainly ork gunship faced him down. He saw two goggled ork pilots laughing uproariously, their hideous faces lit from below by the glowing instruments of their cockpit. They stopped laughing when they saw Kantor standing there unharmed, glaring back at them, radiating raw hate and anger.

The Chapter Master expected them to open fire again, but instead the pilots turned the gunship ninety degrees and presented its left side.

There standing in an open bay-door in the middle of the craft, was a massive figure with red eyes. It glared back at Kantor, and something indefinable passed between them.

Kantor knew instinctively it was Snagrod. He had never seen a larger ork. The warlord emanated an aura of incredible physical power. No wonder he had united so many disparate ork tribes under his banner. Dominance was hard-coded into his genes.

The beast roared, throwing its huge jaws wide, and pointed down towards the landing plate two hundred metres below, the Nolfeas Plate.

Kantor understood. This was between the two of them, leader against leader.

He nodded, and the warlord bellowed something to the pilots.

The gunship swung away. Snagrod and Kantor kept their eyes locked to each other until the gunship moved out of sight.

Kantor turned to the others.

'Anais,' he said. 'Did we lose any critical systems?'

The Techmarine was already checking. After a moment, he said, 'Nothing critical, my lord. I can still get ninety-seven per cent of the remaining defensive systems back online.'

'Do it,' said Kantor, and he strode towards the elevator. 'The moment we have the defence grid back, coordinate with Ruzco and the fleet. Start bringing the reinforcements down. Dorn only knows how the citadel is faring.'

He stepped into the elevator cage.

'My lord,' said Daecor, moving to join him. 'You can't mean to go alone.'

'Agreed,' said Lician. 'Take us with you.'

In the cage, Kantor turned and faced the two sergeants.

'This is my fight,' he said. 'Should it be my last, you will follow the instructions I left with the Chosen back at the Cassar.'

He closed the elevator gate and pressed the rune to descend. Daecor and Lician watched him go, reluctant, but knowing they could do nothing to stop him.

TEN

Atop the Nolfeas Terminal, New Rynn Spaceport

THERE WERE FEW ork flying machines on the Nolfeas Plate, and those there were, sitting silently a few dozen metres from the plate's edge, looked to be in bad shape. Their sides were pocked with holes, their diameter consistent with the damage Hydra rounds inflicted. These craft had been struck by the guns of the Imperial defenders, and had limped back here for repairs. A few gretchin hovered around them, but, when they saw Kantor crossing a covered walkway and stepping onto the edge of the plate, they panicked and disappeared down a small service ramp, screeching and chittering in their crude alien tongue.

Above the plate, the sky was lightening, turning from darkest, star-speckled blue to pale rose. With this colour shift, Kantor could no longer see the tiny lights that told of the battle in space. He prayed to

Dorn that Lord Admiral Galtaire was as good in combat as his service record attested.

He did not like it that so much of his future, and the future of the whole Chapter, rested in the hands of others. No Astartes could be comfortable with that. A Space Marine was used to controlling his own fate. Even in the heat of his most intense battles, he had always known that, live or die, others would fight on. He had always known that the Chapter would go on without him.

Would the coming day see them saved or obliterated?

He crossed to the centre of the Nolfeas Plate. So far, there was no sign of the ork warlord, nor of the gunship, but Kantor was certain he had not misinterpreted the massive ork's intent.

He scanned the skies, senses hyper-alert...

...and heard the roar of jets just a second before the ork gunship surged upwards over the lip of the plate and opened fire on him, stitching the ferrocrete with shells that traced a lethal line towards him.

His dive was almost too late. Chips of ferrocrete smashed against his right side as the hail of fire ripped past him.

He rose to face the craft.

He tracked it as it swung left and loosed a burst from Dorn's Arrow, but the cockpit was heavily armoured, and the bursting bolter-shells left only smears of black on the clear armaplas bubble. One of the ork pilots yanked on the craft's controls, and the gunship swung its nose around to face him head-on again.

Kantor knew only too well the power of the weapons that bristled from under the craft's stubby wings. He saw now that they were indeed looted autocannons. There were two of them, fed by thick, heavy ammo drums that he guessed contained tens of thousands of rounds.

The guns fired again, and again he narrowly avoided being torn apart. Employing his halo again would have cost him power, slowing him down. He couldn't afford that. He had a sense that the ork pilots were toying with him. Snagrod wouldn't let them steal the glory of killing an Astartes Chapter Master. He would want that victory for himself.

The gunship unleashed a third rippling volley, and Kantor tested a theory. He did not move.

It was a deadly gamble to take, but, sure enough, the rounds stitched a path in the surface of the Nolfeas Plate that passed right by him.

The ork pilots were snarling and cursing him. One hauled on his control sticks, and the craft veered away moving to the far edge of the landing plate. Once there, it turned side-on, and again saw his huge nemesis.

The craft lowered unsteadily towards the plate on its vectored jets. When it was still six metres up, the beast called Snagrod dropped from the bay door, landing so hard and heavy that Kantor imagined he felt the plate tremble. Of course, that was impossible. The Nolfeas Plate used anti-gravitic suspension just like the others. Nothing short of a Naval transport could shake it.

Now that Snagrod had landed on the plate, he rose to his full height, and the gunship pulled up into the air, hovering there, drifting drunkenly from left to right as the pilots tried to keep it steady.

Kantor's eyes were on the warlord. Snagrod wore no suit of power armour like other warlords did. His hulking, muscle-bound torso was bare of everything save deep scars and burns, crude stitches and rippling veins as thick as a man's thumb. This lack of armour was the most overt sign of pure confidence and power Kantor had ever seen in an individual ork.

Kantor knew then that he had never faced a beast like this in mortal combat.

For weaponry, the monster wielded no power claw, but he gripped a single massive heavy-stubber in the fingers of its right hand, box-fed with a cruelly ser-rated bayonet slung underneath the barrel. There were close combat weapons slung on the creature's back, too, but Kantor didn't have a good view of them.

The two enemies glared at each other, frozen for a moment, each silently assessing his foe. From around Snagrod's thick waist, a collection of Space Marine helmets hung, swinging on short iron chains that rat-tled from a squiggoth-skin belt. There were four helmets, each coloured differently, each taken from a battle-brother belonging to a different Chapter. One was decorated with the gold laurels of a veteran sergeant.

Inside his armour, Kantor flexed his muscles and felt blood rushing through them, blood and adrenaline. The latter would make him faster, inure him to pain, help him fight fatigue and make his opponents movements seem slower than they really were. But how fast could this monster move? Unhindered by tonnes of iron plate, like that worn by Urzog Mag Kull, Snagrod was a different prospect altogether.

The moment broke suddenly, like glass, and it began.

Snagrod raised the barrel of his gun straight at Kantor and pulled hard on the trigger. Kantor raised Dorn's Arrow and opened fire a fraction of a second later. Shells hammered through the air in both directions... and struck their targets.

Kantor had flicked on the shield of his Iron Halo again, just in time. The ork rounds danced on the energy field, sparking and ricocheting while he fired back.

The bolts from Dorn's Arrow struck true, but Snagrod suffered no damage at all. He, too, seemed to be shielded by some kind of power-field. It was another reason he didn't need a hulking mass of metal plate. The storm bolts exploded harmlessly, sending ripples of strange green energy out over the warlord's body.

They stood there, unleashing the full fury of their weapons at each other, both roaring in hate at rage as they did so. Then, almost simultaneously, their ranged weapons ran dry.

Kantor deactivated the halo's energy field. His armour's power levels had dropped dangerously low. They climbed again now, but never quite reached optimum. He knew he couldn't rely on the halo again. If he came too close to overloading his armour's generator, his systems would lock out to prevent an atomic explosion.

Ammo spent, Snagrod threw his heavy-stubber aside in disgust and charged.

Damn, but he was fast!

His impossibly muscular legs halved the distance to Kantor in scant seconds.

Kantor loosed a battle cry and raced forward to meet him, drawing his sword left-handed from the scabbard at his lower back and activating the power fist on his right.

Snagrod drew the close combat weapons from the slings on his broad back as he ran, two huge chainaxes decorated with roughly painted black and white checks. They growled into motion, teeth blurring.

The two enemies clashed hard, right in the middle of the Nolfeas Plate. Kantor slipped a blistering blow and struck at Snagrod's belly with his blade. Green sparks flew. The monster's energy shield was still in play. Where did it get its power? It had to come from somewhere, but Kantor's eyes couldn't find sign of a device. It had to be somewhere on Snagrod's body, but there was no time to search in earnest for it. Another whistling swipe almost took the Chapter Master's head off. The blade of the left chainaxe missed him by a hair's breadth.

Kantor tried to stay in close. His reach was far shorter than the ork's. It wouldn't help him to pull back. If he stayed here, he stayed within his own striking range, but what good would that do him when the monster was still shielded?

Another swing of the warlord's axes gave Kantor a brief opening, and his power fist flashed forward, a devastating hook that would have killed just about any living thing. The fist's power-field snapped like lightning, and Snagrod's personal shield flashed bright, but the force of the blow was spent on the shield, and the warlord barely even stumbled back a step.

Kantor's adrenaline surged even higher. He felt like a child battling this thing, powerless to hurt it.

Snagrod kicked out while Kantor was focused on the swings of the monster's deadly blades. The kick caught him square in the stomach and launched him ten metres backward, skidding along the surface of the landing plate.

Kantor grunted. Even through his ceramite plate, the blow had winded him.

Snagrod charged straight in while the Chapter Master was still on his back. The beast lifted both chainaxes at once and put all its formidable might into a vertical killing stroke.

Kantor rolled left, every fibre of his body committed to the motion, and the axes bit deep into the plate, lodging there hard. The motors that drove the weapons' wicked teeth whined in complaint.

Snagrod roared and yanked at them, while Kantor leapt to his feet and slipped around to the monster's side. There, at the warlord's back, attached to the squiggoth-skin belt, was a curious looking module.

The shield must come from there, thought Kantor.

In the split second before Snagrod pulled his axes free, Kantor's sword stabbed towards the module, his movement deliberately slowed. Most shields resisted objects travelling at high speeds, but allowed slower intrusions. This was no different. The tip of Kantor's blade pierced the energy field and skewered the module.

There was a snap of ionised air and the green shield flickered off.

Snagrod felt it immediately. With a roar of rage, he swung and batted Kantor aside with the butt of his right axe.

The blow sent Kantor skidding along the plate once more, his right pauldron almost entirely shattered, chunks of ceramite spinning away from him.

But he had achieved more than he'd hoped. The warlord was vulnerable now, and all Kantor's fury and lust for vengeance bubbled up, spilling over his self-control like a torrent of boiling lava.

He was on his feet instantly, ignoring all his pain. His conscious mind retreated, giving way to raw, untempered aggression. With a battle cry that rang out across the landing plate, he launched himself at the ork warboss once last time. There was no holding back. His killer instinct took over everything. He would rip the beast apart or die.

Snagrod loosed a roar of his own and stormed forward to meet him, axes high. The warlord had been undefeated in battle for a thousand years, slaying every last challenger to his rule. No mere human would change that.

They slammed against each other like crashing trucks, ceramite armour against flesh tougher and thicker than old leather. The axes whistled through the air, motors growling greedily again, hungry for meat to rip apart. Snagrod tried to cut Kantor in half with a scissor-like double backhand, but he cut only empty space.

Kantor slipped under in a blur, and, at last, had the warlord right where he wanted him. His sword thrust deep into the monster's side and twisted. Snagrod howled in pain and anger, and tried to knock Kantor away, but the pain robbed the blow of speed and Kantor evaded it, staying inside the creature's guard. He yanked out his blade. Hot blood poured onto the landing plate. Snagrod swiped again and staggered back, his right leg drenched in slick crimson.

Kantor followed the ork's movements, pressing his attack. He launched a savage overhand blow with his power fist, aimed straight at the warlord's head, but the beast rolled with the blow, catching it on his huge shoulder.

The thick deltoid muscle exploded in a grisly spray, revealing the bone and sinew beneath. The impact staggered Snagrod, dropping him to one knee. Kantor leapt at him, kicking him down onto his back and straddling the beast's huge chest. He raised the power fist again for a killing blow, but Snagrod caught it, fingers wrapping iron tight around the wrist.

Kantor's reaction was immediate. He brought his left hand up, still gripping his sword, and stabbed down at the monster's throat.

Snagrod's left shoulder was almost obliterated, almost useless, but not quite.

Through the pain, the ork managed to bring his ruined arm up just in time. He caught the blade of Kantor's sword in his right hand, the edge biting deep into his fingers. With a roar of pain, the warlord wrenched the blade from Kantor's grip. It skittered away across the ground.

Kantor snarled and launched a barrage of punches with his gauntleted left hand instead. There was no deadly power-field over that hand, just hard knuckles encased in armour. It was enough. The fury of his blows was terrible. He rained punch after savage punch on the warlord's face, smashing the beast's tusks, tearing deep red gouges in its cheeks and brow, blinding one of its eyes and breaking its massive jaw.

Snagrod scrambled to defend himself, but, from his back, one arm greatly diminished in strength, the other locked in a death grip around the Chapter Master's power fist, he could do little to resist Kantor's unrelenting fury.

'You destroyed our home!' Kantor yelled as he tore the warlord's face apart. 'You killed my brothers. Now you pay!'

The words were wasted on the warlord's tattered ears, but the meaning was not. Death was close, closer than it had ever come to the greenskin leader before.

With an infuriated roar, Snagrod bridged, thrusting his torso up from the ground with the full power of his thick legs. Kantor was flung off and scrambled back to his feet to continue the attack. Snagrod didn't wait for that. He rose and ran, his huge feet pounding the plate, straight towards the place where the gunship still hovered. Kantor gave chase, but there was a sudden stutter of autocannon and he had to leap back to avoid being torn apart by the shells.

Snagrod kept running, blood pouring from his wounds in red rivers, splashing a great wet trail onto the landing plate as he went. The gunship dipped towards the edge of the plate just as Snagrod arrived there, and the warlord leapt into the open bay-door in the side of the craft, causing the whole gunship to swing unsteadily for a moment.

Kantor roared in frustration as he watched the ship drift away from the edge on tongues of blue fire. The warlord was going to escape!

There was a rattle of fire from behind him, and a patter of storm-bolts exploded on the gunship's cockpit bubble. The armaplas cracked under the hail of shells, but it didn't break. Still, the ork pilots weren't about to wait for another volley of fire. They swung the gunship around and increased its thrust to maximum.

As the ship roared off towards the south-east, Kantor's eyes tracked it.

He saw Snagrod lean out of the bay-door and look back at him.

Incredibly, it looked like the monster was laughing.

Five pairs of heavy footsteps stopped at Kantor's side.

When the ork gunship was gone from view, Kantor turned, and met the visored eyes of Terminator Squad Victurix.

It was Rogo Victurix, the squad sergeant, who spoke first.

'He got away.'

'This time,' Kantor snarled back.

'We have the spaceport secure,' said Victurix. 'Anais has the defence grid online. Ruzco is already guiding in the first of the landers. It is minutes away.'

Kantor looked out across the Nolfeas Plate. The damaged ork bombers were still there.

'We need to clear the tops of the three terminal towers,' he said.

His voice was low, rasping. He was coming down from the adrenaline surge, and even his Astartes physiology felt weary after a battle like that. The pain of the blows Snagrod had landed began to push through to his brain now as the adrenal high seeped away.

Victurix nodded to his fellow Terminators and said, 'I think we can take care of that.'

They would simply push the bombers over the edge of the plate. Together, the Terminators had more than enough combined strength for that. They would clear the areas below of their brother Space Marines first, of course.

'You know, my lord,' said Victurix, his tone suggesting a wry smile under that heavy ceramite faceplate, 'you look terrible.'

Kantor didn't have it in him to laugh, not right now.

The warlord lived.

The secondary sun was rising, poking up just beyond the lip of the eastern horizon.

Golden beams of light kissed Kantor's battered armour. He turned to look north, wondering how the Silver Citadel fared. What of Maia Cagliestra and her people? What of the Old Ones, the Dreadnoughts he had left to fight on the walls. The void-shields had probably fallen by now, or would be close to it. In a few minutes, the first of the Naval landers would be here. The Legio Titanicus were coming, but were they too late? He and his dauntless Astartes had done everything they could. They had seen to the things that were within their power, and at great cost. Much of the Chapter's blood had been spilled. Many brave brothers would be mourned.

What happened next lay as much in the hands of others as it did in those of the Crimson Fists.

Kantor knew this for certain: his Chapter would survive. The Crimson Fists would claw this world back, province by province, metre by metre if necessary. Everything would be put right. If he did nothing else in this life, he would see to that.

He was Lord Hellblade, twenty-ninth Chapter Master of the Crimson Fists, Scion of Dorn, born to wage war in the name of the Emperor.

Alessio Cortez would stand with him, and so would his unflinching battle-brothers, warriors like Daecor, Victurix, Grimm, Deguerro, all of them.

Dark decades still lay ahead, but he would endure.

The Chapter would endure.

EPILOGUE

Remembrance

'It is only on days like today, the anniversary of the day the tables finally turned, that I allow the memories to resurface, that I truly dwell on the totality of the destruction we faced. Despite my rank, despite my years of petitioning, I was never able to gain access to the complete truth of what happened at the spaceport. I know only this: had brave Space Marines not given their lives knowing they would never hear our thanks, not a single man, woman or child would live to remember the war.

'The void-shields of the Zona Regis were close to overload when the greenskin gargants finally turned to engage the fresh Imperial forces suddenly attacking them from the rear. From the relative shelter of the gun towers, we saw Navy landers descend, vast armoured craft studded with guns and missile-pylons, filled to the brim with brave and hardy souls. We saw wings of fighters and Marauder bombers roar out over enemy lines, something we had never thought to see again, and watched those lines blaze yellow-white as deadly payloads hit their mark. Tired as we were, wounded, desperately hungry, we cheered as I know I will never hear men cheer again. We watched the greenskin invaders die by the thousands, then the tens of thousands, and somehow, somewhere, we found the energy to lift our guns again, and lend the last of our strength to the fight.

'Ten years have passed. Ten years to the day. As we do every year, we gathered on Jadeberry Hill, veterans, politicians, survivors, to pay our respects to those that gave everything, men and Astartes both.

'The governor was there. She has aged so quickly since the war. She looks haunted, and rumours abound that she will abdicate in favour of her granddaughter soon.

'Of course, we are all a little haunted.

'At midday, the skies opened. A cold rain lashed down. We took shelter in the memorial building where a string quartet played Guidollero's Vasparda et Gloris, and, together, we stood and wept in quiet gratitude for the souls of all those mighty warriors by whose determination and ultimate sacrifice we yet lived, and who, in this life, we could never hope to repay.'

Extract: *In the Shadow of Giants: A Retrospective*
General Saedus Mir (934.M41-)

ABOUT THE AUTHOR

Born and raised in Edinburgh, Scotland, **Steve Parker** now lives and works in Tokyo, Japan. In 2005, his short fiction started appearing in American sci-fi/fantasy/horror magazines, soon followed by a commission to write for Black Library in 2006. His debut novel, *Rebel Winter*, was published in 2007, followed in 2009 by his second novel, *Gunheads*. *Rynn's World* is his third novel set in the dark future of Warhammer 40,000.

Aside from writing, his interests include reading, gaming, movies, bodybuilding, non-traditional martial arts and wildlife conservation.

Follow his blog at:
www.red-stevie.com/blog.htm

THE ULTRAMARINES SERIES

WARHAMMER 40,000

THE ULTRAMARINES
OMNIBUS

"Great characters, truck loads of intrigue and an amazing sense of pace." Enigma

GRAHAM McNEILL
NIGHTBRINGER • WARRIORS OF ULTRAMAR • DEAD SKY BLACK SUN

ISBN 978-1-84416-403-5

WARHAMMER 40,000

The Ultramarines return in an electrifying new novel

THE KILLING GROUND
GRAHAM McNEILL

UK ISBN 978-1-84416-724-1
US ISBN 978-1-84416-725-8

WARHAMMER 40,000

The return of the Ultramarines!

COURAGE AND HONOUR
GRAHAM McNEILL

UK ISBN 978-1-84416-722-4
US ISBN 978-1-84416-723-2

AARON DEMBSKI-BOWDEN

SOUL HUNTER

A NIGHT LORDS NOVEL

WARHAMMER
40,000

UK ISBN 978-1-84416-810-1   US ISBN 978-1-84416-811-8

WARHAMMER
40,000
A SPACE MARINE BATTLES NOVEL

HELSREACH

AARON DEMBSKI-BOWDEN

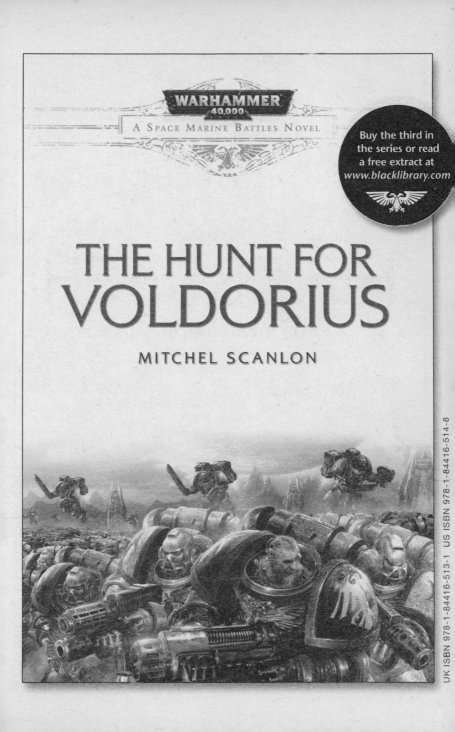

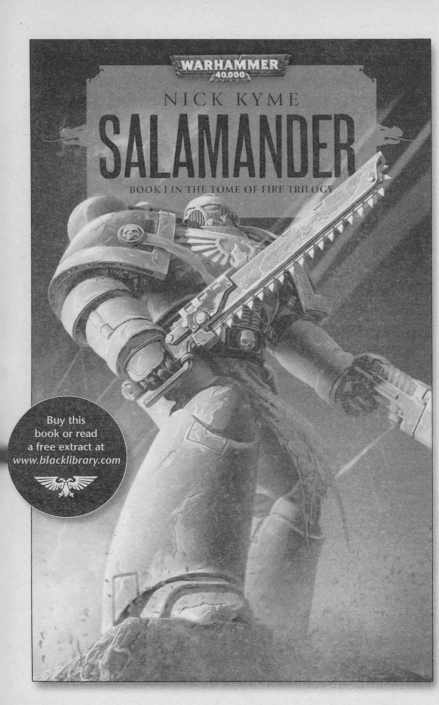

WARHAMMER
40,000

NICK KYME

SALAMANDER

BOOK I IN THE TOME OF FIRE TRILOGY

UK ISBN 978-1-84416-740-1   US ISBN 978-1-84416-741-8

SONS
OF DORN

AN IMPERIAL FISTS NOVEL

WARHAMMER®
40,000

CHRIS ROBERSON

UK ISBN 978-1-84416-788-3 US ISBN 978-1-84416-789-0